Y

...library.ie

Tel./Guthán (021) 4924900

This b... ...he last date stamped below.

...k plus postage.

Canaletto

AND THE CASE OF BONNIE PRINCE CHARLIE

Janet Laurence

Canaletto

AND THE CASE OF
BONNIE PRINCE CHARLIE

MACMILLAN

First published 2002 by Macmillan
an imprint of Pan Macmillan
Pan Macmillan, 20 New Wharf Road,
London N1 9RR
Basingstoke and Oxford
Associated companies throughout the world
www.panmacmillan.com

ISBN 0 333 90768 X

1 3 5 7 9 8 6 4 2

A CIP catalogue record for this book is available from
the British Library.

Phototypeset by Intype London Ltd
Printed and bound in Great Britain by
Mackays of Chatham plc, Chatham, Kent.

To

Professor Michael Horrocks
and the nursing staff of the
Waterhouse Ward,
Royal United Hospital, Bath.

For all the skill and care they gave
to my husband, Keith, during the
last part of the writing of this book.

Acknowledgements

I have to thank His Grace the Duke of Beaufort for showing me Badminton and the two paintings by Canaletto, and also his archivist, Mrs Margaret Richards, for unending assistance in producing documents and answering questions about the fourth duke and Badminton in the middle of the eighteenth century. Both His Grace and Mrs Richards could not have been more helpful.

Others who aided my research efforts include Roseanne Dobson; Bill Murray; Charles Medlam and Ingrid Seifert of the London Baroque; Anna del Conte Waley; and the staff of both the London Library and the Local Section of Bath Library. Any inaccuracies in the following story are mine.

Thanks also to Shelley, Maggie, Wendy and Sarah, 'The Group', whose many comments greatly improved this book.

Apart from certain characters who appear in the pages of history, none of the following characters is based on an actual person, living or dead, and all the incidents are fictitious.

Chapter One

1748

It was April but the shower was far from sweet. London lay under a familiar cloak of heavy smoke and the Warwick stage decanted a load of grumbling passengers into a chilly wind and a sudden downpour.

'Why couldn't it've waited till we'd got 'ome,' grumbled the thin, peevish matron who'd kept up a running commentary on all the unsatisfactory aspects of their journey. None of the relays of horses they'd had was up to the job of pulling such a heavy load, the driver was a lunatic who'd have them in the ditch, the ale at the first stage too thin and at the last too strong.

Canaletto received his grip from the baggage rack and wished his companions a brief farewell. What a relief to see the back of them! He hefted his heavy bag and strode out towards his lodgings at Silver Street. Almost immediately he slid on some rotted cabbage and only just saved himself with nimble footwork from falling into fouler rubbish.

It had been a nightmare journey. A road full of ruts and potholes and a badly overcrowded coach. He had been jerked around worse than if he'd been sitting on a wooden stool on the back of a nervous donkey. And as for the other passengers!

Apart from the ever-complaining woman, there'd been a fellow with a ceaseless sniff who'd cradled a grip as lovingly as any mother her babe but who looked as though he peddled perverted toys for bored nabobs.

Three youngsters continually fought and squabbled over who should sit in the corner and were never corrected by their mama, a woman with the girth of an overfed friar and the softness of a down pillow. Canaletto had found himself squeezed between her and an ancient fellow with a rheum that wheezed through his narrow chest like water through a blocked pipe, and elbows as sharp as giant quills. The elbows found Canaletto's ribs with irritating regularity as their owner was pressed by a large gentleman who indulged in frequent sips from a capacious flask and alternately snored and cursed.

Each time they'd had to disembark to walk up a hill behind the labouring horses, Canaletto had been afraid the aged fellow would expire and they'd be faced with the problem of a cadaver in the coach. Each time they re-entered, he was jabbed by the elbows and had to inch towards the matron. He feared suffocation in her alarmingly pillow-like flesh. If only she hadn't smelled as though she'd spent the winter in a byre full of cows. That and the constant litany of complaints meant every lurch towards London had to be welcome.

On top of that the weather had been miserable and the showers seemed to save themselves for the times the coach approached the steeper hills. By the time they reached London, Canaletto's second best coat was soaked through and his limbs were numb.

Now, though, all that was behind him. Now he could look forward to a refreshing drink of sweet-tasting small ale, a change of clothing, the chance to warm his limbs before a fire and the soothing attentions of his apprentice, Fanny Rooker.

Ah, Fanny! She'd be so happy to see him back. He'd been away so much longer than he'd originally expected, he'd had to send her a letter announcing a delayed return. She would have come to the end of the various tasks he'd left her and no doubt would be longing to show him her progress on a picture of her own. He'd suggested several topographical subjects before he left and it would be interesting to see which she'd chosen.

Canaletto shifted his bag from one hand to the other, disliking its weight, and fended off a suggestion he take a chair. 'Too much,' he told the chairmen. Instead of pressing him, they looked around for a more prosperous mark. At which he felt resentful. All right, at the moment he had to watch every expenditure however small but he was a gentleman, a citizen of Venice, the famous vedute artist, Antonio Canale. He shouldn't be looked at as though he were nothing.

He forced himself to put the incident behind him. It was not much further now and the shower had passed. At the bottom of the Haymarket, Canaletto was happy to catch his breath and study the bill pasted on the playhouse there. Owen McSwiney was always trying to persuade him to visit one with him. Canaletto had avoided the suggestion, as he'd avoided so many other of Owen's socializing schemes. His English had been too halting and he disliked large groups, he felt uncomfortable with a press of people. Owen adored people, and people liked him. That was how he persuaded them into giving him commissions for the artists he liked to recommend. Canaletto wondered if the man had fulfilled his promise to line up more work for his return to London.

The playbill promised a new production of *The Beggar's Opera*. It meant nothing to Canaletto. Having caught his second wind, he picked up his bag and started to climb the hill. Then had to sidestep to avoid the lethal swing of a bale of hay wielded by a hefty bloke in a stained jerkin, only to ricochet off a large matron carrying two enormous baskets of garden produce with as much ease as though they were a fan and she a lady in a drawing room.

Was the whole world taller than he? Canaletto wondered as two strapping youths courteously shifted him out of the way of a cart emerging from a busy stables. He stopped to adjust the set of his wig that had slipped over one ear with the helpful manhandling he'd received. He regretted spurning the chair.

Soon, though, he was in the calm of Golden Square, so neatly lined with well-built houses, the central lawn clipped and orderly. Canaletto found a large kerchief in the back pocket of his damp coat and mopped his forehead. How could he be sweating when the weather was so chilly? Then he trudged the final distance into Silver Street. Home at last!

His landlord's workshop had its doors open. A light carpet of sawdust had blown over the walkway that led through to the studio at the back of the property.

'You whoreson beggar!' boomed out Richard Wiggan's huge voice. There was a thwack and an apprentice shot out of the doorway and lay sprawled in the sawdust. Canaletto put down his bag and helped him to his feet.

'Split the grain again?'

The fellow gave him a shamefaced grin and shambled back inside.

Canaletto missed the gentle cabinetmaker who had been his original landlord. There were no talks over a pint of ale with Richard Wiggan, no interested enquiries about his work. This man had no time for anything but his own cabinet business and he abused his apprentices in what Canaletto considered a disgraceful manner. He would feel ashamed to speak to Fanny the way Wiggan berated his staff. A glance in at the workroom as he passed showed the three apprentices hard at work with their master on what appeared to be a full set of dining room furniture.

Canaletto was glad to see this evidence that London's booming economy showed no sign of faltering. He continued through to the meanly grassed area where chickens clucked and pecked for food. Home at last! He turned the handle of his studio's door.

It was locked.

For a moment Canaletto stood rattling away at the handle, sure it must have stuck and that Fanny would rush to open it from her side.

The door failed to yield and no Fanny rushed to his aid.

Of course, she had had to run an errand. Perhaps to replenish supplies of pigments for his paints, or for more varnish or oil. This was good, for his fingers itched to get painting.

Canaletto found the clay pot of newly sprouting

parsley under which they kept the spare key, pushed away an inquisitive chicken and extracted the key.

As soon as he opened the door, he knew things were not right. The overcast day let in little light, large though the north-facing windows were, and, to start with, all Canaletto could take in was that the fire was nearly out. He dropped his bag and hurried across to coax new life into the embers, carefully placing a little kindling as well as some pieces of coal to encourage a good blaze.

When he was satisfied he'd rescued the fire, he turned to look at the rest of the studio – and stared in disbelief.

All was chaos!

His first thought was that some intruder had been and disturbed his precious painting equipment, perhaps searching for money.

But in that case a window would have been broken or the door lock smashed.

Then, unbelievably, he heard Fanny's light voice raised in song as she approached the studio. He neither knew nor cared what the ditty was.

She stopped in the doorway, the notes dying away. 'Signor, you are back! I did not expect you quite so soon. After your letter, it seemed you would spend longer away. If I had known . . !'

Canaletto was grimly pleased to see that she was babbling. She flung down the workbox she'd been carrying, wrenched off her bonnet and hurried over to the narrow little bed in the corner of the studio. 'I overslept this morning,' she muttered as she twitched the cover into order. Then she picked up the poker and gave a stir to the fire. Flames leaped up, giving a warm and homely glow. She added a few new pieces of coal then swung round again. 'Signor, how was your trip back from Warwick?'

'Wretched,' he growled. 'I freeze and my bones are shaken like Spanish dancer's castanets.' Then he caught himself. Once again he had forgotten the pesky little English article. 'Shaken like *a* Spanish dancer's castanets. You have been buying supplies perhaps?' He was sure Fanny hadn't, she would hardly have taken a workbox to hold such purchases, so what had she been up to when she should have been working for him?

Fanny gathered together the dirty crockery, no doubt the result of her last meal, placed it neatly at the end of the long trestle table that held all the painting impedimenta, then moved two rushlights into their accustomed position. She glanced up at the windows and decided against lighting them.

Canaletto realized the place had been restored to its normal neatness. He didn't feel any better.

'You enjoy yourself with family?' he enquired pleasantly.

Fanny sighed deeply. 'Signor, I am very sorry I was out just now but I did not expect you for two or three more days. In your letter you said . . .'

Canaletto waved a dismissive hand. 'It matters not. Rain finally stop and I finish drawings. No reason for you to wait here every hour of every day,' he finished grandly. 'I am pleased you disport yourself.'

Fanny gave an even deeper sigh, drew out one of the stools from underneath the bench and sat down. 'You're not going to like what I have been doing and I should have told you before but I hadn't done more than approach Mr Hudson by the time you left.'

'Mr Hudson?' repeated Canaletto. His gaze fell on the workbox Fanny had dropped when she entered the studio and the most awful possibility occurred to him.

Chapter Two

'Loyalty, where is Fanny's loyalty to me? Me, Antonio Canale, citizen of Venice?' Canaletto smote himself upon the chest and strode distractedly up and down the studio.

Such was the painter's agitation, he was entirely oblivious to the fact that his wig was once again askew. It hung a little drunkenly over his right eye, pushed there by the need to scratch a flea bite behind his left ear.

Owen McSwiney polished off his mug of ale and reached for a refill. 'Come now, what is the harm in Miss Fanny having a few lessons from another painter?' His hair, powdered but definitely his own, cascaded down the stained velvet coat that sat easily on his slim shoulders. 'Or should no one offer her instruction but you?' he added pointedly.

Canaletto was incensed. 'I greatest painter of vedute there is.'

'Of course, of course,' Owen agreed dispassionately. 'No one can touch you as far as townscapes are concerned.'

'More than townscapes. I do landscapes. I have sketches of Warwick Castle for my Lord Brooke that will make fine paintings.' He swung round on Owen.

'A commission you did not get for me. I get nothing from you for months.'

Owen waved an airy hand. 'I am glad for you, Tonio, but don't think I'm not labouring on your behalf. Why, even now, I am about to land a rich fish for you.'

Canaletto paused, his expression keen. 'Say you so? Who is patron and what will he want? Another view of river, perhaps?'

Owen chuckled. 'I'll say nothing until the thing is set. Except that it won't have anything to do with the Thames.'

'Good!' Canaletto resumed his pacing.

Owen watched him for a moment, his expression amused. 'Come on,' he said after a while. 'What is it about Miss Fanny's painting lessons that is so upsetting you?'

Canaletto stopped, his expression outraged. 'You can ask this? When Fanny Rooker, my apprentice without payment, my apprentice who I instruct in my art as I do no one since my nephew, Bernardo Bellotto, when she, ungrateful wretch, she goes to 'Udson and asks to be taught by him?' He stopped, out of breath.

'Sit, Tonio, please. You make my head dizzy with all this walking about.'

'Your head dizzy because of all ale you drink.' But Canaletto drew out another stool and sat, glaring at Owen.

'Now, my friend, let us see just what it is that poor Miss Fanny has done.'

'I told you,' Canaletto said explosively.

Owen was patient. 'You have told me that Miss Fanny has had some lessons from one of the leading portraiture artists. I see nothing wrong in that nor anything disloyal to you. You are certainly the finest townscape artist there is but what do you know of capturing likenesses?'

'Fanny shall not be portraitist!' fumed Canaletto.

'Because you say so?' demanded Owen.

'Because I teach her vedute.'

'Be reasonable, man! How much demand is there for views? Even you, foremost artist that you are, find commissions difficult. But portraiture, the market for portraits grows and grows so the possibilities for a painter are far greater. Especially for a woman. Think of Rosalba Carriera with her pastels.' McSwiney paused for a moment, thinking. 'Of course, Fanny's social connections are few, she will have difficulty establishing herself in the first rank, but,' he added more positively, 'doesn't she have connections amongst merchants through her brother's wife? That should help begin to secure commissions of a sort.'

'I had no connections when I started,' Canaletto said argumentatively, changing direction completely.

'But your talent is exceptional!'

'Right, you are right but Fanny good painter,' Canaletto insisted.

Owen laughed and flung up his hands. 'Then where is your objection?'

Canaletto began to feel a little foolish. Was it really just hurt pride that he felt because she had turned to someone other than himself for skills to equip her in her chosen career? 'She should have told me.'

Owen tore a piece of bread off a loaf that Fanny had set in front of him before sweeping out to buy a meat pie. 'Wouldn't you have put up all sorts of objections if she had? How,' he asked suddenly. 'How did

she gain access to Hudson? He's as busy as fleas on a
bawd. Portraits trip off his brush like fleas off a dog.'

'Because of his apprentice, that boy she fancy
herself in love with last year,' Canaletto muttered. 'He
take her because of him.'

'Ah yes,' Owen sighed. 'Poor Fanny, doomed love is
always painful. I have suffered many a time myself.'

'You!' Canaletto jeered. 'Your heart is fickle like
butterfly, you sample honey here, there, everywhere.'
To compare Fanny's broken heart and continuing
despair with anything suffered by the effervescent
Irishman was not to be allowed. 'And little wonder
Hudson produce so many paintings, he farms out his
draperies to Van Aken and no doubt more to others.'
His expression grew thoughtful. 'He paints faces indif-
ferent well, perhaps, but they lack . . .' he paused,
wondering how to characterize the painter's work.
'Charm they have, yes,' he continued, 'competent they
are, with great surface gloss, but they do not have . . .'

'Distinction?' suggested Owen, smiling broadly. 'So
now we have it! Poor Miss Fanny has gone to learn
portraiture from a man you do not feel is in the first
rank, is that it?' Another thought struck him. 'How
come she could afford to study with him? Even a cut
rate would be beyond her, I would have thought.'

'She sold two paintings of Golden Square to
someone living in a house there. The buyer pay good
price,' explained Canaletto.

'Perhaps you thought she should have given the
money to you?'

'No!' Canaletto was shocked. 'Never! She offered
me the money, yes, for apprenticeship but I said she

pays by housekeeping. I said she have need of money some day and save it until then.'

'And so this was the need,' murmured Owen.

Canaletto nodded. There seemed nothing further to say.

Owen tore off another piece of bread. 'Is that one of Fanny's efforts?' he asked, pointing at the easel. It held a small canvas covered with a piece of cloth.

Canaletto stared. He'd been so upset, he hadn't even noticed it. He went and gently lifted the cloth off the canvas.

It was a portrait. Of course it was a portrait!

Rebecca Wiggan, the cabinetmaker's wife, gazed out at him, her wiry black hair escaping from her muslin headgear in a way her husband would have found unbecoming. She looked the viewer directly in the eye, her snub nose engagingly raised. Canaletto was used to seeing a silent Rebecca, her eyes downcast in the presence of Richard Wiggan. This was an unfamiliar aspect of the woman; unfamiliar but very attractive.

'Hmm,' said Owen, coming to stand beside Canaletto. 'You are right, she has talent, your little Fanny.'

Canaletto would rather McSwiney didn't refer to her in such terms but he'd given up trying to make his friend accord his apprentice the respect he considered she deserved. So he ignored the comment and continued to study the painting. It was unfinished and lacked sophistication but Fanny had handled the paint well and, though there was something slightly odd about the proportions of the head, she had definitely caught Rebecca Wiggan.

13

Some of his hurt pride and truculence seeped away.

'Come,' said Owen, reaching for his hat and coat. 'Let's not wait for meat pie, let's to the playhouse.'

'You know I do not like the playhouse,' protested Canaletto.

'Tush, man. It's a ridiculous prejudice all due to the fact that you started your career painting scenery.'

'I am not ashamed of the fact!'

'Indeed not,' soothed Owen. 'So come with me.'

'My English is so poor, I cannot understand the action.'

'The action, indeed! No one cares about the action. Just now Garrick is in *The Foundling*, it's of little merit but seems to have caught on. A comedy so you do not need to follow the plot. It will be interesting for you to compare the English way of production with the Italian,' he coaxed. 'In any case, I go, with or without you.'

Canaletto weighed the alternatives. Wait here alone for Fanny to return, when he would somehow have to make things right between them, visit some eating place where the company and the manners would appal him, or accompany Owen to the playhouse.

It was not a difficult choice.

Chapter Three

The theatre was abustle. The boxes were filled with gloriously bedecked men and women. Fans fluttered, hands waved to friends and acquaintances, conversation never ceased, even during Mr Garrick's most pleasing effects. This was a social occasion.

Canaletto found himself transported back thirty years or more, to the youth he'd spent assisting his father painting scenery for the elaborate productions the Italian theatre staged in Rome. Then the ability of canvas and paint to conjure another world, the magical way actors could transport the audience away from everyday affairs, had captivated him

He'd fallen out with his father and said goodbye to the theatre, determined to build a career painting pictures rather than scenery. Since then, he'd buried that first fascination, but his early pictures had been full of drama. Later he'd realized the subtler hold buildings could exert without stormy clouds.

Now here he was in Drury Lane. Canaletto could not make much sense of the piece, *The Foundling* seemed a lot of nonsense to him, though Garrick was certainly entertaining, but there was always the possibility his command of English was not idiomatic enough to catch essential nuances. More interesting to him was the scenery. He was amazed at how skimpy and unimaginative it was. A series of flats plus a back-cloth. No attempt at varying the perspective or to provide special effects. Should commissions ever actually run out in this difficult market, Canaletto told himself, he could always earn money returning to his first profession.

'Tonio, look at the first tier of boxes, second from the left,' Owen McSwiney hissed in his ear.

Canaletto looked.

By the light of the flaring chandeliers, he saw two middle-aged men in curiously checked waistcoats accompanying a woman of uncertain age who was wearing a silk dress of a most beautiful blue. The trio were attracting a certain amount of attention. Eyes looked at them around fans, heads craned up from the pit, whispers were exchanged.

'Why such interest?'

'Sure and it's because they're flaunting their sympathies.'

'Sympathies?' Canaletto thought his command of English was now more than passable, yet he could make little sense of any of this.

'They're wearing the plaid and a true blue.'

Plaid, ah yes, that was what that sort of check was called. 'They are Scottish? In Scotland, that is where plaid is worn, yes?' he enquired. 'And others wear blue,' he added, looking around him. Yet he saw that none of the fashions was that fierce, unadorned blue of the woman's dress. 'Why is it true?'

'Oh, if it wasn't for the plaid, you'd not think a thing. But with that, well, it could not be more offensive!'

16

'Please, you have to explain. Why offensive?'

Owen sighed. 'I tell you so often, Tonio, you do not move enough in society. Has no one told you about the Jacobites?'

'I know about Jacobites.' Canaletto was stung. 'I see, I saw,' he corrected himself, 'the procession when Lord Lovat went to trial.'

'Lord, yes, what a to-do that was. Lovat was the last executed after the forty-five uprising.'

'When the Prince Charlie try to take throne, yes?'

Owen laughed. 'So you really do know about the Jacobites! Well, it was mainly the Scots as supported the Prince so now the Scots' plaid is scorned by all right-thinking folk. And the Jacobites call themselves "true blue", so a dress such as my lady there wears is as offensive as the plaid.'

Was this really so? Canaletto looked again at the trio in the box. They sat gravely, occasionally exchanging a word or two. They appeared impervious to the nudging and whispering that was going on around them. He found it difficult to understand that a few items of clothing could cause such interest. 'Are these aristocrats?' he asked Owen.

But his companion's attention had now been caught by the occupants of the next-door box, a couple dressed resplendently but soberly.

'Here is luck indeed,' Owen said.

Canaletto looked at them more closely. The man was around forty, she some ten years younger. He looked pleasant, she imposing. As he studied them, the woman bowed haughtily in response to a wave from across the auditorium. What was McSwiney's particular interest in them? He seemed to have for-gotten the Jacobites entirely.

'Who are they?'

'The Duke and Duchess of Beaufort,' said Owen. 'This is perfect. Come, I shall introduce you.'

He rose and worked his way out of the pit, followed by Canaletto and the hisses of the people they disturbed.

'The duke's seat is in Gloucestershire,' said Owen as he led the way up to the first tier of the boxes. 'Kent has recently worked most advantageous improvements to the house. Nothing could be more modern or more imposing.'

Hope rose in Canaletto's heart. This must be the possible commission McSwiney had mentioned.

The duke was welcoming, the duchess regal.

'Signor Canale, how good to meet you,' the duke said after Owen had performed the introductions. 'I have already spoken with Mr McSwiney on the possibility of you capturing our beautiful Badminton for posterity with a pair of your famous vedute.'

Two paintings! This was good news. However, 'I would be honoured, your grace.' Canaletto sketched as much of a bow as he could manage in the confined space of the box. 'I trust milord does not require paintings in the immediate future?' Oh, how wonderful his English was so much more fluent now. Canaletto gave mental thanks to Fanny for her patience in teaching him during the long winter evenings.

'We would not wish to wait too long upon your pleasure,' said the duchess, managing to sound at the same time both distant and gracious as well as indicating that Canaletto might not be her first choice as artist.

'Signor Canale has commissions from Lord Brooke for Warwick Castle on hand; any new commission must wait until he has completed these,' put in Owen. 'The signor is always conscious of the duty he owes his patrons.'

Canaletto wondered how Owen could say this with a straight face. No one knew better than McSwiney how in Venice in the thirties the painter had juggled his overwhelming flood of orders with little regard for which had been spoken for first, his only concern had been to keep the most pressing agents away from his studio.

'Signor, I would not presume to suggest our needs have greater importance than Lord Brooke's,' the duke said with an attractively open manner.

The duchess, holding her closed fan against her chin, looked as though that was exactly what should be done.

'Perhaps next month?' murmured the duke. 'I can instruct my steward at Badminton to attend to your every need.'

'The beginning of June, your grace,' countered Canaletto.

'Excellent,' the duke rubbed his hands together in a contented way. 'We plan to be there somewhere around that time ourselves.'

Instantly Canaletto resolved not to allow McSwiney to bounce him into an earlier visit. For if the duke were to be there, Canaletto could discuss with him exactly which views would suit best and save the business of sending sketches for his approval. A few pleasantries and they were once again outside the box.

'You push your luck,' said Owen as they walked along the corridor running behind the boxes.

'Never again do I stay in English country house until weather warm,' said Canaletto firmly. 'I nearly die from cold in Warwick Castle.'

'Signor Canale, I think,' said a tall figure appearing along the corridor from the other direction. 'William Pitt at your service.'

For the Paymaster General to say he was at anyone's service, let alone a humble painter's, was enough to raise suspicion. Canaletto looked at the imperious face with its hooked nose and remembered with painful clarity how this man had involved him in the unfortunate business concerning the building of Westminster Bridge. It had nearly been the finish of him.

'Signor Pitt, the honour is mine,' he said with the deepest of bows. However much he might distrust this encounter, he could not afford to alienate a man of power who knew everyone. Pitt could make sure he had no future in England just when things were looking a little brighter.

'Owen McSwiney, sir,' said the Irishman, holding out his hand. 'If you be wanting the greatest of artists to adorn your mansion, I'm the man to come to. I also have some influence in the theatrical world.'

'Yes, Mr McSwiney, I am acquainted with your talents,' Pitt said with a trace of irony. 'Signor Canale, it is a pleasure to see you again, I trust you progress well in England?'

They stood exchanging conversation of no moment

for a full five minutes before the Paymaster General detached himself and walked back the way he had come.

'Would you look at that, now?' marvelled McSwiney. 'It would seem as if his only purpose was to say hello to us.'

Canaletto said nothing but he feared that Owen had the right of it. Pitt had undoubtedly seen them in the Beaufort box and then waylaid him. What did it mean?

Back in Silver Street, Fanny was sketching in the uncertain glow given by a rushlight. She jumped up as Canaletto entered. 'Tell me about your evening. Where have you been? Can I make you a posset? You must be so tired after all your journeying and then out with Mr McSwiney. You have so much energy!' she marvelled.

It was his own Fanny back again, as though they had never had a disagreement.

Purely for the pleasure of her company, Canaletto accepted her offer of a posset and sat watching her prepare the hot drink, carefully warming the ale and milk, frothing it with a small, wooden mill, then pouring it into a pottery mug and handing it to him, all the while her face intent upon her task.

When they'd first met, Canaletto had thought Fanny a plain girl. Now if anyone, Owen say, dared class her as such, he would angrily deny it. Yes, her forehead was too deep, her nose tended to the same snub that decorated Rebecca Wiggan's features, her mouth was too wide and there were those freckles.

None of this could be denied. But, Canaletto would have said, look at her eyes! They were large and hazel, full of expression. And the copper curls, undimmed this evening by any muslin cap, caught the light in an entrancing way. Her neck was very graceful and in the last two years her body had developed curves. She was no fine lady, unused to work. Fanny was strong, her arms capable of grinding pigments and wielding a brush for hours on end, but her movements were lithe and sweet.

'There, signor, I hope that will ease your travel pains and help you to sleep tonight.'

Canaletto took the drink.

Fanny placed herself upon a stool opposite him. She smoothed down the apron over her plain wool gown, then looked up, her face earnest. 'Signor, I wish to apologize . . .'

He interrupted, 'No need, Fanny. You have right to visit anyone for lessons – so long as you have time for my work,' he could not help adding.

She flushed. 'Indeed, sir, I shall always have that. What I wished to apologize for was not telling you what I planned to do while you were away. That was wrong. Only,' she hesitated, looking down at the hands so neatly clasped over the apron. 'Only,' she looked up again, the hazel eyes searching his face, 'I knew you would not like it.'

Canaletto sat by the fire, feeling himself relax as the slightly alcoholic liquid spread a comforting warmth through his body. 'Fanny, why you explore portraiture so? I am sure Mr Hudson charge large fees for lessons, all your savings disappear.' The knowledge that she didn't believe he could supply all the instruction that she needed was corrosive.

Fanny's expression grew yet more earnest. 'Signor, there is no painter I would rather be apprenticed to than you. No one has such mastery of brushwork, understands colour, is such a draughtsman, is, well, such a complete master.' Her hands clasped themselves ever more tightly in her lap. 'But you do not do faces. You do not paint people, your figures are only sketches. Sometimes,' her voice faltered for a moment, then she gathered up her courage again. 'I think sometimes, signor, that you are afraid to see people in the way you see buildings and landscape.'

Canaletto closed his eyes for a moment, shutting out that earnest face gazing with such concern into his. No one knew better than he how his ability to capture expression and personality in the people that brought life to his townscapes had been reduced to a few quick brush strokes. Was it just the pressure of work, the need to turn out as many pictures as possible during those hectic years in Venice that had meant he'd so debased his gift? Or had he indeed turned his heart away from capturing people with the skill and commitment he'd given to buildings? It was not a question Canaletto wished to answer.

He felt a gentle touch and opened his eyes to find Fanny had placed a hand on his knee. 'Please forgive me, signor, if I intrude, but I have to make you understand why I went to Mr Hudson.'

'You mean,' Canaletto appeared to have a frog in his throat. He cleared it and started again. 'You mean you wish to practise portraiture, not vedute?'

Fanny nodded vigorously. 'I'm interested in

people so much more than buildings, signor. And, well, I think that, as a woman, I will find it easier to gain commissions for portraits than for landscapes.'

Exactly what McSwiney had said.

Canaletto rose and approached the easel. 'I see your portrait of Rebecca Wiggan,' he said.

Fanny said nothing, just looked at him, her big eyes apprehensive.

He caught up the rushlight that flickered on the trestle table and brought it close so that he could see the work clearly. 'You have her vulnerability,' he said slowly. 'Her innocence, such a child-like quality she has. But you have seen also a spirit normally hidden.'

Fanny came and stood beside him. 'There's something wrong with the shape of the head,' she said worriedly. 'I haven't got the proportions right.'

'Pouf!' Canaletto said grandly. 'That will come with practice. Much more important to be able see into heart of sitter. Very easy add accoutrements to illuminate rank and role of sitter, more difficult to give life and personality to the face. That much I know,' he added, somewhat caustically.

'Please, signor, I didn't mean to hurt you by what I said.'

He looked at her, the rushlight gilding her hair. 'Perhaps Fanny right,' he said heavily. 'Perhaps I do not wish be involved in my fellow man. Perhaps I find buildings safer.' He didn't wish to dwell on this. 'Come, I tell you about theatre Owen and I visit this evening. We meet Duke and Duchess of Beaufort.' As he recounted the details, however, his mind was more taken with his encounter with Paymaster General Pitt. Why had the man deliberately sought him out? One thing was for sure, it would cause trouble!

Chapter Four

The next morning Canaletto started work on his paintings of Warwick Castle.

He found it unexpectedly difficult to develop his sketches. Having given Fanny permission to continue her portraiture lessons, he found the studio lonely and empty when she wasn't there and that he quarrelled with her over the slightest thing when she was. He spurned all her attempts to help him and resented the time she spent working on a new portrait of Rebecca Wiggan, this time a more formal one.

His bad temper wasn't helped by hearing nothing from Owen McSwiney regarding arrangements for painting the Duke of Beaufort's property. Had it been a mere aristocratic whim? Canaletto hoped not, he needed this commission, not only for the money but also for the wider publicity it would bring him amongst likely patrons. He regretted not being more eager when the matter had been raised at the theatre.

Several weeks passed in this way, Canaletto's worries about the future mounting, Fanny's painting activities on her own behalf increasing as he continued to shut her out of his work. Then one morning Richard Wiggan gloomily announced that smallpox had struck a house not far from Silver Street. 'And that'll be just the start,' he added. 'Summer will soon be here and then it'll be the plague.'

'The plague?' repeated Canaletto faintly. The hairs rose on the back of his neck. So far in England he had not come into contact with serious infection and he would like the situation to remain so. London had not been visited by a serious plague since the last century but smallpox was bad enough; even if it stopped short of death, it could ruin your health, not to mention your looks. Pitted skin wasn't pleasant to behold and there was a limit to what could be hidden by the patches that were so fashionable. 'Nonsense!' he said. 'There is no plague these days!'

'Doctor, are you?'

'One does not have to be doctor to know when plague is about.'

'There have been two deaths already from the smallpox, that is bad enough,' Richard Wiggan said triumphantly. 'Now that the weather gets warmer, all sorts of infections are about'

Canaletto bade the fellow a hasty goodbye and returned to his studio. But that evening he sought out Matthew Butcher, his surgeon friend. Matthew frequented the Rainbow Coffee House at Fleet Bridge most days after six o'clock. Indeed, such was his patronage of the place, patients in urgent need of his attention would send for him there.

Fleet Bridge was a tidy step from Golden Square but the evening was fine and Canaletto enjoyed the exercise.

The coffee house was noisy with cheerful discussion and exchange of news. A few unsociable souls sat by themselves reading newspapers or scribbling letters but there was a general air of good fellowship. Canaletto found Matthew at the back of the house engaged in noisy debate with two other men. He was a large, untidy figure with a well-creased face. The creases broke into a wide smile as soon as he saw Canaletto.

'My friend, good to see you. Will you join us? Here are Doctor Carter and Doctor Francis.' The two men shook Canaletto's hand. Carter was tall and thin with piercing eyes, Francis small and chubby with a bulbous nose. 'Signor Canale comes from Italy, he is a noted painter.' Neither of the doctors appeared much impressed by this piece of information but they nodded courteously. 'How is Miss Fanny, well I trust?'

'Very busy,' said Canaletto sourly. He joined Matthew on the bench across from the other two doctors. The table was well covered with pots of coffee, glasses of brandy and various papers.

'We debate whether the waters of Bath have merit or not,' Dr Carter said after Canaletto had ordered coffee and a brandy for himself.

'Bath? You mean to immerse body in water? You question is this good?' Canaletto was anxious to get the matter straight in his mind.

Carter leaned forward, 'I think your friend has no idea what we are talking about, Butcher. Have you heard, my dear sir, of the town in the West of England called Bath?'

Canaletto shook his head. London he knew, Warwick he had just become familiar with, Norwich and Bristol he had heard of. That last town was in the west, wasn't it? 'Near Bristol?' he ventured hesitantly.

'Quite right,' Matthew said enthusiastically. 'You have a firm grasp of England's geography.'

Canaletto kept quiet.

'Bath becomes more and more popular and its reputation as a health resort grows every year.'

'Place is built on a bog,' said Francis impatiently. 'And the claims for the mineral waters are manifestly absurd.'

'Far from it,' argued Carter.

'Mineral waters?' asked Canaletto.

'Bath has a source of hot springs with a valuable mineral content,' said Matthew Butcher. 'Originally Roman, they were rediscovered some two hundred years ago. They are taken for a wide variety of ailments.'

'Tush, it's nothing but a story put about by the worthies of Bath to increase the number of visitors,' said Dr Francis irritably.

But the mention of ailments had reminded Canaletto why he had sought out his surgeon friend. What, he asked the medical men, was the present situation regarding smallpox in London? 'Two cases not two streets away from my studio,' he added.

'I have seen no signs of an epidemic, have you?' Matthew Butcher asked his friends.

They shook their heads. 'Of course,' said Dr Francis gloomily, 'summer brings increased risk, especially in London's crowded streets.' He looked across at Canaletto. 'I trust you do not suffer symptoms, my dear sir? For your friend, Doctor Butcher here, is about to depart London and you will be unable to call upon his aid.'

'He wants to make his fortune,' said Dr Carter cynically.

'You are leaving London, Matthew?' Canaletto was

dismayed. He didn't want to lose one of his few friends; a somewhat solitary person, he had not made many since arriving in London two years ago.

Matthew Butcher smiled. 'Don't listen to them. I'm only going to Bath for a short while. My sister is not well and wishes to take the mineral waters. She has prevailed upon me to accompany her. She says I will gain many new patients. I doubt that, there must be physicians enough in Bath. But I am fond of her and have agreed. My friends here have promised to look after my patients in London while I am away, so if you have problems, now you know who to contact.'

Canaletto surveyed the other two men. Nothing about them inspired him with much confidence, Carter's hand as he held his brandy shook and Francis had a permanent dewdrop at the end of that vast nose. He resolved to remain in good health until Matthew returned from this western spa.

He left not long after that, not entirely reassured as to the smallpox situation.

The next day, once again deserted by Fanny, Canaletto prepared himself to start the day alone. Palette in hand, he took a long look at the painting he was working on. It was nearly finished.

There was a knock at the door.

Annoyed at being disturbed and cursing Fanny's absence, Canaletto considered not opening it. But there was a window and whoever stood on the doorstep must have seen that he was inside.

Irritably, he went and opened the door, then stood with his mouth agape. His visitor was William Pitt, His Majesty's Paymaster General.

Chapter Five

'Signor,' William Pitt saluted Canaletto pleasantly. 'I am delighted to find you at home.'

Canaletto could do nothing but stare at him.

'I may come in?' Pitt entered without an invitation.

'To what do I owe this honour?' asked Canaletto, falling back before the tall figure and making an effort to regain his manners and his equilibrium.

Pitt raised an eyebrow. 'Your English has improved, signor.'

Canaletto felt absurdly pleased.

Pitt strolled over to the easel and studied the painting. 'Warwick Castle, I see.'

Canaletto nodded.

'Lord Brooke plans many improvements, I understand. Perhaps he has discussed these with you?'

Canaletto recovered his voice. 'Yes, signor. I am to complete a drawing showing south face of the castle, this same face I paint here, how south face will look after planned works.'

'Indeed!' It was difficult to tell if Pitt was impressed, so high did he hold his face with that imperious nose that always looked as though it was revolted by some aroma. 'And I understand that my lord the Duke of

Beaufort has also commissioned you to capture his seat at Badminton.'

If Pitt could state that with such certainty, maybe the commission was a fact after all. This should have reassured Canaletto, instead a nasty feeling, like the start of a bloody flux, began to grow in the pit of his stomach.

'Signor Canaletto, I may, perhaps, sit?'

Canaletto waved towards one of the studio stools and his apprehension deepened. To see the great man adopting such a submissive position did not bode well.

Canaletto continued to stand, it gave him some small advantage.

'Signor, I come to ask your help on behalf of this country, which I hope is being kind to you.'

Canaletto gave a little, cautious dip of his head.

'The thing of it is,' Pitt said, leaning forward confidentially, 'this country is in danger. Severe danger,' he repeated with emphasis.

Canaletto looked sceptically at him.

'You must have seen the plaid waistcoats the other night at the playhouse?'

'Ah, Jacobites,' said Canaletto, relieved to be able to latch so securely on to an aspect of the situation.

'Exactly! Jacobites!' Pitt said exultantly.

'But English beat the Jacobites in, what was it, forty-five?'

'At the battle of Culloden in forty-six. However, the Prince Charles Edward—'

'Bonnie Prince Charlie,' interrupted Canaletto happily in his Italian accent.

'As he is called by some, yes,' Pitt said smoothly. 'Well, despite all the Duke of Cumberland's efforts and a price of thirty thousand pounds on his head, the Bonnie Prince escaped our militia. He is in Paris and continues his efforts to raise enough support in this country for another rebellion.' Pitt paused for effect. Canaletto said nothing. 'I fear,' Pitt continued, 'there is yet a strong possibility he could succeed. As soon as the Treaty of Aix-la-Chapelle is signed war on the continent will be at an end. . . .'

Canaletto became very excited. 'You mean, the fighting will stop?' The war had brought an end to the stream of young milordi making the Grand Tour, as they called it. In Venice many had been unable to resist the lure of a painting capturing the charms of this most beautiful and unique of European cities. Those who could afford his prices had chosen Canaletto as artist. It was the drying up of those lucrative orders that had stimulated his relocation to London two years ago. For surely the milordi who had ordered so copiously in Italy would be equally desirous to have paintings of their palazzos and the capital city by the painter they so admired?

But ever since he'd arrived in London, Canaletto had struggled to earn a reasonable living.

If the war was indeed over, perhaps he would be able to return to Venice and rebuild his career there! But even before the fighting had started, the demand for Canaletto's paintings had declined. Others would now be in position there with new styles and new approaches. He was over fifty, too old to fight for a new position, Canaletto felt tired at the very thought. No, his future must lie here, in England, where commissions at last seemed to be coming a little more freely. After all, there had been Lord Brooke and now

it seemed the Duke of Beaufort was indeed to commission a view of his palazzo. Things were definitely
looking up.

'However,' continued Pitt, 'a condition of the treaty
will be the removal of the prince from France. If we
are to seal our differences with King Louis, we cannot
tolerate him giving succour to this pretender to the
throne of England.'

'No, indeed,' murmured Canaletto, not quite sure
where this was leading.

'The prince will be without a home. The prince's
father, the so-called "king across the water!",' Pitt's tone
was scornful, 'lives in Rome but father and son have
never dealt well together. And now Charles's brother
has been made a Cardinal, tying the Stuart line yet
more closely to the Church in Rome. As if to offset
this, our spies tell us that Prince Charles Edward is
planning overtures to some of England's leading
Jacobites.'

Pitt stretched an arm along the table with its load
of painting impedimenta. 'With the end of the war on
the continent, English attention will focus more keenly
on home affairs and there are already signs that discon-
tent is growing. At the election in Bedford last autumn
there were riots and demonstrations by Jacobite sup-
porters.'

Canaletto tried to take in the various ramifications
of what Pitt was saying. Since arriving in England, he
had made little attempt to understand politics, all
he understood of Whigs and Tories was that the former
were sophisticates and in power and the latter were
mainly traditionalists with country interests. However,
Pitt's mention of the Beaufort commission and now

this tale of the ci-devant royal family across the water made one conclusion seem obvious.

'Excuse, please, you are saying the Duke of Beaufort is Jacobite?'

Pitt nodded. 'His views are well known. The Somersets – the family name of Beaufort, you must know, is Somerset – well, it was the marriage of Joan Somerset to James I of Scotland in the fifteenth century that founded the Stuart dynasty. You remember that it was James VI of Scotland who became James I of England?'

Canaletto had no such memory but, not prepared to listen to a long-winded history lesson, nodded wisely.

'And it was only relatively recently, under a hundred years ago, that the first Duke of Beaufort renounced Rome and became a Protestant. It was felt at the time to be a political recantation rather than one of belief. So, yes, Beaufort is suspect. We need what I might call a spy in the camp,' Pitt continued. 'You are to go to Badminton, as I understand. You are skilled at discovering what others would conceal. You can be our spy.'

Pitt had gone too far. Canaletto blanched. 'My lord, sir,' he corrected himself, it was difficult to accept that this most arrogant and forceful of individuals was not an aristocrat, 'I am no spy!'

'No, of course not,' Pitt soothed. 'I should have said, an observer, a watcher on the sidelines.' He leaned forward in the confidential manner he had shown earlier. 'Signor, you must understand. This country cannot, in any sense, afford another civil war. Think of the devastation, think of the collapse of the economy.'

Think of the fact that, under those circumstances, no one might want pictures painted, thought Canaletto.

'You do see that we have to guard against any possibility of the prince raising sufficient support to mount another campaign?'

'But surely,' Canaletto objected, 'the Jacobite support is in Scotland. Is it not there you need spies?'

'Not since Cumberland finished off the Scots. There is no appetite there for another campaign. Such support as remains is too busy arguing and falling out amongst itself. No, any uprising will be centred in England. Trust me, the prince will contact Beaufort. Maybe in person.'

'In person? The prince come to England?' Canaletto was highly sceptical. To set foot on English soil was to court betrayal and execution. What man would risk that?

Pitt gave a small cough, it was almost as though he was embarrassed. 'The loyalty this pretender commands is amazing. I told you there was a price of thirty thousand pounds for his capture. Wouldn't you think some poor Scot would have been tempted to give him up? Yet none did.'

It was, indeed, amazing. Such a fortune! For the first time, Canaletto wondered exactly what sort of person this prince was.

'And he's a gambler, a harum-scarum. He loves nothing better than to fool the government and to show his father what he can get away with. He is also a master of disguise. You must remember that he escaped our forces in Scotland dressed as a maidservant? On other occasions he has donned a black wig and darkened his eyebrows and moustache. That is why, good signor, we need your eyes. We need someone who can look beneath the surface of a stranger and pick up hints that he is not what he seems.'

Canaletto had to admit that the thought appealed. His eyes could always be trusted. As could his memory.

'We should, of course, give you recompense for your trouble in this respect,' Pitt added craftily.

That thought, too, appealed to Canaletto. 'You have some likeness of the prince?' he asked cautiously.

Pitt reached into the back pocket of his grey velvet jacket and extracted a folded paper.

It proved to be a sketch of a man in an amazing plaid suit. It was drawn roughly but in a lively manner.

'We are assured that it is a speaking likeness,' Pitt said. He sat back and eyed Canaletto. 'Signor, once before we dealt well together. I was able to help you and you aided me. Perhaps we could similarly assist each other over this matter. The choice is, of course, yours. However, I have to say that you may not like the alternative.' His voice was smooth as silk.

Canaletto stood rigid, staring at him. This was blackmail. Pitt had it in his power to advance or retard Canaletto's career. Canaletto knew exactly how such moves were made. Everything in London was achieved through influence and political influence was the most telling.

Yet if he did what Pitt asked, he would be spying on a patron. That would be unthinkable.

'I need not remind you that if the Duke of Beaufort were knowingly to aid the Prince Charles Edward to incite rebellion, he would be committing treason against the state.' Again, that beautifully smooth voice.

Canaletto took a grip on himself. He thought of the

mayhem that would ensue if, indeed, England should explode in another civil war. He thought of the evaporation of the market for his paintings. 'Signor, you say I am to tell you if Prince Charles arrives at Badminton, in disguise. Well,' he said with relief as he suddenly saw that this would not, after all, be too tricky a situation. 'I do this. If Prince arrive during the two or three days I stay at Badminton, I tell you.'

Pitt looked taken aback. 'What's this, a few days? Surely you cannot paint Badminton, and I understand the duke wishes two views, in a few days?'

'Signor, I paint here!' Canaletto said in amazement, waving a hand at the view of Warwick Castle on his easel. 'At Badminton I sketch, take notes, commit views to memory. Here is where I create.'

Pitt looked nonplussed. 'You must be there longer.'

'Is not possible and sure duke would not wish it.'

'Nonsense! With his entourage, in a house the size of Badminton, he would not notice if you took up permanent residence!'

Canaletto reiterated it was impossible to spend longer than a few days making sketches.

Pitt thought for a moment. Then his face lightened. 'I have it! You must spin out the sketching and note-taking as long as possible. There will be plenty to engage your interest. After that I have a friend, Sir Robert Horton, a recently knighted City merchant, who has acquired an estate very near to Badminton. He is enlarging the house, the building works are, I understand, vast. His family are already there and I happen to know they have a great need of a portrait of Miss Horton. I will suggest that you are the man for the job.'

Canaletto was even more scandalized than when

Pitt had assumed he painted his pictures on site. 'Sir, I am vedute artist, I paint views; I not portraitist.'

'I know, I know,' Pitt said hastily. 'But, perhaps, this once? It would be made worth your while,' he added persuasively.

Canaletto looked at him in astonishment. This noted politician, sophisticate, man of huge intelligence, seemed unable to comprehend that he could no more produce a portrait than . . . 'Sir, could you write novel like Mr Fielding? Or a play like Mr Shakespeare?'

Pitt laughed, his hawkish nose seeming to quiver with his amusement. 'Signor, you have a sense of humour! My skill with the pen is certainly confined to the writing of government documents and private letters.' Then he grew thoughtful. 'So, I accept that you do not paint portraits. I have another idea. You will paint Hinde Court as it will be when finished. Just as you are doing with Warwick Castle for Lord Brooke.'

But Canaletto had seen how several ends could be achieved. How he could extract himself from the vicinity of the deadly infections so near at hand, advance Fanny's career and remove her from the orbit of the painter Hudson.

'Let me show you something,' he said to Pitt and led him to where Fanny's portrait of Rebecca stood in a corner of the studio.

Chapter Six

In the early hours of a June morning, Canaletto and Fanny set out in a post-chaise for Badminton, the Duke of Beaufort's country seat. Canaletto had insisted on travelling in a private conveyance. The very thought of the stagecoach from Warwick made him shudder.

Owen McSwiney had negotiated the deal and arranged for the chaise. It came complete with coachman and a postillion who rode the right-hand front horse of four.

As the drawings and paintings commissioned by Lord Brooke of Warwick Castle were approaching completion, Canaletto had sent word he would soon be ready to travel to Badminton.

The next day he'd received a message from Pitt:

Beaufort arrives at Badminton the first week in June. We believe Prince Charles Edward is planning to visit him there. I rely on your eyes being in position by then. All is arranged with Sir Robert Horton; Miss Rooker is to paint his daughter's portrait, commencing as soon after you arrive as proves convenient. I remain, signor, your servant, William Pitt.

Canaletto read and then reread this missive. An

uneasy feeling told him he should not have agreed to this arrangement. To spy upon a duke, a patron? How could he have allowed himself to be persuaded?

Then he remembered that yet another death from smallpox had occurred in the vicinity of Silver Street. The weather was getting warmer, infections spreading faster. He had to leave London. And there was Fanny and her career to think of.

Canaletto put away Pitt's letter and demanded that Fanny grind more green pigment for paint. 'So much grass at Warwick,' he said.

Fanny put on her painting apron, extracted two lumps of pigment from the bag they were stored in and applied herself to the task of breaking them down in a large stone pestle, all her attention concentrated on her task.

Canaletto worked on his drawing depicting the south front of Warwick Castle after Lord Brooke's intended renovations and told her of the Beaufort commission.

Fanny looked up from her grinding, a little frown on her forehead. 'Two more paintings! That is good news, signor,' but she didn't sound too pleased. With a deep sigh, she transferred the ground pigment to a porphyry slab, took up the flat-bottomed grinder and began the slow business of reducing the grains to a fine powder. Her strong arm moved the glass implement in powerful circles over the hard stone. It took time to produce a result that would please Canaletto.

After she had settled into an easy rhythm, Fanny said, a little dolefully, 'I suppose that means you will be going on a visit to the Duke's house to make sketches, as you did for Warwick Castle?'

Canaletto looked up at her and smiled smugly. 'This time Fanny comes with Canaletto.'

'Me accompany you?' She was puzzled rather than excited. 'Why, signor? Surely you won't be painting there? You do your painting here,' she looked around the studio, today as neat as a newly turned chair leg.

'You are right, Fanny. But you have commission as well.'

She stared at him. For a moment Canaletto wondered if he'd spoken in English. There were times, especially when he was excited, when he slipped back into Italian without realizing.

But after a moment she said, 'A commission, signor?'

So then Canaletto explained about Sir Robert wanting a portrait of his daughter and how he'd been approached to paint her after making the Badminton sketches. 'But, as you tell me, Fanny,' he said, a trifle acidly, 'I do not paint faces. I suggest my apprentice instead and it has been so agreed.'

Canaletto wondered just what pressure the Paymaster General had had to exert on Robert Horton. Did the merchant owe him a favour? Pitt, though, had seemed quite impressed with Rebecca Wiggan's portrait.

Gradually Fanny took in the sense of what he'd said. First the movements of the grinder grew slower and slower, then she raised both hands to her mouth as though she would stop herself from screaming and her wide eyes looked at him over the tops of her fingers. Finally she gave a muffled shriek. 'Signor, you mean, I am to paint a portrait? That is the commission?'

Canaletto nodded.

Fanny looked as if she would burst with the excitement of it. 'Oh, signor, this is your doing, I know it! And I will not fail you, I promise. Oh, this is the best news I have ever had.'

Canaletto had known she would be pleased but her reaction exceeded all his expectations.

'When are we to go, signor? Will I have time to tell my brother, Nicholas? And of course I shall have to tell Mr Hudson. Fancy, he will never have imagined I would get a commission so soon.' Then her expression darkened. 'Oh, signor, will he perhaps think I am not ready? And maybe I'm not.' She dashed over to her second portrait of Rebecca Wiggan.

'It's better than the first but still not very good, signor. I am sure Mr Hudson would say I shouldn't be accepting commissions yet.'

'Fanny,' said Canaletto in exasperation.

She dropped the picture back against the wall.

'Fanny, you are my apprentice, not apprentice of Mr Hudson, yes?'

She nodded.

'I say you accept this commission. You do what I say, no?'

'No. I mean, yes. Yes, of course I do what you say, signor.'

'Huh! I think more often you do what Fanny wants.'

Fanny opened her mouth to protest but Canaletto held up his hand. 'Enough! You will paint good portrait. I will be there to help you. I know you say I don't paint people but I know much. You believe this?'

Fanny flew across the studio, sank before him and

took his hand. 'Signor, I really am so grateful. I will work so hard.'

He looked down at her excited face and thought if anything could make a portraitist of him, it would be the desire to paint her expressive hazel eyes.

She sprang up. 'We shall celebrate. I have a little money left. Shall I buy some wine, signor? And a meat pie for our meal?'

'No, I buy, I also have commission!'

The next few days had been furiously active. There had not been time for Fanny to visit either her brother or Mr Hudson, she had had to send messages with her news. For there had been painting materials to pack and clothes and necessaries for both of them. When asked how long they would be away, Canaletto had been deliberately vague. For as long as necessary, he'd said, then added that it could be a number of weeks. It was unlikely he could spin the time out to cover the rest of the summer but he was determined to stay out of London as long as could be arranged.

Eventually, long before dawn, the post-chaise had arrived.

'This is so exciting, signor,' said Fanny, as the vehicle drew slowly away from Silver Street, the horses' hooves clopping busily on the cobbled street. 'I have never been away from London before.

'Never?' asked an astonished Canaletto.

'I know no one outside, why should I travel?'

Why indeed?

'Will it be very different from the country round London?'

Canaletto shrugged. 'Countryside is different every-where. How it is in Gloucestershire,' he managed the county's name with difficulty, 'I cannot say. I hope perhaps for mountains, rushing waters, grand trees. No mountains near Warwick,' he added. He'd been very disappointed not to come across a more dramatic land-scape on his journey to Warwick Castle.

'Are there mountains round Venice, signor?'

'Not near, no. But north, yes, and south, beautiful mountains. Italian country very lovely.'

'I'm sure the English is as well, signor,' said Fanny.

But though, once they had cleared the metropolis, the countryside was pleasant, rolling and wooded, there was nothing very dramatic to be seen. The post-chaise was infinitely more pleasant than the stage but the springs did not give much comfort. Canaletto found his body swaying and bouncing as the carriage was drawn along roads that were far from even, though an improvement on those to Warwick.

They changed horses for the first time at Hounslow. The activity here was frenetic, ostlers and grooms working, even at that early hour, to change horses on a vast variety of carriages and carts. There was more traffic than Canaletto had ever seen in all his travels. He remarked on this to the postillion as the new team was harnessed to the chaise. 'Oh, ah,' the groom said, his thin face lively. 'Hounslow has stabling for more than two thousand horses.'

Canaletto was impressed. Less so by the postillion's next remark: 'The heath's a right breeding ground for highwaymen, sir, we'd best keep firm hold of our pistols.'

Highwaymen! Canaletto rejoined Fanny in the chaise and said nothing. No point in alarming her.

Hounslow Heath was a desolate stretch of road. Despite the activity in the town itself, there was little traffic and their fast-moving carriage overtook the lumbering stage and a number of slow carts. Soon it seemed to be on its own.

Fanny, observing the starkness of the heath, suddenly asked, 'Have you a pistol in case of highwaymen, signor?'

'I have my sword,' said Canaletto, giving it a little pat.

Fanny eyed it doubtfully. 'What if the highwaymen have pistols, signor? Can you run them through before they fire?'

It wasn't a question Canaletto wished to consider. 'Of course,' he said firmly. 'Pistols clumsy, often fail; a sword will despatch a man in an instant.'

'Oh, my!' said Fanny faintly. She fell silent again, no doubt worrying about the possibility of highwaymen.

'The coachmen have pistols,' Canaletto added, a little sulkily. He would have liked her to feel his sword was as much protection as she needed.

After a while she asked, 'How long will it take to reach Badminton, signor?'

'We hope to get there by nightfall.'

'Nightfall!' Fanny gasped. 'So long!'

'Yes,' said Canaletto grimly. 'So long.' He settled himself in his corner as comfortably as he could and closed his eyes. The last thing he heard her say before he mercifully drifted off was, 'I thought you said there would be mountains!'

The morning passed slowly, the journey punctuated by the stops necessary to change horses and to pay the charges at the various turnpike gates. Fanny always cheered up then, happy to exchange greetings with the tollhouse keepers.

Around noon, at yet another of the inns where the horses were changed, Canaletto had a short struggle with himself then invested in some refreshing apricot shrub rather than small ale, plus some delicious, crumbly jumble biscuits. It was worth the price. As Fanny sipped the sweet, alcoholic drink, fragrant with the fruit, and munched on biscuit after biscuit, her expression lightened. 'Oh, signor, these are so good! I shall have to try and get some when we return to London. I hope it will not be too long,' she added with a slight frown.

'Not too long if you work fast painting Miss Horton,' Canaletto said with meaning. Then regretted his jibe as Fanny grew thoughtful again.

They regained the road, the fresh horses stepping out in a lively manner but the weather looking ever more threatening and the road once again passing through a particularly desolate piece of countryside. 'Maidenhead Thicket next,' the postillion had said while the horses were being changed. His mouth had turned down in a way that to Canaletto indicated more peril. Still, they had passed safely through Hounslow Heath, no doubt they would do the same with this thicket, whatever that was.

'What, signor, do you know of this Miss Horton I am to paint?' Fanny asked. 'Is she old or young? Is she beautiful or am I to make her so? Is the portrait to capture her for posterity before a marriage, or to attract a suitor?'

'Fanny, Fanny,' expostulated Canaletto. 'I know nothing! Pitt only said her father merchant. Is a merchant,' he corrected himself but he should have watched more than his grammar.

'Pitt, signor? You mean Mr William Pitt, the Paymaster General? He that enlisted your help with the building of Westminster Bridge?'

'Ah, well, yes,' stammered Canaletto, aware that he would now be severely quizzed as to why Pitt had approached him once again.

He was saved by a loud 'whoa' and the sudden reigning in of the horses. So sudden that Canaletto had to grasp the leather loop hanging by the window in order to stop himself shooting forward on the smooth leather of the seat.

Fanny was slower to sense the danger and ended up in a bundle on the floor.

'Heavens alive, what's happened?' she said, all agitated as she scrambled up.

Full of trepidation, Canaletto let down the window and stuck out his head. It was as he feared. 'Highwayman!' he said in a high, breathless voice. 'Ambush!'

Chapter Seven

'Highwaymen!' breathed Fanny. Tales of robbery, violence and worse raced around her mind. She knew someone who had been held up on a stagecoach by several men and lost all the money he was carrying. Someone else had been attacked riding across Haywards Heath and been shot in the shoulder when he resisted. Then there were the women who had been ravished. She didn't actually know anyone who'd suffered in this way but everyone knew it could happen.

'How many,' she heard the nervousness in her voice and started again. 'How many men?'

Canaletto ducked his head back inside the coach. 'Only one, I protect Fanny,' he said and drew his sword. The point caught in the leather lining of the coach. Cursing in Italian, he jerked it free, leaving a nasty little gash.

'Oh dear,' said Fanny. There would undoubtedly be a penalty to pay for that! Of much more concern, though, was what was happening outside. She tried to put her head out of the window, only to be pulled back by Canaletto.

'Too dangerous,' he said in an agitated manner.

Fanny dropped back into her seat, now irritated as well as fearful. She wanted to know what was happening and she was tired of the way Canaletto had constantly ordered her about the last few weeks.

The driver shouted in a quavery voice, 'Don't approach. We are armed!'

Fanny waited in a high state of nervousness for the highwayman to demand their valuables.

Canaletto's sword shook in his hand as he edged back against the seat in order to have room for the weapon in the confined space.

'Stay, I say,' came the driver's voice again, this time more authoritative.

Still no 'Stand and deliver' came. Instead Fanny could hear high-pitched sounds of distress that surely came from some animal.

She could bear the suspense no longer. Unlatching the door on her side of the carriage, she jumped down. Without the lowering of the steps, the distance to the ground caught her by surprise and she had to grab at the wheel to prevent herself falling.

From the chaise came Canaletto's anguished voice telling her to come back.

Fanny refused to take any notice. Ahead of her the road was impassable. A horse lay across its breadth, squealing piteously, throwing its head around and trying to rise. One leg, though, was bent in a curious way. Its eyes rolled distressingly, flashing white.

'Fanny,' came Canaletto's voice again. 'It's a trap, horse force coach to stop. Now we are attacked.'

But the highwayman, if highwayman he was, made no attempt to approach them, with or without pistols at the ready. Instead, he knelt and laid a hand on the animal's neck and soothed it until it lay still, its mouth flecked with foam, its eyes still rolling.

50

The man began to examine the bent leg.

The post-chaise horses shifted nervously in their traces. The coachman grasped the reins firmly, keeping the animals under control, while the postillion, astride the lead horse, held two pistols at the ready, the barrels as unsteady as Canaletto's sword.

Fanny started forward.

Canaletto yelled, 'No, Fanny, no!'

The postillion shouted, 'Approach, sir, explain yourself.'

The man looked up. 'Don't be an idiot!' he called. 'Can't you see, my horse has broken its leg!'

The words convinced Fanny there was nothing to fear and she advanced nearer.

The man gave another pat to the horse's head and rose.

Fanny stopped, just in case he was about to pull out a pistol, then was astonished to see that the rider was a priest. His cassock had been up around his waist as he dealt with the wounded animal and underneath it he was wearing riding breeches. He was wigless, his head covered with short, silky reddish curls that reminded her of a small child.

'Has your horse really broken its leg?' she asked nervously, wondering if she wasn't being over rash.

'I'm afraid it has, mistress,' he said, sketching a sort of obeisance that was no more than a nod of the bare head and a backward sweep of his right hand.

The horse had quietened now. It was a bay, the only marking a white sock on the right hind leg.

'Traveller in distress, signor?' asked Canaletto, coming up behind Fanny, his sword held ready in his hand. His support, late though it was, steadied Fanny and made her feel more comfortable.

'I fear so, sir,' the priest said. 'My horse was startled by a rabbit suddenly appearing out of that bush,' he waved a hand towards a large clump of gorse by the side of the road. 'Right under its feet. It reared, threw me, then tried to bolt but caught a leg in that damn ditch.' On either side of the road ran shallow drainage ditches. 'Begging your pardon, mistress, due to this untimely accident, my wits are everywhere but in my head. I should remember better my cloth.' He gave Fanny a distracted smile that transformed his full mouth from a touch of petulance to open charm. His teeth were very regular and white without a single gap.

'Allow me to introduce myself. Father Sylvester at your service. Please do not alarm yourself but I am afraid I shall have to despatch my poor mount. Will you allow me to draw my pistol from my saddlebag without having your doughty-looking servant there fire upon me?' Again that smile as he looked towards the postillion.

'You are not injured, are you, sir?' asked Fanny, warming towards this priest who seemed not at all the pious sort of man the Reverend Williams was at the church she attended in London. Reverend Williams always managed to make her feel uncomfortable, as though he could see all the petty thoughts that filled her brain. This priest didn't make her feel like that at all. Nor was his cassock quite like the reverend's, this had buttons all the way down the front and lacked white lappets at his throat.

Another smile, 'How kind of you to enquire, mistress. A few bruises from my fall but that is all. Now, sir, how say you?'

Canaletto looked at the reverend closely and appeared satisfied with what he saw for he nodded, then turned back to the coach. 'The priest will shoot his horse. Hold your fire, except if he fire on us.'

The postillion nodded his head but kept hold of his pistols, his hands now holding them more steadily.

All went exactly as Father Sylvester had said. He unbuckled the saddle and his bags from the horse and dragged them away from the animal. Then he removed the harness. Finally he undid one of the bags, removed a pistol, cocked it and held it to the horse's head. Fanny braced herself for the shot. Then Father Sylvester lowered his arm, said a short prayer and crossed himself before once again placing the weapon against the horse's head.

Fanny closed her eyes and put her hands over her ears, she had no wish to see the handsome animal meet its end.

The shot was very loud

Fanny dropped her hands and opened her eyes. The horse now lay still on the road.

Father Sylvester looked distastefully at the smoking pistol and dropped it on top of one of the saddlebags. 'Can I ask you, sir, for the help of your servants to move this poor animal's carcass to the side of the road? We cannot have it inconveniencing travellers.'

But the dead horse was too heavy to drag, even though Canaletto tried to help as well while Fanny held the lead horse of the chaise team, soothing it by stroking its nose. Eventually they had to unharness the team and use the horses to drag their poor brother over the ditch. They rolled their eyes and had to be persuaded into the task but finally it was done. Waiting by the chaise, Fanny saw Father Sylvester's wig and hat sitting in the dusty road, no doubt where they must have fallen when the accident happened. She went and picked them up then tried to brush off some of the dirt they'd gathered.

'Why, thank you, mistress. What a sorry sight they are, but no sorrier than myself,' Father Sylvester looked ruefully down at his cassock and stuck his finger through a large rip. 'Still, things could be worse.' He took the wig from Fanny and adjusted it on his head then added the hat. He now looked much older and, with those reddish curls hidden, more, well, more priest-like, thought Fanny. His eyes were a warm brown and twinkled engagingly.

The postillion and the coachman started to rehitch the team to the chaise. Father Sylvester picked up his useless harness and slung it over his arm then looked down at the saddle and the bags. 'I'd walk to the next town and try for another horse but I fear to leave my things here, like this. Some ruffian will come along and help himself, no doubt about that.' He looked at Canaletto. 'Would you be a good Samaritan and give me a lift in your conveyance?'

Canaletto folded his arms across his chest then lifted a finger to his mouth and surveyed the priest for a long moment.

Fanny longed to say, 'Yes, of course, we will.' But it wasn't her place. It had to be Canaletto's decision. Surely, though, he couldn't say no?

Oh, yes he could! But Canaletto lowered his hand

in a gesture of acquiescence. 'Please, we shall be happy for your company.'

Fanny beamed at him.

'Come,' said Canaletto crisply. 'We must journey. Signorina Rooker and I have long way to go.'

'Of course,' agreed Father Sylvester. 'The last thing I want to do is hold you up, I am most appreciative of your kindness in allowing me room in your chaise.'

Canaletto grunted and sent him a sharp look, then climbed back into the carriage, securing the corner he had taken when they'd started out. With a courtly gesture, the priest handed Fanny up the steps and insisted she take the other corner seat. He then superintended the stowage of his gear on to the luggage rack before climbing in and squeezing himself between them. Fanny tried to make herself as slight as possible. The priest arranged his cassock skirts over his legs and Fanny saw again the rip in the material.

'Would you like me to try and mend that?' she suggested a little nervously.

'What an excellent idea,' Father Sylvester said exuberantly, removing the cassock in one easy gesture and revealing a shirt made of a linen much finer than any Canaletto owned.

While Canaletto looked on, amazed, Fanny took the cassock on her lap, then looked in her reticule for her sewing requirements. She just managed to get her needle threaded before the traces were checked, the postillion swung himself on to the lead horse and the chaise, with a nasty jerk, set forward once again along the great west road.

'Well, this is most comfortable,' said Father Sylvester, stretching out his long and well-shaped legs. 'And the tear to my soutane being attended to as well.'

'I hope I shall be able to do a reasonable job,' Fanny said earnestly. 'But it's difficult with the motion of the coach.'

'Your horse, unfortunate accident,' said Canaletto.

Father Sylvester's charming smile faded. 'Yes, indeed. Poor Betty, she was fast and strong, I shall find it difficult to replace her.'

'Betty? Is that what you called your horse?' asked Fanny, managing to achieve some reasonable stitches in the ripped cassock. 'Our first landlord's wife was called Betty, but she and her husband left for the country,' she added sadly.

'Indeed? Then who have you now as your landlord?' asked Father Sylvester easily. Canaletto's eyes gradually closed and he soon appeared to be asleep but the priest seemed to have no difficulty in maintaining a conversation. Fanny thought it was probably a result of having to talk all the time to parishioners. He had an accent that wasn't exactly English and as she told him about Richard Wiggan and how hard he was on both his apprentices and his wife, Fanny wondered where exactly he came from.

'A man has to work hard to get on in the world today,' said Father Sylvester. 'There are great opportunities but only for those who will grab hold of them.'

Fanny thought apprehensively about the commission that had so unexpectedly come her way. She would certainly have to work hard at that. 'I intend taking every opportunity,' Fanny said firmly.

'I am sure you will have success,' Father Sylvester told her with a warm smile. He picked up the cassock she was working on. 'Why, look,' he said, 'how beautifully you are mending my poor garment. Every time now that I put it on, I will think of you.'

The coach gave a powerful lurch and he fell across her lap. She felt his arms go round and hold her tight for a brief moment. Then he laughed and regained his proper place. 'I do beg your pardon, mistress, such a liberty but none of my doing. I trust the mending has not been harmed?'

The brown eyes had such a twinkle in them, Fanny could not help laughing. She was very much afraid Father Sylvester was a bit of a rogue but he had cheered her up. 'Why, sir, I think the stitches may not be as neat as I would like but they are an improvement.' She bit off the last of the thread.

'You are an angel,' he said, slinging the cassock across his legs. 'The Lord was undoubtedly looking after me today. First I broke no bones, then I was swept up into a most comfortable carriage with the most pleasant of company. Would that all journeys offered such enjoyment.'

'Would that all alarums of the road ended so pleasantly,' countered Fanny, feeling, for once, in complete control of herself.

'Heh! What happens?' Canaletto enquired, opening his eyes and looking suspiciously at Father Sylvester.

'Why, nothing! Only that your fair companion and I have a pleasant chat as we travel along. Now, sir, you have my name and business, perhaps you would be kind enough to furnish me with yours.'

'Antonio Canale, at your service, signor,' Canaletto said, a little stiffly, attempting a bit of a bow from the waist as he sat in his corner.

'Canale?' Father Sylvester opened his eyes wide. 'Not the well-known Italian painter of vedute?'

Canaletto thawed just a little. 'Indeed, I am so called.'

'And I am his apprentice, Fanny Rooker,' said Fanny happily.

'And where does the great Canaletto travel today? Which great milordi has enlisted your genius for the immortalization of his country home?'

'Why sir,' started Fanny but Canaletto for once jumped in.

'We explore,' he said. 'We, what is word in English?' He looked at Fanny.

'We reconnoitre, signor?' she suggested, wondering why he should be reluctant to say exactly where they were headed.

He smiled at her. 'Indeed, that is word I seek.'

Father Sylvester leaned back in his seat and smiled again. 'I hope you find subjects worthy of your brush, Signor Canale,' he said.

Canaletto inclined his head. 'Kind, very kind,' he murmured. 'And you, signor, you travel where?'

'Ah, I am, as you might say, an itinerant priest. Originally from Ireland.'

So that explained his accent!

'You know Ireland? No? You must visit one day. Now I travel the country bringing the Mass to those of the Church of Rome who have none to give it to them. You perhaps have found it difficult to attend such a service since you have arrived in this country with its Church of England and the penalization of the Roman Catholics?' The twinkle had left Father Sylvester's eyes and he spoke very seriously.

Canaletto nodded slowly. 'I have been fortunate enough to be invited to a private chapel in London by a family who follow the faith. But I believe there are not so many in this country these days.'

'More than you would think, despite the penalties demanded of Catholics. They cannot hold public office nor vote, however great their possessions, unless the oath of allegiance that denies the faith is taken. There are many who think that too high a price to pay for loyalty to a king who usurped the Stuarts and spends so much time in Hanover.'

Usurped was a strong word, thought Fanny.

'Yet,' said Canaletto, 'is it not true the rising for a Catholic prince did not succeed?'

How had a light conversation suddenly turned to matters of politics with talk of revolution?

Father Sylvester laughed. 'Nay, sir, I am but a humble priest, I know nothing of such dangerous matters.'

'Dangerous,' mused Canaletto. 'Yes, I think dangerous a good word here.'

'Do you have a home, sir?' asked Fanny, hoping to turn the conversation back to more congenial matters.'

'Ah, a home! No, mistress, I merely perch here and there.'

'As a celibate,' said Canaletto pointedly, 'perhaps lack is not important?'

'I would like a home, indeed, sir. Sometimes I dream of four walls to call mine, somewhere with my own hearth where I can burn my own fire, eat my own vittles and drink my own wine. A settled existence, in other words. As it is, I seem doomed to be a wanderer

and can only exist through the courtesy of others.'
There was a ring of sincerity to his words.

'Is that what the Lord has called you to?' asked
Fanny, touched by his emotion.

'Ay, Mistress Rooker, it appears to be so. Now, tell
me of your home and your family, for I am sure you
have one.'

Fanny was happy to tell him of their life in Silver
Street and of that of her brother, the engraver Nicholas
Rooker and his wife, Lucy, and their two sons. And
Canaletto appeared content to let her chatter. The time
passed quickly until, long before Fanny expected, they
drew into Reading.

Fanny and Canaletto left Father Sylvester bargaining
over the price of a horse, his cassock neatly buttoned
over his breeches and shirt, his hat soberly adjusted
on his head. He thanked them most graciously and said
he hoped they would meet again, his eyes twinkling in
the way he had.

Fanny felt sad to say goodbye to such an engaging
companion. After Canaletto and she had started their
journey again, the carriage felt very empty. It wasn't
often, Fanny thought, that you met someone who com-
bined so many attributes: charm, attractive looks and
the ability to make you feel they would rather be
talking with you than anyone else in the world. Fanny
gave a deep sigh.

'He said he was from Ireland, yes?' said Canaletto
as the chaise lurched on to the road once more.

Fanny nodded. 'His accent wasn't English.' She
thought for a moment. 'It's not the same though as

Owen McSwiney's. He must come from a different part of Ireland, the north perhaps.'

'Most like,' agreed Canaletto, then appeared to fall asleep. Fanny thought what a pity it was they were unlikely ever to meet Father Sylvester again. She'd been grateful that, unlike the Reverend Williams at the church she attended, he hadn't once quoted the Bible at her.

Also it had been very pleasant to be with someone who showed her respect and didn't order her about. Her heart ached for the decline in her relationship with Canaletto since his return from Warwick. How on earth were they to get on together at Badminton?

Chapter Eight

Nell Horton was in the still room at her family's new home, Hinde Court in the county of Gloucestershire, making a bag for her mother to smell against the melancholy.

It was no wonder that her mother was depressed, Nell thought as she ground cloves in her large pestle. The banging and clattering that went on day after day as the new building her father was having constructed gradually rose around them was enough to drive all thoughts out of one's head.

'Nell, aren't you to come with us?' Patience Horton, Nell's younger sister, asked. She stood in the doorway, ravishing in her new, primrose silk gown. Her dark curls peeked around a straw hat, its yellow ribbon tied beneath her enchanting little chin.

'You go visiting with Mama?'

Patience came into the still room. 'Yes, Sir Percival and Lady Prout have returned from London, together with their son,' she dimpled charmingly. 'He is apparently delightful and Mama wishes us to meet.'

'Then you do not need me, you know I do not care for visiting.'

Patience came nearer. 'Dear Nell, as Papa says, you make too much of your, well, anyway, nothing is as much fun if you are not there! Not if I can't hear you comment on the Prouts. There is bound to be something about them that you will find amusing. And how will I know what to think of the Prout son if you are unable to tell me?'

'Well, Pattie, you will have to describe him to me on your return and in doing so you may find that you have made up your own mind. Though when you already have an attractive swain paying court to you, I do not know why you should worry what you think of anyone else,' Nell said a little tartly.

Patience opened her eyes wide. 'Attractive swain? Who, may I ask can that be? You cannot refer to Isaiah Cumberledge, surely?'

'Is he not attractive? And intelligent?' Nell coloured a little and picked up the piece of paper on which she'd written out the recipe gained from their friend and neighbour, Lady Tanqueray.

'He does not look at all romantic, not with those ears! And as for intelligence, he may talk to you about science and his experiments – though how Mama can entertain him in the house after your accident, I do not know – but he never addresses any remark at all sensible to me!' Patience said a little petulantly.

'Only because he is overpowered by your beauty. And the accident was not his fault,' Nell said with heat. 'It was no one's but my own.' She waved the receipt at Patience. 'All this says is "Powder of cloves in a gross powder." Do you think this a gross powder?'

Patience looked at the contents of the mortar. 'Darling Nell, how should I know? What do you do with it?'

'It's to help Mama's depression. Now it says

"Powder of mints" but with no indication of quantity. Oh, why does this receipt not give more precise instructions? And why didn't I, wretch that I am, consider what I was copying? Then I could have asked Godmama all these questions.'

'And what a pity that we should not be visiting her this morning and could quiz her for you. Is this the mint?' Patience picked up a bunch of dried leaves.

'Yes,' said Nell, relieved they were no longer discussing Isaiah Cumberledge's attractions. 'I gathered it from beside the brook on the eastern side of the garden and dried it in the portable stove,' she indicated an open cupboard on wheels with lead-lined shelves. 'Damaris complained that it was too long in front of her fire when she needed to roast beef for our dinner so I had to wait until the evening to finish the drying. But how much should I use, that's the question.'

'Why you tolerate the way Damaris rules the kitchen as though it's a kingdom and she its queen, I do not know,' Patience said a trifle fretfully. She sniffed the bunch of herbs. 'This mint is strong.'

'So is the powder of cloves. As for Damaris, you know how well she cooks and understands our little fancies. We were in a sad state until she appeared. Well, I'll try the same amount of mint as cloves.'

'Then what do you do with it?' Patience asked as she checked the fit of her long lace gloves.

Nell indicated a large glass jar of rose petals. 'Mix it with these. Then all go into a muslin bag and I sew it up for Mama to take to bed with her.'

'Charming,' said Patience. 'I am sure it will help her sleep. Cloves and mint sounds a delightful combination. Perhaps I will ask you for one myself.'

Nell smiled at her sister. 'Sweetheart, you have no need of a bag against melancholy, nor to sleep well of nights.'

'No,' agreed Patience happily. 'But why should I not enjoy such without the need?'

'In that case, I shall make another for you.'

'That would be most kind. Well, if you really will not come, I must find Mama, the carriage is already at the door.' Patience drifted out of the still room, leaving behind her a trace of the violet scent that perfumed her gloves.

Nell smiled to herself, removed her ground cloves from the mortar to a dish, replaced them with a goodly quantity of dried mint leaves and once again picked up the pestle.

Soon she was mixing the ground spices with the rose petals. But before she could start filling her bag, there was another interruption. This time it was Thomas Wright, Sir Robert's steward. He was agitated.

'Miss Horton, I regret I have to ask you this but he is very importunate.'

'Who is very importunate, Thomas?' For one breathless second Nell wondered if Isaiah had come looking for Patience. If he had, she would have the pleasure of a tête-à-tête with him undisturbed by either her sister or her mother. But then she remembered that at this hour Isaiah would be otherwise employed.

'Captain Farnham, Miss Horton.'

Thomas was always so correct with her, it irritated Nell, who counted him a friend. Her brother James might complain that she was too informal with their steward but she didn't care what James said, the steward was a rock she could rely on. Now that her father was abroad and James was in charge, someone as efficient and knowledgeable as Thomas was needed. He had a pleasant demeanour as well. Maybe a sense of humour was lacking, but Nell was always happy to spend time with him, discussing the progress of the building and household requirements. It wasn't his fault his respectable birth had not been matched with a suitable income and he had had to find employment. Sir Robert had reckoned himself lucky to have secured his services. 'Knows which end is up,' he'd said after Thomas's interview with him. 'Got a keen sense of the value of things as well. He'll more than do to keep control of the household.'

Patience had declared it was too romantic. 'He is just like a long-lost prince, he's so tall and got such a strong face and have you noticed how straight his nose is?' she asked Nell soon after he arrived. 'And have you seen the way he looks at you, sister dear? I think he has a *tendre* for you,' she added with an engaging chuckle.

Nell had told her not to be so nonsensical. But over the months Thomas had been with them, she had formed a firm friendship with him. He had been very kind to her after the incident she refused to dwell on. She appreciated his common sense and if sometimes she saw a particularly warm look in his eye when he was with her, well, it was very pleasant to be admired. If only, though, he could sometimes find life amusing!

Nell let go of the pestle and wiped her hands on a towel. 'Captain Farnham? What is the matter with him? Lead on, Thomas, don't let's keep him waiting.' She shooed him out of the still room and down the short corridor towards the main hall.

'He would have talked with Mr James but after I explained your brother was not at home and unlikely to return before dusk, he asked for you.'

'I am happy to speak to the captain at any time,' Nell said composedly.

'I fear he is not in a good temper.'

'And do you know what has upset him?'

The steward stopped. 'It's the plans for the village,' he said, reluctantly.

Nell stared at him. 'What plans for the village?'

The steward's handsome forehead frowned. 'Mr James hasn't discussed them with you?'

'James, as you well know, does not discuss anything with either his sisters or his mother. According to him our dear father reposed complete trust in his ability to carry forward all the plans for the estate,' Nell said tartly. 'He says the fact that the building work is so behind is none of his fault. So where is my dear brother?'

Thomas looked even more uncomfortable. 'I think, that is I believe, he has gone abroad to see, well, to see about a horse.'

'You mean a cock fight!' Nell's tone was resigned. 'Take me to our visitor, Thomas. Let the captain tell me his complaint himself.'

The hall was the most ancient part of the old house. Panelled and two stories in height, it was held to date back to the fourteenth century. When Sir Robert had suggested it might be better to demolish everything and start again, his wife and daughters had protested that he could not destroy such beauty. So it had been decided that an extension would be built to provide the modern, spacious mansion Sir Robert needed to reflect his status as London's leading merchant.

Striding up and down the hall's ancient flagstones, his limp now hardly perceptible, was Captain Humphrey Farnham.

The captain was a tall, lanky figure, his skin brown and weather-beaten, his dress plain, serviceable and very worn. On his introduction to the Hortons, Nell's mother had been worried. 'I am sure Sir Robert would not approve. He would think the captain of no great moment. Hardly a decent rag to his back and such rough manners!'

'Oh, but, Mama, his pedigree is most respectable and he is under the protection of the Beauforts,' Patience had said in her soft voice. 'You know how Papa approves of everything the duke does. After all, isn't that why he sought an estate in this part of the world? So that he could be a neighbour to Badminton?'

All this was certainly true. Lady Horton had sighed and said no more at that time. Later, to Nell, she said, 'I didn't like to mention it to Patience, one has to be so careful what suggestions one makes to your sister, such a romantic as she is. I cannot help thinking, though, that there is something *dangerous* about Captain Farnham.'

'Dangerous, Mama?' Nell had been amused at the idea of her mother, usually so involved with household matters that she hardly took in more than a visitor's name and credentials, making such a judgement.

'There is something about his eyes,' Lady Horton fiddled with her gown. 'The way he looks at one, as though, as though one is an animal in a menagerie! It is no laughing matter, Nell,' she said indignantly. 'Both you and Patience are of marriageable age. Single gentlemen, and I suppose one has to consider that Captain Farnham is a gentleman, what with his mama being a Russell and his papa a Seymour, dead though both now are. Well, gentleman he may be but I cannot think your father would hold him at all *comme il faut* as a suitor for either of you. A soldier of fortune, and wounded!'

'He is unlikely to try and fix his interest with me,' said Nell straightforwardly. 'And in time his wound will heal.'

Her mother looked at her fondly. 'Darling Nell, you are such a treasure, any man would value you as a wife.'

'Of course, Mama,' agreed Nell pleasantly. 'But I do see that Patience might view the Captain as a romantic figure and she is beautiful enough to turn the head of a war-sick warrior.'

But the captain, whilst seeming to enjoy his social calls on the Hortons, had shown little sign of trying to attach the interest of either the elder or younger Horton daughter. Patience he treated as someone hardly out of the schoolroom and Nell as a comrade.

The captain's lined face as he turned to Nell was set and angry. Her heart sank. No wonder Thomas Wright had been disturbed. This could be no ordinary dispute Humphrey had come about. What plans could her father and brother have? For an instant she wished she were better prepared for this meeting. Then she caught herself. Humphrey Farnham might have quarrels with others but to her he had always been courteous. Indeed, she'd thought she could count him as a friend.

'I cannot believe that you didn't tell me what was intended,' he grated out, his expression bitter and hard.

'I have tried to explain to you, Captain Farnham,' Thomas Wright started, his pleasant countenance anxious.

A swift downward stroke of the captain's hand cut him off. 'Quiet! My quarrel is with the Hortons. All of them.' He glared at Nell, who felt anger rise.

'Well, Humphrey, just what is it that you want to argue with the family Horton?' she demanded, holding herself ramrod straight and looking him in the eye.

'Why, your plans to raze the homes and buildings of your tenants,' he rasped out.

'Raise the village?' queried Nell. 'Raise it how?'

'To the ground,' said the captain through his teeth. 'That is how.'

'Oh, that sort of raze,' said Nell, enlightened. Then she realized exactly what it was he'd meant. 'Oh, sir, you cannot mean what you say. There is no plan for destroying the village.'

'You cannot be that naive,' Captain Farnham said scornfully.

'I am afraid, Miss Horton—' started the steward at the same time.

Nell looked from one to the other, appalled. 'Are you telling me,' she demanded of Thomas. She stopped for a moment, unable to believe what it appeared she had to believe. 'Are you telling me that my brother has ordered the village to be razed to the ground?'

'Not immediately,' he said quickly. 'New homes are to be built at the eastern end of the estate.'

'But why?'

'Homes and farms that families have lived in and

tended for centuries are to be demolished on the whim of a nouveau riche family who have bought their lives along with the estate. Merely so that they can enjoy a better view from their grand new house.' Humphrey Farnham's voice dripped with disgust. 'I've met more honour among armies than here.'

Nell looked at Thomas, who gave a reluctant nod. Her heart sank. How on earth was she to handle this? 'Maybe they will like their new homes better,' she said.

'They do not want to move. They have told me so,' he assured her. 'How would you like to be forced to leave a house you know and love and land you and your family have cultivated for years, adding nourishment and tending it until it harvests as you wish?'

Nell had a sudden memory of how shocked her mother had been at the news that her husband had bought an estate in Gloucestershire and was planning to enlarge it to a splendid mansion.

'Oh, sir, the housekeeping!' had wailed Abigail Horton. 'Just as I have at last achieved things the way you want here. You know how difficult it is to get good servants in London, and you so definite in your ways as to what you expect from them, and from me! I am sure they will not welcome a move to the country. Of course, some may come, but so far from town! And the winters, so cold! And the house will be difficult to heat, these country places always are. And what of your business? You will never be able to carry on your affairs from those depths. We shall end in penury, I know it! And then how will our daughters find husbands?'

'Hush yourself, my dear. We shall keep our London house. As you say, it is now just as I like things to be and we shall spend part of the year here. If you feel the winters are too severe in Gloucestershire, then we shall return to London until the snows vanish. But soon Hinde Court will be as comfortable as here,' he'd glanced around the walnut wainscoted room where he and his wife sat, she sewing, he with a pile of papers on the table by his side. 'I have engaged an architect to build us a house that will be everything modern and quite as beautiful as Badminton.'

Lady Horton wasn't yet over the distress she had felt in being uprooted from her London home. Nell could imagine just how upset the villagers would feel at having to leave their homes. But if they were to have much better accommodation?

'Thomas, bring us the plans,' she said. 'And some Marsala for the captain.'

'You'll not bribe me with drink,' he said coldly.

'Humphrey, don't be impossible!' Nell said in exasperation. 'Can't you see I'm trying to be of help? I could be telling Thomas here to send you packing for insolence.'

'He might try, he'd never succeed,' the captain said dryly.

'Thomas, do as I say,' Nell repeated with some heat.

'But Master Horton said . . .'

'I don't care what James said, he is not here and I am. Now go and get the plans and then bring us Marsala.'

The steward looked as if he would protest again, thought better of it and left the hall.

'I cannot believe my father would order anything so drastic without consulting the villagers,' Nell said to Captain Farnham.

Humphrey Farnham looked at her and some of his anger seemed to seep away. 'My dear Nell, your father is a businessman and used to making decisions with no other rationale than that they will make him money. When he comes into the country, he will have seen no reason to alter his methods. Indeed,' he added in a defeated tone, 'there are landlords of many years' standing who do the same without thinking twice. Which does not make the action any less reprehensible,' he concluded.

'Let us see exactly what the plans are,' suggested Nell as Thomas re-entered carrying a large roll of papers. She took them over to a round oak table set next to a window, unrolled and anchored them with various items, an ape's head, a large piece of sparkling quartz, a small piece of petrified wood and a stuffed sea bird, all picked at random from the collectibles that Sir Robert had hastily arranged around the hall before his departure.

Nell studied the first plan.

Humphrey Farnham came up and stood next to her. 'See, here, where the new village is planned, the ground is marshy and the wind comes across shockingly'

'So you say,' murmured Nell. 'One would need to inspect it before making such a judgement.' Her mind was racing. Had this move truly been planned by her father, or was this James taking things upon himself? Ever since Sir Robert had unexpectedly had to leave for the West Indies to attend to his properties there and left his eldest son in charge of the building operations, James had been impossible. All his love of architecture had come to the fore but also his sense of superiority over his sisters and mother, not to mention his propensity for gambling. If this was his idea, maybe something could be done. But perhaps the villagers really would be better accommodated in the new houses.

Nell released the right-hand two corners of the paper and allowed it to roll itself up and so reveal the next plan. This proved to be for the houses themselves.

'Why, these are most handsome,' she said, encouraged by what she saw. 'Model homes indeed.'

'Model homes,' scoffed Humphrey. 'It's damp there and the winds are wretched. Where they are now, the villagers enjoy a healthy climate and fertile soil. It is proposed to move them to an area where farming will fail and they will suffer from the miasmas. And never mind what the new houses look like, they will be cobbled together, just like so many of the dwellings now erected in London that fall down before their mortgages are paid.'

'Now there you are all wrong,' spluttered Nell. 'Any building undertaken here is performed most carefully. Why, didn't I take you round a few days ago to see how the work was going and you yourself admired how it was being carried out?'

'What an innocent you are, Nell. Of course the work on Sir Robert Horton's own house will not be skimped. James has enough sense to see to that. But the opportunities for shaving corners on innocent villagers' houses are too great. Particularly with a master who knows not how to keep track of expenses.'

'Thank you, Thomas,' murmured Nell, taking a glass of Marsala from the steward. 'But James is most careful to look after matters here exactly as father intended.'

'If you say so,' the captain said indifferently. He looked at the glass that the steward was offering him and for a moment it seemed as though he might refuse the refreshment. Then he took it and gulped down a good half of the wine.

Nell sighed. Humphrey's manners were shocking. She supposed it was a result of spending so much of his life in the company of rough soldiery. But he had seen and experienced so much and, when you could persuade him to talk, had such tales to tell, of chicanery, double-dealing, fighting and political Machiavellianism. He had even met Prince Charles, the young pretender. When Patience had heard that, how she had quizzed him. She'd wanted to know everything, how the prince looked, what he said, and, most of all, whether he was really as handsome and charming as everyone declared.

'As to that, you cannot expect me to say,' Humphrey had growled at her. Patience's charms never seemed to attract him the way they did most others. 'He certainly has courage and ambition. He endured five months scrambling around the highlands of Scotland evading capture with no more than a few barbaric Scots for company.'

'To wish to be King of England needs ambition,' Nell had said dryly. 'Without that he would indeed be nothing.' She was by no means in sympathy with the Jacobite cause, which she thought could bring nothing but disaster to the country.

'How did you find out about these plans, Humphrey?' she suddenly asked. 'As I told you, I knew nothing of them until now.'

The captain looked her straight in the eyes. 'Walter Cary is up in arms at the idea. He is threatening action.'

'Not Barnaby's father?' Nell said. The Cary family already had one cause to wish the Hortons had never come near Gloucestershire. And Walter was discontented at the best of times. He'd led a delegation of villagers to her father the day after they'd moved into Hinde Court, petitioning against the possibility of enclosure of the common land.

Nell had been proud of the way her father had greeted the delegation. He'd offered them refreshment and said he welcomed the opportunity to talk and get to know them. They'd left disarmed by his approach but Walter had been heard to mutter on his way out, 'Sweet words are easily swallowed, actions are what we'll watch for.'

And it was true Sir Robert had made no firm promises not to enclose land.

Later had come the accident to Barnaby.

Walter Cary could prove a dangerous enemy, particularly, Nell realized now, if he had Captain Humphrey Farnham standing alongside him.

Chapter Nine

Fanny never forgot her first sight of Badminton House. The chaise had rolled up through a charming street of delightful cottages, then entered a long drive. Finally, they approached an enormous mansion, classical in proportions, solid and dark in the gathering gloom. It seemed to encapsulate all the weight and power of ducal authority. This is where they were to stay for at least a couple of days while Canaletto prepared the sketches for his paintings.

They passed outbuildings and went through a large forecourt before turning a corner and coming to a stop in front of a columned doorway.

The postillion let down the steps and assisted Canaletto and Fanny to descend.

It was the silence that struck Fanny first. There seemed no noise at all. In London, at whatever hour, there was always something astir. Even at night-time carousers and late revellers were about, guided by link-boys with flaring torches; there was the noise of horses' hooves and carriage wheels rattling over cobbles, and the watchman calling out the hour on his rounds. Here there was nothing. Just this immense building with its many, many windows, and the sound of the horses that had brought them to this mansion breathing noisily as they rested first one leg and then another.

The postillion rattled the great doorknob. Without delay the door was opened and a porter invited Canaletto and Fanny inside.

'First I will see my luggage safe,' Canaletto announced. He looked on anxiously as two footmen appeared and removed the baggage from the back of the chaise. 'Careful,' he said warningly as a large, rectangular box was taken inside. '*Camera obscura*, very fragile.'

'Don't you be worrying, sir, we knows how to handle all precious objects,' said the larger footman, a fellow of splendid muscles and handsome aspect. Both footmen were dressed in smart breeches and shirts that were plain but of excellent quality. As the box was cradled securely in their enormous hands and taken up the steps, a man of aristocratic bearing came down to greet them.

'Most happy to see you arrived, Signor Canale and Mistress Rooker. Will you enter?'

'About the men and the horses,' Canaletto began but was stopped by a regal gesture.

'They will be taken care of, please do not trouble yourself about anything. I trust your journey was not too tiring?' The man stood back and gave a wave of his hand up the steps.

This must be the duke. Fanny had met the Duke of Richmond the previous summer when Canaletto had painted the view from his window overlooking Whitehall. Fanny resolutely refused to remember any of the unhappy events that followed, instead, she recalled how courteous and pleasant the duke had been. This man, though, was far grander.

'Thank you, my lord,' she said, giving a neat little bob.

An indefinable expression crossed the aristocratic-looking face. 'I am the duke's butler, Briggs, at your service, mistress.'

Fanny felt herself flush with embarrassment as she followed Canaletto up the steps.

The butler ushered them through a great hall into a corridor and towards a graceful staircase, its balustrade elegantly carved. 'The duke has ordered that you are to be offered every facility,' Briggs said. 'Your accommodation is arranged and a small repast awaits you. Would you prefer to have this downstairs or in your rooms?'

Fanny's excitement suddenly vanished. She had been tired when they started the journey, what with trying to juggle her portraiture activities with keeping the increasingly fractious Canaletto happy, and now she was exhausted. The journey had been long and her body ached from the jostling of the carriage. Canaletto had said that the private chaise was a great improvement on the public stage he had travelled on to and from Warwick Castle. Fanny could only wonder that his temper had not been much worse when he'd lashed out at her on his return. She felt bruised in every part of her body.

But suddenly she didn't want to be parted from Canaletto. Badminton House was too large and overwhelming, she needed a friend.

Canaletto though brushed a weary hand down his

coat. 'The room will be most pleasant, please. We meet in morning, Fanny, yes?'

What could she say?

'This way, miss,' said the older footman, and led the way upstairs.

The room Fanny was shown to on the first floor seemed huge. There was a large bed with the whitest of sheets and pillowcases and a beautiful embroidered cover. A fire burned in a small grate, an elegant table held a silver mirror with a stool in front of it. A most comfortable-looking upholstered chair was drawn near to the fire and a small round table stood beside it. In one corner was a washstand with a handsome porcelain bowl and accessories. Fanny's bag stood on an intricately patterned carpet.

Also standing in the room was a young girl wearing a simple gown with a large apron and a mob cap. As Fanny entered, she gave a little bob. 'I'm Hannah, I'm to serve you, miss,' she said in a voice with comfortingly broad and slow vowels.

A maid to serve her? Fanny could not believe it. 'Hannah, I'm very happy to meet you,' she said, holding out her hand. 'But I'm sure I will not need you to wait on me.' Then she thought of the size of the house. She had no idea where Canaletto was sleeping, nor what was expected of her the following day, or even how to find the entrance hall again. 'But if you can tell me how I should go on and where I can meet with my master, Signor Canale, tomorrow, I would be very grateful.'

'Of course, miss,' said Hannah, shaking the outstretched hand solemnly. 'I'll take you downstairs tomorrow morning. Oh, your supper's here, miss.'

The other footman, the younger, handsome one, entered. He was now wearing a green velvet coat with gold braid and carried a large tray. He put this down on the round table beside the fire and lifted a domed silver cover to reveal a bowl of hot soup. There was also a roll, some slices of rare roast beef, a small curd tart and a flask of red wine. 'There, now, miss. That should put you to rights,' he said in the same slow accent as Hannah's. 'Them's the cook's best preserved oranges,' he added, indicating the slices beside the meat. 'Go a treat with the beef, at least, that's what he says. Not something we get in the servants' hall of course.' He winked at Hannah and she coloured slightly. 'Anything else I can get you?' he asked Fanny.

'No,' she said faintly, finding it difficult to take in the care and attention she was receiving from this ducal household. 'It's most kind of you.'

The footman gave her a little nod of his head and left.

'That soup won't be hot long, miss,' Hannah warned. 'Let me take your wrap. Would you like me to unpack while you're eating? Or come back and do it later?'

'No need for that,' Fanny said, a little shocked at the idea of having someone sorting out her few bits and pieces. 'I'm sure I can manage.' She sat down in the comfortable chair. Hannah immediately organized the table closer to her and once again removed the domed cover. An enticing aroma of chicken came from the soup and Fanny's mouth watered. She hadn't realized how hungry she was.

'Is it true, miss, that you're a painter?' Hannah

asked as she stood holding the silver cover. Her expression was almost reverent.

Fanny nodded and began to feel that she had achieved a certain status. With her first commission, life suddenly looked exciting. In one way it was terrifying, her sessions with the portraitist Hudson had shown her there was so much more to the art than capturing a sitter's features. There had to be a series of clues to the subject's identity. The setting, the pose, the accessories that would proclaim status, position and interests, could be as important as the actual face. Fanny knew nothing about this Miss Horton and she would have to find out a great deal before she could start on a portrait of her. But she was sure she could overcome all problems. After all, her second portrait of Rebecca Wiggan had proved so much more successful than the first, that Richard Wiggan was actually thinking of buying it!

'Oh, miss, that's wonderful,' said Hannah, setting down the cover by the fire. 'Fancy being able to do something like that!'

After Canaletto's crabbiness over the last few weeks, Hannah's admiration was very soothing. Just why was he being so difficult? Was it because she, his apprentice, didn't want to follow in his footsteps? Or could he be concerned about his own abilities to fulfil this important commission to capture Badminton for posterity? Fanny dismissed the thought as soon as it came. Canaletto was the leading vedute artist of the day, he was, quite simply, a genius. No, it must be because of her decision. But in that case, why had he helped her to gain this first commission? Considering it now as she sipped the sustaining and delicious soup, his aid seemed positively suspicious!

She looked at Hannah. In the face of the girl's obvious respect, she felt she could unburden herself of one embarrassment.

'I made a fool of myself when we arrived,' she said. 'I thought Mr Briggs was the Duke of Beaufort!'

'Ooh, that'll have given him a thrill,' said Hannah with a giggle. 'He thinks he's such a grand person when in fact it's Mr Capper, the steward, who heads the servants here.'

'Is Mr Briggs very like the duke?' asked Fanny, finishing her soup with a contented sigh.

Hannah shook her head and giggled again. 'The duke's much kinder and not nearly so grand. He always asks how I am and how my mother is. She used to work at Badminton, you see. She was a sempstress, looked after the linen and all that, that's how I got here. It was she who approached Mrs George, that's the housekeeper, and asked if she'd take me on. It's ever such a good start I'm a housemaid really but Mrs George has said I can train to be a ladies' maid, that's why she said I could attend you. Only I'm not very good with hair, yet, miss,' she added anxiously. 'I practise on the other girls when I can but often there isn't time.'

Fanny smiled to herself at the idea of being classed a lady. 'I don't think we need worry about my hair, Hannah, really I don't.'

'Mother says if I work hard, I could end up a house-keeper.'

So, Hannah had ambitions as well!

'Mother says she should have done that instead of

83

marrying Dad. She gave up her ambitions, she says I should not do the same,' Hannah said seriously.

'And what does your father do?' Fanny found herself liking the girl more and more. This huge house was a world on its own, very different from any she'd ever inhabited before and this girl could be an ally.

'Dad works on a farm,' Hannah said abruptly. Her mouth clamped shut, she turned away, undid Fanny's bag and started taking out her clothes.

Why had her ready flow of words suddenly dried up? Fanny wanted to know more. 'Both my parents died when I was very young,' she said sadly to Hannah's back. 'I'd love to have had a father who could take an interest in what I was doing.'

'Huh!' Hannah lifted out some of Fanny's things from the bag. 'My father doesn't approve of me. He says living here gave Mother ideas above her station and he didn't want that for me. And when Mother asked him what else he thought I could do, he said become a good wife to an honest man!' Hannah set Fanny's change of linen in a drawer with some force. Then she extracted a bodice and skirt of figured lawn from the bag, her face shone and she forgot about her father's disapproval. 'Oh, this is pretty, miss.'

'It belonged to a friend of mine who died, I inherited several of her dresses,' Fanny explained. No need to mention the clothes had been given to Mary by a well-off lover. 'There are muslin ruffles and a muslin apron that go with it.'

Hannah had already found them and held them against the sleeves admiringly. Fanny felt very grateful that, thanks to poor Mary, she'd been in a position to bring with her dresses that would enable her to look respectable in this grand house.

'Is there an honest man you would like to marry?' Fanny asked.

At last another giggle, 'Who's to say who's honest? But, no, there's no one, not at the moment. And I don't want to live on the land, right uncomfortable it is! I prefer to have a good roof over my head and know where my next meal is coming from. Oh, miss, this is lovely.' Hannah shook out the folds of a green silk dress Fanny had never yet worn.

'I don't suppose I'll find occasion for that but since we were coming here, I put it in,' she said, feeling just a little foolish.

'Quite right, miss. When the duke's here, there's all sorts of parties and things, people are always coming and going. The duchess likes to be social. Though not so much as the previous one, or so I'm told. The third duchess was a right one for the entertaining.' Hannah carefully shook out the skirt, caressed the lace that finished the sleeves of the bodice and then hung both parts of the dress with Fanny's other clothes on the wardrobe pegs.

'The duke has been married before?' Fanny finished her soup and, still hungry, started on the beef. This was as good as the soup and the roll was beautifully light, with a wonderful white crumb. She spread butter generously.

'Do you not know about him, miss?'

Fanny, her mouth full, shook her head.

'It was his brother as was duke before him and it was his duchess that loved entertaining. Right one she must have been, she ran off with another man!'

Hannah paused to let the effect of what she had said sink in. 'And then, about five years ago, the duke divorced her. Divorced! Fine old scandal that was.' Another pause. 'About a year after that, the duke died and his brother inherited. Everyone here says the new duke's a much better man than his brother but that his duchess is a bit of a tartar. We're polishing everything like mad, I can tell you.'

Fanny wondered briefly if a divorced sister-in-law mattered if you were married to a duke, or if the new duchess felt she needed to live down the disgrace. 'Do you like working here?'

Hannah nodded enthusiastically. 'It's lovely. I have two dresses and four aprons,' she glanced down at her neat appearance. 'And everything's laundered for us. And I have a bed to myself and lots of friends.'

'You mean friends among the staff here?' Fanny finished the last bite of the light little cheese tart then sat holding a glass of the red wine, loving the depth of its flavour and the warmth it sent through her.

Another enthusiastic nod, then Hannah said, 'Shall there be anything else, miss?'

Fanny was suddenly conscious she was keeping the girl when she probably wanted to go off duty. 'No, Hannah, thank you, I don't need anything. Except, perhaps, would it be possible to have a little hot water so I can wash before I go to bed?' she asked apologetically.

'Oh, of course, miss. I'll always bring you a jug before you retire and another in the morning. Will nine o'clock be all right tomorrow?'

'Is that when breakfast is available?'

'You can have it any time. The others usually eats

theirs about eight but I thought after such a long journey you wouldn't want to be that early.'

'You mean the duke and the duchess?' Fanny couldn't believe she was being invited to breakfast with the duke and his family.

'Oh, no, miss. I thought you understood, them's not at Badminton yet. We expect them the day after tomorrow. That's why we're having such a time getting everything ready.'

'A lot of work, I should think,' said Fanny, wondering who else would be having breakfast if it wasn't the duke. She thought for a moment. 'I'm used to rising much earlier than eight, so I think if you could bring me the water a little before then, I should be quite rested.'

Fanny woke long before Hannah came with the hot water. It was both a luxury and a frustration to have to wait on someone else's action before she could start her day. It seemed that as long as she could remember, her duties had begun at dawn. First she had worked for the couple who had taken her and her brother in after their parents had died, then she'd worked for her brother the engraver as his apprentice and housekeeper. Now she worked for Signor Canale. But soon, maybe, she'd be independent, she had no indentures to work out, what was needed was enough commissions to set up a studio of her own. But even after achieving that, there would still be no chance to lie abed. She should make the most of this opportunity.

Fanny slipped out of bed, drew back the heavy curtains and looked out of the window at the day.

How bright the sun was! And how amazing the view! There were no great mountains or rushing falls of water. On the contrary, the landscape was benevolently smooth, rising gently towards the horizon. But as far as the eye could see, lines of carefully planted trees led in a dozen different directions, all radiating out from Badminton House. To the left there was a long lake with a bridge. Alongside the water was a small Chinese-looking pavilion. Fanny thought how very different this view was from anything Canaletto usually painted. She would be very interested to find out how he approached the problem of satisfying the duke with a picture that would celebrate his estate.

That reminded her of her own problem. How was she to satisfy the Hortons with a portrait of their daughter? 'A painting that will bring out her true beauty,' was what Canaletto had told her was required. If the Horton daughter was indeed that lovely, then she was probably vain as well. Mr Hudson had told her that vain people were the most difficult to capture. 'It's not so much the likeness,' he'd said, 'but the fact that you can never match their own opinion of their beauty.'

She thrust away the problem of the portrait to wait until she actually met Miss Horton, and looked again at the view. The sun was already up and the air was so clear, she could almost make out each leaf on each tree. Such a difference from the smoky atmosphere of London.

There was a knock at the door and Hannah entered with the promised jug of hot water. 'Would you like me to help you dress?' she asked.

'No, indeed!' Fanny was shocked. Was this what it

was like to be a lady? It seemed a very complicated life, always dependent on others.

'Shall I come back in a little and show you the way downstairs?' suggested Hannah, sounding a little disappointed.

'Oh, please do. I shall be completely lost else.'

Hannah gave a little bob and left.

Fanny washed then looked at the clothes she'd brought with her. Canaletto would be sure to want to get to work immediately. She took out her linen bodice and skirt, then added a muslin apron and cap. The smock could wait, there would be no painting today.

By the time Hannah knocked again on the door, Fanny had brushed her hair, added a muslin cap and was ready. She followed the girl down the same fine staircase she had ascended the previous evening. Now, in the light of day and fresh from sleep, she could appreciate her surroundings. Such fine paintings and wood panelling. Fanny, her eye educated by living alongside a cabinetmaker's workshop, noted excellent pieces everywhere she looked. She was staggered by the wealth that must lie behind such displays.

On the ground floor doors were open into enormous rooms. Fanny saw dustsheets being whipped off chairs and sofas, maids polishing windows, shirtsleeved footmen on steps attending to chandeliers. Maids wearing huge aprons and hauling buckets of soapy water passed her. Everywhere there was the smell of beeswax.

Much to Fanny's relief, the breakfast room was quite small.

Already at the table were two men, one young, the other rather older.

They both rose to their feet as Fanny entered and bowed courteously.

'Isaiah Cumberledge, at your service,' said the younger of the two. Mid-twenties, Fanny guessed, with an open countenance that couldn't be called handsome, his eyebrows were much too black and heavy, the nose looked as though it had been broken at some stage in his youth, his mouth was too wide and his ears stuck out so much it looked as though they were needed for holding up his rather untidy wig, but the overall effect was pleasant and friendly.

'Humphrey Farnham, equally,' said the elder man. He had a darkly weather-beaten and lined face and a supercilious air that vanished when he smiled at her.

'He's Captain Farnham,' said Isaiah, straight faced.

'And he's a schoolmaster,' said the captain, as though making a joke at the other's expense.

'For the moment only,' the other said sharply.

'A schoolmaster?' Fanny remembered the crabbed man who'd taught her her letters and tables. He'd peered out at the world through thick glasses, his coat had been snuff stained, his breeches shiny with wear and he'd been far too ready with the cane if you stumbled on your lessons. She would much have preferred someone with Isaiah Cumberledge's easy manner, even though his suit was as ill-fitting as her old teacher's.

He gave her an engaging smile and relaxed a little. 'Well, after all, teaching is a respectable profession. And we have the pleasure of meeting?'

'I'm Fanny Rooker,' she said, giving a little bob.

'How delightful to meet you, Miss Rooker.' The captain held out a chair for her to sit. 'Isaiah and I are thoroughly bored with our own company.' He was perhaps forty. His face looked careworn and as though life was a burden but he sounded in good spirits. 'Can I help you to some breakfast? There is an excellent ham and I shall be delighted to carve you some slices.'

The table was well supplied with cold meats, rolls, butter, preserves and some pastries. Fanny sat down and allowed the captain to furnish her with a plate of the ham, its flesh beautifully pink, the fat gleaming white. Despite her late supper the previous evening, she was hungry.

'Will you have coffee, claret or porter?' asked Isaiah. 'Or perhaps hot chocolate, there is none here at the moment but we have only to ring the bell and order you some.'

'Coffee?' This was something Fanny had never tasted before. Coffee houses were not for females and it was far too expensive for her and Canaletto to indulge in at home. 'I think I should like some very much.'

Isaiah poured her out coffee and hot milk.

'And what brings Miss Rooker to Badminton?' asked the captain, sitting down again.

'I'm here with my master, Signor Antonio Canale.'

'Ah, the great Canaletto!' said the captain. 'We heard that he was expected. He is to capture the duke's estate and house, is he not?'

Fanny nodded. She sipped at the coffee, wondering whether she really liked its slightly bitter flavour, then finding a rich subtlety in its depths that was very satisfying.

'And are you are a painter as well?' Isaiah asked exuberantly.

Fanny nodded.

'How splendid. Will you also paint Badminton?'

'No, I assist my master with his sketches. Then I am to paint a portrait of a neighbour, a Miss Horton.' Fanny thought the taste of these words much more pleasurable than that of the coffee.

'A Miss Horton?' repeated the captain. 'Do you mean Miss Horton herself or her sister?'

Fanny looked at him in dismay. 'I did not know there was more than one, sir.'

'It must be Patience,' said Isaiah with certainty. 'Is it not Miss Patience Horton you are to capture?'

Fanny looked from one to the other. 'I only know it is a Miss Horton.'

'It cannot be Nell,' said Isaiah decisively.

'Why not?' enquired Humphrey Farnham silkily. Fanny was not sure she liked the captain, there was something a little, what, about him? Dangerous, she immediately decided. If it had been he with a fallen horse on the great west road, she would certainly not have approached him in the way she had Father Sylvester.

'Why not?' exploded Isaiah. 'You have to ask that?'

'I am told I have to try and capture Miss Horton's true beauty,' Fanny offered.

'That's settled it, then. It's Miss Patience.'

'On the contrary, I think that shows it is most certainly Miss Horton,' said the captain.

The two men eyed each other across the breakfast table, Isaiah Cumberledge looking heated, the captain very cool but with a decided spark in his eye.

'We shall have to wait until I meet Sir Robert Horton,' said Fanny equably, wondering a little at the strength of the discussion. 'But do I understand that Miss Patience is an undoubted beauty?'

'Like a diamond of the first water,' said Isaiah lyrically. 'She shines like the stars in the sky, no, more like the moon. Her eyes . . .'

'Spare us, for heaven's sake,' the captain sounded disgusted. 'We know you are besotted with the girl but how, intelligent fellow that you are, you can ignore the far greater charms of her sister, is something I will never fathom.'

'You said you are a schoolmaster, sir?' asked Fanny, hoping to turn the conversation; interesting though it was, it seemed likely to cause dissent.

'For his sins, he teaches the Badminton estate children,' grunted the captain, leaning across the table to help himself to the claret jug.

'Merely as a favour to the duke. As soon as he finds a more suitable candidate who can be given a permanent appointment, I shall cease my task without regret.'

'You do not enjoy teaching?'

'Enjoy banging letters and sums into boneheaded children who would rather be out in the fields, working with their fathers?'

'It was obviously a stupid question,' said Fanny, rather amused at the young man's rhetoric. He seemed to have such energy, he was always reaching for something or other across the breakfast table or shifting his position in his chair, as though he found it difficult to sit still. 'A pity, because I'm sure your teaching would be much more fun than the instruction I received as a child.'

'See, I told you so, Cumberledge.'

'I wonder you don't take over the job yourself, Farnham, you are always telling me how worthwhile it is. I would be very happy for you to do so. Then I could get on with my real work.'

'And what is that?' asked Fanny with interest.

'He calls himself a scientist,' said the captain.

Fanny could tell that the captain actually rather liked the schoolmaster, even though he tried to make fun of him.

'And the duke has given him accommodation here at Badminton so he can carry out his experiments.'

'One of the duke's ancestors, the second Marquess of Worcester, was a scientist also,' said Isaiah eagerly. 'The duke is very sympathetic to my ambitions. I am lucky to have him as patron.'

'Indeed you are,' said the captain rather sourly. 'I would I had your luck.'

'You have been enjoying the ducal hospitality just as I have,' Isaiah said in a pointed manner.

'So I have,' the captain said but his tone was just as sour. 'Still,' he added on a more cheerful note. 'My plans to improve my lot are coming to fruition, soon you may see a changed man.'

'That fortune you always claim you're so near to making?' Isaiah said sceptically. 'The only way you'll achieve money is to marry it.' Then, in a very different tone he said, 'That's not your plan, is it?'

The captain tapped his long nose with one finger. 'Best to say nothing until all has been achieved, don't you think?'

Isaiah's face was comical in its dismay. 'You're not after Patience Horton?'

Humphrey Farnham laughed. 'You have no need

to worry yourself, dear boy, little Patience, attractive as she is, has no mind to speak of. I couldn't possibly contemplate spending the rest of my life with such a feather-brain.'

'It's Nell then?' Isaiah sounded astonished.

The laughter vanished. 'I would not foist such a poor figure as myself upon Miss Horton, she deserves far better.'

Fanny liked the way he said that but she wondered what it was about Miss Horton that so concerned these two men. Obviously she was not a beauty and Isaiah had sounded as though he thought it incredible the captain might want to marry her.

'Oh, no, it's not my aunt, is it?' asked Isaiah.

'You will get nowhere by such questioning. My business is my own and it will remain so. Should you not be preparing to leave for your class?'

Isaiah removed a timepiece from his waistcoat pocket and flicked open the cover. 'By Jove, you're right.'

As he rose, Canaletto came into the breakfast room.

'Ah, sir, I am honoured to meet you,' said Isaiah, offering his hand. 'I hope we may have an opportunity to talk soon. Just at the moment, however, I am required elsewhere.' He looked back at Captain Farnham, 'I shall not ask what occupies you today.'

The captain raised an eyebrow, 'Best not, dear boy, but shall I present your compliments to your aunt, were I to see her?'

'Damn your eyes, Farnham, one never knows which way to take you!'

'Tush, dear boy, ladies present.'

Isaiah looked at Fanny. 'A thousand apologies, Miss

Rooker, this mountebank makes me quite forget my manners.' He gave her a small bow and left the room.

Canaletto stood looking at the closed door as though he had not understood a word of what had been said.

Indeed, thought Fanny, she wasn't sure she had.

Chapter Ten

On rising that morning, Canaletto had immediately gone outside so he could catch Badminton House in the early light.

Dew lay on the ground, the air was fresh, birds sang. Canaletto felt a deep peace as he walked around the huge building. The stone glowed gold in the sun and everywhere was green, the grass, the leaves of the trees, the shrubs. So many greens, such subtle shades, they seemed to exude peace and a rich quiet. He gazed around him, all this space was so very different from the crowded buildings in the urban scenes that were usually his subjects. Very different also from Warwick Castle. There he'd enjoyed contrasting the rugged medieval magnificence perched on a rock with the carefully tended landscape that surrounded it. Here was none of that drama.

Feeling stimulated and happy, he made his way back into the house and found the breakfast room.

His good mood was jolted by finding Fanny obviously enjoying herself with two personable gentlemen. Her sweet smile of greeting did little to improve his temper.

After the younger man had left, he nodded curtly

to the one remaining at the table. 'Antonio Canale at your service,' he said, taking one of the chairs.

'Indeed, signor, and I, too, am honoured to make your acquaintance. Captain Humphrey Farnham at your service.' The captain half rose and gave a small nod of greeting.

'An army man?' enquired Canaletto, looking at the darkened complexion and harsh angles of the face.

'Until recently. I was wounded on the continent and have been recovering my health.'

'Now with this treaty, perhaps no more battles?' Canaletto probed.

'You may indeed have the right of it, if it ever gets signed. I understand negotiations continue. May I help you to some of this excellent ham? Or would you prefer beef?'

Canaletto expressed a preference for the beef and held out his plate with a murmur of thanks.

'I have been drinking coffee, signor,' said Fanny. 'It has a most uncommon flavour.'

'Will you take coffee also?' enquired the helpful captain. 'Or would you prefer claret or porter?'

Canaletto accepted a glass of red wine and realized that here was someone who might be able to increase his understanding of the current political situation.

'Perhaps, captain, if the Prince Charles Edward lands here and claims the throne, you may fight again?'

'Heaven forfend that should happen!' said the captain forcefully.

Canaletto swallowed a slice of beef. 'Then you think it could be possible?' he probed further.

The captain shrugged his shoulders. 'The sun rises each morning and goes to bed each night, that I know.

Whether Charles Edward Stuart can muster an army that will raise rebellion in England is not nearly so certain.'

'He did it once.'

'Indeed, signor, he did. And was sent back to France with a veritable hornet at his backside.'

'Yet I hear there are many who would welcome his return?' Canaletto reached for a dish of pickled pears.

The captain's face darkened. 'You may well have heard that but I would not repeat it, if I were you, not unless you are happy to be arrested for treason.'

Fanny looked horrified.

'As for me, I wish the prince and all his relations at the bottom of the ocean. My brother died at Culloden, hacked to pieces by a Scottish sword. My mother died shortly afterwards, I don't think I was enough to keep her attached to life when her firstborn had gone. They were the last of my family. I have no love for civil war.'

'Then you do not want a return to the Stuart family on the throne?' Canaletto was extremely pleased with the captain's reaction. If one of the duke's guests could be so against the idea of restoring the Stuart dynasty, maybe Pitt was mistaken in the possibility of the duke being sympathetic. Maybe, after all, there was little chance of the prince turning up at Badminton.

The captain was almost spitting in his condemnation of the Jacobites. 'James II forfeited his right to the throne. Attempting to bring back allegiance to the Church of Rome is against the law. At the time he tried, that law had been in place for over a hundred years, thank heavens. No, the situation now is that the country has accepted the accession of the house of

Hanover and I have given my allegiance to King George II.'

'Indeed,' murmured Canaletto. 'Our host, the duke, does he agree?'

The captain's eyes narrowed. 'If I had a mind to my health, I would forget any such question.'

'*Scusi*, you must forgive the foreigner. I just interested in situation, you understand?' Canaletto tried to sound disingenuous.

'A foreigner should be more circumspect,' barked the captain.

'Where have you travelled on the continent, sir?' Fanny asked hastily.

His little apprentice was eager to defuse the situation, thought Canaletto. And she was right, he had gone too far and it was best to leave the subject entirely. But the captain's attitude interested him enormously. He was not sorry he had pressed in the way he had. Nor did he resent Fanny's intrusion. She always had his best interests at heart and he found himself warming towards her again.

The captain seemed willing to acquaint them with a short account of some of his travels, mellowing as he talked. 'And in Paris I once met with Charles Edward Stuart. I cannot say I was impressed.'

'I have heard that he is very charming,' said Fanny, looking fascinated.

'Oh, that he is. And relies too much on it. Always chasing the women and he's too fond of his wine. Not much of a commander either, can't recognize which of his generals is the most skilful, and he's too hot headed and too full of his own importance.'

'You talk with prince?' Canaletto enquired eagerly, too eagerly.

'Yes, why?'

'He sound interesting fellow,' was all Canaletto could think of to say. But he was delighted. Here was someone who could identify the prince.

'Interesting? It depends on your point of view. I have to say I told him I hoped he would never show his face in England again. He did not take kindly to that. He believes in his divine right to rule.' Captain Farnham bared his teeth in what Canaletto assumed was meant to be some sort of smile. 'I hope our paths do not cross again.'

Better and better! The captain was unlikely to protect his identity if Prince Charles Edward by any chance did show up at Badminton. However, this was now seeming more and more unlikely. Perhaps, after all, this commission could be completed without him having to make difficult decisions.

After breakfast Canaletto asked Fanny to find the *camera obscura* and meet him outside the north front. Then he collected his tripod, his sketchbook and some tracing paper and started across the large gravel semi-circle that lay outside the front door. Beyond lay the green sward that led to lines of trees radiating out as far as the eye could see. As he walked, Canaletto wondered if the duke's estates were large enough to encompass each of the lines or whether his neighbours had been persuaded to continue the rows that proclaimed all paths led to Badminton.

He had not got far before someone hailed him.

From the direction of the large forecourt on the west façade came a small, puffing figure.

'Mr Canal, isn't it?' he said as he approached. He took off his hat and wiped a sweating brow with a large kerchief, then stuffed it into a back pocket of his shabby black jacket. Equally shabby black breeches, a shirt liberally decorated with the remains of what must have been the last two weeks' meals and an untidy cravat completed his ensemble. 'My word, sir, it's fortunate I saw you striding out there. Saves me from having to chance curiosity by enquiring for you at the house. And if it was one thing Mr Pitt said I must avoid, it was arousing curiosity.'

All Canaletto's delight in the beauty of the scene vanished.

'Mr Pitt?'

'He sent me, sir,' the little man gave a small bow. 'Joshua Bland at your service. I attend on matters for Mr Pitt in Bath – you know he is a Member of Parliament for the city?'

Canaletto felt a certain despair. That Bath was no great distance from Badminton had been pointed out to him by Matthew Butcher. The surgeon had come to say goodbye just before he left for the spa. When Canaletto had revealed the details of his new commission, he had pressed his direction upon him, saying, 'You would enjoy a visit to Bath, according to my sister, there is much building of a very high quality there.' Canaletto had murmured something non-committal. He had not realized, though, that the Paymaster General had such a close interest in the place. There seemed no way he could avoid his influence.

'Mr Pitt suggested I ride out to Badminton and

make contact. Just to reassure you that, when you have something to report, you have only to get the information to me and I will see that it is immediately sent on to Mr Pitt.' Joshua Bland had an annoying habit of sniffing at the end of each sentence. 'Here is my card.' He handed over a piece of pasteboard bearing his elaborately printed name and an address in Bath. 'You haven't, I suppose, anything to report at the moment? No unexpected visitors to the duke?'

'The Duke of Beaufort is not yet in residence,' said Canaletto carefully. He mentally reviewed the two men he had met that morning. One, surely, a little too young to be the prince, and with no sense of that self-importance the captain had spoken of, the other too old. Neither bore any resemblance to the sketch he'd been provided with. 'I have seen no man who could be the pretender prince.'

'Excellent, sir! We're right glad to have you here, where you can keep a close eye on the situation,' Joshua Bland pulled down the corner of one of his eyes in a graphic gesture. 'Just remember, I shall be in close contact.' It sounded a threat.

'Tell Mr Pitt I conscious of my duty,' Canaletto said stiffly.

'He'll like to hear that, sir, and so I shall report. I shall be seeing you, then, sir.' Joshua Bland gave a huge wink to Canaletto and strolled off, back to the courtyard.

Canaletto found he was sweating and it wasn't because the day promised warmth. He slipped the piece of pasteboard into his pocket without looking at it again. But he was shaken, he had had no idea Pitt would keep such a close eye on him at Badminton.

'I'm sorry it took me so long, sir.' Fanny appeared, bearing the big rectangular box wrapped in a cloth that had so concerned Canaletto the previous evening. 'They had locked the room it was put in and I had to apply to the steward for the key.'

'Well, we must commence to work,' Canaletto said sharply and strode forward, leaving Fanny struggling with the box.

Level with the lake, Canaletto stopped and Fanny put down her burden with a sigh of relief. 'This must be aspect for my view,' he said. 'See, grand pediment and cupolas.' As Fanny looked towards the top of the house, a window on the first floor was raised and a feather bed thrown over the sill. Then another window shot up and a duster was vigorously waved.

'Signor, don't you love the rows of trees?' asked Fanny, turning to the view behind her. 'Can you see them from your bedroom?'

Canaletto was not to be deflected. 'Tomorrow we look at view from house, today it is house we sketch.' He decided that more distance was required and continued to walk.

'How much further, signor?' Fanny asked in an anguished voice. 'I'm not sure I can carry this much longer.'

'Is not very heavy,' said Canaletto dismissively and strode on. He was anxious to complete as much as possible of the groundwork for his pictures before the duke arrived with his family and entourage with all the bustle and activity that would follow. Plus the possibility of the wretched Stuart pretender turning up.

Canaletto was not surprised that the prince was considered likely to approach the Duke of Beaufort for funds. Everything about Badminton House, its size, the number of its staff, its lavish furnishings, said that here must live one of the richest men in England. He'd seen a most impressive carved sarcophagus in the hall, a classical antique without a doubt, and glimpsed an elaborate cabinet of the finest marquetry he'd seen. Though Pitt had said the Duke of Beaufort did not concern himself with the governance of the realm, surely his potential power must be vast!

Canaletto was determined not to spy upon a patron. It did not fit with his notions of honour at all. But if he didn't, Pitt could make his life in England impossible. Just when he seemed to be attracting the commissions he needed. And when he had his studio so nicely organized with Fanny making him so comfortable. He tried to tell himself that if the duke encouraged the ambitions of a pretender to the throne, he was committing treason against the state.

But what if the treason succeeded? Could it then be called treason?

Oh, it was such a conundrum. At the moment it seemed as though the only way Canaletto could emerge from the situation with his honour intact was if the prince failed to turn up at Badminton.

Canaletto heaved a great sigh and gave his attention again to the view while Fanny set down her burden with a cry of relief.

The house was handsome, no doubt about that. The cupolas either side of the central pediment added considerable interest, as did the wings. The question was, how best to present it to reflect the power and magnificence of its owner. From an angle? Made dra-

105

matic with thundery clouds behind? Foliage to be introduced where no foliage existed?

'So much grass,' said Fanny doubtfully. Then she added cheerfully, 'But it will offer great scope for the characters you populate your views with.'

Canaletto said nothing. Already his mind was assessing possibilities with lightning speed. Finally, carefully ensuring he was standing at the dead centre of the building, he set up his tripod and made certain it was steady. 'Bring me the camera,' he ordered Fanny. She unwrapped the box she'd been carrying, revealing a long lens at one end, and brought it over. Together they fixed it securely on the tripod.

Canaletto took out a sheet of tracing paper from his portfolio, then opened the top of the box, revealing a ground-glass screen. He carefully placed the paper on this, felt inside the back pocket of his jacket and brought out a lead-tipped stylo. 'The cloth,' he said.

Fanny picked up the dark material that had been wrapped around the box and gave it to Canaletto, who flung it over his head and then stood looking at the screen.

Now a view of Badminton House was reflected on to the glass beneath the tracing paper. And now a figure appeared walking towards him. Even reduced in size, as it was by the lens, the newcomer was not difficult to recognize. With a certain sense of fatality Canaletto heard Fanny say, 'What a surprise to meet you, father.'

Canaletto removed his head from its covering. The priest was no longer wearing his soutane, instead he was dressed in a dark-blue coat and breeches with a fine lawn shirt and neat cravat.

'No sooner did you start to work, signor,' said Fanny, 'than I saw Father Sylvester approach from the trees behind there,' she waved a hand towards the little Chinese pavilion.

'Signor Canale, it is a great pleasure to meet with you again.' Father Sylvester held out his hand, seemingly unperturbed at running across his travelling companion at this grand estate.

'Do you take the air on this bright morning?' asked Canaletto. 'I trust you still have your new horse?'

'Indeed, though he is, I regret to say, not much of a stayer. Still, he carries me safely enough.' The priest turned to look at Badminton House. 'Mine host at the inn I found refuge at last night commended the beauty of this house, I thought I would ask to be shown around, I gather the duke is not at home?'

'You know milord?' asked Canaletto, studying him curiously.

Father Sylvester waved a hand deprecatingly. 'We have acquaintances in common, one in particular.'

'They are very busy getting the house ready for the return of the duke and duchess,' said Fanny doubtfully.

'They will be here soon, then?'

'Tomorrow.'

'And you think no one will have time to show a visitor around today?'

'You could always enquire.'

Another wave of the hand. 'I would not like to trouble such people. Better, perhaps, to wait until the duke is back and then to present my credentials and offer him greetings from our mutual friend.'

Before Canaletto could enquire into the name of this friend, Father Sylvester's attention was caught by

the box sitting on its tripod. 'What is this?' he asked
with a lively curiosity.

'It is my *camera obscura*,' said Canaletto.

'*Camera obscura?* A dark room? How interesting.
May I ask its purpose?'

Canaletto could never resist real interest in his
work. 'It captures a view, one can draw skyline most
accurately. Put your head here and cover it with this
cloth. A mirror inside throws picture on to glass, see?'

'By all that's wonderful,' came Father Sylvester's
muffled tones, 'Badminton House in miniature! This is
truly remarkable.' He started to describe the glories of
the view as he saw it but Canaletto saw that someone
else was now approaching. Covering the ground at a
rapid rate despite his slight limp was Captain Farnham.

'At work already, I see,' the captain said as he drew
near. 'Is this the view you have chosen?' He turned
back and looked at the house. 'I have to say, it is quite
a prospect. When I saw what William Kent had done
to embellish the place, I was quite taken aback. Charles
had told me his brother had started all sorts of works
and that he was continuing with them but I had not
expected quite such changes.'

For several minutes Canaletto, the captain and
Fanny looked at the splendours of Badminton House.
'Who would have thought,' the captain continued, 'that
a pediment and a couple of cupolas could make the
house look so much more impressive.'

In his mind's eye, Canaletto removed these
additions and had to agree that they added considerably to the house's stature.

'But what is this that you have there?' asked the
captain, turning again and indicating the camera.

108

'Ah,' said Canaletto. 'It is very useful aid for my work. 'Father Sylvester is studying the view from inside,' he added. 'But when he has finished, you may see.'

'Why, signor,' said Fanny in surprise, 'Father Sylvester has gone!'

The cloth lay draped over the instrument. While the three of them had been looking at the house, the priest had quietly departed. Looking around, Canaletto saw him walking rapidly in the direction of Worcester Lodge, the banqueting house that sat on the horizon.

How very strange!

Chapter Eleven

Damaris Friend, cook at Hinde Court, woke in the early hours of the morning.

For a few moments she lay in her narrow bed at the top of the old house and wondered what could have roused her.

Had it been something at the back of her mind? She'd been worried about the cream in the dairy. The weather that evening had been overcast and humid, it had threatened thunder and everyone knew that thunder could turn cream. Lady Horton would not be pleased if the cream for her morning chocolate was not sweet.

Then there was the matter of the apricots steeping in spring water that she and Mistress Nell were to make into apricot wine. Damaris had been charged with the duty of removing them before nightfall but she'd been interrupted and the task had quite escaped her memory.

Damaris moved voluptuously on the hard, straw pallet as she remembered just how she had been interrupted and she ran her hands down the inside of her thighs then up to her full breasts. It was no wonder she had forgotten the apricots!

Damaris's thoughts drifted from why she had

woken to wander through the treasures in her memory. She wasn't an introspective girl. Life so far had taught her to live by her wits, to make the most of every opportunity and let other people take care of themselves. She was, though, the first to admit that it had been a lucky day when Nell Horton had answered her knock on Hinde Court's kitchen door. Even luckier had been the day when she'd gone out picking sorrel from the hedgerow for a ragout. Oh, what a sweet afternoon that had been! Her mind filled with the delights of dalliance, Damaris lay awake. Never in her life had she been so happy before and she was determined that, whatever it took, she would keep her happiness. None knew better than she, though, what dangers she was running.

Suddenly she sat upright, all thoughts of sexual play banished. Now she knew what had woken her. There it was again, a crackle like a small pistol shot. And she could smell smoke. Hinde Court was on fire!

Damaris leapt out of bed and drew on her gown with no thought of petticoats or chemise. That damned James Horton, she thought, smoking in bed again. He never listened to anything anyone said.

The thought of his room full of smoke and him asphyxiated where he lay, bed curtains and posts aflame, made her heart race. She rushed for the door, petrified she would find the corridor outside full of smoke. There was nothing. Not only that, the air there smelt sweet and the crackle of the fire was less than in her room.

She stood still for a moment, wondering if she could have imagined it. No, there was the sound again and now she could see wisps of smoke curling round the window frame. On the other side of that was the grand new house being built for the Hortons. It must be alight!

Damaris banged on the door of the room next to hers where the three maids slept, then went on to the housekeeper's. At present there was only one male servant in the Horton household who slept at the court, Thomas Wright the steward-cum-butler. His room was on the other side of the staircase and woe betide any female found in that part of the house. Damaris ignored the prohibition and banged on the steward's door. 'Fire!' she yelled, banged again then dashed down the stairs and beat loudly on James Horton's door. When she got no response, she flung it open. 'The house, it's on fire,' she shrieked and shook his sleeping figure, his nightcap askew over one eye.

'Eh, what's up?' he groaned, turning over. 'Damaris? What the hell?'

'The house, it's on fire,' she repeated, even louder. 'Do something, you pitiful specimen of a man.'

Without waiting for his response, she flew out of the room and into the one shared by Nell and Patience.

Nell woke first. 'Fire?' she breathed, her eyes wide and terrified. Then she swallowed hard and spoke more firmly. 'My mother, the babies?' she asked as she slipped out of bed and drew on her robe. 'Go to them, Damaris, I'll wake my sister.' Damaris left her shaking Patience and telling her in a quiet, reassuring tone that the house was on fire and she had to get up. The sound of Patience's shriek followed Damaris down the corridor.

By now footsteps were pounding down the narrow stairs from above accompanied by panic-stricken cries from the maids and the commanding voice of the housekeeper calling for order. And the smoke was curling down from the upper floor into the main part of the house.

Waking Lady Horton was beyond Damaris. Laudanum, she thought grimly, as she left the sleeping woman breathing loudly and dashed on to the nursery at the far end of the corridor. The nurse was deep asleep, as were the three little ones. Beside herself with fear, knowing all too well how quickly fire could spread, Damaris shook the nurse remorselessly. 'Get the children out, never mind their clothes,' she ordered in a low, vibrant voice as the woman groped her way up from dreamland. 'It's fire.'

'Fire!' the woman stared up at her, a fat plait of hair falling over one shoulder and down a thin breast. 'Fire!' she repeated on a note of fear and struggled from the bed.

'Sshh,' said Damaris urgently. 'Don't alarm the babes.'

'Oh, the poor little darlings!' the nurse moaned, at last managing to release her limbs from her bedclothes.

Damaris was already kneeling by five-year-old Jack. 'Come on, love,' she said softly. 'We're going to have an adventure. We're going to see what moonlight is like.' He opened his eyes, instantly awake in the way children can be and gazed at her wonderingly. 'Bikkies?' he said, reaching out a hand for one of the biscuits Damaris kept for his visits to the kitchen.

'No, darling, just a run to see the stars. You will all count how many you can see.' Jack slid out of bed, looking expectant.

'Theo can't count but I can.'

'Of course you can. Put this on,' Damaris snatched up a jacket from a nearby chair. 'Now run down the stairs.' She found another jacket and helped three-year-old Theo into it. The nurse had already wrapped baby Katie and stood waiting with her in her arms as though she needed to be told what to do next.

'Take them downstairs,' Damaris ordered shortly. 'Go,' she urged, flapping her hands at the woman. Jack was already whooping down the corridor, crying out, 'I'm counting stars, everybody!'

Finally galvanized, the nurse followed, holding Katie and leading Theo by the hand.

Damaris returned to Lady Horton's room to find Nell bending over her mother and imploring her to wake. 'You won't do it, I've already tried, she's right out. We'll have to carry her.'

Smoke was infiltrating the bedroom and there was the sound of a crash above. 'That's my bedroom ceiling,' the cook said matter-of-factly. 'We can't wait.'

Nell slipped an arm beneath her mother. Damaris did the same and together they lifted a groaning Lady Horton out of the bed. Reaching with one arm, Damaris scooped up a robe from the embroidered silk bed cover. Then she decided the effort needed to put it on the drugged woman was too great so slung it over her arm instead.

Only the smoke had so far spread down to the first floor but the flames couldn't be far behind. Together Damaris and Nell forced the semi-conscious woman towards the bedroom door. Groaning and muttering under her breath, Lady Horton did her best to resist them. Suddenly she waved a hand wildly and hit

114

Damaris on the nose. 'What's happening?' slurred Lady Horton.

Damaris pushed the hand away and Nell took a tighter hold around the ample waist. 'The house is on fire, Mama, we have to leave.'

There was a long moan of distress. 'Fire? Fire? Where's Robert?'

'Father's abroad,' said Nell succinctly as they negotiated the doorway.

'Abroad?' the word was badly slurred. Then, 'Fire?' on a rising note of distress.

'Don't worry, Mama,' gasped Nell as they yanked her along the corridor, almost lifting her off her bare feet. As they approached the stairs, Damaris felt her lungs fill with the choking smoke now pouring down from the upper floor. She stopped.

'We'll never get through there!' She could hardly manage to speak.

Nell gasped, 'Scarves, that's what we need. Hold her.' She released her grip on her mother and dashed into her bedroom.

Damaris put both her arms round Lady Horton and pushed the woman's head into her shoulder, burying her own in the thin hair. The acrid smoke was terrible. Above her she could hear the hungry crackle of the flames. Was it her imagination or could she feel heat coming through the ceiling? How could Nell be so calm and quick-thinking?

A wet piece of material was wrapped around her nose and mouth. 'Help me put one round my mother,' said Nell, her voice muffled through the scarf that was wrapped around her own face. A moment later, they were all equipped for escape from the burning house.

Now better able to breathe, Damaris approached the staircase with caution. What if it was smouldering? What if the flames had already reached their little landing?

The heat of the fire came down from the attic floor and the smoke, even through the wet scarves, threatened to choke them, but the staircase was intact. It was narrow and twisted round several times as it wound down to the flagstoned hall. Damaris went first. Immediately she felt the weight of the semi-conscious woman pressing on her.

Then there was a terrible screech and Puff, the house cat, slid past Damaris up the stairs, followed by Jack, just failing to grab its tail. 'Go back,' shrieked Nell.

It was too late, the cat had threaded itself through Lady Horton's feet and, with a gasping cry, she staggered, then collapsed on Damaris, dragging Nell down with her. In a confused bundle of legs and arms, the loose bed robe tangling them further, the three women fell down the remaining stairs on to Jack. He gave one terrified scream then fell heartbreakingly silent.

Damaris lay winded and helpless underneath the weight of both Lady Horton and Nell.

It seemed a lifetime but it could only have been a moment before Nell picked herself up and attempted to pull her mother off Damaris. Damaris heaved as best she could from below. For one awful second she feared the woman would come crashing down on her again but then the balance shifted and Lady Horton was upright, swaying dangerously but held in place by Nell.

Desperately aware that every moment they

delayed, the fire could sweep down on them, Damaris scrambled to her feet. Unbelievably, she seemed to have all her limbs intact. But lying senseless in a huddle at the bottom of the stairs was the boy.

'Get your mother out,' Damaris said to Nell, pushing them past her. 'I'll bring Jack.'

She bent and pulled Jack's nightshirt over his head to protect him from the choking smoke then tried to get his slight, limp body over her shoulder.

'I'll take him,' said a voice.

'Thank God,' Damaris breathed. At last here was Thomas Wright.

He stooped and lifted the small boy in his arms. 'Are you all right?' he jerked out.

'Yes, go,' she gasped and stumbled after him out into the clean, clear air.

Outside, the night was dark, the moon obscured by heavy, threatening clouds. But its light was hardly needed as bright flames sparked their way up from the roof of Hinde Court and illuminated the chaotic scene.

Someone, it had to have been Thomas, had organized the maids into hauling water out of the pond at the side of the house. The two grooms who slept above the stables had been awakened. One was up a ladder and the other was passing buckets of water up to him. Trying to douse the fire was a hopeless task for flames were now licking out of the soffits all around the house. Taking no part in the rescue attempt was James, who sat on the low wall that edged the little formal garden in the front of the house, his head buried in his hands, an embroidered robe billowing around his bare legs. Beside him, Patience tried to calm an excited Theo and the nurse held a miraculously still sleeping Katie.

Also sitting on the wall was Lady Horton, her bewildered gaze trying to take in the magnitude of the fire.

Nell left her mother and came hastily towards Damaris and Thomas.

'How is he?' she asked urgently, smoothing back a lick of hair from Jack's forehead.

The steward lowered the boy gently on to the wall. 'I think his arm is broken and he must have cracked his head. Forgive me, I have to try and save the house.'

The house! Damaris looked up at Hinde Court. The blaze at the moment was still confined to the top floor. The flames were strongest at the junction of the new part with the old, in the centre, exactly where her bedroom was – or had been! As she watched, more roof fell in, sending showers of sparks high into the dark night.

Thomas Wright walked swiftly towards the scaffolding reaching up the bare walls of the new building, his tall figure outlined by the flickering light. For a moment he looked up towards the roof, then he turned and called to James. 'Sir, we need all the help we can get to put out the fire. You must stay with one lad here while I take the other and try to get some buckets up the new part of the building; that seems to be where the flames are worst.'

James groaned and lifted his head. 'My father, what will he say?'

Pusillanimous was the word for him, thought Damaris. How could she ever have thought he had anything to offer her? She felt desperately tired. Her body ached from the bruising she had received in the fall and she longed to be able to lie down somewhere, anywhere, and cry herself to sleep. Instead, she had to keep all her wits about her if anything was to be rescued from this terrible situation.

Damaris returned to Nell, who held the still unconscious Jack slumped against her shoulder. One arm hung oddly. Damaris gently examined it. 'I think it's broken,' she said.

'Oh, Jack, my darling,' moaned Lady Horton. 'What shall I do if I lose you?'

After Patience, Damaris knew that five children had been born and died before Jack had appeared. Lady Horton was not the most sensible of women but she had had much to bear.

Out of the corner of her eye, Damaris saw a movement in the shrubs that bordered the garden. In a moment she was there. Just in time to grab a lad who tried to escape her firm grasp.

The light of the flames hardly reached this spot but Damaris easily recognized the scarred face 'Barnaby Cary, what do you here?'

'Nothing, miss,' he said in a frightened voice.

What he'd been up to could wait. 'Can you ride, Barnaby?'

He stared at her, his damaged face inscrutable in the dark. 'A horse, miss?'

'Yes, Barnaby, a horse. I'm going to harness one for you then you must ride and fetch help.'

'I don't need a horse to go to the village, miss. 'Tis only a step.'

Damaris ignored the interruption. 'Wake your father and tell him we need men to handle buckets of

119

water or the Court will burn to the ground. Then ride to Badminton, and wake them, too.'

'Badminton, miss?' Barnaby's one wide eye was enormous. 'The duke's house?'

'You can wake him, too, if he's there,' retorted Damaris. 'Now, go!' She gave him a push.

Only the manpower that Badminton offered could possibly save Hinde Court from being consumed by fire.

The question was, how on earth had it started?

Chapter Twelve

At first Canaletto thought it was thunder that had woken him. Then the noise came again and he realized that someone was knocking at the side door of Badminton, knocking so loudly it could have been the devil at the gates of heaven.

Canaletto's inveterate curiosity aroused, he left his comfortable bed, so much softer and wider than his London one, threw up the window and craned out his head.

He could only see the rosy flush of dawn. But he could hear heavy bolts being drawn back and the slow drawl of the porter, followed by the high, excited tones of a boy. Then both vanished inside. And now Canaletto remembered that his room didn't face east. He looked again, the warmth in the sky had a flickering quality that said it came not from daybreak but fire.

Footsteps pounded up the service stairs not far from his room. There was more banging on doors on the floor above, where the servants slept.

Canaletto could not resist finding out what was happening. Hurriedly he dressed. Hurriedly, yes, but with his usual care. Canaletto never presented himself less than immaculately.

By the time he made his way downstairs, he found

a scene of extraordinary commotion. The great hall was dimly lit with side sconces, no one had taken the time to light the chandeliers. Milling around were a large number of male servants dressed in ordinary breeches and hessian jackets that looked as though they had been pulled on without any thought as to their set.

On the edge of the scene, trying to attract the attention of the steward, John Capper, was the young man Canaletto had met at breakfast the previous day, Isaiah Cumberledge.

Canaletto went and presented himself. 'Signor, Antonio Canale at your service. Can you tell me, please, what happens?'

Isaiah, his other name was far too difficult for Canaletto to apply to him even in his thoughts, looked strained and distracted. 'A neighbouring house is afire. I am trying to find out which.'

'You have friends in that area, no?'

'What? Oh, yes, yes, I have.'

Isaiah's obvious wish to talk to the steward was frustrated by Briggs, the duke's sanctimonious butler. 'By all means send over to the stables for the lads to fight the fire, Mr Capper, that I will allow to be only right. But to let the footmen go when there's his lordship and her ladyship to be attended to later today, all tired as they are after their journey and wanting to see that everything here is in order – no, that I cannot allow.'

'Mr Briggs,' said the steward in awful tones, 'who is master here, you or me?'

Isaiah sighed, 'Those two are constantly at war.

122

Briggs refuses to admit his position is inferior to that of Capper.'

Canaletto looked at the two senior members of the household. 'You say Briggs is butler? He is not on level with steward?'

'Indeed, no! The steward concerns himself with the whole household, the butler merely attends to matters of the table.'

'Ah!' Canaletto saw the butler draw himself up, preparing to launch another attack. But just then came the jangle of a bell from within the house.

'His grace has summoned me,' announced the steward with ineffable dignity.

'Now we shall see how he would have his household ordered,' retorted the butler.

'Fry,' called the steward. One of the men stepped forward. Middle-aged with a weather-beaten face, Canaletto recognized him as the head groom who had taken charge of the post-chaise when he and Fanny had arrived at Badminton. 'Harness up one of the carts and take all the ground staff over to the fire immediately. But leave Richards ready to take the inside servants in another as soon as I have confirmed his lordship's wishes.'

Fry nodded and left, followed by some half dozen of the men. The steward left the hall.

'He did not say where the fire is,' murmured Canaletto to Isaiah.

'I know,' the young man said in anguished tones. 'There are several substantial houses in that direction. Oh no,' he groaned.

Canaletto followed his gaze and saw a small boy huddled on a chair. His face was badly mutilated, perhaps as a result of another fire for the skin was discoloured and badly puckered and one eye completely gone.

Isaiah hurried over to him. 'Barnaby, is it Hinde Court that burns?'

The boy looked up and scowled. 'It's not my fault,' he whined. 'It was nothing to do with me.'

Isaiah crouched down until his face was on a level with the boy's. 'Of course not,' he said robustly. 'You have brought the news and summoned help. You've done well. But are they all safe, all of them at Hinde Court?'

Obviously, he'd meant to ask after one particular person, most probably a girl. Hinde Court was the address of the Hortons. Was the daughter whose portrait Fanny was to paint the same girl he was interested in?

Barnaby's one eye scowled at Isaiah. 'I saw all the family come out, sir, and the servants. But Master Jack tried to catch the cat and it ran back into the house.'

'You mean he followed it? But he came out again?'

Barnaby's expression became sly. 'Told you, didn't I, all the family was out?'

Isaiah put a hand on his shoulder. 'That you did, Barnaby and I thank you for it. Now, I must ride there and help to put out the fire.'

'They'll never do it, sir,' Barnaby said scornfully. 'The roof's burning, you can't get enough water up there to put it out.'

As though in answer to him, the wall sconces were dimmed by a blinding flash of lightning. It was followed almost immediately by a deafening roll of thunder. Then came the first lash of rain, driven hard against the windows. It was as though heaven had had a bath and was now emptying a vast container of water. No line of men handing up buckets could have such an effect. If anything was to save Hinde Court, it had to be the weather.

'We'll not need to go now,' said Briggs with enormous satisfaction. 'You may return to bed, men.'

It was hard to say whether the servants were relieved or disappointed but just as they started to move out of the hall, John Capper returned. 'Stay,' he said imperiously. 'My lord wishes the Horton family and servants to be offered the hospitality of Badminton. Richards,' he said to the groom who'd been deputed to take the indoor servants to the fire. 'Harness the big coach, take it to Hinde Court, hand over to Fry and tell him to bring back the family. Once they are safely here, he is to return for the Horton servants. You will bring back the cart with our men when they have done all that is needful.'

The man hurried out.

The butler gazed horrified at the steward. 'All the family and the servants to come here?' he enquired faintly.

'All the family and the servants,' repeated the steward. 'I will wake Mrs George and inform her. Mr Barton, you will please produce some soup, the Hortons and their servants will be wet, exhausted and severely distressed, soup is what will be needed.'

The head cook left the hall.

Soon everyone had been given their tasks.

Isaiah, the need to ride to Hinde Court superseded, stood with Canaletto and watched a fire being built in the huge grate, his hands flicking restlessly by his legs.

A little later, the duke himself came into the hall dressed in plain brown breeches and a buff coat.

'Ah, Signor Canale and Cumberledge, you, too, have been aroused by the dreadful circumstances I see.'

Both men gave a respectful nod. 'Indeed, Your Grace,' said Isaiah. 'Terrible, isn't it? But I am vastly relieved that it seems no one has been injured or lost. Barnaby tells me,' his gaze swept the hall but the boy had disappeared. 'Barnaby tells me that little Jack went back into the house after a cat. But he came out again, the Lord be praised. To think of that youngster, all energy and mischief, caught by the terrible force of flames would be too much.'

'Yes indeed. We have to give thanks that no lives seem to have been lost this night.'

The duke spoke easily and seemed rested. He and his family had returned the previous evening, slightly in advance of when they were expected. As soon as the family's arrival had been announced, all the servants had gathered in the hall to greet them. Canaletto, Fanny and Isaiah had stood quietly at the back.

'It's good to be home,' the duke had said, shaking hands with everyone. 'We made such good time, we are ahead of ourselves.'

The duchess had given a slight nod of recognition in the direction of Isaiah, then had swept from the hall, followed by her children and their attendants.

After the duchess had disappeared and the servants had gone back to their duties, the duke had greeted Isaiah warmly. He gave Canaletto and Fanny no less courteous a welcome to Badminton. 'I shall look forward to discussing your views with you, signor, when we are rested from the road,' he'd said before disappearing for the remainder of the evening.

The rain was still battering down outside. The duke advanced towards the grate and held his hands out to the flames. 'I wonder how this fire arose? I make all my household aware of its dangers. A spark from a log, an ill-tended chimney, a candle that falls and fails to snuff itself out, all can cause such devastation. Fire makes all our lives comfortable but it has to be one of life's worst hazards. Who will ever forget the awful devastation that was wrought in London some eighty years ago?'

'Quite,' murmured Isaiah.

'It will be up to you scientists to find ways of harnessing and taming its power so that we can enjoy its benefits without the dangers,' the duke added kindly.

'That is such a challenge,' Isaiah said with enthusiasm. 'There are so many mysteries waiting to be unlocked by those who care to study how nature works. Mr Boyle and Mr Newton have answered many questions but many more remain.'

'Yes indeed,' agreed the duke. 'If I understand you aright, isn't it steam that interests you in particular?' He moved a chair away from the wall and sat beside the fire.

'Just like your ancestor, the Marquess of Worcester, I want to find out how to harness its power.'

'I am sure you will make, at the very least, a valuable contribution to such a discovery. Indeed, it is for that reason I suggested you pursued your researches here.'

Isaiah shifted his weight uncomfortably from one foot to the other. 'I am immensely grateful, sir. I could wish I had not fallen out with my aunt, though, then I would not have to impose on your hospitality.'

'I, too, wish you had not disagreed with your aunt, but not for that reason. Tell me,' the duke asked in a different tone, 'I have yet to meet with Humphrey Farnham? Is he not still here?'

'He was certainly here at breakfast yesterday,' said Isaiah. 'But I haven't seen him since. How about you, signor? I left you both talking.'

Canaletto thought back. 'Yes, I meet captain at breakfast and again in park. I prepare sketches and will soon have view of the house to suggest to you, milord.'

'Capital, capital! But the captain, you haven't seen him since?'

Canaletto shook his head.

'And he has left no message saying he was going on a visit?'

Isaiah shook his head.

'Strange!'

Briggs the butler appeared with the news that the head cook had prepared soup for the Horton party and he proposed that it be served to them in the breakfast room.

But behind him came Capper the steward. 'Mrs George informs me that all the beds are now prepared and she suggests that, distressed as our visitors will be, they should be offered sustenance in their rooms.'

Steward and butler exchanged veiled glances.

If the duke was aware of the rivalry between the two men, he gave no sign of it. 'All sounds admirable. I think we should offer our guests the choice.'

Both servants bowed in acknowledgement and

turned together to leave the hall. Then the steward, perhaps not wanting to have to battle with the butler for the right to leave first, hung back and said, 'Would you have me light the chandeliers, my lord?'

'There is light enough, I think, now that the fire is burning up.'

The steward nodded and left.

'My mother had a marvellous way with servants,' said the duke, apparently apropos of nothing very much. 'Knew exactly how to handle them. My brother, well, he was a reserved man who showed his feelings on too few occasions. His wife, on the other hand, perhaps inclined too much the other way. I never expected to inherit the dukedom, you know? I was a third son and I always thought Henry, my brother, would breed. Still, here it is and I must make the best of it.'

Canaletto nodded his head gravely and thought that making the best of a dukedom with a country seat as noble as Badminton was no hard task.

'I wish Humphrey was here, though.' The duke looked around the hall as though the missing captain might just be lurking in one of the corners. 'We were at Oxford together, you know?' he said to Isaiah. 'In those days we ranked with each other. Both younger sons, both with a future to carve out. Humphrey opted for the army and I, with my brother's help, entered parliament. As a Tory, of course.' His face darkened. 'The Whigs will be the ruin of this country. All they see is the opportunity to line their own pockets. Loyalty, patriotism, all gone, gone with the Stuarts.' He thrust his hands deep into his pockets and gazed gloomily at the fire.

Canaletto waited, hoping to hear more, but the duke seemed disinclined to develop the subject. He came a step forward, 'In Venice commercial interests are rule for many hundreds of years,' he said. 'We are, of course, a republic, our doges are voted for by, by,' he sought for the right word, 'by those of the same station as themselves.'

'Their peers,' suggested the duke, cheering up a little. 'I am sure Venice is admirably governed. But here we have a monarchy, a king – or queen – who rules by divine right.' He paused and Canaletto waited. Surely, now, in this strange hour that bore so little resemblance to reality, in this dim hall with its flickering lights throwing vast shadows on the high walls, the duke would show where his true feelings lay.

But at that moment there came the sound of horses' hooves and carriage wheels.

'They are here,' said Isaiah in excitement.

The duke rose and came forward. The butler reappeared and headed for the door. Behind him came the housekeeper, Mrs George, a stiff figure in black.

Briggs flung open the door and ushered in the refugees. Canaletto watched with keen interest.

The first to enter was a middle-aged, bewildered woman, dressed in a sodden robe and lovingly supported by a girl with bedraggled hair. Her face, though, was one of the most beautiful Canaletto had ever seen, a perfect oval with a small, neat nose, wide apart eyes and a delicious mouth. He would have to wait until daylight to see the colour of her eyes but he had no doubt that they would in some way match the rest of her perfection.

'Patience,' said Isaiah in a passionate voice. He

130

made his way past the duke to her side. He then seemed to be lost for action and hovered uselessly beside her.

She smiled in a weary way at him.

'Welcome to Badminton,' said the duke.

Lady Horton blinked at him then turned to her daughter. 'I don't understand,' she wailed. 'Why are we here?'

'Come with me, your ladyship,' said Mrs George. 'A room is all prepared and hot soup waits.' She gently guided the woman and her daughter out of the hall. Isaiah was left looking yearningly after them both.

Next was a nurse carrying a baby with a small child clinging to her wet skirts. Both the baby and the child were crying, grizzling little wails that said just how tired and unhappy they were.

Snivelling rather than crying were several maids. Trying to encourage them to cheer up now that they had reached this haven was a woman of striking looks, her tall, well-shaped figure shown off to full advantage by the way her wet dress clung to all its curves. Her strong features were enhanced rather than marred by the long wet hair that revealed the fine lines of her skull. An Amazon, thought Canaletto in admiration and could understand the protective manner of the man who followed her.

'Well, Wright,' said the duke. 'Where are Miss Horton, Mr Horton and young Jack?'

'Master Jack has broken his arm and Miss Horton insisted they take him to the doctor. Forgive me, my lord, I must return to Hinde Court immediately but I had to see the family safely here.'

Canaletto looked at the soaked coat and breeches of

the man and his battered boots, then at the bedraggled appearance of the women and the crying children.

These were indeed refugees. They were people without dignity and Canaletto knew it was unfair to remain as voyeur to their plight. Murmuring excuses, he left the hall.

As he climbed back up the stairs, though, he mentally reviewed the beauty of the girl Isaiah had called Patience. It was no wonder the young man had been so concerned for her safety. This must be the girl that Fanny was to paint, Canaletto realized with a certain amount of dismay. She would not have an easy task. More to her taste would have been the amazonian looks of the servant.

Canaletto's last thought as he returned to bed for a few more hours of sleep was to wonder just what had happened to Captain Farnham.

Chapter Thirteen

After the drama of the storm, the morning was clear and bright, the landscape sparkling after the rain, the light full of a lambent innocence that made everything look new minted. Canaletto gazed out of his window in satisfaction and his fingers itched for his stylo. Today he would sketch the view from the house.

After breakfast he asked to be taken to a window offering a view from the first floor of the north front.

He and Fanny were shown to a magnificent bedroom furnished with a bed and hangings in the Chinese style. The room was on the west side of the front and gave Canaletto a slight angle on the park with its fascinating lines of trees and, perched on the arch of the distant horizon, the banqueting hall.

'Oh, signor, to think that I slept all through such commotion!' Fanny sighed as she stood at the window at his side. 'And you saw the girl I am to paint and you say she is beautiful?'

'Very,' he said shortly.

'Even though she was just in a sodden bed robe and her hair was all undressed and all wet?'

'Yes,' Canaletto said shortly. Yesterday Fanny had insisted on repeating everything that had passed at breakfast before his arrival and now she was insisting on hearing all about the arrival of the Hortons. Distracted from the view, he looked instead at the room's wonderful bed.

'Only just installed,' Mrs George had said proudly, lovingly stroking the cover with her hand. 'Carved by one of our foremost cabinetmakers, sir, Mr Linnell.'

'It is to be oils, is it not, signor? Not pastels?' asked Fanny.

'Oils?' he asked, wondering what it was about the room that nagged at his attention.

'The portrait that I am to paint of Miss Horton,' Fanny said impatiently. 'I would not feel happy with pastels, my experience is with oils. But even with oils the thought of having to capture such exceeding beauty is very daunting.'

'It is oils,' Canaletto said tersely. He suddenly knew what had seemed curious to him. It was that Lady Horton had not been deemed worthy of laying her head on the pillow of that magnificent bed. There could not have been a grander room available. Was it being reserved for someone else?

'How long do you think the Hortons will be staying at Badminton, Signor? Will I have to start the portrait here?'

This aspect of the fire at Hinde Court had not occurred to Canaletto. If the Hortons were to stay at Badminton for any length of time, he would be perfectly placed for identifying the prince, should he turn up. 'It may be so,' he said and returned to contemplate the view through the window.

For a few moments Fanny studied it with him and was blessedly quiet. Then, 'Signor, it is good this view is so central. Everything out there is so very . . . so very *ordered*,' she said. 'Look at how regular those lines of trees are, they all march in such a carefully controlled way.'

'You have reason, Fanny,' he said approvingly.

But all that grass and trees! What else was there of interest? On the left was the long lake with, beside it, the little Chinese-type pavilion. Canaletto smiled to himself at the reiteration of the Oriental theme, the architect had a sense of whimsy – or was it the duke? In any case, it would make a nice feature in his painting.

'Would you like the *camera obscura*?' asked Fanny, hovering behind his shoulder.

He stood for a moment, absorbed in the view. 'Yes,' he said after a moment. He wasn't at all sure he would need it, the view was simplicity itself, no complicated roof line, no eye-straining architectural details to be captured, but sending her to fetch the instrument would at the very least ensure him ten minutes or so of solitude.

'Signor, I will be back in a moment,' said Fanny happily. 'You do not need anything else while I am gone?'

'I have all I need,' he said and gave a wave of his hand to encourage her on her way.

At last he was alone and could give his whole attention to the problem of his painting, except that a few minutes later an open carriage drove round the corner of the house, coming to a stop in front of the entrance. It was a remarkable equipage, the coachwork picked out in gold, the interior leatherwork a bright red, tassels everywhere. It was pulled by six prancing black horses, their coats ashine, red plumes on their heads. A postillion rode the lead horse, a coachman was perched on the front of the chariot, a groom by his side, all dressed in black and gold liveries. All Canaletto could see of the passenger as the carriage drew up at the front door was a wide-brimmed black hat, trimmed with all manner of red and white silk flowers and finished with a trailing black feather.

As the carriage drew to a stop, the groom descended, opened the door and let down the steps then helped his mistress to descend in a froth of scarlet silk skirts that billowed around scarlet satin shoes stepping nimbly to the ground.

As the hat vanished beneath his window, Canaletto found himself sniffing the air, as though to detect the fragrance that must surround such a fashionable looking creature. He wished he could have seen her face, it must surely be one of great beauty.

No scented aroma rose to the window. Canaletto gave a small sigh, dismissed all thought of feminine loveliness from his mind and returned to contemplating his view.

Oh, but England was so green! All nature's sweetness and prodigality seemed summed up in the tapestry of verdant richness laid before him. When before had his palette had to capture such a range of tranquil greens?

Then a second carriage drew to a stop in front of the house. It was large and imposing but not as outrageously stylish as the previous one and carried no groom. While the coachman controlled the restive horses, a young man, sketchily dressed, slippers on his feet, pushed open the door and jumped to the ground. He banged the door knocker then returned to let down the steps. Reaching into the interior of the carriage, he received the limp figure of a small child, its left arm bandaged, which he carefully carried into the house. A female form followed him from the coach. No creature of fashion she; enveloped in a dark cloak, she was hatless, her hair loose and disgracefully wild. She moved, though, with a youthful ease. Lifting a hand in thanks to the coachman, she hurried inside after the man and his burden. They must be the missing part of the Horton household, the brother and sister with the injured boy. The doctor had no doubt given them hospitality after attending the child.

Canaletto retrieved his sketchbook and stylo from his back pocket and once more gave his attention to the view. The coach had gone and the scene was as tranquil as it had been before. Only in the distance was a lone figure walking away from the lake to the west. Canaletto was reminded of the previous day when he'd been interrupted in his work by the approach first of Father Sylvester and then Captain Farnham. This figure, though, was too far away for recognition to be possible. It was, in any case, much more likely to be one of the Badminton outdoor servants, for the captain hadn't been at breakfast and if Father Sylvester was in the vicinity, he would be walking towards Badminton, not away.

Once again Canaletto turned his mind towards how he was to capture the park to the duke's satisfaction and his own. It was going to require a subtlety of approach greater than any he had previously had to produce.

Time passed.

Fanny did not return. Perhaps she had met with Patience Horton and was discussing the portrait with her. Canaletto felt that was doubtful, though. Perhaps Fanny was quizzing someone else about the events of last night. Canaletto did not care. He was totally immersed in the challenge of the prospect before him. Very gradually, though, he became aware that something was wrong. Unlike the previous night's drama, it did not announce itself with a bang. There was no commotion, no running feet, no sudden eruption in the park. Just a very gentle, hazy drift of grey from the Chinese pavilion. So gentle, it took time for Canaletto to realize its import.

He stood staring at it for a good minute. Then a bright yellow flame licked its way out of one of the small windows and galvanized him. Stuffing his pad and stylo back in his pocket, he ran for the stairs. It was only an ornamental pavilion that was burning, but Canaletto was sure the duke would be seriously upset to see his Chinese folly razed to the ground. Still, no need to shout and alarm those poor people who had only just escaped from a far worse conflagration.

As he reached the bottom of the stairs, Canaletto saw a servant. 'Fire,' Canaletto gasped. The fellow gaped at him. 'In the park, the Chinese pavilion. It's on fire!'

Chapter Fourteen

Fanny never reached the room where the *camera obscura* was stored. Losing her way, she was redirected by Bob Hawkins, the handsome young footman she'd met on her first arrival.

'You'll find it safely set in the storeroom beside Mr Briggs's pantry, miss. Shall I fetch it for you?'

'Thank you, but I am used to carrying it for my signor. If you'll just show me which way to go, I'd be grateful.'

'I know, you don't trust me not to drop it, right?' He gave her another of his engaging grins.

'Can you trust a bird not to sing?' said Fanny gaily, she thought she knew all about young men like Bob Hawkins.

'Oho, Hannah has given me quite the wrong impression of you,' Bob said with an even wider smile.

Fanny was just about to tell him that she thought neither Hannah nor he had the faintest idea what she was like when Mr Briggs appeared. 'Miss, her ladyship would be pleased to see you in the drawing room,' he said, giving Bob a look that said he should be about his business.

Fanny drew herself up. 'Please to show me the way, Mr Briggs, I am sure Signor Canale would wish me to attend to her ladyship's requests,' she said, speaking with what she hoped was proper dignity.

The butler led her back along the corridor to an imposing polished wood door set in an elaborate architrave. Knocking lightly, he opened the door and advanced a couple of paces into the room. 'Miss Rooker, your ladyship,' he announced in a voice that nicely suggested a person of little importance.

Fanny told herself that she had met a duchess before and that no one could have been kinder to her than the Duchess of Richmond, and entered. 'Good morning, your ladyship,' she said cheerfully and dropped a bobbing sort of curtsey.

As she raised her head, she saw immediately that this woman was very different from the Duchess of Richmond.

Her ladyship the Duchess of Beaufort was steely backed with a pleasant but remote expression. Trying to sum her up, as if preparing to paint her portrait, Fanny decided the duchess was the sort of person who worried more about her effect on the people she met than the people themselves. This thought helped her relax.

'Miss Rooker, I am pleased to meet you,' the duchess said with stiff courtesy. 'I trust my staff have made you and Signor Canale comfortable?'

'Indeed, your ladyship, extremely so,' said Fanny.

'Please, will you take a seat?' The duchess indicated one of a number of wide-seated chairs with graceful arms that stood around on the finely patterned carpet.

Fanny sat down on the red damask upholstery, then realized for the first time that there was another woman in the room. Having noticed her, it was impossible to believe that she had overlooked her before. This was a woman who stamped herself on your consciousness with an authority that was completely missing in the duchess.

'Lady Tanqueray, may I introduce Miss Rooker,' the duchess said, waving a hand towards Fanny.

Two very blue eyes surveyed her. But it wasn't the eyes that demanded attention, nor the scarlet silk dress or wide-brimmed hat loaded with floral finery. It was the face. Plastered thick with paint, it was almost white. The bones were delicate, chiselled, they belonged to a face that once had been ravishingly lovely and now was a ruin. But the eyes were dauntless; full of life, they gazed at Fanny with extraordinary vigour.

'I asked to see you because I heard the other day that you have been commissioned to paint Miss Horton's portrait. Is that so?' Lady Tanqueray said abruptly.

Fanny nodded.

'You are very young,' Lady Tanqueray said, her voice as bright and pretty as if she was twenty instead of the fifty Fanny reckoned she must have reached.

'I am at the start of my career,' Fanny acknowledged firmly.

Lady Tanqueray smiled, her rouged lips cracking the white mask of her face. 'A good answer,' she approved. 'Everyone has to start somewhere. But I wonder if Miss Horton is the right subject for one so obviously inexperienced.'

The butler reappeared, came over to the duchess and spoke briefly in her ear. The duchess rose. 'Letitia, Briggs tells me Nell and James have arrived with Jack. I must go and see how they are. Will you come?'

'Your ministrations will be more welcome than mine, my dear. Miss Rooker and I will continue our interesting discussion,' Lady Tanqueray said firmly. After they'd been left alone, she said, 'I have to ask if you are the right painter to capture my god-daughter?'

'I am told Miss Horton's looks are out of the ordinary,' Fanny said slowly. 'But everyone to me is out of the ordinary and I look on my job as one that celebrates the individual.'

She saw immediately that she had startled Lady Tanqueray and Lady Tanqueray did not appear a lady who startled easily. Fanny felt a small jolt of satisfaction.

'Have you met my god-daughter, Miss Rooker?' Lady Tanqueray enquired.

'Not yet, my lady, but she has been described to me.'

'In what terms?'

Fanny thought of Isaiah Cumberledge's lyrical words. 'In terms of great beauty. It was a young man, your ladyship, and perhaps he exaggerated?'

Lady Tanqueray gave Fanny a smile that showed her teeth, small, pearly and sharp. 'Isaiah, my nephew? I think, Miss Rooker, he was describing Miss Patience Horton.'

'And your god-daughter, my lady, is Miss Nell Horton?' Fanny said slowly. 'I was told my commission was to capture the true beauty of my sitter. Captain Farnham felt that meant it was Miss Nell Horton who was to be my subject but Mr Cumberledge was insistent it must be Miss Patience.'

'My nephew is an idiot,' Lady Tanqueray said

impatiently. 'I am quite out of sympathy with him and have broken off our relations.'

'Indeed?' Fanny's eyebrow rose. She didn't feel she could comment further.

'But you mentioned Captain Farnham. He is a gentleman of acute perception. Have you seen him this morning?' Lady Tanqueray's bright-blue eyes looked into Fanny's with extraordinary concentration.

Something was up here!

'Not since yesterday morning,' Fanny said. 'Signor Canale was assessing the viewpoint for his painting of Badminton house and the captain came and had a conversation with us.'

'And after that?'

'After that,' said Fanny, speaking more slowly. 'He walked off, I think it was in a westerly direction.'

'West,' repeated her inquisitor. 'Hmm.'

'Forgive me, your ladyship, but you seem very concerned for the whereabouts of Captain Farnham. Is there a particular reason?' Fanny felt that, having displayed such a depth of interest in the captain, the advantage in this small battle of wills had passed from Lady Tanqueray to herself.

Lady Tanqueray's gaze dropped to her hands. Small and gnarled with arthritis, they fiddled with the lace gloves she held as she conducted an inward debate with herself. Finally she looked again at Fanny. 'The captain was engaged to me for dinner yesterday. He did not come nor was any note delivered from him. It was,' she paused then concluded, 'unlike him.'

Fanny thought she discerned an unexpected tremor of feeling in the light and charming voice. She sought the right words. 'Perhaps he met with some friends,' she suggested.

'And forgot his arrangement with me?' the voice was caustic now. 'You have an unpleasant way of offering reassurance.'

'You are feared for his safety, then?' Fanny said gently. 'Captain Farnham seems to me a gentleman most able to look after himself. Is he not a soldier? And has he not survived many wars?'

Lady Tanqueray suddenly smiled. 'I see you are a rational creature. You are quite right, of course. Of all men, Humphrey is the most resourceful. He will turn up in the near future with an explanation that will show me for the silly woman that I am.'

'Forgive me, my lady, but you do not seem to me to be at all silly,' Fanny said robustly.

The smile Lady Tanqueray produced was as charming as her voice. 'We shall leave the captain to his own devices and return to your suitability to capture the likeness of my god-daughter. Perhaps I should offer you a small explanation of my concern. I know Nell does not wish for a portrait and for my part I cannot understand why my old friend, her father, has commissioned any painter to carry out such a task against her desires. Even less can I understand why he has chosen someone who, whatever her talents,' another piercing look at Fanny, 'cannot have the experience which must be necessary to handle such a delicate task.'

Fanny was becoming more and more curious about Nell Horton. But their conversation was interrupted by the sound of feet running in the corridor outside the drawing room and voices raised in excitement.

Lady Tanqueray and Fanny looked at each other.

'Did I hear the word fire?' asked Lady Tanqueray faintly.

'Look!' said Fanny, pointing out of the window. Men were running across the gravel semicircle towards the park.

Both she and Lady Tanqueray went and looked out. More men came running and now Fanny recognized Canaletto.

Then she saw that the Chinese pavilion was ablaze. Flames shot out of the little windows and rose over the pretty roof and a light wind wafted sparks towards the heavens.

'Another fire!' Lady Tanqueray clasped her hands together. 'How could this have happened?'

'In London there are often fires,' said Fanny slowly, wondering who could have lit a fire or a candle inside the ornamental folly and then proved careless of the danger offered.

The drawing room door opened. 'Aunt Letitia,' said a light voice. 'The duchess told me you were here and I had to come immediately, I knew you would want to know about Jack.'

Fanny turned, then stood frozen.

Nell Horton's appearance could never be classed respectable. Her hair was unkempt and her gown, obviously hastily donned, had skirts that were too short and her neat little feet were shod in bedroom slippers. But it wasn't her dress that was shocking, it was her face. It was grotesque. The right half was pretty enough with a young girl's freshness of skin and feature. The left half had suffered some terrible accident, its skin was puckered and livid, the scars running right down to her mouth. Only the eye had escaped injury, that was as lovely as the right, a powerful blue invaded with violet. Was this the girl whose portrait Fanny had been commissioned to paint?

Chapter Fifteen

Canaletto ran with the other men towards the pavilion. Already he could feel the heat of the fire. There was a rumbling from behind and a cart loaded with buckets and pulled by several men passed in the direction of the lake.

Soon a line of men had been organized to pass water-filled buckets from the lake to the burning pavilion. Canaletto was in the middle, his jacket removed and flung on the ground, his breeches being splashed with the water as it passed along the line. He could only hope that they would dry without staining.

Soon it looked as though the pails might be having some effect. The flames began to die down, to be replaced by smoke. Cries of encouragement came from the men nearest the pavilion.

Efforts were redoubled.

Canaletto couldn't judge how much time had passed before Capper the steward said, 'I think we've done it, men!' but the sun had passed its zenith, his shoulders were aching and he was very much afraid a blister was appearing on one of his blackened hands. He laid the bucket that had just been passed to him on to the ground and straightened up, easing his stiff shoulders.

The pavilion was still standing, just. The walls and roof were blackened and charred, tiles lay smashed on the ground.

'Thank you, men,' said the duke. 'A fine effort by everyone.' Then he saw Canaletto. 'Signor, I must thank you, there was no requirement for you to expend your valuable efforts on our behalf. I trust you are not too exhausted?'

Canaletto murmured a modest denial.

'We must look after you particularly well,' the duke promised him. 'And Wright, you too. How is Hinde Court?' he asked of a tall man that Canaletto recognized as having brought up the rear of the Horton refugee party.

'Without the rain, it would have been a ruin but, thanks to the heavens opening when they did, I think the damage can be made good. The builders are assessing the situation.'

'Then you will want to speak to James Horton as soon as maybe. He, his sister and little Jack arrived just before this fire was noticed. We shall not allow any of you to return to Hinde Court before everything there has been made comfortable again.' The duke gave a small nod and passed on to stand just in front of the smoking ruin of his little folly. 'What could have caused such a conflagration?' he asked in general.

It was a question that was exercising Canaletto's mind also.

'My lord, please, there will still be too much heat,' said John Capper, his steward as the duke appeared ready to enter the ruin.

He quickly changed his mind. 'You are right,' he

said. 'I can feel it from here. We shall not be able to examine the inside for some hours, I fear.'

'Should we not continue with the water for a little time yet, just in case there is sufficient heat left to cause the fire to flare up again?' said the steward.

Soon the bucket chain was again in action.

'This is so sad,' said the duke. 'It was a perfect Oriental retreat. The tiles came from China. We brought paper from London for the walls, there was furniture in the style of bamboo, both chairs and a table. My wife and I had the idea we could enjoy sitting here and reading, sample a small repast, play with the children, I had some special toys sent from London, there was a wooden horse for Henry. It was all quite, quite charming.' He sighed deeply. 'Carry on, men. There will be ale and sustenance for you afterwards. But you, signor, your efforts are finished. I think a cognac is called for and we must ask Mrs George to attend to your clothes.'

Canaletto saw with dismay that his breeches were drenched and his shirt besmirched with smuts. He hoped that no holes had been burned in either garment. In anticipation of a meeting with the duke, he'd worn his second best this morning instead of his working garments.

'I gather that it was you, signor, who raised the alarm?' continued the duke.

'I was beginning to sketch a viewpoint from your window up there,' he waved towards the house, 'when I saw first the smoke and then flames.'

As he and the duke walked back towards the house, Canaletto saw an audience standing on the semi-circular sweep of gravel. It seemed all the female

149

servants were there, the duke's family and some of the
Horton family as well. In the front were several small
children. A boy who could not long be out of skirts ran
up, 'Father, Father, what a fire! I wanted to carry a
bucket but Mama said I couldn't.'

The duke ruffled his curls. 'Soon, Harry, soon you
will be able to carry buckets.' Then he turned to the
onlookers. 'The drama is over. Back to your duties,
please!'

The servants hastily withdrew and the nurse gathered up the children and removed them also.

Amongst those left on the gravel, Canaletto saw
without surprise, was Father Sylvester. As on the previous day, the priest was not wearing his soutane,
instead he was dressed in a fine suit of light-blue coat
and dark-blue trousers and a white waistcoat orna-
mented with a broad band of embroidery.

The duke strode forward. 'My lord, I am indeed
honoured to see you here.' He took the hand the priest
held out and it seemed to Canaletto he would have
kissed it but Father Sylvester took it back with a light
laugh.

'You do me too much honour, my dear duke,
perhaps you mistake me for my brother, I am not a
cardinal yet nor never likely to be.' Then he turned
towards the painter, 'And so we meet again, dear sir.
Your Grace, Signor Canale and his apprentice rescued
me from an accident upon the road. They thought I
was a highwayman and I would not have been surprised if they had drawn a pistol on me, I must have
looked a desperate fellow indeed,' he said with a laugh.

'You exaggerate, sir,' said Canaletto, his mind alive
to all the nuances of this exchange of greetings. 'For

moment, yes, perhaps you highwayman but when we see priest, we are content. Indeed, we are grateful for your company.' He turned to the duke. 'Father Sylvester make journey,' he paused to think of an appropriate English word. 'He make journey fly! Fanny and me very sorry he leave at Reading. Very nice surprise to meet him here yesterday.'

The duke looked questioningly at the priest.

'My lord, I thought you might be at home and, if not, that I might view it.'

'I will certainly guide you over Badminton myself. May I say I am very pleased indeed to welcome you, your, that is to say, your reverence.'

Canaletto realized that Fanny was trying to attract his attention. He excused himself.

Fanny was standing with a woman whose hat Canaletto recognized. But where he had expected a young and beautiful face beneath it, there was only a painted mask.

'Lady Tanqueray, here is Signor Canale. Signor, Lady Tanqueray is the godmother of Miss Horton whose portrait I am to paint.'

Canaletto made a graceful leg. 'My lady, I regret my appearance.'

'Sir, you are a hero!' she said and held out her fingers in a graceful gesture.

'Alas, my lady, I cannot take your so kind hand.' He showed her how his were blackened from the fire. But only half his attention was focused on Lady Tanqueray for he recognized that Fanny was upset about something. It must be to do with the portrait commission. 'Has Signorina Rooker had honour to meet Miss Horton?'

Fanny nodded, it appeared she did not trust herself to speak.

'In commissioning this portrait, my husband's old friend, Sir Robert Horton, did not see fit to explain certain difficulties,' Lady Tanqueray said to Canaletto. 'I am extremely fond of my god-daughter and I am distressed on her behalf. I ask you, Signor Canale, to discuss this matter most carefully with Miss Rooker. Both of you should talk with Miss Horton. Unless my god-daughter wishes this portrait to go forward, I shall take it upon myself to cancel the commission.' She eyed them both with an expression that said they were not to doubt that she could do this. 'The duke will back me. Miss Rooker,' she turned to Fanny. 'Whatever the outcome of your discussion with Miss Horton, it has been a pleasure to meet you. I wish you every success in your career, though I doubt that it will commence with painting my god-daughter.'

Lady Tanqueray nodded to Canaletto then walked with small, determined steps into the house, her scarlet gown billowing as she went.

Fanny seemed torn between tears and anger. 'Signor, it is such a thing. Lady Tanqueray expressed such doubts about my experience and then, and then Miss Horton herself came in. Oh, signor,' and now tears did come. 'She is such a person! One side of her face is fair whilst the other, the other is the ugliest you have ever seen!'

'Ugly?'

'She has been in some accident which has quite destroyed her looks. Signor, she does not want her likeness captured and if I were in her place, I would not either.'

152

Here was a thing! Without Fanny painting Miss Horton's portrait, there would be nothing to keep Canaletto at Badminton. His sketching could not be spun out for more than a couple of days at most. And Pitt had his agent, Joshua Bland, keeping an eye on him. Unless Canaletto stayed in place, he was certain that Pitt would make it impossible for him to remain in England. Somehow, whatever the state of her face, he had to persuade Miss Horton to allow Fanny to paint her portrait.

Chapter Sixteen

'*Al diavolo*,' Canaletto said explosively. 'Here is pickle! We must talk with Signorina Horton.'

Fanny nodded vigorously. 'Of course, signor. But perhaps not until she has recovered from last night's fire at her home.'

'You are right, Fanny. Now, I change clothes then continue sketches. I not require you.'

Fanny watched Canaletto's retreating back in dismay. Why couldn't he have thrown orders at her as usual and given her things to do, not left her to worry about Nell Horton and the portrait. And why was he so positive the commission was not to be cancelled? Was it because he wanted it for her? Was she wrong in thinking their comfortable relationship had been torn into rags and tatters?

Then there was Miss Horton herself. Fanny tried to imagine what she would feel like if her face looked like that. She knew she wouldn't want her likeness captured, that much was certain! But was her career to be finished before it had actually begun?

Exasperated beyond measure by the impossibility of being able to do anything about the matter at present, Fanny went to get her own sketchbook and some chalk so that she could try to lose herself in capturing some of the Badminton staff.

First she found a maid making butter in the tiled dairy, so clean and ordered. Jenny was a small girl with rosy cheeks and strong arms. She giggled at Fanny's request but had no objection to being sketched as she pounded the butter churn, the muscles in her upper arms showing clearly through her rolled up sleeves. She looked at the finished drawing with astonishment and more giggles. Then Fanny went along to the laundry and found another maid ironing linen sheets. When done, she hung them to air in waves from lines stretched wall to wall just below the ceiling. Fanny sketched her with her arms raised, her face tense with the effort needed not to crease the smooth linen.

As she wielded her chalk, Fanny's inner turmoil gradually began to ease. Work always calmed her. And as she sketched, she wondered about Nell Horton. What had happened to the girl? And why oh why did her father want her portrait painted? Was he a sadist? Or did he want the artist to paint the girl with both sides of her face unscarred? Painters regularly ignored smallpox pittings, warts and all manner of other defects in their sitters. If Canaletto could capture an image of a refurbished Warwick Castle before Lord Brooke's plans were put into effect, then Fanny could paint an undamaged Miss Horton. Would that be the 'true beauty' that Sir Robert had called for?

After sketching the laundry maid, Fanny went back inside the house. There were sounds of activity in the kitchen, no doubt the day's main meal being prepared. Would sketching in the kitchen be acceptable to the cook or should she try to find less involved subjects? She walked along the corridor towards the main part of the house. A door to one of the offices suddenly opened and a striking looking young woman half emerged, then turned back to address someone still in the room. 'You are a snake in the grass, John Capper, and never try that trick again with me. You'd better watch out or the duke could hear things you'd rather he didn't.' She shut the door and swept up the corridor.

Fanny's feelings of guilt at being an inadvertent eavesdropper vanished beside her enchantment at the glimpse she'd gained of the woman's profile: strong nose, long dark lashes, elegant cheekbones and determined chin. She caught up with the woman at the door to the kitchen.

'I apologize for detaining you,' she said.

The woman paused, her expression still stern.

'I am Fanny Rooker, assistant to Antonio Canale, and I'm sketching some of the inhabitants of the house, could you spare me a few minutes so that I can catch your likeness?'

'Catch my likeness? Well, Fanny Rooker, that will be a first. I've never been caught in that manner before, though many times in other ways. But I cannot mislead you, I am not part of the duke's household, I am cook to the Hortons.'

'It doesn't matter,' Fanny said. She wouldn't have minded if the woman had wandered in off the fields.

'Where will you catch me?' the cook asked, glancing around.

'Perhaps outside? The light is best there.'

Out in the courtyard was a mounting block. Fanny suggested she might sit on this. The woman looked at it critically, then arranged herself on the top with her feet on the steps. 'How do you wish me to look?' she asked.

'You are a cook, I should have asked you to bring a tool of your trade.'

'Oh, if that's all, I can oblige.' The cook felt in a pocket of her skirt and brought out a knife and an apple.

Fanny fetched a bucket from a corner, turned it upside down and sat on it, then studied her model. The statuesque figure had arranged herself very well, her buff skirt falling away in interesting folds, her apron neatly lying over them. Her back was very straight, which emphasized her generous bosom. The bodice was partly unlaced and her breasts strained at the linen under her bodice as though the clothes had been made for a slighter person. The strong bones of her face, though, suggested that here was a woman of principle. Dark hair was tidied away beneath a linen coif. She had a timeless look.

'Would you like me to be peeling this?' The cook held up the apple.

'An excellent idea.' Fanny brought out her tools. She'd chosen buff paper as a base for red chalk together with white for highlights. Remembering what Mr Hudson had told her about making her sitters feel at ease, she said, 'Tell me what you could do with the apple. And go slowly with your knife, please,' she added as a couple of rapid strokes with the broad knife released a curl of peel.

The woman laughed. 'Do you want a cooking lesson? Shall you want to take over my job as well as my face?'

'You could say I already cook with pigments,' Fanny said, starting to sketch. 'As you mix flavours, so I mix colours.'

The cook let her hands with the apple and the knife fall into her lap. 'I have never thought of painting like that. Tell me, how did you learn? Or is one born knowing how to capture an image and place colour on a canvas?'

She was as easy to talk to as Father Sylvester and Fanny found herself relating a good deal of her background as she sketched. Mr Hudson said one of the prime talents of a portraitist was to be able to talk as one worked. Canaletto, though, could concentrate entirely upon what he was doing, he never had to make a building relax.

Afterwards, Fanny couldn't remember exactly what she had said. She'd been too involved in keeping that alert look on the cook's face and capturing it on her paper. Every now and then something she said brought laughter. 'Miss Horton, my mistress, would appreciate your company,' the woman said at one point. 'She doesn't have many friends, being how she is and too intelligent for her own good.' Good servants always understood the people they worked for, Fanny thought.

'Will you hold up your apple and knife again, please? I'd like to capture them now.' Such strong and shapely hands, such skill in dealing with the apple, such interesting talk of fritters, pancakes, paste, a tansey, a marmalade and a cream, was there any end to what you could do with an apple? Fanny finished a quick study of the hands and started on a full-length sketch of the figure.

'My, but you're clever with your pen,' the cook said

when she was able to see the finished drawings. 'Is that what I look like?'

'Do you never see yourself in a mirror?'

'It's not a tool we use in the kitchen.' Her laugh was a deep, attractive sound that was infectious. 'What does one need a mirror for, anyway? You can see in someone's eyes if you are attractive to them and what else matters?'

What indeed?

Fanny thanked her for her time.

'I have few duties at the moment. A skivvy in a ducal kitchen, not an enviable position. The sooner we can return to Hinde Court, the better.' The cook looked at her speculatively. 'In return for my time, though, perhaps you can give me some information.'

'If I can, certainly.'

'You must have come across Captain Farnham?'

Someone else asking about the captain?

'I met him at breakfast yesterday morning but I have not seen him since.'

'He's gone off somewhere, then.'

'So it would seem.'

'And will no doubt return when he's ready. Well, I should be about my tasks again.' The woman returned the knife to her pocket and sank her white teeth into the pared flesh of the apple as she made her way back to the house.

As Fanny watched her stride off, she realized she hadn't asked her name. She went to find Hannah, the source of most of her knowledge about Badminton.

Hannah was laying the table in the grand dining room for dinner. As Fanny described the woman, she smiled. 'That's Damaris Friend. Right character she is.

All the Horton servants were invited here for a party last Christmas and you should have seen her dance. Like some sort of goddess she was. All the men were after her.'

'Including Mr Capper?' asked Fanny, remembering what she'd overheard.

Hannah looked shocked. 'Mr Capper is too grand for that. The staff think he's after Mrs George.'

Interesting, thought Fanny, then asked if she could sketch Hannah as she worked. Like the other two maids, Hannah giggled but, like Damaris, she was interested in Fanny's work.

'Will you show me what you do?' she demanded, smoothing the spotless white tablecloth she'd spread over the long table.

'Of course,' Fanny said. 'If you like the sketch, you can have it.'

Hannah brought a tray of cutlery to the table.

'How many are we for dinner?' Fanny asked as they both set to work, she to draw and Hannah to arrange knives and forks.

The previous day Canaletto, Fanny and Isaiah Cumberledge had been served dinner in the breakfast room. The prospect of eating in this grand salon with its mirrors and portraits and beautiful furniture was very attractive.

'Well, miss, I'm not rightly sure. The duchess has said she'll probably eat upstairs, one of the little children isn't well, sickly little thing she is and the duchess worries about her. But the duke should be with you, then there's his chaplain and his agent, Mr Cumberledge and Captain Farnham . . .'

'If he reappears,' Fanny interposed.

'Oh, he often takes off. Now that the duke's here, he'll return. Then, of course, there's yourself and Mr Canal.'

'Signor Canale,' corrected Fanny.

'Quite, miss. Well, as I was saying, the two of you and then there's the Hortons what arrived last night, though Miss Nell is tending little Jack, he's still unconscious and Lady Horton is suffering from a nervous decline because of it, so they probably won't come down. But there's Miss Patience, I'm laying for her, and then there's this Father Sylvester what the duke has invited to stay.'

'Really, to stay?' Fanny said, startled to hear this. 'Is he a friend of the duke's?'

'No use to ask me, miss, I never met him before but her ladyship didn't seem too pleased about it. I was there when she told Mrs George the duke wanted her to prepare the Chinese room for him.'

'The Chinese room? We saw that this morning, it seems very grand.'

'It's the best for guests in the whole of Badminton. And Mrs George queried it, miss,' Hannah added, pausing in her work. 'And the duchess went all dignified, like she does when anyone questions an order. She said that Father Sylvester was an old and valued friend of the duke and would Mrs George please just get the room ready and tell Bob Hawkins he's to act as his manservant. Apparently the father has been separated from his. Bob says his things are in no end of a mess!'

Hannah left the room and Fanny thought about Father Sylvester. Meeting him again was a very strange

161

coincidence but it would be very pleasant to talk with him some more.

Hannah returned with a tray of glasses and started to put them round the table.

'Who are the Hortons, Hannah?'

'Oh, they're old friends of the duke's. At least, Sir Robert is. Mr Capper says they knew each other in London, before the duke was married. Mr Capper says Sir Robert bought Hinde Court because he wants to be a landed gentleman. Mr Capper says he's ever so rich but my father says he doesn't know how to be a gentleman and he'll be the ruin of us all.'

'Your father?' Fanny remembered how reluctant Hannah had been to talk about him the night she'd arrived.'

'He's one of Sir Robert's tenants, miss,' Hannah said abruptly.

Fanny finished off a sketch of Hannah leaning across the table to place salt cellars and asked, 'What happened to Miss Horton's face?' She waited in keen anticipation for Hannah's response.

Hannah picked up her empty tray. 'Oh, miss, that were terrible. It was some sort of experiment that went wrong. Mr Cumberledge tried to explain something about it but it didn't make any sense. I only know that my brother looks worse than her.'

'Your brother?' Fanny told herself she had to stop repeating what Hannah said.

'My brother, Barnaby. He was helping her, you see, miss and he got the worst of it. He's lost an eye and the use of an arm and no girl's ever going to look at him. Mother's ever so upset and Father's that angry because Barnaby can't work on the land any more. He says the Hortons must pay.'

'And how does Barnaby feel about it?'

'Oh, miss, I don't know. Sometimes he's that bitter and swears he'll do for the Hortons and other times he says Miss Nell will see him right and he'll get to do all sort of things.'

'What sort of things, Hannah?' Fanny asked, starting another sketch now that her subject was facing her and still for a few moments.

Hannah shrugged her shoulders. 'He's not right in the head now, miss. Half the time he don't know what he's saying.' Then her face brightened. 'But when the house started burning, Miss Nell says it were Barnaby as raised the alarm in the village and rode here, he manages very well with his bad arm, and got the men sent to Hinde Court. If the rain hadn't come, then he'd perhaps have saved the house, or part of the house. She told me that he was a hero.'

'You seem to know the Hortons very well, Hannah.'

Hannah nodded. 'My younger sister was taken on as a maid at Hinde Court as soon as the Hortons arrived. And, as I said, Father's one of Sir Robert's tenants. He says it was a bad day when Sir Robert bought Hinde Court. Says he doesn't understand how things should be done, not like old Mr Procter did. Sir Robert's gone to the West Indies but father says Mr James is even worse to deal with as he doesn't know nothing but can't admit it. And Captain Farnham says Father's quite right and he's trying to stop the village being moved.'

'How can you move a village?'

'I said it can't be done. But Father says it's easy

enough if you don't mind destroying folk's homes. Captain Farnham came back ever so angry from visiting Hinde Court the other day. Said there should be a law against it.'

Fanny changed her red chalk for the white. 'Do you know Sir Robert has commissioned me to paint Miss Nell Horton's portrait?'

Hannah stared at her. 'Never!'

'It's true, Hannah. It's my first commission and now I understand that Miss Horton is against it.'

That she would be, if you pardon me saying so, miss. Meg, that's my sister, she says Miss Nell won't have a looking glass in her room. Sir James has plans for a whole set of mirrors in the new drawing room and Miss Nell has had a huge fight with him, says if he loves her, he'll cancel them. At it hammer and tongs they were. With him saying she's a poor thing to worry so about what she looks like.'

'He didn't!'

'And after the accident he told Barnaby it'd be the making of him.'

'What a strange man!'

'So will you be painting her portrait, miss?'

Fanny had a brief fight between her sympathy for Nell Horton's feelings and her desire for her first commission then said firmly, 'Not if she doesn't want it.'

'But if Sir Robert wants it done?'

'He's abroad.'

'But Mister James says he's got his father's authority and everything's supposed to be taking place just as if Sir Robert was here.'

'No one can force me into painting Miss Horton if she doesn't want her portrait taken.'

164

'No, miss,' said Hannah in obvious disbelief. 'You finished, miss, only I'm supposed to be helping you dress.'

'Dress?' Fanny looked down at her linen gown. 'Oh, you mean for dinner?' She put down her chalk and dusted her fingers with her apron. 'I didn't realize so much time had passed.' What it was to be staying in a house where you changed your clothes to eat your dinner!

'The duchess likes to eat at three, miss. We thinks it's very late but that's what she wants.'

'Then I'll go and prepare myself but I can manage, Hannah, you don't have to wait on me.'

'I would like to, miss. Maybe I can do something with your hair.'

Before Fanny could think of a kind way to tell Hannah that she was happy with the way her hair was, Isaiah Cumberledge entered and collapsed into a chair. 'I've been looking for you,' he said to Fanny. 'What did you learn with the schoolmaster you said I would be an improvement on?' His voice was so intense and the query so extraordinary that Fanny felt bewildered.

'Why, reading, writing, my sums, some history, the kings and queens of England, all that sort of thing.'

'Reading and writing? And your sums?'

Fanny nodded. 'As I said.'

Hannah had left the dining room but now returned with a china stand which she placed in the centre of the table and started to arrange fruit in.

'Did you attend the Badminton school, Hannah?'

'Why, yes, Mr Cumberledge.'

'And what were you taught?'

'Reading, sir. And a few sums and sewing.'

'You can't write?'

'My mother taught me a little, sir, before I started work here. But she says I am very slow and now, of course, there isn't time. But, then, I don't need writing.'

'You will if you want to advance in the world, Hannah,' Isaiah said forcefully. 'What is your ambition?'

Hannah looked a little shy. 'Why, sir, I'd like to be like Mrs George. Not here, of course, somewhere smaller, but in charge.'

'You'll have to be able to write for that,' he insisted. 'There'll be all sorts of lists to be kept and letters to be writ to suppliers, and much else.'

'That's what Mother says. But Father says it's a lot of nonsense. He says he doesn't know how to write, it's not for people in his station of life.'

'And he thinks that you belong in the same station, I suppose?' Isaiah sounded angry.

'Why, of course, sir.'

'Does this have to do with the school where you are teaching?' asked Fanny.

Isaiah took a deep breath. His mouth looked sour and his brown eyes very tired. 'I have just had an interview with the duchess about the school. The first duchess set it up and my lady is now a trustee. Her interest in it is very strong. I've been asking for slates so that the children can learn to write their alphabet.' Isaiah began to stride about the room, his eyes sparkling with anger. 'The duchess tells me slates aren't needed, the school was set up to teach children to read and for girls to learn needlework. There was nothing in the foundation, she says, about learning to write. When I suggested they would find it very valuable, she said it wasn't the place of village children to learn to write.' Isaiah looked as if he would explode.

'I have heard of such a thing before,' Fanny said. 'There is a Children's Foundation in London where the same thing happens. And no end of prominent folk are governors there.

'Indeed?' said Isaiah, sitting down again. 'A foundation? For what sort of children?'

'Why, orphans, and those whose parents cannot keep them.'

'And what sort of children are they? For what are they educated?'

'The boys go into the navy or become apprentices, and the girls go into service, I believe,' Fanny said, thinking of the little boy from there that she'd become involved with and all the things he'd told her about life in the foundation. 'They are extremely well meaning, I think.'

'And is it well meaning to send children out into the world without the skills to improve themselves if they are capable of this?' demanded Isaiah. 'The duchess is very keen on education for her own children, she wants them to learn as quickly and well as they can.'

'They have a great position,' said Fanny. 'They will need the best education they can get.'

Isaiah scratched at his head, pushing his wig off and revealing a head of short dark curls that made him seem much younger. 'I don't dispute that, but what of Hannah and what of you?' he suddenly shot at her. 'Do you not need to read and write in order to advance? If you cannot correspond with possible patrons, how are you to obtain commissions?'

167

'Indeed, sir, you are right. I practise the best hand I can. My master, Signor Canale, has most beautiful writing.'

'There you are!' exclaimed Isaiah. 'No matter how talented an artist you are, unless you can write, you won't fulfil your potential.'

'Potential,' Hannah said suddenly, 'that's what Miss Nell said Barnaby had and look where it's got him.'

'It was a terrible accident,' agreed Isaiah. 'But Barnaby is bright, he can overcome his looks, if he works at his letters. It is all wrong that your father refuses to allow him to continue with Miss Horton.'

Hannah got pink around the eyes and pressed her lips tightly together. Fanny tore out the last sketch she had made and handed it to the girl. 'I promised you should have this,' she said quietly. 'What do you think?'

Isaiah took a look. 'I say, that's you, Hannah, to the life.'

Hannah traced one of the lines with a doubting finger. 'Is that how you see me, miss? Do I really look as determined as that?'

'Indeed you do, when you are attending to your work.' Fanny was pleased with the sketch, she'd managed to capture the way Hannah's underlip slightly jutted out as she concentrated on a task.

'You are very talented, Miss Rooker,' said Isaiah admiringly. 'Your mother will like to have that, Hannah, you must give it to her.'

'I will, sir,' Hannah said. 'But now I am to attend Miss Rooker, to help her change. I'll see you in your room, miss,' she said with a meaningful look as she left the dining room.

'She means me to chase up the stairs and spend

time allowing her to do things to my hair,' Fanny said
with a laugh to Isaiah. 'You know, sir, it turns out that
it *is* Miss Horton that I have been commissioned to
paint.'

'No!' he said in astonishment. 'Have you met with
her?'

'Very briefly. But a Lady Tanqueray spoke with me
and said it was not to be.'

'Aunt Letitia has been here? No doubt she heard
about the fire. She is very close with the Hortons. Her
late husband was a compatriot of Sir Robert's.'

'She said she would cancel the commission.'

'Did she indeed! She is a redoubtable woman and
while Sir Robert can stand up to her I don't suppose
James can.' Isaiah looked at Fanny with full attention
for the first time. 'Will you be very disappointed?'

She nodded, 'It was to be my first portrait.'

'Ah, I understand. What a pity Sir Robert did not
want you to paint Patience, she would be a most fitting
subject for your pencil.'

'I have not yet met Miss Patience Horton.'

'When you do, you will itch to paint her.'

Fanny wondered if Miss Patience could possibly
live up to the expectations of beauty Isaiah had raised
in her. Now she had another reason to look forward to
dinner.

Chapter Seventeen

Patience Horton did not come down to dinner. Indeed, few of the household appeared that day. The duke and duchess kept to their rooms. Father Sylvester was nowhere to be seen and the Horton women were concerned with the condition of little Jack. He had not regained consciousness and the doctor who had attended him the previous night had been sent for.

Canaletto was surprised, though, to see that Captain Farnham had not reappeared. 'I cannot think where he is,' Isaiah said as he gathered in the dining room with James Horton, Canaletto, Fanny, the duke's chaplain, the Reverend Elias Sparks, and a middle-aged man who introduced himself as Mr Bertie Burgh, the duke's agent.

'Lady Tanqueray was very concerned that he had not kept an engagement he had with her,' said Fanny.

Isaiah stared at her. 'She said so? To you?'

Fanny coloured. 'She asked to see me over the matter of Miss Horton's portrait and the captain's name came up. She was anxious to know if I had seen him.'

Canaletto was pleased with how well his apprentice handled herself and wondered how soon they could manage to return to their previous relationship. He wanted very much for her to trust him and turn to him the way she used to. She was the only female present at the meal and Canaletto had been delighted to find her seated next to him instead of being separated from the gentlemen, as would have been the case had other ladies been present.

The conversation turned to the drama of the Hinde Court fire.

'I cannot imagine how far this will set back our building works,' James Horton said fretfully, allowing a footman to help him to soup Lorraine, refusing the sweet-breads that were offered with it but accepting the sliced lemon.

James was very unlike his sisters, thought Canaletto. He had seen enough of both elder girls to note their height and slenderness. James was short and chubby. He had the sort of face that should be cheery – his small eyes should twinkle, the full red lips should smile, the snub nose be a happy chance that tied the whole comical visage together. Instead, he looked both sulky and dour. And Canaletto was sure it wasn't just because of the damage to his home, the lines of his face indicated that his customary expression was one of disappointment. And he so young!

'It was coming on so well,' said Isaiah, accepting the invitation of a footman to carve a capon. 'Such an edifice!'

'My father should have been well pleased with how I've handled matters in his absence. I hope he will realize he should have given me control of his City affairs as well,' James said.

'You have worked in your father's office?' asked Canaletto politely.

'That is nothing to the point, such matters as

import and export are easily understood. And I have ideas for new areas of interest, my father has little business with Cathay and Chinese is all the fashion at present.' James at last showed enthusiasm for something.

'Such a barbarous society,' objected the chaplain. 'We should not welcome their fashions here.'

'There's money in them, though,' said Bertie Burgh, the agent, a thin, cadaverous man with a trail of snuff down his waistcoat. He allowed Isaiah to place several slices of breast on his plate. 'You could have something there, young man.'

James preened himself.

'We admired the Chinese room here at Badminton this morning,' said Fanny lightly. 'There is the most marvellous bed.'

'I must get my father to see it when he comes back,' said James morosely.

'Will that be soon?' asked Canaletto.

James shrugged hopelessly. 'Who knows! He talked of returning within three months. That time is up but we have had no news from him.'

Canaletto's brief hope that Sir Robert might appear imminently to sort out the commission of his daughter's portrait, dimmed. Should he and Fanny talk to this young man or his sister? Whichever, it would be important to see the girl with the damaged face.

His wish received almost instant gratification for a few moments later Nell herself entered the dining room.

Canaletto was used to deformities, one saw them every day in the streets of London, the hunchbacks, the club feet, the bowed legs, heads too large for their bodies, wall eyes, skin disfigured by various excrescences, purple birthmarks that could sometimes cover half a face, limbs that had been broken and healed awry, not to mention the damage inflicted by smallpox. And not only the poorer folk, the gentry were by no means immune to any of these unfortunate disfigurements. So he should be inured to any ugliness the body could suffer. But the contrast between the two halves of this girl's face was shocking, there was no other word for it; he admired, though, the way she bore herself as though unaware of her appearance.

All the men rose. 'Please,' she said, 'be seated. I apologize for disturbing you but I must speak with my brother.' James touched his mouth with his napkin and waited. He made no attempt to leave the room so they could be private. 'I am so worried about Jack, he is still unconscious. The doctor can't suggest anything and his expression as he looked at poor Jack sent Mama into such a state. Oh, if only dear Doctor Carter had not departed this life and left this nincompoop in his stead!' Even in her distress, the girl was dignified and spoke with a low, musical voice.

A footman produced a chair and placed it beside James's. Isaiah gently took her arm. 'Do sit, Miss Horton, let us see if we can't suggest some amelioration of this terrible situation. Shall I send for the duke?'

She sat and smiled up at him. Her mouth had escaped disfigurement and its curve was very sweet. 'This doctor I have so little confidence in is the same one as attends on the Badminton household, so I wouldn't like to trouble his lordship.'

James Horton was visibly disturbed. 'Damn it, Nell,

what do you expect me to do? I know no medical man. Does anyone?'

'Only in Bath,' said Bertie Burgh, the agent. 'And then none I can personally recommend.'

Canaletto gave a small cough, the sort that calls for attention. 'Please, Signorina Horton, to introduce myself. I am Antonio Canale, artist. I am preparing sketches of Badminton for his lordship. I have surgeon friend now residing in Bath. That is far from here?'

'With a good horse less than a couple of hours, perhaps more coming back, there are some fearsome hills,' said Isaiah, seating himself again. 'What is the name of this friend of yours?'

'Dr Matthew Butcher, he practises in London,' said Fanny eagerly. 'He has an excellent reputation.'

'Doctor Butcher!' Nell Horton repeated in some excitement. 'Why, I have heard of him. A friend of my mother's considers he saved her life. Would he come to Badminton, do you think?'

'Get a message to him and he will be here,' said Canaletto, thinking how very good it would be to see his friend again so soon. 'I can supply address,' he added.

'The duke will send a servant to Bath, he is always so generous,' said the agent. Something about the way he spoke struck Canaletto as false. This man didn't believe the duke generous, he thought he was foolish.

Nell rose. 'I can send someone.' She turned to one of the footmen and asked him to find her servant and send him to her. 'I'll instruct him immediately, if you will be good enough to give me the direction of your surgeon friend, sir. Perhaps he would be able to come this evening, I am sure the duke will offer him hospitality for the night.'

Canaletto leapt up from the table and insisted on going to his room that very instant.

Having copied out the address Matthew had given him, he presented it to Miss Horton and then rejoined the diners. The second remove was on the table. He surveyed the grilled salmon and fried gudgeons, the crammed chickens, the roast virgin pullets, puffs of cheese curd, kidney beans and peas and realized he would be expected to dine this way for the remainder of his stay at Badminton. The simple fare he and Fanny existed on in London was no preparation for such feasts. He wished his stomach had greater capacity and saw Fanny refuse dish after dish then accept a raspberry and cherry tart. A good choice, he thought, and said to the footman that he would have one too. He would like to have drawn her into conversation but her attention was given elsewhere.

Isaiah, the chaplain and James Horton were deep in some discussion about classical texts and, much to his surprise, Canaletto heard Fanny make an observation on Tacitus.

'When did you read such works?' he whispered to her as the conversation moved swiftly on.

'Mr Hudson says that a sitter likes to feel his likeness is being caught by someone of his own standing and being able to converse on the classics, Mr Hudson says, is a sign of a good education.' She gave an enchanting little giggle. 'I borrowed some books from my brother to study in spare moments. I think, though, that it will take a long time before I can conduct a conversation such as these gentlemen are having.

175

What did you think of Miss Horton, signor? Is she not a tragic sight?'

He nodded, delighted she was talking to him so freely. 'A portrait of her needs to be carefully posed. But with right lighting and perhaps three-quarter profile, much may be done. Her mouth is perfect.'

Fanny did not look convinced.

After a lengthy meal, spun out with fruits and sweetmeats and generous quantities of various wines, the party gathered in the small drawing room. There they were joined by the duke, who brought Father Sylvester with him. Canaletto wondered what needed to be kept so private they felt they could not join the main party for dinner. They appeared to have done themselves well, however, for Father Sylvester's face was flushed and his conversation inane. The duke was sombre.

When they arrived, James Horton, the chaplain and the agent were playing cards, Fanny was occupied with crewel work and Canaletto was glancing through a portfolio of architectural drawings. The sun still shone brightly outside; they were approaching the longest day and it was still not more than six o'clock so no candles had needed to be lit.

The duke looked around and said, 'Captain Farnham has not appeared?'

'No, my lord,' said Isaiah. 'It is a puzzle to know where he has taken himself.'

'And no word?'

'No, my lord.'

The duke absent-mindedly caressed the ear of a spaniel that had accompanied him. 'The duchess is sorry not to have been able to join you all this evening, she sits with one of our daughters, who has a rheum. James, how is your little brother?'

James explained about sending for Dr Butcher.

'Butcher, what a name for a surgeon!' said Father Sylvester irrepressibly.

The duke was not amused. 'Signor Canale,' he said, 'I am most grateful you have been able to supply the name of a reputable surgeon. Doctor Carter's loss to our community has been great indeed. We must encourage one of the many Bath medical men to move nearer to us.'

Father Sylvester approached Fanny and admired her needlework. Then he sat down beside her, his arm reaching negligently along the back of the couch, his legs fashionably disposed.

There was the sound of running footsteps outside the drawing room and a cry, 'My lord, my lord!'

The duke opened the door. 'Why, man, whatever is the matter?'

In came a gardener followed by Mr Capper.

'I am sorry, my lord,' the steward said, 'I could not stop him.'

The gardener's eyes were huge, his face a picture of distress. He bent over to catch his breath, hands on knees.

The duke placed a hand on his shoulder. 'In your own time, Finlay,' he said.

Finally the man managed to blurt out, 'My lord, in the pavilion, there is a body!'

Chapter Eighteen

'A body?' said the duke. 'What do you mean?' He looked at the steward.

Mr Capper shook his head. 'My lord, I know nothing of the matter.'

'Tell us exactly what has happened,' the duke said to the gardener.

'The boss, Mr Parsons,' Finlay spoke slowly, his breath gradually coming more easily. 'He said I was to go to the pavilion. I was to check for any sign of fire, see?'

'Very sensible,' said the duke.

'Eh, but it's a mess, my lord. All charred wood and broken tiles. Chunk fell off the wall as I went in. Nearly hit me head.' Finlay rubbed his cropped hair. 'Well, it gave me a fair turn. Leaped back, I did and slipped, what with the water and the ash and all.' There was a streak of ash down one cheek. 'And that's when I found meself right beside a corpse. Burned to a cinder it is, looks something dreadful, but it's a corpse, as I live and breathe, Lord be thanked,' he added, crossing himself.

For a moment there was silence, then the chaplain said, 'Lord have mercy on his soul, whoever he is.'

'My God,' said Isaiah. 'You don't think it could be . . .' his voice tailed away.

'You'd better show me,' said the duke decisively.

Canaletto felt a sense of inevitability. 'My lord,' he said hesitantly. 'In Italy I experience occasion like this, and I able to discover what happened. Perhaps you allow me look at this,' he hesitated for a moment, wondering what term would be best to use. 'This incident?'

The duke looked at him, his head slightly on one side, his gaze very direct. 'Incident?' he repeated.

Canaletto, as so often, cursed his lack of fluency in English. Such a complicated language, so many words that were so near in meaning yet not the same. 'Perhaps accident be proper word?'

'I think Signor Canale would be an excellent witness,' said Father Sylvester unexpectedly. 'And though it is obviously too late for the last rites, I can perhaps perform a blessing on the corpse?' It was said modestly and yet with authority.

Canaletto looked at this mysterious figure who had shown up at Badminton so unexpectedly and had exchanged his religious robe for a most fashionable outfit. Why should a humble priest be received by the duke with such great civility? A dreadful possibility bore inexorably into his mind. Once there, he couldn't imagine why it hadn't come before.

'I think, as his lordship's chaplain, I should be giving any blessing,' said the Reverend Elias Sparks. 'It is, I am sure, a Protestant corpse.'

The duke looked distinctly put out. 'This is not a circus,' he said. 'Signor Canale, please do accompany us. And Father Sylvester, since you were so kind as to offer first, and I am sure a Catholic blessing will serve as well as a Protestant one, you may come too. Mr

179

Capper, you as well. Right, Finlay, take us to the pavilion.'

The little party set off through the hall and out of the north front of Badminton House.

'This incident to which you referred, signor,' said the duke as they went towards the ruins. 'What happened, exactly?'

Canaletto was quite happy to give him details. 'The palazzo of a leading family, my lord, in Venice. A young English milord stayed. One night a fire. Alas, fires start so easily. Of course, in Venice, much water available to fight flames and palazzo is saved. Then they discover body of the young milord. My friend Guiseppe Smith, is called.'

'Ah, yes, Joseph Smith,' murmured the duke. 'He is English consul, is he not?'

'Now, yes, but then, no. But he advisor and guide to young English who perform, you call it the Grand Tour, *si*?'

'Indeed, yes,' the duke agreed.

'Guiseppe arrange for me to paint so many vedute for the English, he and I friends, and because I know the back ways, of city and also of people, Guiseppe, he ask me for help many, many times when milordi in trouble. So now he comes again. This grand family anxious not have grand scandal, you understand?'

'But, unhappily, people often die in fires,' the duke protested. 'It is no scandal.'

They had reached the edge of the gravel semicircle and started across the swathe of grass.

'No, my lord,' Canaletto said smoothly. 'But this milord have big, big argument with son of family. Milord say son do dreadful things, he is heard saying he tell authorities and there be big trouble.' He paused for a moment, 'There will be much trouble,' he corrected himself. 'There is another English milord who say family's son wish dead youth harm.'

'How very unpleasant,' the duke said.

'Alas, the ways of the world can be full of deceit and chicanery,' said Father Sylvester.

'What happened?' asked the duke as they crossed from the gravel area to the grass of the park.

'I get surgeon friend of mine in Venice to examine body of young milord,' Canaletto said. The pace the duke was setting started to tell on him. 'Even though body burned, he examine bones. He find that injuries match fire injuries. No bones broken, only head damaged by falling beam. He say that fumes of fire often kill people before flames consume them. There nothing to suggest death caused by another person.'

'So, no scandal,' murmured the duke.

'No, my lord.'

Though matters had happened exactly as Canaletto had told the duke, he had not been happy with the final findings in that sad case. The fire had come too pat upon the quarrel. It would have been too easy for the son to have knocked out the young milord and left him to burn. And Canaletto knew the son for a vicious and malevolent young man. The father also had an unpleasant reputation. But nothing could be proved and, indeed, he might have misread the situation.

Why, he asked himself as they walked, was he so anxious to accompany the duke to see this corpse? As had been said, many people died in fires. The body could be that of a vagabond who had broken into the pavilion for a comfortable night and then been over-whelmed by the fire.

But Canaletto disliked coincidences. Fires were common, yes, but the pavilion burning so soon after the Hinde Court fire? And what about that extra-ordinary meeting with Father Sylvester on the road here and then finding him turning up at Badminton behaving as though he had a position of special privilege?

That same morning was the last time he'd seen Captain Farnham and both men had been interested in his *camera obscura*. Though Father Sylvester had melted away before the two men could meet.

It was a brew that to Canaletto smelled rank.

'We shall have to report the presence of this body to the constable,' the duke continued. 'It must be some vagrant, no doubt seeking shelter from the storm.' It was exactly the scenario that Canaletto had thought most likely. 'Perhaps death came to claim him in the night. Or perhaps lightning struck him and he lay in the pavilion with a part of the building smouldering away until it burst into flame. Something like that must have happened. And you will be able to confirm this to the satisfaction of the constable.'

The duke appeared perfectly happy with the way he had summed up the situation.

On the duke's other side, Father Sylvester nodded vigorously. 'I am sure Signor Canale will discover that something like that is what happened. Nature can be devastating, can it not, signor? We are all likely to be called into the presence of God at any time.'

Canaletto swiftly crossed himself. At just over fifty

182

years of age, he felt fit and hearty but time was passing at an increasingly rapid rate.

They reached the ruin. The gardener, Finlay, looked increasingly uneasy. No man would care to view more than once a body that had been consumed by fire. And Canaletto himself had already viewed one such body during his lifetime. He found now that he had no inclination to view another.

Father Sylvester looked across at Canaletto. 'Shall we enter? The servant of God and the man who captures nature's beauties?'

Canaletto forced his mind into observation mode, a state during which his eyes could note facts without his emotions being engaged.

The priest led the way into the ruin.

The floor of the little pavilion was indeed a mess. Canaletto remembered the way the duke had described its appearance. It was impossible now to recognize any aspect of what had once been a charming retreat for the ducal family. Plaster from the ceiling, soaked and shattered, lay everywhere, as did the pretty green tiles that had been imported from the Orient.

The corpse was lying face down, head turned to one side, half buried under the debris not far from the entrance. It was only possible to say that he had been tall. His head was horribly disfigured, hair burned away, skin blackened, eyes gaping holes, nose barely recognizable as nose. In the perverse way of some fires, however, his clothes were not completely destroyed and sufficient remained to refute the suggestion he had been a vagrant.

'*Mio Dio*,' said Canaletto.

'My God,' said the priest and crossed himself. 'Alas

that I do not have any holy water with me,' he added rapidly. Then he closed his eyes and began the last rites. Canaletto paid no attention to the Latin phrases. He knelt beside the body and started to clear away bits of plaster, tiles and charred wood.

Then, lightly, delicately, he felt around the charred skin covering the dead man's head. Almost at once his fingers sank into a break in the skull. Something had given the dead man a violent blow. The question was, had he been hit before the fire started or had he lain dead or unconscious and been struck by a piece of falling debris?

Father Sylvester continued to intone Latin.

In the doorway, the duke hovered with the steward behind him.

How had the conflagration started, Canaletto wondered? Had it indeed been a bolt from the heavens the previous night that had ignited some piece of the pavilion? Fire could do curious things, it could smoulder away for hours before bursting into flames. If, though, lightning had not started it, had the man who was now lying dead in some way been responsible? Had he, for instance, come into the pavilion for shelter from the rain and chosen to smoke a pipe? If so, he would have had a tinder box on his person.

Canaletto scrabbled around in the debris near the corpse but there was no sign of the remains of a tinder box. However, a more systematic search might uncover something. Would the duke think that was worthwhile?

Canaletto sat back on his heels and studied the half-destroyed walls of the pavilion. After a moment or two his attention was caught.

Rising, he went and picked up a piece of charred

beam then poked around at the foot of one of the walls, disturbing several layers of ash. He found a small piece of what could once have been leather. He smiled grimly to himself, slipped it in his pocket, then returned to the corpse. Now he saw that one of the arms had been caught underneath the body. He looked at the priest, who was crossing himself having reached the end of his prayers. 'Father, I would turn the body.'

'My son, be gentle with these poor remains.'

Canaletto told himself he had heard many a priest who had sounded as insincere as Father Sylvester, it need not mean anything.

'Father, I will.' For a long moment the priest and Canaletto looked at each other and it was Father Sylvester who dropped his gaze first.

Carefully Canaletto turned the awful remains of the corpse on to its side. On the little finger of the hand that had been protected from the worst effects of the fire was a signet ring, blackened but intact. He steeled himself and then withdrew the ring from the finger.

It came easily, the inside bright and shiny.

'What have you found?' asked the duke, peering into the ruin from where he stood in the entrance.

Canaletto rose, took a handkerchief from one of his pockets, polished the ring and handed it to the duke. 'Perhaps you recognize, no?'

As he studied the ring, the duke's expression was horrified. 'Humphrey,' he groaned. 'It's Humphrey Farnham's. Show me the corpse.'

Father Sylvester took the duke by the elbow. 'It is a sad sight, my friend. Prepare yourself to be much distressed.'

185

Canaletto dropped back and let the two of them approach the dead man.

The duke gave one look at the ghastly head, shivered and turned away. 'One cannot say aught about such a sight,' he muttered. 'Jones, organize a stretcher, take the captain's remains to the church. He will lie there for the moment.'

Canaletto fingered the little piece of burned leather in his pocket and wondered whether to say something to the duke now. Better later, he thought, alone.

The duke walked back towards the house with a bowed head, the signet ring clasped in his hand. Beside him walked Father Sylvester.

The steward walked with Canaletto. 'You spent a long time studying the walls of the pavilion. Did you find anything? Anything that would suggest how the fire started?' he asked.

Such curiosity was, of course, natural, Canaletto told himself. He shrugged, 'So much mess,' he said. 'How is one to see anything?'

John Capper shot him a sharp look but all he said was, 'I must see about that stretcher' and strode out ahead.

'Signor Canale,' said the duke as they regained the house. 'I would have words with you before we send for the constable. It will, I am sure, be just a formality but I would be grateful if you could tell him, as you did the authorities in Venice, how accidental Captain Farnham's death has been.'

Canaletto gave him a deep bow. 'My lord, my friend, Doctor Butcher, arrives soon, I hope. Perhaps, after he has seen Master Horton, he may examine body, if it pleases your lordship?'

'I see no reason for that,' the duke said stiffly. 'Captain Farnham is quite expired. I take it you do not claim your doctor friend can raise men from the dead?'

'No, my lord, but perhaps he able to tell more about how captain die.'

Father Sylvester stared at him, 'Say you so?' He turned to the duke and said gracefully, 'My friend, if this man is indeed able to reveal anything of how the good captain died, can I suggest he be allowed to examine what he will?'

The duke hardly hesitated. 'Well, if you think it wise, it shall be so.' He laid a hand on the priest's arm. 'Come, you shall help me see the body of my friend carefully disposed.'

Canaletto watched them walk round the end of the great house and it seemed to him that the aristocrat deferred to the man of God. Was the Duke of Beaufort indeed at heart a Roman Catholic? Was he also preparing to finance an invasion of England? To commit treason?

Chapter Nineteen

Matthew Butcher arrived an hour or so later and was taken straight upstairs.

Afterwards Canaletto joined him as he was served refreshments in the breakfast room. They told the servants attendance wasn't necessary and were able to be quite private.

'How is the boy?' Canaletto asked.

The surgeon was wearing a well-cut dark-brown coat and buff riding breeches with a buff waistcoat and a shirt and stock of fine linen. He looked as smart as Canaletto had ever seen him.

Matthew helped himself to more slices of cold beef. 'He has just become conscious and, if he can be kept quiet, I think he will do well enough.'

'Good news!' Canaletto rubbed his hands. He took a glass from the sideboard, sat down and helped himself to the decanter of wine on the table. 'I congratulate you.'

Matthew grimaced. 'Nothing to my credit, I just happened to be there as the boy came round. Nature was the doctor. But first I reset his arm. The doctor who attended to that is a charlatan, he should not be practising. It was as well the lad was still unconscious at that time, else he would have swooned away again.'

'Miss Horton be pleased.'

'Ah, that's the girl who was nursing him? Excellent female, never blenched when I got her to hold the bone in place while I fixed the splint. Nor did she fall into hysterics when the boy opened his eyes and asked for Puff. I thought he might be having delusions but it was explained that Puff is a cat.'

'Ah, I understand boy chased cat into burning house. So ridiculous!'

'Miss Horton had her sister there, quite a different girl. Dazzler to look at but full of the vapours. Burst into tears and almost strangled the lad as he came round. Takes after the mother. I was asked to see her as well. Nothing much wrong with her that a firm grasp on reality wouldn't help. I will never be a fashionable doctor, I can't be doing with the vapours.'

Matthew finished his food, recharged his wine glass and sat back. 'I owe you thanks for this introduction, signor, it will up my stock in Bath no end to be known as a surgeon who attends the Duke of Beaufort.'

'You enjoy Bath?' Canaletto asked, wondering how soon he could bring up the matter of the burned body.

'Enjoy? My dear signor, the place is one continual round of enjoyment from sun up to sun down. My sister starts the day by dressing in some fancy linen garments. She gets herself taken to the baths straight from her hall in a sedan chair. No end of fashionable folk cavort about there, it's a social session. Later she sips more of the waters in the Pump Room and exchanges gossip with others. On to Simpson's Assembly Rooms for a little card play and more gossip. Dinner can be taken as late as four o'clock and most evenings there is music or dancing or a lecture on some worthy matter or other.'

Canaletto was amazed. 'Matthew, you do all this too?'

'Need you ask? I tell you, if it wasn't for the fascination of finding out as much as I can about the efficacy of the spa waters, I would have been bored into returning to London before this. As it is, I spend most of my days at the hospital that has been established in connection with the baths.'

'You attend patients?'

'Aye, and ask questions. If I'm not careful, I shall become as calcified as the waters.'

'But you do not mind leaving baths to visit Badminton?' Canaletto said a little slyly.

'As I said, it'll up my reputation considerably. My sister is happy for me and does not mind my leaving her for a night. Apart from that, it is good to see you again, my friend.'

'And I you. Matthew, before you return to Bath, there is serious matter I ask if you can attend to.'

The surgeon put down his wine and tore a hunk of bread off a loaf. 'What sort of matter?' he growled. 'Another patient? Not little Fanny?' he asked with sudden concern.

'No, no, Fanny is fine.'

'That's good. I look forward to seeing her.' Matthew cut himself a large piece of the cheese that sat in a wooden holder on the table. 'Excellent provender here,' he added, taking a bite with the bread. 'So, what else is it you want me to attend to?'

Canaletto refilled both their glasses. 'There was fire

here today, in small pavilion. Later a man's body was found in the ruins.'

Matthew groaned. 'And you want me to look at the corpse, is that it? Any particular reason?'

'The duke wishes to confirm nothing sinister about his death. I,' Canaletto brushed some invisible dust from his linen cravat in a modest manner. 'I have reason to believe death not so innocent.'

'Indeed, why?'

Canaletto waved his arm airily. 'Something about way fire started. And skull is broken. But maybe accident. If you examine body and say all is innocent, then duke happy.'

'Another of your darned investigations! And you give me the choice of pleasing the duke by finding nothing or you by confirming your suspicions! It is as well I am an honest man and look to the truth of things, not to political advantage.' He finished his wine and rose. 'All right, lead me to the body.'

Canaletto took him out through a side door and round to the church. As they went, he said, 'The captain old friend of duke, he very distressed he dead. He want to know truth.'

'If I can discover aught. But with a burned body,' Matthew shook his head. 'I cannot guarantee anything, my friend.'

'If nothing found, nothing lost,' Canaletto said cheerfully.

Matthew's eyes twinkled. 'Nothing found, nothing lost? My friend, you will have to watch it, you are beginning to make jokes in English!'

The skies were clear and the pearly twilight as the sun prepared to set was very attractive. It took a moment or two to adjust to the dark interior of the church. As they entered, there was a curious sound that Canaletto couldn't immediately identify.

'Who is that?' whispered Matthew.

Now that Canaletto's eyes were adjusted to the dim light, he could see that the stretcher had been placed across several stools and was covered with an embroidered cloth. Beside it, on the floor, a figure lay collapsed and he realized that the sound he'd heard was low sobbing. Someone, a woman judging by the spread of skirts, was desolate.

Canaletto walked up the aisle with Matthew and summoned his best English. 'We are sorry to tread on your grief,' he said gently.

'Intrude,' whispered Matthew in his ear. 'The word is intrude, not tread.'

Canaletto ignored him.

The figure lifted her head, her eyes reddened and swollen, and revealed herself as the woman with the splendid facial bones whom he had seen arrive with the Horton party the previous night.

Brushing Canaletto's helping hand aside, the woman got to her feet. 'He's gone,' she said in a voice more desolate than any Canaletto had ever heard. She grabbed his upper arm in a strong grasp. 'You are the painter, are you not? That saw the pavilion was on fire?'

Canaletto nodded, wincing from the power of her grip.

'Tell me, did you see him? Did you see my Humphrey go into that place?'

'No, signora, I not see the captain. Last time I see him was previous day.'

'We met there sometimes,' she said dreamily. 'Such a pleasure palace it was for him and me.' She looked at the bier. 'I can't bring myself to lift the cloth, to see what the fire has done to his dear face. And yet, until I do, I cannot accept that he is dead. Will you,' she faltered, took a deep breath and tried again. 'Will you, sir, lift the cloth for me?'

'Is a terrible sight,' Canaletto warned her.

'I know it will be ugly beyond imagining but unless I see, I will imagine even worse. Please, sir, lift the cloth.'

Canaletto went to the head of the bier. Someone had placed a heavy gold cross on the embroidered covering. Carefully he moved it off the body. Then he lifted up the cloth and revealed the blackened head. It seemed to have shrivelled slightly and become, if anything, even more repellent to look at. He prepared himself to deal with hysterics from the woman.

Instead, she gave a sudden intake of breath, raised her hands to her mouth and stood quite, quite still. Then her arms dropped to her side, she moved forward and stood looking down at the terrible travesty that was once the face of Humphrey Farnham.

Satisfied she was not going to break down, Canaletto took a step back and allowed her to stand alone at the head of the bier.

Incredibly, she reached out a hand and gently stroked the head that bore so little resemblance to anything that could be called a man. 'Goodbye my love,' she said in a low voice, then turned and strode out of the church, never hesitating or turning.

The door swung shut behind her with a crash.

Neither man said anything for a little, then

Matthew raised one shoulder in a small gesture of resignation. 'That was a woman who loved too well.'

Canaletto agreed but he did not want to consider the implications of the woman's presence beside the corpse now. There were more urgent matters to attend to.

Matthew pulled the coverlet further down. For a long moment he looked at the charred remains. Then, like Canaletto before him, he felt the bare, blackened skull. 'Ah, here is the contusion you found. It will need investigating. As will the body. Are you expecting me to perform an autopsy now? I do not think there is enough light left.'

The church was almost dark now. Canaletto looked up at one of the windows and saw by the red streaks in the sky that the sun was setting. In a few minutes it would be gone. 'You are right,' he sighed. This meant delay. But a good light would be essential. 'Early tomorrow morning, yes?'

Matthew carefully replaced the coverlet. 'Yes, at first light. I will need to see the boy again and return to Bath by noon if possible. You will arrange a suitable place for me to hold the autopsy?'

'I speak to duke.'

They made their way back past the windows of the drawing room. The candles had been lit and a large chandelier sparkled, casting its faceted lights upon the company. Where it might have been expected that a sombre mood would prevail, there was an air not perhaps of gaiety but certainly not funereal.

A group of men that included James Horton was chatting in one corner. Isaiah sat beside Fanny, her sewing abandoned in her lap as she spoke in an animated fashion. In her green silk gown, matching ribbons threaded charmingly through her lace cap, she made a delicious picture. Any man should have been delighted to be seated beside her. But Isaiah's attitude was not attentive. Instead he was glowering at the couple seated opposite them.

On another sofa was the lovely girl Canaletto had first seen wet and bedraggled on the night of the storm. Now polished and presented to perfection she radiated beauty. Beside her, seemingly entranced by her company, was Charles Sylvester.

'Why, there's little Miss Fanny,' said Matthew happily. 'Let us join the company.'

'Let us indeed,' said Canaletto as he looked at the mysterious priest who was now acting as though he had never claimed a religious vocation.

Chapter Twenty

Patience Horton had not wanted to go downstairs.

'I want to stay here with you and Jack,' she'd said to Nell.

'Darling Pattie, Jack is back with us but he needs to be very, very quiet now, Doctor Butcher was most insistent.'

'I can sit here quite quietly.' Patience rearranged her skirts around her chair. She had dressed ready for dinner, in yellow silk with a blue stomacher that matched her eyes, then had been too worried to go downstairs. 'How can I enjoy food and wine and company when Jack is lying here all unconscious and Mama is in such a decline?' she'd said.

Since the fire at Hinde Court and the accident to little Jack, Lady Horton had suffered a nervous collapse. When Patience had called in on her earlier, she had wailed for her husband and asked how he could abandon them in this hour of need. Then she had called on God to explain why he had brought such trouble on them. Patience had become far too upset to remain with her.

But now Jack had opened his eyes and spoken. Patience had cried. It had been so emotional, she had wanted to smother Jack with kisses. Dr Butcher had visited Lady Horton and given her a soothing draught and then Nell told Patience that she should go and join the rest of the Badminton party. 'They will soon have finished their meal. We will eat something up here, for I am very hungry even if you are not, then you can join them.'

'Can I not sit with Mama, I might calm her.'

'Doctor Butcher said she will soon sleep. Anyway, she would only fret that you are not astonishing the ducal gathering with your beauty,' Nell grinned at Patience. 'You must know Mama has set her heart on your marrying some aristocratic title and where better to meet one than at a duke's table?'

'There's none here at the moment but us and Isaiah and you know he is the last person Mama would want me to be affianced to.'

'Patience!' Nell caught herself and continued more quietly. 'Isaiah is most respectable. He has a future. Any girl would be fortunate to attach him.'

'Oh, Nell, I know you like him but Mama has made it clear that Papa will never countenance a match with a penniless schoolmaster, no matter how well connected.'

Nell drew a chair alongside Patience's. 'Tell me, Pattie dear, are you truly not at all in love with Isaiah? He is so deep in love with you.'

Patience gave a low laugh. It was unlike Nell not to know exactly what she was thinking. 'Transparent,' that's what Nell called her. 'Isaiah makes me feel like some precious doll that lives on a shelf only to be taken down and played with every now and then. I do not want to be a doll, Nell, I want to share my life with someone I can talk to.'

'But you and Isaiah talk all the time!' Nell said in surprise.

'Chitter chatter, that is all.' Patience made a face. 'I cannot understand when Isaiah talks of his scientific interests; I'm not like you, able to discuss Mr Boyle's discoveries and what importance he and Mr Newton have to science. So I tell him what I do with my day and ask him what the little children he is teaching have done. And he gazes at me with eyes like a puppy dog,' Patience brought a small fist down on to the arm of her chair in frustration. 'Love should be romantic. I should be able to feel passion.' Patience stopped abruptly. Nell would never understand how she longed to give her heart to someone exciting.

Nell looked sad. 'Poor Isaiah. If you were able to return his love, Pattie, I'd tackle Papa when he returns. Isaiah's parentage is more than respectable and I am sure he will be a man of distinction one of these days. His ideas are so radical and he works so hard at his research. If it's your dowry you're worried about, I'm sure I can persuade Papa to drop this nonsensical idea you are to have none until I am married. I will convince him that I shall never marry.'

Patience couldn't bear to hear dear Nell talk like this. She took her sister's hands in hers. 'Dearest sis, anyone who knows you doesn't see your damaged face and, truly, it gets better every day.'

Nell put a hand on her sister's cheek. 'Sweetheart, it is not because of my face I say I won't be married. Can you imagine there is a man who will put up with my constant questioning of everything I see that I do not understand? Men want their women to be submissive and I can never be that. Maybe the accident was God's way of showing I was not born to be a wife.'

Patience looked up at the damaged face she loved so dearly. That awful explosion had been such a shock. But she had got used to the scars and Nell was so much more than her features. She sighed. 'One of these days, all will change for you. You know, if there is no one else, I am sure you could marry Thomas.'

Nell looked at her in astonishment. 'Thomas? Thomas Wright? Oh, Pattie, I don't mean that I consider him beneath me, far from it. His birth is better than ours. But, well, his interests lie elsewhere.'

'You mean with Damaris? Nell, you are such an innocent.' Patience felt worldly-wise compared with her sister. 'He stopped spending all his time in the kitchen weeks ago. And haven't you seen how assiduously he attends to all your needs and wants? He is handsome, too,' added Patience, delighted that for once her intelligent sister couldn't see something so obvious.

'Pattie, I am sure you are wrong. But it doesn't matter. Thomas could be the most eligible man in the world and it would mean nothing to me.'

'If you insist.' Patience rose. 'If there really is nothing I can do, by all means send for some food and then I will go downstairs and perform as Mama would wish.'

So it was that Patience eventually found her way downstairs.

As she came down the last step and turned towards the drawing room, she gasped as her elbow was taken in a firm grasp. 'You have come as an angel from heaven to help a lost soul,' said a voice.

Patience turned and found herself looking at one of the most attractive men she had ever met. Warm brown eyes laughed down into hers and a well-shaped mouth was curved in enjoyment of the picture she made. He was tall and slender and dressed in a beautifully cut coat of light blue over darker trousers with a white waistcoat embroidered in silver. There were silver buckles on his shiny black shoes. All this Patience took in with one quick glance as she raised an eyebrow at him and gently freed her elbow.

He gave her a graceful obeisance. 'Charles Sylvester at your service. I am trying to find my way back to the drawing room. May you, by some wonderful chance, be on your way there too? If not, tell me where you are going and I will accompany you there instead.'

Patience had to smile, the voice with its slightly foreign accent was so very charming. She bobbed him a little curtsey and offered her hand. 'Patience Horton at your service, Mr Sylvester, or should I say,' she paused for a moment, 'Lord Sylvester, perhaps, or Sir Charles?'

'Plain Mr Sylvester suits me very well, Miss Horton,' he said and raised her hand to his lips. Never had Patience so regretted the etiquette that said gentlemen did not actually kiss your hand. 'My dear Miss Horton, I will follow you to the ends of the earth. Or we may just stand here while you tell me all about yourself.'

Patience gave her silvery laugh. 'The drawing room is this way.' She attempted to take her hand back but Charles Sylvester continued to hold her where she was.

'I should perhaps warn you,' he said. 'There has been sad news. One Captain Farnham met his end in the pavilion that burned down and we are mourning his demise. Did you perhaps know him?'

'Humphrey?' said Patience in dismay. 'Humphrey Farnham? Yes, indeed I did. Is he really dead?' She gazed at Mr Sylvester, appalled. She had found the captain too disturbing to like in life. She had always felt that he didn't approve of her, that he found her too silly, too flippant. But now she wished that, instead of seeking excuses not to be in his company, she had made more of an effort to be kind to him.

Blinking rapidly, she extracted her hand from Mr Sylvester's and turned towards the drawing room. He followed her and flung wide the door. 'Look, beauty has come to cheer us,' he announced.

Even if Mr Sylvester hadn't said anything, Patience would have known immediately that something was wrong, there was such a sad atmosphere in the room. Isaiah and James talked together desultorily. The Reverend Elias Sparks, a man Patience found singularly unexciting, sat reading a book with a very sulky look on his face. Sitting on a sofa was a pretty girl with copper curls, wearing a green silk dress and working some embroidery, her forehead creased in concentration. Nobody was enjoying themselves.

'It's wonderful to see you, Miss Horton,' said Isaiah, jumping up. 'How is little Jack?'

She looked across at her eldest brother. 'He has regained consciousness, James, it would do your heart good to see him.'

'I shall visit him in the morning, sis,' he said and picked up a book.

Ever since Sir Robert had left James in charge of the family, he had become more and more impossible.

'Come and sit down.' Mr Sylvester led her to another sofa. Isaiah looked first hurt and then furious. He flung himself down beside the girl in the green dress, who immediately put down her embroidery and appeared happy to converse.

Patience allowed herself to be seated beside Mr Sylvester and found herself looking again into the warm brown eyes that had no hint of the lost puppy about them. Then she noticed his eyebrows. They were arched in a questioning sort of way that she had never seen in a man before.

She gave him a warm smile. Patience was used to the effect her smile had on men, that slight widening of the eyes, the way their interested gaze became even more alert, how they would lean a little closer to her. It was something she would giggle over with Nell. Never before, though, had she received such an attractive smile in return. Her own eyes widened and she felt her breath come a little faster.

'You are staying at Badminton, Mr Sylvester?' she asked hopefully.

'For a few days. May I ask what has been the matter with your little brother?'

Patience had no difficulty in telling this deeply interested audience all about the fire at Hinde Court and how Jack had been injured.

Mr Sylvester was all sympathy and concern. 'How very distressing for you. You are very brave to join us this evening. What a pity that I had to tell you such sad news.'

'It is indeed a tragedy. We were all very friendly

with Captain Farnham, especially my sister. He visited her the day before our fire, while I was out visiting with my mother. I hope Nell does not hear of his death until tomorrow, she is quite worn out with nursing my brother. I would have stayed with her but she positively forced me downstairs.'

'I shall have to try and repay your sister for, as you say, forcing you downstairs.'

'Have you known the duke long, sir?'

'Yes, indeed. I brought my father's compliments to him,' he said.

'You mean your father is the duke's friend?'

Mr Sylvester looked amused. 'That is perhaps one way to describe their relationship, yes.'

'And does your father live abroad, sir?'

'Now, how did you guess that, Miss Horton?'

She waved her hand airily, 'There is something about the way you speak, sir, which suggests you may have been raised in another country.'

'You are very perceptive, Miss Horton.' The interest in his eyes deepened. 'It is not often one has the pleasure of meeting a young lady who is not only beautiful but has such sensibility as well. Have you travelled at all?'

Patience gave an exasperated little sigh. 'Papa has promised we shall visit Paris but Nell and I are anxious to go further, we want to see the Italian Alps, Venice and Rome, but Mama says it will upset her nerves too much to take to the sea to cross the channel and so we haven't been. I am sure you know Paris, sir.'

He looked delightfully amused. 'Yes indeed, I do.'

'Should we like it, sir?'

'It is a place full of pleasures and vices, entertainment and despicable practices, fashion and political chicanery.'

'Why, it must be exactly like London, sir,' Patience dimpled demurely at him.

His eyes twinkled merrily back at her. 'Oh, vastly more so in every way.'

'Good heavens,' Patience said. 'It sounds rather like wine, delicious to taste but after a little you can be quite overcome with sensation.'

'Now there is a sensible suggestion.' Mr Sylvester rose and pulled the bell. 'As soon as someone comes, we shall ask for some wine.' He returned to his seat. 'Miss Horton, you are delightful. Tell me more about yourself. So far I know you arrived last night in the middle of a thunderstorm, with your home burned down and your brother injured. Does disaster follow your family?'

What a suggestion! But such was Mr Sylvester's charm, Patience could only smile. 'No more than any other, sir. And the storm saved the house from total ruin. Indeed, our steward says much of it still stands and he rescued us a supply of clothes. They smelled vilely of smoke, we have had them hung in the open air all day.' She sniffed and found the odour still clung to her. 'I shall not mind if you say you are unable to sit next to me, sir.'

'If you had not mentioned the matter, I should have been unaware of any aroma of smoke. Anyway, it's a small price to pay for so delightful a creation as you are wearing,' Mr Sylvester said with a smile that seemed to Patience more honest and sincere than his previous ones, charming though they had been, and she suddenly felt very comfortable with him.

Just as they were getting on so well, the drawing room door opened and in came, not a servant to offer refreshment, but Dr Butcher and another, much smaller man.

Patience rose. 'Doctor Butcher, thank you so much for saving my brother's life.'

'I did little,' he said gruffly. 'What he needs now is careful nursing.'

'Oh, that he will get from my sister and myself, I assure you,' she said, then was surprised to find him moving away to greet the girl sitting on the sofa with Isaiah.

'Antonio Canale, at your service,' the small man said, giving her a graceful bow.

'Oh, isn't it you who gave my sister Doctor Butcher's name and direction?' she said, determined that this man at least should be charmed. 'You have our most profound thanks.'

A servant appeared and almost immediately, it seemed, wine and brandy were produced. Supplied with full glasses, the party seated itself again. Patience had no clear idea how it had happened, it was certainly none of her doing, but she found herself sharing the sofa not with Mr Sylvester but Signor Canale.

However, Mr Sylvester was hanging over the back of the sofa, right by her shoulder, which was almost a better arrangement.

'Miss Horton has been telling me what a time she and her family have had,' he said to the Italian.

'I so sorry to hear of fire,' Signor Canale said. 'How did this come about?'

'Damaris, our cook, woke us and she says it started in the new part of the building – for you must know that my father has commissioned a great deal of construction – and it burned through into her room and then spread down the stairs. Thomas, our steward, says the top floor was almost totally destroyed before the storm came and put the fire out, and that water has flooded everywhere.' She looked up at Mr Sylvester with wide eyes.

'But your closet preserved your clothes,' he said gravely. 'What a very fortunate circumstance.'

Patience dropped her gaze. 'Was it not, sir? To have been left without clothes to wear, how difficult that would have been.'

'A tragedy,' he said, laughing, as he went to replenish his glass.

Patience turned to the Italian. 'From where do you come, signor?' she asked.

'I citizen of Venice,' he said. 'You like Venice very much I think. She is most beautiful city in all the world.'

Patience had found conversing with Mr Sylvester an intoxicating experience but talking with this man was slightly unnerving. He had such sharp eyes, they seemed to take in every aspect.

'And what do you do at Badminton?'

'I am artist, I paint vedute, signorina, what you call views.'

'You are not the artist commissioned to paint my sister?' Patience asked in dismay.

He shook his head, 'That is my apprentice, Miss Fanny Rooker. That is she, on the sofa.' Patience looked again at the girl, still talking animatedly with Isaiah. She wondered what they could be talking about, surely not science!

'I paint landscapes, not portraits,' the Italian went on.

Patience wondered if she should have heard of Antonio Canale. Her father bought paintings, large affairs with gods and goddesses disporting themselves in various ways. He said that the agent he had bought them through had sworn they were by old masters. Patience could not remember the names of any of the artists.

'I thought if you could paint anything, you could paint everything.'

The painter shook his head. 'Experience proves talent lies in particular direction.'

Mr Sylvester sauntered over with his refilled glass. 'Come Signor Canale, you are monopolizing the most beautiful woman in the room. It won't do. Allow me to take my seat again.'

Patience felt her breath taken away by the impudence of it but loved how much he wanted to sit beside her.

The Italian looked up at the tall man standing over him, looking positively regal, and rose. 'Miss Horton certainly very beautiful but I happy to talk to other beautiful woman here.' He waved a graceful hand towards the girl in the green dress. 'Take my seat, Father.'

'Father?' Patience repeated, looking at Mr Sylvester, impatiently waiting for his place beside her. For an instant she thought she saw a flash of anger in the brown eyes.

Then he raised a hand in the manner of a swordsman acknowledging a hit. 'When I met Signor

Canale and Miss Rooker on the road from London, I was wearing my priest's dress.

'Then you are a priest?' Patience could hardly believe it for no man could look less like one. 'A Roman Catholic priest, not a vicar of the Church of England?'

Mr Sylvester stood with a hand on his hip, he looked very proud. 'I am Roman Catholic and I have chosen to be a priest, yes,' he said.

The evening turned to ashes in Patience's mouth.

Chapter Twenty-One

Before breakfast the next morning, Canaletto met Matthew in the church.

Matthew had his surgeon's case with him and Canaletto had arranged with the duke for them to use a well-lit outbuilding for the autopsy.

Together they carried the stretcher out of the church, Canaletto finding his end a heavy burden, and into a room that looked as though it was usually used for storing bags of flour. A trestle table had been set there and they placed the body on this. A bulging linen bag stood in a corner, its contents most definitely not flour.

'I will need containers for the innards,' Matthew said as he got out his knives. 'I doubt the fire has fried the good captain's vital parts.'

Canaletto accepted this without revulsion. He went to the dairy and borrowed two large earthenware bowls from the maid working there. After taking them to the surgeon, he went and fetched a bucket of water from the stables.

'Excellent work,' said Matthew approvingly. He had cut off the charred remnants of the captain's clothes and the body was now naked. 'Right!' he said. 'Since we are dealing with military remains, let battle com-

mence.' Really, faced with a corpse, Matthew was
damnably insouciant. The fellow acted as though it
was the most ordinary thing in the world to carve up
a body, no more than slicing into a roast joint of beef.

'First of all,' the surgeon went on, 'I have examined
the front and back of the body. The fire has wrought
great damage to the face, as we can see. The cadaver,
however, has to a certain extent been protected by the
clothes, particularly the front, which was lying against
the floor. Which is why you were able to rescue the
ring from his finger.' Matthew moved the head slightly.
'Now this is the contusion in the cranium I found last
night and that you noticed when you first looked at
the corpse.'

Canaletto nodded.

'As you so rightly concluded, there is nothing to
say whether this injury occurred before or after he
died. No hair remains on the head and such is the
charring, I cannot tell whether blood was round the
wound, which might indicate a pre-death contusion,
or not. It is on the back of the head, in a position that
might well have attracted a falling tile or beam as the
body lay on the floor. Was there anything on the body
before it was moved that might have caused such
damage?'

Canaletto thought back. 'Too difficult say exactly,'
he said. 'So much rubbish, bits and pieces. Maybe
something drop and, how you say, bounce?'

'Hah! Bounce, that's good, my friend. Bounce
indeed it might have! But the deceased might have
been hit hard with a club or something similar. Not a
sword nor anything sharp.'

'You can tell that?'

Matthew nodded. 'By how the bone has been broken. In layman's language, it has been bashed, not cleaved.'

That was something Canaletto could understand. Though so far he had learned nothing he did not know before, he was content to let Matthew proceed in the manner he preferred. You did not tell a professional how to do his job.

'Now, when I examined the front of the body, it had been, as I said, protected from the fire to a certain extent. Although the flesh is discoloured, it has not suffered much from charring.'

Canaletto tried to force his mind to be dispassionate. It was difficult, particularly as he kept remembering the captain as he had been in life, prickly, contentious and intelligent. Opinionated but with good sense. Canaletto wasn't sure he would have warmed to him but he would have liked the opportunity of hearing more of his views, particularly on the Jacobite cause and Prince Charles Edward.

'Now look, my friend.' Matthew pointed his knife at the chest. 'Here there is a slit in the skin. The fire has damaged it slightly but I can say with certainty that a knife entered the chest of this man.'

'Ah!' Canaletto gave a great sigh.

Matthew looked at him with a good deal of understanding. 'You have suspected as much? That this man had been despatched by more than an unfortunate fire?'

'Too many coincidences,' said Canaletto.

'You have too suspicious a mind, my friend. And a devilishly astute one where murder is concerned. Now,

I will uncover the ribs and the heart and we shall discover if there is anything else to be seen.'

While Matthew proceeded with his dissection, Canaletto tried to imagine the captain approaching the pavilion, with his mind on – what? And just why had he entered the pretty little folly? Did he know the person who must have been lying in wait for him? Did he struggle or was the killer, surprising him, perhaps from behind the door, able to fell his victim with some heavy stick so that it was easy to knife or run him through with a sword?

The surgeon peeled back skin and muscle from bones. 'See,' he said, revealing the ribs and dipping an old flour bag in the bucket of water to wipe the bone. 'Here is where the blade struck before entering the heart.' He pointed to an easily recognizable scar on the cleaned rib. A few minutes later, the heart had been removed from the body cavity and Matthew could show Canaletto where it had been stabbed.

'Must have been sword,' the painter said decisively.

Matthew held the heart in his blood-streaked fingers, flexing it so that the cut was better seen. 'If so, it was very wide, a broadsword such as are used in campaigns. But just as likely is a knife such as a butcher would use.'

'Dead man back from wars.' Canaletto wondered if anyone had seen the captain carrying a broadsword recently. Could he have feared death waited for him in the pavilion and gone in there armed? Only to have his weapon taken over by his killer? Canaletto tried to visualize the fight that could have taken place between the athletic captain armed with a heavy sword and his murderer. Even with the victim's limp, it would have to have been a young, very fit and determined man to overcome such an experienced fighter. Unless, of course, the murderer had managed to surprise him with such a blow the captain was knocked unconscious before he could defend himself.

Matthew placed the heart in one of the earthenware bowls. 'Why should anyone have wanted to kill him?'

'That, my friend, is important question.'

'Have you any ideas?' Matthew proceeded to remove the lungs and bowels from the corpse.

Canaletto was used to disgusting sights but somehow the knowledge that he owned organs no different from the ones being mauled was painful. He turned his mind towards reasons for the captain's death. 'I have little knowledge of captain. But why men kill?'

The question was intended to be rhetorical but the surgeon saw it as an invitation. 'Revenge? Gain? Passion? Remember the woman in the church,' he added, wielding his knife expertly. 'There is one that men would kill for.'

'You think so?'

Matthew nodded. 'If the captain was cutting someone else out of her affections, I can imagine that person wishing him dead.' He might well have a point, Canaletto had thought the Amazon a striking woman the first moment he'd seen her with her wet and wild hair.

But there was something else. 'Wishing not same as deed,' Canaletto said. An idea had hit him with the force of a crossbow, an idea with such dire implications, he could hardly take it in. 'There is another reason – fear of discovery. If someone think captain could betray them, maybe quick thrust remove danger.'

'Possible, I suppose.' Matthew looked up. 'Is there something the captain might have known that could offer such danger to him?'

'Perhaps,' said Canaletto. He almost wished the idea hadn't occurred to him. He had no idea how he could prove it and he would have to be very certain before making any such suggestion to either the duke or Paymaster Pitt. It would cause such difficulties and lead into such dangerous waters, he was tempted to discard the theory altogether. But to do so would mean abandoning any investigation into the captain's death and Canaletto didn't think he was ready to do this. However, there was something else that was essential to be done first.

'Please, see if left leg recently broken,' he said to Matthew. 'Necessary we know we have correct man. Maybe signet ring put on another's hand.'

'My, you are suspicious enough to please the heart of any scientific follower,' said Matthew with a grin. 'Very well, then.' He fell to dissecting the corpse's blackened left leg.

'There you are,' he said with satisfaction a little later. 'See, quite clear break of the tibia and fibula.'

Canaletto saw two thickened portions interrupt the smooth flow of the lower leg's parallel bones. 'Body captain's,' he said.

'Fell from his horse, did he?'

'He not say.'

'They were knitting together well, it is a waste,' said Matthew. 'I have finished. I can find nothing else of import. What should we do with these poor remains now?'

'He must be restored as much as possible.'

'Sew him up, you mean?'

Canaletto nodded. 'I suggest to duke we dress captain in best clothes, then he respectable.' He went to the bag sitting in the corner, opened it and took out a set of garments. 'He arrange for these.'

'And you will tell him the result of the examination?'

'Indeed, yes! Captain his guest, his friend.' Canaletto watched Matthew take a large needle and some thread from his bag. 'He not like, he will not like,' he corrected himself, 'your findings but he must know. He must tell Constable the circumstances of fire and death.'

'He may not thank me for my discoveries, all the goodwill I won over the boy will be dissipated.' Matthew, though, sounded resigned as he started the process of closing up the corpse. Then together they performed the difficult task of dressing the body.

After that they carried the captain's remains back to the church, covered them with the embroidered coverlet again and added the cross. Then they returned to the room they'd been using. The bowls of organs still stood on the floor. 'Heart should be preserved,' said Canaletto, looking at it with no more emotion than if it had been offal for sale.

'I have no fluid with me,' said Matthew. 'However, a bottle of brandy?'

'I get,' said Canaletto.

'See if you can find a jar, too,' Matthew called after

him. 'The kitchen may have one for preserving fruit and suchlike.'

So it proved. Armed with a heavy glass jar plus lid begged off the cook, Canaletto went and found Mr Briggs in his pantry, carefully washing the glasses they'd been drinking out of the previous night. There was no difficulty in being supplied with a bottle of brandy once the butler had found the right key to unlock the right cupboard.

As Canaletto carried the spirit back across the forecourt, he was almost run down by Father Sylvester on a powerful-looking dappled grey horse. 'Apologies,' the priest laughed, wrenching the animal around the Italian. 'Miss Horton and I go riding.'

Sure enough, behind him came Patience Horton, mounted on a frolicsome bay mare she seemed to have little trouble managing. She raised her whip in a salutation to Canaletto and trotted after the other rider.

Grasping the brandy and the jar tightly, Canaletto proceeded on his way. He doubted that the powerful-looking horse could have been the one Father Sylvester had bargained for in Reading. The duke was obviously generous with his horseflesh.

'Here, brandy,' said Canaletto to Matthew. The heart, having been put in the jar and covered with the spirit, was carefully stowed in the surgeon's bag. The remaining organs were disposed of in the midden pit, the bowls that had held them sluiced out and returned to the dairy.

At last everything had been done.

'Do you intend to pursue the question of who despatched the captain?' asked Matthew as they walked back to the house.

'Perhaps,' Canaletto said. 'Maybe duke not want.'

'Be strange if he doesn't.'

'Indeed,' agreed Canaletto. But you never knew with the rich and powerful. So often they preferred to cover up possible scandal. The duke, though, must surely want to find out who had murdered his friend. Unless the answer was one he would prefer not to contemplate.

Apart from any desire of the duke's, however, for his own satisfaction Canaletto needed to find out who had been responsible. He had been outraged to discover that he, the observer who saw everything, had been sketching a murder scene without picking up a single hint that so dastardly a deed had been committed. He couldn't even identify the figure he'd seen walking away from the pavilion.

The only person still at the table as they entered the breakfast room was Fanny, sitting over a cup of coffee. 'How is the boy this morning?' she asked, welcoming them with a warm smile.

'I shall see him shortly. First some vittles, then the patient,' Matthew said, piling his plate with meat and pickles. Neither he nor Canaletto explained what they had been doing. While he ate, Matthew regaled Fanny with the delights of Bath.

'I think you enjoy yourself very much,' she said.

'My medical researches, yes, the fashionable activities, not at all,' he retorted, reaching for a sweet white roll.

After breakfast, Canaletto told Fanny to meet him in the hall in about half an hour and then went in search of the duke, only to find that the duchess's brother had arrived for a visit and was closeted with

217

the duke. Canaletto was not too displeased at having
to postpone his interview, it promised to be a difficult
one.

What now, though? Canaletto thanked Mr Capper,
the steward, for his information then stood thinking.
After a moment he remembered something Fanny had
mentioned the previous evening during the account
she'd given him of her day.

Canaletto went and found a groom in the stables
and asked for some directions. By the time he made
his way to the hall, Fanny was there waiting for him,
well in advance of the half hour he'd suggested.

'*Bene*, but you need hat, we go visiting,' he said.

'Visiting, signor, who?'

'You will see,' he said.

Chapter Twenty-Two

Fanny dashed upstairs for a pair of net gloves and her straw hat. She tied its cream ribbon under her chin, angling the bow against her cheek, and checked the result in the splendid mirror in her room. The ribbon had drawn down the wide brim so that it framed her face. Satisfied, she set off again, and ran into Matthew Butcher and the Horton cook emerging from a room near to hers.

'Light meals,' the surgeon was saying to Damaris Friend. 'Soup, a little chicken, buttered eggs, nothing too rich.'

'I understand, sir.' Damaris looked drawn and tired. 'I will bring him sops now and a nourishing broth in a little while.' She vanished towards the servants' stairs.

'An excellent-seeming woman,' Matthew told Fanny. 'Between her and that sensible sister, the boy will do.'

'Are you leaving us?'

'I'll be back in a day or so to see how my patient does and take another look at his mother.' He gave her a wide smile. 'This connection needs encouraging. What a ravishing bonnet, where do you go?'

A compliment from Matthew, normally never one to notice a woman's appearance, was to be prized.

'We go visiting but ask me not where, my master keeps all very secret.'

'Ah! Well, say goodbye to him for me.'

At the bottom of the stairs, Fanny parted from him with a quick wave of her hand.

Outside the front door Canaletto paced impatiently up and down the gravel. The moment Fanny arrived, he set off, without so much as a glance at her hat.

It was another fine day and very pleasant to be away from the smoke and noise of London, able to walk without dodging passers-by or risking being run down by horses and carriages. London was plentifully supplied with pleasure gardens but you needed leisure and money to visit them. Here you merely stepped outside the door and you were in the countryside with the sun shining, birds singing and beautiful greenery everywhere.

Then Fanny realized they were walking in the direction of the burned-out pavilion. 'Surely you do not want to see that dreadful place again, signor!'

'There is something I would show you, Fanny. Would you mind entering this place?'

Fanny did indeed not want to go inside but she knew Canaletto must have a good reason for asking her. 'Is this something to do with the captain's death, signor?' she asked, stepping gingerly through the empty doorway, holding up her skirts to protect them from the dirt and charred rubbish that littered the floor.

'Come, over here,' he said, picking his way through the debris.

Fanny followed carefully. She couldn't help

thinking about the captain lying burned to death on the floor. He'd escaped gunfire, cannons and the sword, only to end in this funny little building.

'What am I to look at, signor?'

Canaletto stood in front of a pile of ashes at the base of one of the walls.

'Here I find this.' He fished something out of his pocket and handed it to her.

Fanny turned the fragment over several times. 'It looks as though it was a piece of leather once,' she said. 'Red, perhaps? If you rub it on this other side,' she said, 'the charring comes off,' she ignored how dirty it made her fingers. 'See, signor, it's the underside of leather and it has been dyed red. What does it mean?'

'Look, Fanny, at how thick the ashes are in this place. And different from ashes elsewhere here, no?'

'Well, signor, I see lots of ashes all over the place. And there are pieces of blackened wood here but also elsewhere.' she looked around her distastefully. The smell of burning was still in the air. 'But more here,' she added.

'Exactly, Fanny, more here. Look at wall. You recognize?'

She looked up. 'Why, those are shelves, signor, with books, or the remains of them.' The lower shelves had been more severely burned than the higher. On the top two were the charred remains of several leather volumes but the bottom shelves appeared to have been empty. Fanny suddenly saw what he meant. 'Do you think someone removed the books from the lower shelves and used them to start the fire? She looked at the little piece of leather in her hand. 'But this couldn't have come from a book, signor, the leather is too thick.'

'*Bene*, Fanny. No, red leather not from book. The duke say he send a rocking horse down from London for his son. I think that is from saddle of horse. Horse, chairs, books, all put here to start fire. That is why so much more ash here. Killer, he think to hide how captain die.'

'He didn't burn to death, then?'

'Why should healthy man die in fire here?'

'He limped, signor. Perhaps he fell over, broke his leg again and couldn't get up.'

'Bravo, Fanny, good idea!' he clapped his hands together delightedly. 'You think well. But wrong! The captain stabbed to death.'

Fanny stared at him. 'How do you know?'

'Come outside, not nice in here.'

Very willingly she followed him out of what she now thought of as a charnel house, a house of death.

'We continue to walk and I tell you everything.'

They skirted the edge of the long lake with its ornamental bridge and continued over the park. As they walked, Canaletto told Fanny how Matthew had performed an autopsy on the captain that morning.

'So Matthew prove that captain already dead when fire start.'

'Good heavens,' said Fanny, almost tripping over a hummock in the grass. She thought back to the acerbic man she'd met only a couple of times. 'Captain Farnham, signor, seemed to me the sort of man who might have enemies. But to kill him, who could have wanted that?'

'Who, indeed, Fanny?'

'Do you suspect someone in particular, signor?'

Canaletto hesitated and she was suddenly sure that

he did suspect someone but was not going to tell her. 'You don't think it could be that nice young man, signor?'

'You mean Father Sylvester?' he said, putting sardonic emphasis on the 'Father'.

Fanny stared at him. 'No, I meant Isaiah Cumberledge. He is a scientist and I thought that maybe using fire to cover up a crime would be the sort of thing a scientist would do. But you think it's Father Sylvester, don't you?' she demanded. 'Why, signor?'

He shrugged, 'It could be anyone, it could be that young Cumberledge as you suggest.'

'But you don't think so,' Fanny persisted. 'You suspect Father Sylvester. Why?'

Canaletto walked in silence for a moment then he said, 'Do you not think Father Sylvester's behaviour strange for a priest?'

'Well,' said Fanny after a moment's thought. 'He hasn't been wearing his priest's dress. And, now that you mention it, I remember thinking it was a little odd that he didn't constantly quote from the bible. All the vicars I've met throw bits of the gospels at you all the time. But it's only a small thing.'

Again a pause. Then Canaletto said, 'You remember at breakfast that first day at Badminton the captain against Jacobite Prince Charles Edward?'

'Why, yes, signor, he was almost, you might say, vituperative about him.'

'Vituperative?' Canaletto articulated each syllable precisely.

'It means very abusive.'

Canaletto looked pleased as he stepped around a large pothole in the road. 'Exactly what I meant. And captain come up when we in park with *camera obscura*. And Father Sylvester, that is Charles Sylvester, is there and suddenly is not there.'

Fanny stopped dead. 'Signor, you don't think that Father Sylvester is . . . But that's impossible!'

'Why impossible?'

'Well,' said Fanny. Then, 'You really believe that he is?'

'Perhaps. I do not know. But it makes sense, yes?'

'You mean that Father, that is, Mr Sylvester, recognized the captain and didn't want to be recognized by him?' Canaletto nodded. 'And so he killed him?' The idea was so outrageous Fanny couldn't say anything more for a moment. 'No,' she said. 'It may very well be that Mr Sylvester is who you say but I do not believe he would kill the captain.'

'Because he is such a charming young man? Because you have lost your heart to him?'

'No, signor! I have not "lost my heart to him" as you put it. It's just that he doesn't seem the sort of man who could murder anyone.'

'He may ask another to do so.'

'Who?'

'I hear Mr Sylvester have manservant who supposed to be lost. Maybe he not lost.'

'Someone no one has seen? Or heard about? Signor, I cannot believe this.' They left Badminton Park, Canaletto turning right on to a rough road. 'Where are we going now?' Fanny asked.

'We seek more information.'

'Have you spoken with the duke on the captain's death?'

Canaletto gave an exasperated sigh. 'I have tried to

talk with my lord duke but he is busy. So you and I investigate together, eh, Fanny?'

Fanny didn't know what to think. On the one hand for Canaletto to choose her as an assistant was very flattering. On the other, the path his suspicions were leading him down was one she instinctively felt would not take him anywhere. 'What do you want me to do when we get to this mysterious place you are taking me?'

'You only have to be Fanny,' Canaletto said, his short legs striding out well. 'I think the person we talk to respond better if you there.'

Fanny knew nobody could be more obstinate than Canaletto. But he needn't think he was going to get her co-operation automatically. Particularly if it meant incriminating Father Sylvester, who Fanny was sure couldn't be guilty of anything other than being a bit of a rogue.

After walking some time in silence, they reached the drive of an estate. 'Ah,' said Canaletto. 'This, I think, is our destination.'

A gatekeeper came out of a small lodge, a little child playing around her skirts. 'Can I help you, sir?' she asked, her ample figure dipping a small, bobbing curtsey.

'Is her ladyship at home?'

'You will have to apply at the house for that, sir, but her carriage has not come through this morning.'

'Excellent, we will approach,' said Canaletto.

'Lovely day, isn't it?' said Fanny cheerfully as the woman opened a small side gate for them. 'And what a dear little boy, how old is he?'

'Two and a half, miss, and a right handful,' the woman smiled at her.

As they started up the drive, Canaletto said, 'You have way with people, Fanny. They like to speak with you.'

'Why, I only say what I think,' she said.

'Then stay thinking and saying.' Almost in spite of herself, Fanny warmed a little towards him.

The drive wound round in wide sweeps. Just as it seemed they would never reach its end, a bend unfolded to reveal a grey stone house with mullioned windows and a creeper growing up the front. Beside Badminton it would seem miniature, a house for a doll, but it had grace, was a comfortable size and looked prosperous.

A stylish open carriage stood by the front door. As Fanny and Canaletto approached, Lady Tanqueray emerged, her face looking even whiter above a black ruffled silk manteau.

She beckoned her unexpected visitors towards her. 'I cannot think of any two people I would rather see at this minute,' she said and snapped her fingers at the groom holding open the door of the carriage. 'Take it away, Luke, but be prepared to bring it back a little later.' The groom folded up the steps and closed the door. 'Come inside, I must hear everything about the death of Captain Farnham, which I have to say I do not understand at all.'

She swept back into the house, her black skirts rustling around her. She unbuttoned her manteau and dropped the garment on to a footman's arm. Still wearing her wide black hat, several plumes swooping down to caress her lined cheek, she said, 'Madeira and ratafia biscuits, William.'

The drawing room was not large but displayed some fine and well-polished examples of the cabinet-maker's art. Fanny looked appreciatively around her as she sat on a well-upholstered chair.

Lady Tanqueray arranged herself in a wing chair next to a gently smouldering fire. Beside her was a round table carrying an eccentric mix of necessities: a piece of crewel embroidery, a small pile of books, a writing box, a jar of preserved fruits, a deck of cards. In the middle of the clutter, something moved and Fanny gave a small scream. A little mouse stood on back legs, balanced on its long tail, tiny pink nails waving in the air.

'That's Horace, he won't do you any harm,' Lady Tanqueray said. The mouse surveyed Fanny unblinkingly for a full minute, then came down on to all fours and scurried away. 'He keeps me company sometimes,' she added.

A mouse to keep this fine lady company? Were there so few social possibilities in the country, Fanny wondered. In London people were always visiting each other, taking tea or a glass of something; in the winter they played cards or made music, in the summer perhaps visited a pleasure garden. Maybe living in the country wasn't such a delight after all.

'We came to tell you that Captain Farnham is dead,' said Canaletto in his best English. 'But you know already.'

'Dear Nell sent me a note early this morning by Thomas Wright, their steward. What a personable fellow he is! She must be distressed herself, Humphrey

227

frequently visited Hinde Court. I was just about to call at Badminton to elicit all the details. Maybe you can save me the journey. Perhaps, also, you can set my mind at rest on the condition of Jack Horton. Nell says he has recovered consciousness, for which heaven be thanked. I was distressed to hear he had been seen by that oaf who has taken over from our invaluable Doctor Carter, his death is such a loss.'

'Yes, my lady,' said Canaletto. 'I was able to suggest excellent surgeon presently staying in Bath. He attended last night and boy recovered consciousness.'

'Doctor Butcher saw him this morning as well and says he will do well,' Fanny added.

'God be praised!' Lady Tanqueray gave them both a brilliant smile.

In came William, the footman, bearing a tray with glasses, a decanter and a plate of almond biscuits. Fanny found she was hungry and gladly accepted a biscuit with her glass of Madeira.

As she accepted the richly golden liquid, Fanny could sense the rigid patience with which Lady Tanqueray waited for the wine to be served. At last the servant left and Canaletto gave her the full story of how Captain Farnham's body had been discovered. While he talked, the bright blue eyes never moved from his face. Fanny realized, though, that Canaletto had failed to tell their hostess that the captain had been murdered.

'So, he really is dead, then?'

'You had doubts?' he asked.

Very briefly the blue eyes closed and opened again. 'A body burned to death, unrecognizable except for his ring? There were grounds there for hope but, really, I had none. When Captain Farnham failed to arrive two evenings ago, I knew something was wrong. But what was he doing in that little pavilion and how did it catch fire?'

Canaletto said, 'These are indeed questions I ask.'

'You mean it was not an accident?'

Canaletto shrugged. 'I have to talk to duke.'

A long, cool look. 'It does not ring right to me, Humphrey escaping war and getting cornered in a ridiculous fire that no one can give a satisfactory explanation for.'

'Duke suggested the building struck by lightning, took time for fire to break into blaze,' said Canaletto without expression.

'Lightning, huh!'

'You maybe talk to captain about his life on continent?'

The blue eyes narrowed. 'You are not suggesting some incident there pursued him here?'

Fanny thought how quick Lady Tanqueray's understanding was. She would be a dangerous enemy and Fanny was glad she had decided not to paint Nell Horton.

'As an intimate, you would know,' Canaletto continued as though there had been no interruption. 'The captain's feeling on restoration of Stuart monarchy?'

'Jacobitism?' Lady Tanqueray gave a bitter little laugh. 'It was the only matter on which we seriously disagreed.'

'You wish James Stuart on the throne?' Fanny asked. She could not imagine throwing out a monarch in favour of someone else.

'Ah, Humphrey would have liked to hear you say that.' Lady Tanqueray put down her glass of Madeira and leaned forward. 'I will tell you what I told him. James II was a true king deprived of his throne, why should not this German princeling be sent back to Hanover and the son of the deposed king be restored to his rightful place as ruler of our country? The country would welcome it. The Hanovers constantly quarrel amongst themselves, the king and the Prince of Wales keep separate courts, some even say that the Duke of Cumberland would seize the succession in front of his brother. I have heard there are a number of Whigs who would join with Tories and Jacobites to work for the restoration of the Stuarts.'

'And captain would say?' asked Canaletto.

'Humphrey said that James lost his throne because he would make England a Roman Catholic country again, under the domination of the Pope,' another bitter little twist of the mouth. 'He said he would be damned before he knelt before a foreign power.' Suddenly she looked sad. 'He could not understand that for the true faith there can be only one head of the church and that ecclesiastical power should not be equated with political power.'

'You are a Roman Catholic?' asked Fanny. 'But you said Miss Horton was your god-daughter.'

'Ah, yes. It was not strictly accurate.' Lady Tanqueray waved a negligent hand. 'I should perhaps have said my daughter in God. Nell is the child I never had, we have a special bond. And her father did ask me to be her sponsor when she was born but, alas, I had to explain that, given my religion, it was impossible. Following the Roman Catholic faith is unfashionable and constricting, my husband was unable to hold any

office, but our families have always kept to the true
path.'

There was something odd about this proud
woman's declaration of her faith. Up until now, she
had seemed completely worldly, a woman of principle
but one dedicated to her own self-interest.

Lady Tanqueray eyed Fanny. 'Do you think I
cannot look beyond my paint and my clothes?' she
demanded. 'I tell you, the pleasures of Mammon are
as nothing beside the glory that is God.' A mischievous
glint came into her eyes, 'One has to say, though, that
the pleasures of Mammon are highly enjoyable.'

What rare discussions the captain and their hostess
must have had together, thought Fanny.

'My lady,' said Canaletto, 'it is privilege to know
you. I, too, belong to true faith. When I arrive in
England, it was difficult to find Mass.'

The bright eyes were watchful but the head with
its huge hat gave a slight nod of acknowledgement.
'Catholic priests are not many in England.'

Fanny saw this as her cue for finding out more
about the man who called himself Charles Sylvester.
'We met a priest on the road coming to Badminton,'
she said, 'and now he is staying there. Isn't that a
coincidence? Have you met Father Sylvester?'

'I have,' said Lady Tanqueray with a careless air.
'He is young but charming.'

This told Fanny nothing. On the other hand,
wouldn't such a keen observer as Lady Tanqueray have
noticed that Charles Sylvester was not like any priest
she'd known? In which case, why not mention it?
Had he charmed her? Had he charmed Fanny herself?
She had to admit that twinkle in his eye was very

231

disarming. And he had a way of making you feel he would rather be with you than any other female in the world that was very seductive.

Canaletto picked up her lead. 'I wonder if he will hold Mass at Badminton,' he said.

'The duke is Protestant,' said Lady Tanqueray sharply.

'Then maybe at some chapel hereabouts? You have one here, perhaps?'

'I have but I do not expect Father Sylvester to be holding a Mass for me.' The comment was sharp and final and the bright eyes looked suspiciously at Canaletto.

'I commiserate with you, Lady Tanqueray, in the loss of your friend,' said Fanny. 'I only met Captain Farnham a couple of times, but I found him a most interesting man. I should like to have known him better.'

Lady Tanqueray gave a sad smile. 'You are right, Miss Rooker, he was indeed an interesting man. One who could see down to the heart of people. When he was with me, I did not feel a raddled old woman but rather the society beauty I once was. To think I now have to rely once again on Horace for company! When I had reason to think, well, no matter what I had reason to think. Still, how I look matters not to a mouse and he never contradicts what I say.'

'Any man of discernment would value the company of my lady,' Canaletto said.

She threw him another suspicious glance. 'I would like to know why you are so interested in Humphrey Farnham and his death, Signor Canale. What is your interest?'

Canaletto spread out his hands deprecatingly. 'I involved in fire in pavilion, I examine corpse and I have investigated other cases of unexpected death.'

'Really? That is very strange for a painter, especially a painter from abroad.'

'I am observer, my lady, and I not involved in English life. I see with clear eye.'

'I hope indeed that is true. Well, Signor Canale and Miss Rooker, I am grateful to you for coming today. I am not sure you have got what you came for but I can offer nothing more, other than another glass of Madeira, perhaps?'

Fanny knew that they were now expected to leave. She rose. 'Lady Tanqueray, you have been most kind. I hope we meet again on a more auspicious occasion. I must tell you,' she added deliberately, 'that I have enjoyed also talking with your nephew, Isaiah Cumberledge. He is a most interesting man as well and full of principle. He and the captain seemed good friends, perhaps you can enjoy talking with him now?'

The eyes flashed and the painted mouth pursed itself. 'Isaiah and I have quarrelled irretrievably.'

'Irretrievably?' repeated Canaletto, placing his empty wine glass delicately beside the decanter on its tray.

She merely fixed him with one of her autocratic looks, yet Fanny felt Lady Tanqueray found it difficult to control her emotions. Then it was her turn to withstand the basilisk stare. 'I trust, Miss Rooker, that you have now abandoned your intention of painting a portrait of Miss Horton, my daughter in God.'

Canaletto and Fanny spoke together.

'As to that, your ladyship,' started Canaletto.

'Yes, your ladyship, I have decided I shall not accept the commission,' said Fanny and sensed rather than saw the glare that Canaletto sent her.

There came a knocking at the front door.

'Dear me,' said Lady Tanqueray, 'I am fortunate to receive so many guests today. I think this must be dear Nell, able to leave her patient long enough to set my mind at rest.'

But William announced, 'Mr Cumberledge, my lady.'

Isaiah came into the room, hat in hand, wig neatly on head, boots dusty from walking. 'Dear aunt,' he said. 'I had to come. I know what Humphrey meant to you.' Then he saw Fanny and Canaletto and stopped.

Lady Tanqueray sat very straight in her chair. 'Isaiah, Humphrey's death has changed nothing between us. I cannot approve of your life. Unless you change your ways, I will have nothing more to do with you.'

Isaiah flushed deeply and tightened his grip on his hat. 'Aunt, I cannot abandon what I see as my duty to my calling in life, nor prostitute myself to suit your notions of what is best for me. However, I hope that some day we may be reconciled, I shall continue to have your best interests at heart.'

'Your duty, boy, is to your family and the principles with which you were brought up. Can you not see that?' she demanded.

Isaiah glared at her.

'In that case, go!' Lady Tanqueray said. 'My best interests are served by your instant removal from my house.'

Chapter Twenty-Three

'Why did you say that to Lady Tanqueray?' demanded Canaletto as he and Fanny walked rapidly down the drive. Behind them, they left Isaiah arguing with his aunt.

'Because I have decided I cannot accept the commission,' Fanny said.

'Decisions must be discussed with me, your master.' Canaletto could not believe that his apprentice was throwing up this chance to start her career. He was as angry as when he'd found Fanny was taking lessons in portraiture.

'But, signor, this is something I have to make up my own mind about.'

'You are my apprentice, your duty is to obey me.'

At the gate, Canaletto turned towards Badminton. For several minutes the two of them walked in silence.

At length Fanny said, 'Signor, I do realize what I owe to you and that I must do as you say.'

Canaletto felt forgiving.

'But in this instance,' Fanny continued, 'I cannot insist on accepting the commission to paint Miss Horton's portrait. How can I when she won't sit for me?' she added.

Canaletto's moment of warmth vanished as though

it had never been. 'It is not decision for Miss Horton,' he said. 'Her father wish portrait, her brother place commission. Her brother must deal with her. If he decides commission cancelled, fine.' Not fine at all, thought Canaletto, for then he and Fanny would have no further excuse to remain in the area. Unless, that is, the duke wanted him to investigate the captain's death. But how loyal would the duke be to the memory of his friend if it looked likely that that loyalty could expose what he would prefer to be kept secret?

It was everything Lady Tanqueray had not said rather than what she had that had convinced Canaletto that Charles Sylvester was no more a Catholic priest than he was. And there could surely be only one reason for donning such a disguise.

If the fellow was the prince and he was caught at Badminton, he would undoubtedly be arrested on a charge of treason and then would be executed. Despite all his reservations regarding Charles Sylvester, Canaletto could not help admitting to himself that the fellow was very attractive. It would be a tragedy to see him lose his head. And he was under the auspices of the Duke of Beaufort, who was Canaletto's patron and deserved his loyalty. A loyalty that surely had to come before his duty to Paymaster General Pitt. But what if the duke was planning to back the prince in revolution?

Somehow Canaletto had to find out if this was the case.

How long, though, before Joshua Bland came to hear of the personable young man staying at Badminton and became suspicious? What would happen then?

And what would Pitt say if Canaletto took the sensible course, had his sketches approved and left for London with Fanny? Canaletto shrank from imagining the revenge he would take for having his wishes flouted.

And who had murdered Captain Farnham?

For all sorts of reasons, Canaletto had to remain at Badminton. Which meant that Fanny must undertake the portrait of Miss Horton. He couldn't understand why she should jeopardize her career in this way.

Fanny marched alongside him, her mouth mutinous, her eyes fixed straight ahead, her shoulders rigid. He could tell that she was determined to stick to what she saw as her principles.

After a little she said, 'I should tell you, signor, that there is someone else who could have wanted the captain dead. At breakfast, the first day we were at Badminton, before you came down, Isaiah Cumberledge practically accused the captain of wanting to marry his aunt. Lady Tanqueray is obviously well off and has no children. Maybe Isaiah Cumberledge expects to inherit her money if she doesn't remarry.'

'Lady Tanqueray very much older than captain,' Canaletto said. He was not impressed with Fanny's suggestion.

'If he didn't mind that, I don't suppose she did,' Fanny said.

'Fanny, this nothing to do with portrait,' Canaletto said. For the rest of the journey back to Badminton, he treated her to a sermon on the duties of an artist to his patrons. Fanny said nothing.

As they approached the house, Fanny asked, 'Have you any need for my services at present, signor?' in a very stiff way. Canaletto wanted to shake her, make her realize how stupid she was being. But he said, curtly, that he did not need anything from her for the rest of the day.

So off she went, her skirts swinging from her small waist, her shoulders stiff with tension.

Oh, what an obstinate little goose she was!

Canaletto shook his head in disgust, then dismissed her from his mind. He had to decide what his next step was. He took a little time to go over what he had learned from Lady Tanqueray, pacing back and forth across the green of the park. He dismissed quickly Fanny's suggestion regarding a motive for Isaiah Cumberledge to despatch the captain. Maybe if an engagement had been announced but without that, murder seemed an unnecessarily drastic measure. Finally Canaletto decided that he could proceed no further until he had spoken to the duke and went and collected his preparatory sketches of Badminton.

Tracking down the patron proved difficult. Briggs thought both his lordship and her ladyship were discussing plans for new landscaping with the head gardener.

All Canaletto could find was an undergardener who said the head gardener was indeed discussing new plantings with the duchess but he thought his lordship might have gone riding.

In the stables, a groom said the duke hadn't taken a horse out that morning, but that the duke's agent had arrived and no doubt his lordship was meeting with him.

Back inside Badminton, Canaletto found Mr Capper, the steward, who told him that, yes, the duke had been talking with his agent in the library but he believed that his lordship was now free.

Canaletto made his way to the library through a small, inner hall. Ahead of him he saw the cadaverous agent, Bertie Burgh, who had joined them at dinner the previous day. He was carrying a sheaf of papers and disappeared into the library. He failed to shut the door completely behind him and so his voice came through clearly. 'I have those other accounts now, your lordship, and I think you will see exactly what I meant earlier.'

'I hope not, Burgh, I can't believe the situation is as bad as you suggest.'

'If you will just look here, your lordship, and here.'

There was silence from the library and Canaletto imagined the two men poring over the accounts.

He retraced his steps thoughtfully, returned to the garden and found the duchess and a stranger talking with the head gardener.

'Ah, Signor Canale,' she said. 'The very man. Norborne, this is the famous Italian painter who will capture Badminton for the duke. Signor, may I introduce Mr Norborne Berkeley, my brother?'

Canaletto bowed to a pleasant-seeming man who did indeed bear a resemblance to the duchess. 'Come and see what I propose for the new flowerbeds,' the duchess continued. 'I would value your opinion as to the effect I want to create.'

She sounded more welcoming than she had at any of their previous meetings. 'I very sorry but my knowledge of garden plants is small,' Canaletto said as they passed through a parterred area. 'In Venice we have few gardens.'

'Let me show you what I intend,' said the duchess. The gardener muttered something about checking the progress of the grapes in the glasshouse and left them.

Canaletto found himself listening to lists of plants and watching wide sweeps of her ladyship's hand as she explained her ideas for this part of the garden. As she spoke, she constantly referred to her brother, who showed as deep a knowledge of plants and gardens as she did. There was obvious affection between them. Perhaps it was being with her brother or talking on what had to be one of her favourite subjects but the duchess's manner continued to mellow, her eyes glowed and Canaletto found himself conversing with an attractive woman. He played upon this unexpected rapport by asking questions as to the colour, height and nature of the plants that were new to him. 'Good colour, interesting pattern,' he said approvingly. 'And ingenious use of seasonal variations.' In fact he was none too certain exactly what the beds would look like but hoped that the phrases summed up what he had caught of her intentions.

It seemed he said the right things.

'I have sketches for views to propose to my lord duke,' he said when they had exhausted the planting ideas.

'Indeed?' she said courteously but with less warmth. 'My husband will be interested to see them. He is anxious for you to capture Badminton in all its glory.'

'What a wonderful change has been wrought,' said Mr Berkeley. 'By your poor brother-in-law and then by you and Charles.' They had walked round to the north front and he turned to admire the building. 'Those cupolas were a brilliant stroke. What vast sums you must have spent! How glorious to be a Beaufort.'

'So many people seem to think so,' said the duchess. It seemed to Canaletto that she found it a burden.

There was a sudden whooping and round the corner came a small boy on a pony, led by one of the grooms. 'Mama, Mama,' he cried. 'Look at me!'

'Henry,' she said severely. 'Remember your dignity!'

The boy coloured and fiddled with his reins.

'The Marquess is a natural rider,' Mr Berkeley said in a kindly way. 'Look at his seat.'

The duchess softened again.

Canaletto saw an opening. 'Stables most splendid, guests enjoy your horses. Miss Patience Horton and Father Sylvester look very happy on their ride.' He waited expectantly.

'Patience Horton and Father Sylvester?' repeated the duchess. 'They are riding together?'

Canaletto nodded, beaming brightly.

Mr Berkeley looked at his sister 'Is that wise?' he asked.

The duchess glanced at Canaletto. 'We wish all our guests to enjoy themselves,' she said.

'Charming fellow, Father Sylvester,' murmured Canaletto. 'Last night, he entertain Miss Horton most exceedingly.'

'Exceedingly?' questioned the duchess.

'Mama, you must watch me ride!'

She smiled. 'Of course, Henry. I am proud of you.'

The groom led the horse off and they all watched young Henry's progress across the gravel to the park.

'Shall we hunt today?' asked Mr Berkeley.

She shook her head. 'Charles has too much business with his agent. Always when we arrive at Badminton there is business.' She sighed deeply, 'Ownership of Badminton carries so many responsibilities, so much expense,' she added in a low voice that perhaps Canaletto was not intended to hear but his ears were as sharp as his eyes. 'Signor Canale, I am sure the duke will be anxious to see your proposals as soon as maybe. Perhaps if you were to apply to Mr Capper, he would obtain an appointment for you with his grace.'

Canaletto was not disappointed at his dismissal, he had gathered much valuable information.

Back in the house he found Mr Capper in his room talking to Mr Burgh. On the table before the steward were spread what looked like accounts. The moment he saw Canaletto at the door, the steward rose. 'I believe his lordship is in the library. If you will come with me, Mr Canale, I will see you settled in the hall while I ascertain his lordship's availability.'

Canaletto allowed himself to be led through to the hall, where he stood examining the huge paintings that were displayed there. Large expanses of horseflesh were not to Canaletto's taste but he could admire the technique that was on show.

'James Wootton is the artist,' said the duke, quietly appearing at Canaletto's side. 'He was originally a page to my aunt, she encouraged his talents and sent him to Rome. Magnificent animal,' he added, with a nod to the horse in the painting Canaletto was studying.

'You are fond of hunting, I believe, my lord?'

'Indeed I am! Marvellous sport we have here. I hope we may achieve a buck or two tomorrow. Now, signor, I believe you have sketches to show me? Perhaps you would care to come to the library so that we can study them in comfort?'

This was true politesse, Canaletto thought, the duke coming to find me himself instead of sending Mr Capper. 'I have had most pleasant talk with duchess and her brother on gardening,' he offered as they walked to the library.

'My wife is an expert on planting,' the duke said proudly. 'As is my brother-in-law. He lives not far from here, the Berkeley family is well known, Signor Canale. Mr Berkeley is considering instituting proceedings to establish his right to the barony of Botetourt.'

Canaletto thought of the dignified woman he'd talked with this morning. She would undoubtedly prefer her brother to be a lord rather than a mere mister. Then he realized there was a yet more interesting aspect of this information. 'Very good to regain titles,' he said approvingly. 'No existing Lord Botetourt, I suppose?'

'No, indeed,' said the duke, opening the door into the library.

'So not like Jacobite king, who must remove Hanover king to reclaim his title?' Canaletto said. 'Perhaps I should not mention this?' he added humbly. 'But as foreigner I find most interesting so many people believe in Stuart inheritance.'

'One cannot equate the divine right of kings to rule with the legal entitlement to a peerage,' the duke said. 'Nor is the Stuart cause one that can be discussed in these times, even with a foreigner.' He turned and gave Canaletto a charming smile. 'We will talk, instead, of your designs for capturing the glories of Badminton, hmm?' He cleared away papers from the surface of his desk.

Canaletto took two sketches out of his portfolio. 'Perhaps one painting of north front, your so grand façade,' he said, putting the first sketch in front of the duke. 'And for second, a view from house across park.' He put down the second then stood back and watched the duke study the two pieces of paper.

'Hmm. This I like, I like very much,' the duke said, raising the one of the house. 'It will show the embellishments perfectly. But this,' he tapped the other view with a forefinger. 'Bit plain, perhaps, hmm?'

'Difficult to show effect without paint, without colour, my lord,' Canaletto said cheerfully. He had anticipated this problem. 'Here we show world of Badminton, the great park, the fine view, trees that lead from all parts to here, centre of this universe.'

'Universe,' repeated the duke thoughtfully. Then his expression darkened. 'You have included my Chinese pavilion in your view.'

Canaletto nodded.

'That's a sad, sad business.' The duke sat back in his chair and looked through the window. Then he swung round to Canaletto. 'Has your surgeon friend viewed my poor friend's body?'

Canaletto nodded again.

'What did he discover? Did he find something more about how he died?'

'Yes, milord.'

The duke's eyes narrowed. 'And?'

'I try to see milord sooner because I think you want to know this but I know how busy milord is.'

'Quite, quite. Get on with it, man.'

'Doctor Butcher, he say captain stabbed in chest. Maybe also hit on head with something not sharp.'

'Blunt,' the duke said automatically. 'Hit with something blunt.'

'Thank you, milord. Blunt.'

'How can Dr Butcher be so sure of this, eh? The body was burned, badly burned, I saw it myself.'

'Doctor examine very carefully, with medical eye,' explained Canaletto, not sure how much the duke would want to know about the autopsy.

The duke continued to view him sceptically. 'I still cannot be convinced that Doctor Butcher can be so certain. And we have to be sure here,' he added with emphasis. 'You understand why?'

'If captain stabbed, it means he was killed unlawfully,' he said carefully.

'Quite and the constable will have to be informed and he will want to be convinced.'

Which meant that the duke also needed to be certain before he would lay such information before the constable.

'Under burned clothes, the skin was not so damaged,' Canaletto said.

'Did Butcher inspect the ribs, the heart?' The duke was sharper than Canaletto had realized.

'Yes, milord.'

'And this was how he established my friend had been stabbed?'

'Yes, milord.'

'Could he tell what sort of weapon had been used?'

'He think a broadsword or a knife for butcher.'

'Hmm. Humphrey's army sword is still in his room.'

Interesting! It seemed likely some other weapon was used.

'I trust he left the body in a decent state?'

'Indeed, milord.'

'And the question now has to be, who could have done such a thing?'

'Milord,' Canaletto started but the duke held up a finger to stop him.

'Signor Canale, will you come with me up on to the roof?' the duke asked, rising.

For just a moment, Canaletto hesitated. Once someone had tried to throw him off the roof of a house sufficiently similar to this to give him pause. Then he said, 'Of course, milord.'

They climbed the stairs, a couple of small dogs yapping at the duke's feet, up past the main floor of the house and then out on to the lead roofing. Here was a world of chimneys, parapets, cupolas, pediments and wide open sky.

The duke walked into the area beneath one of the ornamental cupolas. Canaletto followed and immediately saw something of interest. He tapped at one of the corner supports.

'Stone would have been too heavy,' said the duke. 'Wood gives the effect without the weight.'

'Very clever, milord.' Together the two men studied the scene laid out before them.

'Lord of all I survey,' said the duke sardonically. 'Now I am responsible for all this,' he waved his hand, 'and so much more beside.'

'It is a great estate,' agreed Canaletto, wondering where all this was leading.

The duke leaned against one of the cupola pillars

and faced Canaletto. 'I think I told you earlier that I met Humphrey Farnham at Oxford when we were both younger sons and that he became a soldier while I entered Parliament. Humphrey's family fortunes declined and he could not gain the advancement his talents warranted. I, too, suffered but through my political persuasions. As a foreigner you may not know that in England if you are to succeed financially, you have to obtain sinecures carrying valuable income. For that, at this time, you need to follow the Whig persuasion. The Whigs do not care for the country, all they are concerned with are their own commercial ambitions and to ensure Roman Catholicism shall never be an acceptable religion in this country. Well, you are not interested in all that.' He caressed the little dog that pawed at his stockings for attention.

'To return to Humphrey. Just after he was wounded, we learned that a peace was about to be agreed in this war that has cost us dear over the last few years. I am happy for the country but I knew that Humphrey would be anxious how it would affect his career. I suggested that he came and stayed at Badminton.'

He looked again out at the panorama before him. Some deer had advanced out of the lines of trees and were grazing on the grass. 'I was looking forward to discussing various possibilities with him. We were to enjoy renewing our friendship after a long period apart. Instead,' he spread out his hands. 'Instead I find that he has been killed by person or persons unknown. I cannot allow whoever did this, this murderous deed, to go unpunished. Yet the constable, to whom I am bound to report this circumstance, is a nincompoop, a minor official who will fluster and flounder, deny the possibility of a malefactor, then, when it is proved to him – and I am sure the good doctor can prove it – he will arrest some poor idiot who has no idea how to protest his innocence and the real culprit will escape.' The duke sighed deeply.

Canaletto could not bring himself to mention the possibility that the man known as Charles Sylvester could be involved. Not until he knew a great deal more about Captain Farnham and his stay at Badminton.

'Milord, perhaps you will permit me to talk to people?'

A ghost of a smile appeared. 'Dear sir, I can hardly stop you talking to people!'

'But if I had your permission to ask questions?'

The duke drummed his fingers on the parapet. 'You mean, you would see if you can find who was responsible?' He looked extremely sceptical. 'You think you could do this?'

'I have done so before.'

'You have?'

So Canaletto told him of the case he'd been involved with the previous year, when he'd found the murderer of two girls.

The duke folded his arms across his chest and listened with deep interest. 'Well, signor, I have to say that you surprise me!' He thought for a moment. 'I cannot see that you can do much harm by asking a few questions and if your enquiries uncover the malefactor, then we shall all be delighted. I will tell my steward you are to be given every facility.'

'No, milord!' Canaletto was alarmed. 'I go where I want, talk to people I want but no one know Canaletto investigate death of captain. Otherwise, someone else may be found dead, maybe me!'

'My dear sir! We cannot have that. If this is as dangerous an enterprise as you suggest, then you must not be involved.'

For a moment Canaletto was tempted. But if his suspicions had any substance, he doubted the duke's ability to find an official who could conduct the investigation with any hope of success and he badly wanted to identify the scoundrel who had committed murder under the observant eye of Antonio Canale. 'Milord, I can question without suspicion, I think. Give me a few days.'

The duke looked at him thoughtfully. 'We had been told you would only require a couple of days to produce sketches but no reason why you should not continue here for a few more days.'

'There is another reason for me to stay longer, milord,' Canaletto said, not at all sure what the duke's reaction would be. 'My apprentice, Miss Fanny Rooker, was commissioned by your friend, Sir Robert Horton, to paint his daughter, Miss Horton.'

'Miss Horton? You mean Miss Patience Horton?'

'No, milord, elder daughter.'

'Nell?'

'Before he leave for West Indies, he ask son to arrange this.'

'What an extraordinary thing! What does Miss Horton herself say?'

'Matter has not been discussed with her.' That was no more than the exact truth.

'But you have met her?'

Canaletto nodded.

The duke rubbed his chin. 'That accident was the very devil. She was a very attractive girl. Now she keeps herself at home, only visits such old friends as she feels comfortable with. Sir Robert is much distressed with the situation, he has discussed it with me. He is another old friend. For some time my family was involved with the East India Company, with which he is closely concerned. He has provided me with wise counsel many times and it is a happy circumstance he has found an estate so near to Badminton. The duchess is very fond of the girls. And James, of course,' he added.

'Sir Robert said portrait is to celebrate true beauty of Miss Horton.'

'True beauty, eh? Interesting concept, don't you think, signor?'

'Very.'

'But is an apprentice the right artist to carry out such a difficult, nay, delicate, commission?'

Canaletto stood as tall as his short stature would permit. 'Miss Rooker has considerable talent,' he said. 'I should not have suggested her else. And I shall guide her,' he added.

The duke did not look reassured. 'I shall speak to James Horton,' he said.

Canaletto gave a little bow of his head.

'But to return to the matter of Humphrey Farnham's death, I suggest you speak with Isaiah Cumberledge. The two have been living here together for some time, if anyone can throw light on what might have led to Humphrey's death, it will be him.'

'He seems intelligent young man,' Canaletto said.

'Perhaps too intelligent for his own good. The

duchess tells me he's got fixated on the idea that the village children have to be taught how to write. As if they don't find reading difficult enough. There is no point educating them above their station, it only leads to trouble.'

This was not a conclusion that Canaletto could agree with but there was little point in arguing with his powerful patron. Instead he saw, galloping towards him across the park, a perfect opportunity for sounding out the duke on a matter he had already ascertained the duchess's views on.

'Why, there are Miss Patience Horton and Father Sylvester making a race of it,' he said jovially, leaning ostentatiously over the balustrade.

Along one of the avenues, helter-skelter, came the riders, the girl in the lead, presenting a most stylish picture on her bay mount, Charles Sylvester close behind, urging on his dappled grey, the deer scattering from the open grass as they emerged from the trees. They approached the gravelled semicircle in front of the house and Patience pulled up her mare. 'I won!' she cried joyously, her voice reaching clearly to the two men standing on the roof. Canaletto had no difficulty making out her smiling face or the flirtatious way she turned to the man behind her. 'What fun that was,' she said, panting a little, her little head held high, a feather dancing in her chic riding hat.

The duke bent over the balustrade beside Canaletto, education forgotten, his attention all given to the scene below.

'Your horsemanship is as spellbinding as your beauty,' Father Sylvester told her, his voice carrying equally clearly. He leaned over his horse's neck and stroked it with a slow, sensuous movement as he exchanged a long look with the girl. Then Patience slapped the mare's rump and rode off towards the stables. The man sat and watched her for a moment, admiration plain on his face. Then he spurred his horse to follow.

'What an idiot,' groaned the duke. 'Can he not see the danger?'

Chapter Twenty-Four

Fanny was furious. Furious with Canaletto for insisting that she had to accept the commission to paint Nell Horton and furious with herself for not being able to put her case more effectively.

Of course she owed Canaletto so much for securing the commission in the first place, never mind about the matchless tutoring she was getting as his apprentice. But he should allow her to decide whether she was to accept the task of painting Nell Horton or not.

And there was another thing Fanny was angry about. She couldn't believe that Father Sylvester, whether or not he was a pretender to the throne of England, could be responsible for murdering Captain Farnham, even at second hand.

Canaletto had behaved as though she was love smitten. This was definitely not the case. Charles Sylvester was certainly attractive, certainly great fun, might even be a prince, but he had not touched her heart, she was quite sure of that. Fanny's heart had been broken very effectively the previous year and it would be a long time before she gave it away again. Certainly not to a plausible rogue, however high his station.

And why hadn't Canaletto considered more

seriously her suggestion that Isaiah Cumberledge could have had a motive for killing the captain? Fanny did not really think the young man was capable of murder, any more than she thought Father Sylvester was, but surely the possibility deserved more consideration than Canaletto had given it?

As she left Canaletto and went towards the gravel semicircle, it struck Fanny that it would be a fine thing if she could find out who had killed the captain. She had assisted Canaletto before in his investigations, why not see if she could solve this case for him?

Whom should she talk to? Isaiah Cumberledge was an obvious choice, he knew the captain well and she might be able to gauge from him how serious matters had become between the captain and Lady Tanqueray. But he would be teaching the children this morning. However, last night Patience Horton had said that the captain had visited her sister only a day or so before his death. Maybe Miss Horton knew something that could be pertinent. Anyway, Fanny had to let her know that she would not accept her brother's commission to paint her portrait.

Her first commission and she was refusing it! It was difficult enough for any artist to get established and she didn't move in the sort of circles that produced commissions. The only influential contacts she had were Canaletto and Owen McSwiney and after this she couldn't see that either of them would put themselves out for her. Whereas a successful portrait of Miss Horton, intimate of the Duke and Duchess of Beaufort, would undoubtedly have given her career a flying start.

Successful, though, that was the thing to remember. And how was a portrait of poor, scarred Nell to be successful? A profile that hid her injured side altogether would be an easy way out but hardly true to the sitter. And exactly what had Sir Robert Horton meant by showing her true beauty?

Forgetting for a moment that she had no intention of painting Nell Horton, Fanny puzzled about the problem as she opened the front door. The hall seemed to be full of children. A couple of infants were crawling about the marble tiles, two young girls were fighting over the lead of a large dog and an equally young boy was bouncing a ball on a racket. A baby was in the arms of a nurse who, with another, was trying to keep the nursery party in some sort of order. 'Into the garden, children,' she said while the second servant shooed the little ones towards the front door.

Fanny longed for her sketchbook so she could capture the scene, then had an idea. 'How is the little Horton boy who broke his arm?' she asked the nurse who wasn't holding the baby.

The girl beamed at her. 'He makes a good recovery, thank you, miss. His sister is with him.'

'Would he welcome a visit?'

The girl frowned a little. 'As to that, it isn't my place to say but I do know that Miss Horton is having a right time keeping him in bed and amused. Such a scamp he is!'

Taking off her hat and swinging it by the ribbons, Fanny mounted the stairs full of resolve. First she deposited the hat in her bedroom and found her sketchbook and a lead-tipped stylo. Then she found the bedroom door Matthew and the Horton cook had emerged from that morning and knocked gently.

A voice invited her to enter.

In a large bed, his face flushed and fractious, was a boy of about five years with his arm in a sling.

Sitting beside the bed with a book in her hand was Nell Horton.

'Yes?' she said.

'Doctor Butcher told me young Master Horton was on the road to recovery so I have come to see how he does.'

Nell's face lightened. 'Oh, Doctor Butcher has been such a help. Jack is so very much better since his visit.' She wore a very simple cream-coloured dress with a soft fichu round her neck. In profile, Fanny could hardly see the scarred side of her face and she looked attractive with her simply dressed dark hair, straight nose and firm chin.

Fanny came up to the bed, 'Do you read to Jack?'

Nell nodded. 'Not that he's interested in moral tales, are you?' she said to him with a broad smile.

'You know I want to play in the garden with the others, Nell. It's not fair to keep me in bed, 'specially when it's so sunny outside. All the others have gone into the garden, why can't I?' His voice grew more and more petulant, a lock of dark hair fell into his eyes and he pushed it back with his good hand. His eyelashes were long and dark and his nose was as straight as his sister's, his chin as determined. He looked at Fanny. 'Who are you?'

'Fanny Rooker, at your service. I thought you might like to play at drawing with me.'

Immediately some of the petulance fell away. 'Drawing?'

She brought out her sketchbook and stylo. 'When I

came in, there was such a gaggle of children and babies in the hall, you've never seen such raree show.'

'Raree?' he asked in a lively way.

'Have you never heard a travelling showman calling out to passers-by to come and see his raree show?' Fanny started sketching. 'I think he probably means something out of the ordinary. And that's what was in the hall just now. I wonder if you can tell me which of the children are Hortons because I'm sure there were more than Beauforts there.'

'Show me, show me!'

Nell sat back with an amused expression on the undamaged half of her face.

'You must wait a minute while I try and catch the various children. I have to remember how they were, seeing that they aren't in front of me any longer.'

'Are things usually in front of you when you draw?'

'Usually,' agreed Fanny, sketching at a furious rate. 'There!' She gave him the book and Nell stood up to look over his shoulder.

'I say,' he exclaimed delightedly. 'What a raree!' The page was filled with rough but very telling sketches of the children. 'That's Kate,' he pointed to one of the infants crawling on the floor. 'She can't talk yet, she's very boring. All she does is cry,' he added in a super-cilious way. 'And that's Theo,' he moved his finger to the boy bouncing the ball on the racket. 'Theo's three, he makes all our lives a misery,' he announced tri-umphantly.

'Jack, he doesn't!'

'Yes he does, James said so and he's always trying to spoil whatever I'm doing.'

'Who are the other children?' Fanny asked, very amused.

Jack yawned. 'I don't know, prob'ly they're Beauforts 'cos they have a lot of smallies.'

'Henry isn't there,' said Nell, looking more closely at the sketch. 'It's all the girls. Oh, dear, I hope Theo behaves himself.'

'Draw me,' Jack demanded, making a small wooden horse gallop across the bedclothes with his good hand.

It was exactly what Fanny had hoped for. Her stylo moving rapidly over a new page of the sketchbook she said, 'Have you had your likeness captured before, Master Horton?'

He shook his head vigorously.

'You have to keep still, otherwise I can't catch your expression.'

'What's 'pression?'

'Oh, whether you are smiling or sulky or sad. I would like to catch you smiling. What do you like best in the world?'

'Puff, I like Puff best.'

'And who or what is Puff?'

'Puff's my cat.' The grey eyes suddenly filled with tears and the little red mouth puckered. 'Puff got burned!'

'No, Jack, we don't know that Puff didn't escape. She's probably catching mice in the barn, waiting until we come back,' said Nell.

'Do you think so? Really, really think so?'

'That cat hasn't started on its nine lives yet. I'll bet you she's still alive. After all, we are, aren't we?'

He nodded slowly.

'I saw a little boy on a horse out of my window

while I was getting my sketchbook,' said Fanny. 'Do you think that was Henry? And do you like riding?'

'Yes, I'm a great rider, aren't I, Nell? And when Father gets back he's going to get me a new pony 'cos Theo's going to have mine. Have you caught my 'pression?'

'Nearly, just a few more minutes. You know, I've been asked to catch a likeness of your sister here but she doesn't want it taken so I'm not going to do it.'

Nell gasped. 'Is that why you're here? To persuade me otherwise?' Her dark eyebrows came together and she stared fiercely at Fanny, the scar tissue deepening in colour.

Fanny looked up. 'No, indeed, it is just as I said. I respect your decision. I shall not be persuaded nor try to persuade you.'

'You will not be persuaded?' Nell said sharply. 'Is my brother trying?'

'I have not spoken to your brother on this. It is my master, Signor Canale, who tells me that an artist's duty lies to the person who commissions a portrait, not to the sitter,' said Fanny, a trifle bitterly.

'Have you finished? I want to see,' pressed Jack.

'Almost, just a few more lines and I shall be able to show you,' Fanny said, speaking more and more slowly while her pen moved faster and faster. 'There, what do you think of yourself?' She held out the sketch-book for him.

Jack reached forward eagerly but Nell intercepted the book.

'It's me, I should look!' protested Jack.

'You shall have it in a moment. I have had the task of nursing you for so long I think I deserve first sight.'

She laughed at him. Then her laughter faded as she studied the drawing.

'It has been done very swiftly,' Fanny said as no comment was forthcoming.

'You have caught him excellently. There, Jack, do you agree?' Nell gave him the book.

'Is that me? Do I look like that?'

'Shall I fetch a mirror?' teased his sister.

Fanny took back the book, sketched some more then handed it over again.

Nell leaned over. 'Why, Jack, do you see, she's added your bandaging and your horse and the beautiful bedspread. Before it was a picture of a little boy, now you know it must be you, don't you?' She looked across at Fanny. 'I didn't realize there was more to portraiture than just catching a likeness,' she said slowly. 'So that's why there are all those accessories in a painting of someone, so that they can recognize exactly who and what they are?'

'That is how it is supposed to work,' Fanny agreed in a throwaway manner.

'I like my horse,' Jack said, then tossed the book aside, yawning.

'Shall I draw the curtains so that you can sleep a little?' asked Nell. He snuggled down under the bedclothes. She rose and pulled the heavy material across the window, then arranged one side so that a small amount of light was allowed to filter through. 'There, when you wake, I shall bring you a bowl of soup,' she said quietly and indicated to Fanny that they were to leave the room.

Picking up the sketchbook, Fanny followed her through the door.

Outside, she tore the drawing from the book and offered it to the other girl. 'Perhaps Lady Horton may like to have this?'

Delight lit Nell's face. 'Do you mean this? Oh, she will be so pleased. When it looked as though we might lose Jack, my mother mourned that she would have no likeness of him.'

'Now she will have both. Would you like to walk a little outside? It is such a lovely day and I think you have been shut up here for some time. If you are worried about your brother,' she added as Nell threw a glance back towards the bedroom door, 'we can ask Mrs George if Hannah or some other maid can keep an eye on him.'

'I own I would very much like a walk outside,' said Nell. 'Ever since the fire I have been tied to Jack's bedside and I long for a look at the sun and to be able to breathe fresh air.'

Fanny was delighted with the success of her suggestion. Now she would be able to hear about the captain.

Chapter Twenty-Five

The duke was silent as he led the way back down to the ground level. Canaletto wished that he knew his thoughts.

Was the duke willing to back another insurrection by the Stuarts? If he was, Canaletto had to send word to the Paymaster General immediately. But surely if that was the case, he would have told Charles Sylvester by now and the pretend priest would have moved on.

Instead he was still here and paying the sort of attentions to Miss Patience Horton no prudent pretender would indulge in.

What was it the captain had said that first morning? The prince was full of charm and relied too much upon it. He was too self-confident, too fond of the women, indulged too much in alcohol and was too hot-headed to be a reliable leader of men. The captain had had little respect for his intellect either.

All of that seemed to fit the fellow they'd picked up from the highway and left at Reading only to find him turn up here at Badminton.

Once back on ground level, the duke took a courteous but abstracted farewell of Canaletto. 'We will meet again quite soon, signor, when you will tell me what you have discovered regarding my poor friend's death.'

Canaletto went into the great hall and wondered when Isaiah Cumberledge would be free from his schoolroom duties. The young man would know, Canaletto was sure, just what the captain would have done had he recognized Prince Charles Edward in Father Sylvester.

But did Canaletto really think the prince would take the desperate step of despatching the captain in order to avoid discovery?

Wasn't it much more likely that he would have kept clear of Badminton until the duke arrived and then appealed to him to keep his old friend in order?

Headstrong and hot-headed, yes. Murderous? Canaletto couldn't decide.

However, he made up his mind that he would visit the school and see what was going on there. Perhaps he and Isaiah could walk back together, allowing them to talk without fear of being overheard.

Before he could put this plan into action, James Horton came into the hall. 'My word, this is a fortunate meeting, Signor Canale. I have been wanting to talk to you. But I have to ride over to Hinde Court to meet with my steward and discuss various building matters. Will you come with me?' He smiled engagingly at Canaletto, who realized the young man was not much taller than himself. This gave him a good feeling.

James Horton's suggestion was timely. It meant Canaletto could not only discuss with him the difficulties surrounding the portrait commission but also Captain Farnham, who Lady Tanqueray had said frequently visited Hinde Court. And maybe he could find out something about how the fire there had started. If the Chinese pavilion was a case of arson, maybe Hinde Court had been also? There was no obvious connection but Canaletto distrusted the coincidence of two fires happening so close together in both time and place. Yes, there were a number of reasons for Canaletto to be pleased with the suggested outing. However, 'I have no mount,' he said.

'The duke's stable will be happy to furnish you with one. Come with me.'

Canaletto might also have said that he had little experience of horses. Riding was not a skill needed by Venetians and none of his various journeys had he done on horseback. Walking and carriages, whether public or private, were his usual methods of transport. Still, when he'd lived in Rome as a youth, painting scenery with his father, he'd occasionally travelled by horse. No doubt it was a skill that would return.

For a moment he wondered whether to send a message to Fanny telling her what he was doing, then decided that he was still far too cross with her. Let her chase after him, there was no mischief she could get up to while he was away.

It was a decision that later he was bitterly to regret.

Canaletto trotted out of the stable yard behind James Horton, mounted on what the groom had asserted was a gentle animal, 'You'll be all right on her, sir, never shies nor bucks nor takes it into her head to go her own way,' he'd said.

The young man was on a frisky bay that took exception to a cat walking by and then started at the sound of a bucket being dropped on the cobbles and took off across the yard and into the park.

Canaletto thanked heaven for the solid good nature of his mare and followed more slowly.

Young Horton managed to gain control of his mount halfway down one of the long avenues and reined it in to wait for the older man. 'Hasn't been out for a couple of days,' he said breathlessly as Canaletto caught up with him. 'Wright, my steward, brought him over with my sisters' mounts yesterday but that was hardly enough to reduce his energy and no doubt the duke's grooms have overfed him.'

'Perhaps you should give him a gallop,' suggested Canaletto uncertainly. But James thought that a splendid idea.

'Be back in a moment, you just follow this avenue,' he said and then was off, his face exultant, the horse's hooves kicking up the odd piece of earth as he went.

Canaletto patted the neck of his horse and thanked her for being so well behaved. He jogged along slowly, thinking that perhaps young James Horton wasn't quite as staid as he seemed and wondering how best to approach the subject of his sister's portrait.

Eventually, puffing slightly, James Horton returned, his horse blowing through its nostrils. 'I hope that has rid Thunder of some excess energy,' he said.

'Tell me of your building activities,' Canaletto said quickly, not yet ready to talk about the commission.

James was happy to expound on his father's plans for Hinde Court. 'It will be a veritable palace by the time we have finished,' he said. 'We were not able to engage William Kent but have the services of another excellent architect. Is not Badminton a fine house?'

Canaletto agreed that it was indeed a very fine house.

'Well, Hinde Court will match it in degree and appearance, if not in reputation. One cannot rival a duke, after all, can one?' James said in rhetorical fashion.

For the rest of the short journey, Canaletto listened to the young man on the necessity for a portico to attest to the Horton standing, the requirement for a pedimented façade, how he had encouraged his father to embrace the French style and have an *appartement de société*, where the Hortons could entertain their friends, as well as an *appartement de parade*, for more formal occasions. Then he became lyrical on the ornamentations he was commissioning for the interior, the plaster works, the pilasters, friezes and murals.

'I have not been able to tour the continent, due to the war conditions,' James continued while Canaletto mused upon the wealth that all these elaborate plans indicated. Sir Robert Horton had been described to him as a merchant, now he realized the man must be a prince amongst merchants. 'However, I have visited many of the great houses in this country. Whilst I was studying at Oxford, it was a pleasure I frequently indulged in. My notes have been of inestimable value now that we are building our own edifice.'

James Horton spoke with condescension, he was a young man evidently convinced of his superiority to other beings.

Following first a bridle path and then a rough road after they left the park, Hinde Court was soon reached. Canaletto realized that the distance from Badminton could be walked without difficulty. There had been no opportunity to bring up the captain's name but Canaletto wondered how often he had journeyed between the two places.

The approach to the house was through a jumble of village cottages, mostly of a mean sort. Dogs and infants playing in the lane scattered before the horses. James spurred his mount on with a cavalier disregard for any in his way and through an open wrought iron gate set in a low stone wall. A short drive led to a grey stone house with mullioned windows, its roof a ruin. Charred beams capped the second storey and a lone chimney rose above the devastation.

At first Canaletto was unable to equate this attractive building with the grandiose schemes that had been related to him by James Horton. True it was, or had been, a sizeable dwelling, but it hardly matched what he had been led to expect.

His companion led the way past a large pond, where a small child was occupying itself making stones bounce across the water, and through a collection of outbuildings on the left of the main house.

As they emerged from a stable yard, scaffolding and massive building works announced the site of the new construction. 'Now you can see the scope of my vision,' said James.

Canaletto sat on his horse and stared. Before him was nothing less than a Palladian mansion. On to the charming old house was being erected a building at least three times larger. When finished, it might well stand comparison with Badminton.

'Eventually you will not see the old house at all,' James said proudly. 'Father's plans ended as you see but I have asked for a design that will include wings and a southern façade. It will offer a most modern kitchen, dairy, laundry and brewery.'

'Indeed?' murmured Canaletto.

'Father did not allow sufficient place for all the servants we shall require, nor a ballroom. I also have a notion for a billiards room, it is all the coming thing, you know! We shall want to entertain considerably when the house is ready. And, of course, I am employing a landscape artist to transform the setting into the most rarefied of natural landscapes.' James waved a hand at the farmland all around. 'There are some trees that will serve for the moment but there will have to be a grand planting.' He had a lot more to say about the new movement that replaced formal gardens with vistas of parkland cunningly in-corporating hills, lakes and a variety of arboreal treasures. 'We shall have temples and gothic follies as well,' James added. 'The village is being moved, of course. We cannot have that raggle-taggle of cottages on our doorstep.' He spoke as though there was nothing to moving a dozen or so families from their settled existence.

As a painter, Canaletto was well used to the necessity of creating a more satisfactory view than actually existed but this wholesale reorganization of nature, a reorganization that could move people with the ease of a flock of sheep, took him aback.

He turned his attention once more to the building. The architecture interested him but not as much as learning more about the fire. 'I see no damage to new construction,' he said.

'There's been enough,' James said aggressively. 'It's

put the building back by several weeks if not months. Ah, there you are, Wright.'

In front of what would clearly be a most impressive portico approached by wide steps, the Horton steward leaned against an embryonic pillar. He slipped a notebook into his pocket and came down to hold James Horton's horse so that he could dismount.

'Have you discovered yet what started the fire?' his master asked.

'The builders are fairly certain it's arson, sir.' Wright threw a glance towards Canaletto. 'We'll have a word later on as to who could have been responsible.'

'Damn it all man, no need for discretion, it was obviously Cary and his wretched son. They're the ones who have the grudge against us and Barnaby was found in the garden that night.' Barnaby was the name of the disfigured boy who'd raised the alarm at Hinde Court, Canaletto remembered Isaiah questioning him. 'You must turn them off!' His face red with anger, James flung his leg over the saddle and slid to the ground. 'How go the repair works? When will we be able to move back in, my sister, that is, my mother is anxious it should be as soon as possible.'

The servant moved to help Canaletto. 'Mr Harris has got several men clearing out the damaged roof area, sir, and he is preparing estimates for the repair work. He hopes Lady Horton and your family will be able to return to the house in a few weeks or so.'

The painter dismounted with some difficulty and, too late, remembered how riding exercised muscles one never knew one had. 'Fire great tragedy for you,' he said, walking gingerly around as the steward led the horses back to the stables. He looked up at the building, shading his eyes from the sun. The front of the house would face north, he noted approvingly. The main rooms would not receive the sun's damaging effects.

James whacked his thigh with his riding crop. 'It's the very devil,' he said to Canaletto. 'Curse the Carys. They must have meant to burn us in our beds. Which would have happened but the cook roused us. Apparently the fire started outside her bedroom window.'

'Why, then, she saved your lives!'

'I suppose so,' James said sulkily. 'Though no doubt we should all have realized what was happening before too long.'

'Many a person die without waking in a fire,' Canaletto reminded him. 'I may explore the construction?'

'But of course, my dear signor. I shall be most interested in your comments. And perhaps you may provide us with a view when all is finished?'

Assessing the wealth that must lie behind this place, Canaletto realized he could ask a price that would make the commission worthwhile in financial terms, even though it would not carry much social cachet. He left James Horton with his steward and entered the building.

The ground floor area had been divided up with both stone walls and upright beams that would later be filled with lath- and plasterwork. Cross beams were in place but had not yet been boarded over to provide floors. Stepping carefully, Canaletto explored what promised to be a grand entrance hall then went through to an embryonic major salon. It would be lit by long windows that were presently only apertures in the stonework. How they would show off the paintings that must be hung on these walls. Would the ceilings be painted? Or decorative plasterwork? For a few moments Canaletto indulged himself in imagining the finished grandeur. Then, turning to the wall that had been built alongside the old house, he saw debris.

Scattered over quite a wide area was a quantity of ash and pieces of charred wood. The ground floor beams were also charred in parts. All had been soaked through by the blessed rain. Looking up, Canaletto could see gaps in the beams for the two upper floors, their partly consumed and broken ends dark witnesses to the lethal power of fire.

Canaletto looked again at the mess at his feet. The damage on the upper floors was far greater than down here, which suggested that the fire had started up there.

There was no staircase in place yet but Canaletto found a ladder leading to the next floor and climbed up. Here, again, walls and beams were in place. Odd boards had been put across the beams to provide an easy way to access the various areas. Canaletto made his way towards the damaged beams. Now, looking up again, he confirmed that the beams for the second floor had suffered even greater damage than those for the first

Canaletto found another ladder that led up to the second floor. This was as far as construction had reached and now it was very evident that the new building was more generously proportioned than the old. Only the first foot of the second floor wall had been built but already it reached across the dormer windows of the existing attic. When finished, the second floor would rise above the roof of the original house.

The new frontage and wings had not been constructed on to the outside wall of the old building but rather built as a self-contained unit. Doors leading through from one building to the other had been incorporated, though not yet broken through. Because the new ceilings were higher than the old, however, the first floor levels would require steps to lead from one part to the other. By the time the second floor had been reached, any attempt to give access had been abandoned. Soon the second floor wall would cut off all light to the old dormer windows.

On this level there weren't so many boards set across the beams and progress was more difficult but, by dint of changing the position of what boards there were, Canaletto managed to see the burned area.

It was immediately obvious that was where the fire had started. Here the dormer window had been totally burned away and what could be seen of the room behind was a scene of devastation. Men were working to clear the debris so that rebuilding could start. A canvas chute had been organized outside one of the dormer windows and pans of rubbish were being shovelled down to rattle their way to the ground.

Canaletto studied the blackened roof beams. What a blessing the heavy rain had been, without it the house would have been destroyed.

Could the fire have started in the old house and then falling debris ignited the beams in the new part? Canaletto thought not.

It looked as though, somehow, a fire had been built on the new beams. It was no distance from there to the wooden frame of the cook's window. Set that alight and the rest of the roof must follow. Canaletto looked around. Further along the construction work was a platform of boards that held a pile of stones ready for building. Immediately he saw how a similar platform could have a pile of brushwood added to it, perhaps with branches leading towards the window frame. Nobody opened their window at night, unhealthy humours had to be guarded against. In any case, all those dormer windows opened outwards and the new wall would prevent any attempt. The brushwood could have been added at dusk, after the builders had left. Some paper and a lamp could have provided ignition.

Canaletto decided he had seen enough. He made his way back to the ladder. Just as he reached it, there came a sound that might have belonged to an enraged bull. Instead of descending, Canaletto made his way to the front of the building, grabbed hold of the scaffolding supports and looked over the shallow wall.

Round the side, wielding a pitchfork and making straight for James Horton, came a burly fellow in rough breeches and smock, roaring fit to stampede a herd of cattle.

James was alone, the steward nowhere in sight. His only weapon was a riding crop, hopeless against the long and cruelly sharp fork. Shouting for the steward, James turned and ran, tripped over a length of wood, fell and lay on the ground, screaming piteously. The labourer came on, his weapon raised.

Looking around, Canaletto saw another platform of stones not too far from him. Feeling slightly dizzy from the height, he trod carefully from beam to beam, clutching at the scaffolding as he worked his way across to it.

The man paused exultantly with his pitchfork poised above the helpless man. He was shouting now and Canaletto strained to make sense of the broad accent. 'You whoreson bugger, you'll not throw us out of our house, no, nor no one else neither.'

Canaletto reached the stones and took hold of one of the smaller ones. It was almost too heavy to lift but with a great effort he managed it. Aiming was an impossibility but a falling stone might startle the man enough to let James Horton escape.

He dropped the missile over the wall, through the scaffolding. It thudded down but made no impact on the infuriated labourer. At that moment, however, help arrived from two different quarters.

From round the west end of the building works came Thomas Wright. Picking up a length of wood from the ground, he advanced towards the demented man and said, 'Now then, Cary, put that fork down, you'll do no good this way.'

From the other direction flew an angry woman, a coif around her head, linen skirts pinned up. 'Walter!' she shrieked. 'Give me that!' She grabbed the fork and wrenched it away from the startled man. 'You idiot!' she screamed at him. 'You'll do for us all. You can't leave things to me, can you? No, you know best.'

The disarmed man gave a frustrated roar.

'Mrs Cary,' began the steward.

'You leave Walter to me, Tom,' she said firmly. 'I promise you, Mister Horton, he'll not trouble you again.'

'Betsy, you knows what they're going to do!' Her husband reached for the pitchfork.

She whipped it behind her. 'You'll not stop them, not like this,' she said angrily.

'That you won't,' agreed James, scrambling to his feet and brushing soil and bits of this and that off his breeches. 'You'll be off my land by sundown or it'll be the worse for you.'

From his bird's-eye view, Canaletto saw the woman look towards Thomas Wright and he give her a small shake of his head.

Betsy Cary tugged at her husband's sleeve. For a long moment he glared at James Horton then he shook off his wife's arm and stomped off.

'Where the hell were you, Wright?' James Horton was very angry, his face as red as the roses blooming at the edge of the building site. 'One moment you're there, the next you're gone and that maniac is coming down on me.'

'I'm sorry, Mister Horton,' the steward said steadily. 'I went to fetch the estimation the builder gave me yesterday for building stone. I found that I'd left it in my office. I did tell you that was what I was doing.' He brought out a paper from a capacious pocket in his serviceable jacket and handed it to the irate young man.

'See that Cary goes, Wright, I'll take no more from him.' James snatched the paper from the other man.

Canaletto worked his way back to the ladder and then down to the ground, his aching legs threatening to give way as he negotiated the last steps. He returned to the debris he'd seen earlier and studied it carefully. After the first fire and then heavy rain had done their work, it was impossible to ascertain whether it was the remains of more than the beams. One thing was certain, there had been a lot of ash, which proved the fire had been very hot.

He made his way outside. James Horton was examining the paper his steward had given him and neither man paid any attention to Canaletto as he walked round to the front of Hinde Court. There the door stood open.

Canaletto entered and had no difficulty in finding his way up the narrow stairs to the attic floor where the men were working. Not much had yet been cleared. The mess was indescribable, soaked ash mingling with broken tiles and charred wood. Damaris Friend's room had been at the end of the corridor. A half-burned door stood open on ruination. The ceiling had fallen in and smoke stained what remained of the walls. A heavily charred bed frame was just identifiable. Canaletto imagined the girl with the strong facial bones lying there. She could so easily have been overcome by the smoke and the flames. As it was, she had had a fortunate escape.

Slowly he made his way downstairs again. Everywhere there was the smell of smoke but the fire seemed to have been confined to the attic floor. Water had caused a certain amount of damage but nothing serious.

How dark and poky these old English houses were! Canaletto could understand James Horton's desire for the elegant rooms the new building would afford. Quietly he let himself out of the front door and stood wondering for a moment about the scene he'd just witnessed. When Thomas Wright had suggested the fire might have been deliberately started, James had been very ready to suggest the malefactor was Walter Cary and the man's attack on him seemed to prove the likelihood.

Canaletto walked down the short drive and stood by a small wrought iron gate looking at the jumble of cottages along the approach road. Outside one stood Betsy Cary, talking urgently with another man. He had the appearance of respectability but little more. There was a sense of familiarity between them. There was no sign of Walter Cary. As Canaletto watched, the man took a hurried leave, raising a hand in a farewell salute, and walked through the wide gate leading to the out-buildings. There was nothing to show whether he had noticed Canaletto or not. The woman disappeared inside the cottage.

Making his own way back to the building area, Canaletto found James Horton in conversation with the steward and the man he had just seen with Betsy Cary. Canaletto strolled up to join them.

'This will be a most excellent building,' he announced. 'The façade, the proportions, the vision, all first class.'

James Horton beamed. 'I'm pleased to hear you say so, sir. And what think you of the standard of building? You must have a vast experience of buildings both in England and Italy.'

Canaletto felt wary. 'Is very good,' he said carefully. 'Stonework excellent. Shame about burned beams. Much work needed to replace, I think? Yes?'

Both Thomas Wright and the other man nodded vigorously. 'Damn me but you're right,' said the newcomer. 'And so I've just been saying to Mister Horton here.'

'Mr Harris is the master builder in charge of the construction work at Hinde Court,' said the steward. 'I am sure he is very pleased to hear you think the work of himself and his men is of a good standard.'

'Indeed, yes,' nodded Mr Harris vigorously. 'You are, sir,' he said to James Horton, 'getting a bargain of a building here. A bargain of a building,' he repeated, nodding emphatically.

'It's certainly costing enough,' James said a little resentfully. 'My father will be questioning all the accounts when he comes home.'

'And you will be able to show him how well his money has been spent,' agreed Mr Harris, his round face weather-beaten and beaming. 'I would have you visit Bath in the near future to confirm the stone for the portico and pediment and also I need to discuss the carving of the Horton arms for the portico.'

James nodded.

Canaletto wondered how long this conversation on the building of the new house was to take. He was tired from scrambling around the construction works and he was stiff from the unaccustomed ride. He wanted to sit quietly and think about what he had learned. And he wanted to discuss his discoveries with Fanny. She was such a sensible girl. Above all, what he did not want at this particular moment was to have to discuss the awkward matter of the portrait commission.

As the talk turned to the work involved in making good the fire damage, Canaletto murmured something about finishing sketches for the duke and slipped away to find his horse. He would have preferred to leave the animal there and walk back but his legs were now so sore, he wasn't sure he could make it on foot.

He found the mare tied up in the stables. He led her outside, took a firm grip on the reins and then looked up at the saddle. How on earth was he going to manage to get himself up there? There was no groom to help. Nor could he see a mounting block.

Just then there appeared the young lad with the damaged face he'd seen at Badminton on the night of the fire.

'Want a leg up, sir?' the boy asked.

'Yes, most kind, Barnaby.'

'Me arm's no use, sir. You'll have to put your leg on me.' So saying, Barnaby bent over and offered his back.

Canaletto hesitated but only for a minute. Then in a twinkling he was mounted. 'You are bright boy, you live here, at Hinde Court, yes?'

'In the village, sir.' Once you got used to the vile scarring of his face, the boy had an intelligent look in his one good eye. 'Is me uncle still here? Me mam wants him when he's finished.'

'Uncle?'

'Mr Harris, the builder.'

The boy's mother must be Betsy Cary, the woman Canaletto had seen the builder talking with. Which meant that Barnaby was about to find himself homeless. 'He talks with Mr Horton and Mr Wright, about the building works.' Canaletto felt in one of his pockets and found a small coin. 'Here, for your trouble.'

'Thanks, sir.' The boy looked delighted. Unlike

279

London urchins, he didn't bite the money to test it was proper coin, but immediately pocketed it.

Canaletto turned his gentle mount and rode out of Hinde Court considering the matter of arson. All the evidence suggested the fire had been aimed at Damaris Friend.

Chapter Twenty-Six

Fanny soon arranged for Hannah to watch over Jack while Nell took some fresh air. 'Do the girl good,' Mrs George said to Fanny. 'She's hardly moved from the lad's side since he was brought here.'

Emerging on to the gravel semicircle, Nell averted her eyes from the ruined pavilion. 'Do let's walk in the other direction,' she said. 'I cannot bear the sight of that dreadful place where Captain Farnham met his end. Particularly since the last time we talked together we quarrelled.'

Had they indeed! 'I did not have much opportunity to talk with the captain but I thought he was a most interesting man.'

Nell was very happy to talk about her friend, his career on the continent and the frequent visits he had paid to Hinde Court. 'Mama feared he might try and fix his interest with one of us,' she said. 'My sister, Patience, is such a romantic.'

'And a soldier with a limp must offer plenty of scope for romance?' suggested Fanny. 'Your sister is very beautiful, I can imagine many men trying to fix their interest with her. Indeed, last night Father Sylvester was exceedingly attentive.'

'Who, pray, is Father Sylvester?'

'He is a priest, a friend of the duke's,' said Fanny. Even if Canaletto was right as to his real identity, it was best to keep to Charles Sylvester's description of himself.

'A priest!'

'I am sure the good father is a gentleman.'

'Faced with my sister's beauty, I can imagine any gentleman losing his principles,' Nell said dryly. 'I can only hope a priest is more sensible.'

'Was the captain interested in your sister?'

'He did not appear to be,' said Nell, sounding a little puzzled.

Happy she had the conversation away from Charles Sylvester, Fanny asked Nell to tell her more about the captain. 'Signor Canale and I feel his death is most mysterious.'

'Oh, and so do I,' said Nell. 'Captain Farnham was so experienced a soldier, so enterprising, I cannot understand how he can have been overcome by fire. Why, all of us escaped conflagration the other night and he had such a simple building to quit, not a house with narrow stairs.'

'In fact,' said Fanny with great seriousness, 'my master, Signor Canale, believes he was assisted out of this life by a malefactor. He is looking into his death and I am helping him. We worked together on another mysterious death last year and discovered the killer.'

'No!' It was difficult to tell whether Nell's astonishment was because the captain's death was being investigated or because this was not the first case Fanny had worked on. Fanny hoped she wouldn't ask for more details, it was too soon for her to be able to discuss any aspect of that dreadful case with any sort of equanimity.

'You said you had words with him the day of his death, that you quarrelled,' she said hastily. 'Would you care to tell me what about?'

'You cannot think what we discussed had anything to do with his death,' Nell said, looking aghast.

'My master says light can be thrown in mysterious ways from the most unexpected of sources,' said Fanny. She had never actually heard Canaletto say this but she felt he might very well have done. 'Only if you let us know what you talked about with the captain can we assess whether it had anything to do with his death.' She sat down on a low wall and patted the space beside her. 'We could sit and admire these roses while you talk.'

'I must ask the duchess their name and if perhaps she will give us a cutting,' said Nell distractedly, pulling at the head of one of the red and white striped blossoms. 'She professes to prefer London to Badminton but she is mightily keen on the garden here.'

'You do not wish, perhaps, to tell me what you and the captain quarrelled about?' suggested Fanny. She was liking this disfigured girl more and more. The way she'd nursed her brother, her evident distress at the captain's death, her frank and open manner, all were attractive – and so very different from the social manners of her beautiful sister.

Nell discarded the rose petals and fiddled instead with the ends of her fichu. The sun was very bright on her scarred cheek. She did nothing to hide the damaged skin, wore no paint, arranged no trailing hair, no scarf. 'It could have had nothing to do with his death,' she repeated finally. 'It had to do with my father's plans for the village, something I felt could easily be sorted out.' But the way she twisted the soft material around her fingers showed that whatever it was they'd argued about had concerned her more than she wanted to allow. 'Who could have wanted him dead?'

Fanny grasped at the first idea that came into her head. 'It might perhaps have something to do with a rival in love,' she suggested. Passion, Canaletto had once said, lay behind so many crimes.

A figure strode towards them and Nell looked up with relief. 'Mr Cumberledge, have you finished schooling your pupils for today?'

He took off his hat and swept her and Fanny a bow. 'What a picture the two of you make, sitting on that wall in the sunshine. Will you not paint it for me, Miss Rooker?'

'It would be difficult if I am to be part of it as well,' Fanny said.

'I will fetch a mirror. Don't artists paint themselves with such an aid all the time?'

'It saves money,' Fanny laughed. 'You don't have to pay yourself to be a sitter.'

Nell, though, was not amused. 'You know my feelings towards mirrors, Mr Cumberledge.'

'I know you will not look in one,' he said gently. 'But I am happy to look at you.'

Her eyes suddenly filled with tears and she looked away.

'Surface beauty is beguiling,' he went on. 'But what is beneath is so much more important.'

'Would you be so charmed by Patience if she was not so beautiful?' she asked in a constricted voice.

'Ah, Patience,' he sighed. 'Her loveliness goes all through. If she lost her looks today, I would still feel just as much for her.'

Nell gave him a brilliant smile and, with a sudden leap in understanding, Fanny sensed that Isaiah meant a great deal to her. Such a girl would love deeply and would not easily show her feelings. 'Pattie is indeed a dear, sweet girl,' Nell said quickly. 'Mr Cumberledge, you can perhaps help. Miss Rooker is assisting her master, Signor Canale, to discover how Captain Farnham met his death, they feel there is something sinister about it. You made a remark once that occasionally he would not appear for meals because he was meeting a girl. Then you were embarrassed at mentioning such a matter. But I understand the ways of the world,' she said quaintly. 'Was it one girl in particular? If you told us who she was, it might help to find out why he died. Miss Rooker feels it could have involved a rival in love.'

Fanny held her breath, would what she'd so casually suggested actually lead to the truth?

Isaiah sat down on the ground at their feet, his hat still in his hand. He looked very worried. 'You cannot believe that Farnham's death is anything but the most dreadful accident,' he said robustly, but Fanny didn't like the way he avoided looking at either of them.

'Signor Canale believes it was something quite other,' said Fanny seriously. 'So there must be a question of who would want to remove him from this world.'

'I see,' he said slowly. 'And you think because he

disported himself with some female, that that could be a reason for his demise?'

'Tell us who it is, then we can question her and perhaps find out.' Fanny held her breath.

He drew an invisible pattern on the lawn where he sat. 'I should not be talking of such things to two young ladies,' he said. 'Maybe I should talk with Signor Canale.'

'I do not know where he is at present,' Fanny said hastily. 'Since we have broached the subject, you can see that our sensibilities are not such that we will be upset. Unless,' she added suddenly. 'Unless you have to protect the name of the woman involved.' Could it be Lady Tanqueray? If Mr Cumberledge refused to discuss the matter further, it would have to mean that his aunt was the woman the captain had been dallying with. She was sure he would not allow such a great lady's name to be associated with the dead man.

But Isaiah laughed. 'Protect her name! My dear Miss Rooker, I tell you she has no name to protect, as Miss Horton here will be the first to admit, fond though she is of her.'

Nell stared at him for a moment, then she said, 'You cannot, surely, mean Damaris?'

'Why not? Has she not had her name linked with other men? Including the steward here?'

'Mr Capper?' enquired Fanny. She remembered the little scene she had overheard between him and the Hinde Court cook.

'The very same.'

'No!' said Nell forcibly. 'I will not hear such things said about Damaris.'

Isaiah looked at her fondly. 'My dear Miss Horton,

your attachment to her is laudable but even you have to admit that her morals leave much to be desired. Indeed, I do not know why Lady Horton has not turned her off before this.'

'If my mother knew,' Nell began, then bit her lip. 'But you mean, Captain Farnham was dallying with Damaris?'

'He told me he met her gathering herbs from a hedgerow looking, he said, like an earth goddess. That from Farnham who, as you know, was the most plain spoken of men!'

'And when he was such a constant visitor to your aunt!' Nell sounded shocked.

Isaiah plucked at the grass by his knee. 'Oh, they were merely sparring partners. Both of them love, or rather loved, a good discussion. Now, I think I have told you all I can and I must return to battle with the duchess on this matter of slates for the school.' He picked himself up from the grass. 'Ladies, adieu, I thank you for your company.'

And he was gone.

Nell looked after him thoughtfully. 'Strange, I had not realized he was so little concerned about the friendship between the captain and his aunt.'

'He visited her this morning, to enquire how she did.'

'Oh, that was good of him. Lady Tanqueray was so very fond of the captain. Indeed, more than once when she spoke of him, I wondered if there was something more than friendship, but I told myself that that was unlikely, she being older than the captain by some ten years or so.'

'If neither thought that an obstacle, then it would

not have been,' Fanny said, feeling a good deal older than the other girl though there could not be more than a couple of years between them. 'Is that why Mr Cumberledge fell out with his aunt?'

'No, indeed, that happened before Captain Farnham arrived. Lady Tanqueray acts as a sort of godmother to me and I respect her deeply. However,' Nell sighed. 'She remains philosophically in the last century. She believes God created everything in the world and that to attempt to separate nature from man, is to reduce God's miracles to a scientific dissertation, and to establish laws and orders is an offence like to blasphemy. As long as Mr Cumberledge commits himself to unravelling nature's mysteries, she will have nothing to do with him. She cannot see,' Nell rose from the wall and strode about, her hands on her hips, her nose raised belligerently to the air. 'She will not admit how important the work he and others do is! The world is moving on apace and we need to understand so much.' She stooped and yanked off another rose, seemingly impervious to the thorns on its stem, and started to pull off the petals as she walked. 'Mr Cumberledge will contribute important discoveries, he is particularly interested in steam and its propellent powers. I know he will become a great man and it distresses me that Godmama, as I call her, cannot understand this. But since my accident, she will not admit any conversation on the subject with me at all.'

Fanny longed to ask what had so ravaged her face but didn't want to disturb the rapport that was developing between them. 'Indeed, it is a great shame Lady Tanqueray takes that line. As painters, Signor Canale and I work all the time for a greater understanding of pigments, how they can be used, what new ones can be discovered. There is Prussian blue, for example. Until recently lapis lazuli had to be used, which made a Madonna's robe or an intense sky a matter of great expense. Now this other blue can be obtained at a lesser cost. It may not match scientific understanding of steam,' Fanny added, suddenly conscious that pigments were not a matter everyone was as concerned with as herself, 'but for artists it is important. Now,' she went on, determined to pursue the course she'd set herself. 'Tell me more about your cook and her adventurous life, that is, the men she consorts with.'

Nell tossed away the ruined flower and came to a stop in front of Fanny. 'Adventurous life is in fact right,' she said, smiling a little. 'If Mr Cumberledge really is correct when he says she has consorted with many men, Mama will be so upset. And,' she frowned, 'she will blame me. For it was I who persuaded her to employ Damaris.'

'Shall we walk a little again while you tell me her story?' suggested Fanny.

While they strolled through Badminton's formal flower beds and well-trimmed hedges, Fanny listened to a tale that belonged more in the pages of one of Mr Fielding's novels than to reality.

Damaris Friend, Nell told her, was the offspring of a well-born woman who had married a gambler. After she'd borne him a daughter, he'd lost all he'd owned plus her fortune and shot himself. A second husband was just as much of a gambler and no more successful than the first. At the age of twelve, Damaris found herself placed as stake for a last, desperate bet. When

the cards made her stepfather the loser, her mother
had shot him. She was hanged and the orphaned girl
was taken in by her uncle, who made of her a skivvy.
She worked in the kitchen for several years then, tired
of constant beatings from both the uncle and the cook,
ran away.

'She is so brave,' Nell said admiringly. 'She said
she did not want to be hanged like her mother so she
couldn't bring herself to kill her uncle but she was
determined to escape his thrall. And so put herself on
the market as a cook.'

'A good cook must find a position without difficulty,'
said Fanny, thinking of all the complaints she had
heard from her sister-in-law over the impossibility of
securing one.

'If you do not have references, one in a respectable
household is not easy,' said Nell ruefully. 'So Damaris
found herself working for an old roué who raped her.'

'No!'

'Alas, yes. Damaris said she would not have minded
if his breath hadn't smelled so foul and his legs hadn't
been so thin.'

Fanny couldn't help laughing.

'That is Damaris,' acknowledged Nell with a smile.
'When she again ran away, she met with some Romany
folk who took her in for a while but two men fell out
over her and one of the women threw her out and
threatened her with a knife, saying she would ruin her
beauty for ever if she ever returned.' Nell fingered
her devastated face absent-mindedly. 'The weather was
fine and for a few days Damaris walked and slept
under the stars, applying for work at the houses she
passed.'

'If she found a position difficult without references, how much more must one have been to find when living from hand to mouth!'

'Indeed, Fanny, you have the right of it. But she knocked on our door just as we were desperate for a cook. The one mother brought from London had left after two weeks, saying she couldn't stand the quiet. We had had three others, all hopeless and we were in despair of ever receiving a meal worth eating again. Indeed, Mama was saying we should have to return to town ourselves!'

'So you were willing to give Damaris the opportunity to prove herself?'

'Luckily, it was I who was in the kitchen the day she knocked on our door. I think Patience, and certainly Mama, would have given her short shrift but maybe they would have been as charmed by her as I was.'

Fanny thought of Father Sylvester, a traveller in distress without references, and how he had charmed her and Canaletto. 'And so you took her in?'

'I said we would give her two weeks' trial and she could do the same with us.'

'And she proved herself a good cook?'

'Damaris is a marvellous cook. Some of the other staff find her difficult, especially the kitchen maid, for she stands no nonsense. Patience says she rules the kitchen like a queen, and it is true. But how we enjoy the food that comes out of that realm! And I enjoy being with her. We are, I think, friends.'

'But you had no knowledge of her association with Captain Farnham?'

Nell shook her head. 'Absolutely none. We thought

the captain came to visit Hinde Court to see us. And even now I find it difficult to believe he left by the front door only to go round to the back!'

'Perhaps they met somewhere outside?'

'Maybe. Damaris is always collecting herbs from the hedgerows for her dishes and her remedies. She is clever with simples.'

'Did you already know she was friendly with Mr Capper?'

Nell laughed, 'Oh, yes! That is Damaris for you. There was a party here at Christmas in the servants' hall to which our staff were invited. I heard she was the belle of the ball and several men were mightily smitten. I believe she did dally with Mr Capper a little but not for long. There is something wild about Damaris, she says it's the same quality that made her mother choose two fools for husbands, it picks out the worst of men and finds them attractive. When she told me this one day, I said that my mother would not countenance loose behaviour under her roof. She claimed she understood this. Can she have been deceiving me?' Nell sounded aghast. 'I must talk to her at once.' She started to walk hurriedly back to the house. 'I must learn the truth.'

Fanny tried to call her back but the girl had gone. She started to run after her, then stopped. Why should she feel so anxious? Was it just that events were starting to move too fast? But too fast for what?

Chapter Twenty-Seven

Nell found Damaris cutting vegetables for soup in the Badminton kitchen, working quietly in a corner while the cook issued orders to his staff for the main meal of the day. On being applied to, he reluctantly released his assistant and Damaris followed Nell out of the kitchen.

'Ouf, I am glad you rescued me from there,' she said, removing the coif from her hair and running her fingers through the dark tresses that, though she was still in her early twenties, were already shot with silver.

Nell had intended to tackle Damaris immediately on the matter of Humphrey and loose behaviour at Hinde Court but, as so often with her cook, she found herself diverted from her chosen path. 'Is he working you very hard?'

Damaris shook her head, her heavy hair swinging from side to side. 'Just enough to keep me busy, stop me thinking. I'm grateful for that. But he won't keep his hands to himself. Doesn't care who sees it. The kitchen staff are placing bets on how long it's going to take him to get up my skirts.'

'Damaris!' Nell couldn't help but be shocked. Yet at the same time she admired the cook. She would like to be able to express her thoughts and feelings with the same careless ease as this girl. Some people might call her coarse, Nell felt she was completely natural.

Damaris gave a wan smile, quite unlike her usual self. 'I might just let him, see if his French training has had any effect on his love making.'

Nell laughed. She had no idea exactly what Damaris meant but it was easy enough to make a guess.

They reached the large courtyard outside the kitchen. Once in the open air, Damaris spread out her arms to the sun and held up her face.

For the first time since the news of Humphrey's death, Nell saw her properly and she was shocked at the look of strain on her face, at how reddened her eyes were and at the deep shadows underneath them. 'You did love him,' she said impulsively.

'Love him? You know about Humphrey?'

Nell nodded, her eyes fastened on the other girl's face.

Damaris hugged herself, it was as if she was trying to recapture the feel of her lover's arms. 'I never expected to, I never expected to feel about any man what I felt for him, but, yes, I loved him. I don't think he felt as deeply for me but we had some fine discussions.'

'He was good at talking,' said Nell sadly.

'Almost as good as at love making,' Damaris agreed. Then a ghost of a smile gave way to tears. They welled up in her dark eyes, apparently spontaneously. She made no effort to brush them away and they ran down the olive skin of her cheeks as though following a well-trodden path.

Nell put her arm round the girl and held her tight. Damaris gave a great sigh and leaned her head on

Nell's shoulder for an instant, then she drew away. 'But all that's past now. One cannot look back, if I've learned anything from life, it's that.'

'It was only this morning, before that I had no idea you and the captain . . .' Nell said awkwardly.

'I know! I told him I'd be turned off if any of you found out. We used to meet away from Hinde Court.'

'Oh, Damaris, what you have suffered!'

'I'm suffering now, all right, but not then. Then was marvellous!' Damaris threw open her arms again in an exultant gesture.

A maid passed through the courtyard and stared curiously at the two of them.

'Let's go to the church,' said Damaris.

Inside it was dark with the faint odour of damp that always seemed to hang around churches and caused Nell's nostrils to curl in disgust. There were enough smells around in life for her to feel a sense of blasphemy in resenting this particular one but she couldn't help it. It conjured up dark, earthy fungi and white, crawling things that never saw the light of day, all areas of the devil, not God.

'Heavens,' said Damaris, sniffing hard. 'Another day and poor Humphrey will be decomposing before our eyes.' She approached the bier and stood there silent for a moment. Nell hung back. Damaris should be allowed to pay her respects alone.

Then Damaris shuddered. 'When will they bury him? Surely it is time?'

'I don't know. There are questions about his death. Perhaps that is why.'

Damaris turned. 'Questions?'

'Will you sit? I need to talk to you.'

With a last look at the cloth-covered corpse, Damaris slipped into a pew beside Nell. All around were tablets commemorating past lives and Nell felt the pulpit hovering over her with a sense of doom.

'You said questions about Humphrey's death. What questions?'

'Signor Canale says it wasn't an accident.'

'Not an accident?' Damaris drew in her breath sharply. 'You mean the fire was set deliberately? The question of why he didn't escape has haunted me, Humphrey was so resourceful.'

'Signor Canale says he was killed before the fire started.'

Damaris sat very still. 'Who is Signor Canale?'

After Nell had explained, she said, 'There were two men here last night. One was Doctor Butcher, who attended Jack, and one was a much smaller man.'

'Signor Canale is not very tall.'

Damaris thought about this, everything about her very still. 'Why would anyone want to kill Humphrey?'

'That is what Signor Canale's assistant, Miss Rooker, would like to speak to you about. She is helping to look into the circumstances of the captain's death. Mr Cumberledge feels that you were probably the last person to see Humphrey alive.'

'Mr Cumberledge?' Damaris asked sharply. 'How does he know anything about Humphrey and me?'

'I don't know. He and the captain have been together at Badminton for some weeks, maybe Captain Farnham told him things.'

'He'd never have told him about us, surely?' Suddenly Damaris didn't sound so certain. 'But that's men for you. They say women gossip but they're as bad if not worse.'

'Do you not like Mr Cumberledge?'

Damaris shrugged. 'He is an idiot.'

'Damaris, he is not! He is a highly intelligent man.'

'He is an idiot.'

'Why do you keep repeating that?'

'Because he prefers your sister to you.'

'Patience is beautiful,' Nell said firmly. 'Inside as well as out.'

'That's as maybe but she does not have your strength of character, your spirit. That man can see no further than his eyes. You should find someone who will value you. Love can be wondrous but only if there is something there on both sides. To have to hug it privately to yourself offers no sustenance at all.'

'Oh, Damaris,' Nell was half laughing, half indignant. 'You are a philosopher!'

'I've never found philosophy offered me any delights. Whereas men, well . . .,' she left the end of her sentence hanging in the air.

'You are a terrible girl. How many men have you had?'

'Nell, you don't expect me to tell you, surely!'

'Mr Capper?' Nell asked severely.

Damaris gave her a sideways glance, 'Once or twice, no more.'

Nell took a careful breath and asked, 'What about Thomas Wright?'

'Oh, that was another fleeting experience, over long ago.'

'Is there anyone male in the area you haven't bedded?'

Damaris laughed and refused to answer.

Nell was filled with a mixture of emotions she didn't want to analyse. Finally she said, 'Well, will you speak to Miss Rooker?'

'Is she the one who is supposed to paint your portrait?'

'Well, yes, so it was proposed. But I do not want it done and she says she will not carry it out if I am not in agreement.'

'Then she sounds a girl of sense.'

'I think she is. You will speak to her? Or if not to her, then to Signor Canale?'

'I cannot think anything I have to say could throw light on Humphrey's death,' Damaris said slowly. 'Even if, as you say, he was killed and the fire started deliberately.' She paused for a moment, thinking. 'It's strange, though, that Hinde Court should be burned also.'

'You don't think there could be a connection?' Nell asked in astonishment.

'That would indeed be sinister.'

'Talk to Fanny or Signor Canale.'

'How is Master Jack?'

Nell sighed deeply. She would get no further with Damaris this morning. 'Much better. I've left Hannah looking after him, I must go and relieve her.' She got up from the pew. 'We'll talk again later.'

Nell was on her way upstairs before she realized that there was one very obvious candidate for Damaris's bed who hadn't been mentioned.

Jack woke up as she returned and asked if he could get up now.

'Tomorrow,' Nell promised him. 'If you are a good boy and stay quiet today.'

As she played spillikins with him, Nell wondered whether she should be worried about Patience and Father Sylvester. But men constantly paid court to her sister and Patience never seemed to have trouble in keeping them at a distance. The sisters shared all their experiences and Nell knew Patience would tell her when romance entered her life. Just as she must now tell her about the doubts surrounding Humphrey Farnham's death. Exactly what Damaris had been up to, though, she decided, need not be gone into.

Lady Horton came in as Jack jumbled up the spillikins for another game. She seemed much recovered. She was wearing one of her best day dresses and her hair had been attractively arranged. 'Darling boy,' she said, rushing over and hugging Jack. 'You are so much better!'

Jack submitted to being smothered. 'I feel all better, Mama. Nell tells me I cannot get up yet.'

'Of course not, my precious, not for a very long time yet, we do not want to lose you.'

'You will not lose me, Mama, I can find my way around very well, I promise you.'

'Will you be here for a little, Mama?' asked Nell. 'Perhaps play a game with Jack?'

'I should like that very much,' Lady Horton said.

As Nell left Jack's room, Patience, dressed in riding clothes, advanced up the staircase.

'Oh, Nell, isn't it the most wonderful day?' she said, giving her sister a brilliant smile that was disturbing in its self-absorption.

'Is it?'

'How can you ask such a thing? Have you not seen how the sun shines and the air, how soft and fragrant it is? I am so pleased we are not in grimy, hot and smelly London now. Oh, how could I have forgotten! You have been with Jack, of course. How is he?'

'Much improved. It will be difficult to keep him in bed until tomorrow. Mama is with him now.'

'I must go to them.'

'Pattie, can you spare me a little time to talk? There is something disturbing I must tell you.'

'Disturbing? Nell, what has happened?'

'Come to our room.'

Nell was actually sleeping at present in the truckle bed in Jack's room but now she sat on the bed that had been assigned to her and watched Patience take off her riding hat with one of her graceful gestures.

'Tell me, Nellie, what is disturbing you.' Patience listened in mounting horror as Nell told her the doubts about Humphrey Farnham's death.

'You are never telling me he was murdered!' she cried at the end. 'That cannot be!'

'Not only that, Damaris thinks the fire at Hinde Court could have been started deliberately.'

Patience's face grew white. 'Someone set fire to our home? But why?'

Nell went over to the window and stood looking out over the rose garden where she and Fanny had talked with Isaiah. 'Someone who had a grudge against us, maybe. Captain Farnham told me the day before he died that Father planned to move the village so that our house might have a better approach. The villagers are not best pleased.'

'Nell, this is terrible! Can anything be done?'

300

'Signor Canale and his assistant are looking into the captain's death. They want to speak to Damaris.'

'Why her?'

Nell found that she had to tell her sister at least something of their cook's activities. 'It appears that she and the captain were involved,' she said. 'Please do not tell Mama anything of this,' she added. 'She has been so overset by the fire and Jack's accident, learning anything of this will bring on another nervous attack.'

Patience sat on her bed looking appalled and Nell regretted being as frank as she had. 'You have been riding this morning?'

Immediately Patience's expression lightened. 'Oh, yes,' she breathed. 'Such pleasure, Nell.'

'With whom did you ride? Thomas, perhaps?'

'No, indeed. Thomas had to meet with James at Hinde Court. I rode,' she blushed a little and fiddled with a button on her bodice. 'I rode with Charles Sylvester.' She looked up at her sister with an eager face. 'You haven't met him yet, Nell, but when you do, you will find him everything you could ever want in a man.'

Nell's heart plummeted. 'Tell me more, Pattie,' she invited, coming over to sit next to her sister and taking her hand.

'He is so handsome, Nell, the brownest eyes you ever saw and such a straight nose. But it isn't his looks, he has such a way with him. He makes me feel, oh, he makes me feel I am a person of worth, someone who has more than surface beauty.'

Nell wished her sister could have heard Isaiah declaring that she was lovely all through. 'Forgive me, sweetheart, but I have heard that this Charles Sylvester is a priest?'

Patience's colour deepened but she looked frankly at her sister. 'It was explained after we met that he was.'

'He does not wear a habit?'

'Not all the time, no. He told me in the strictest confidence but I can tell you, my dearest sister, that he is giving up the priesthood. It is a circumstance that was forced upon him and he is determined to follow it no longer. Especially, he says, since meeting me!' Patience glowed as she said this. 'Oh, Nell, I am in love and he is in love with me. He says so!'

'My sweetest sister, do you know what you are saying? What sort of man is this? Of what family, what background? How can he give up such a calling so lightly? And what will be his place in the world now?'

Patience jumped up. 'Nell, I cannot believe you can be so prosaic! He is a gentleman, what matters except that?'

'Pattie, sweetheart, can you imagine what our father will say?'

Patience's mouth set in an obstinate line. 'Papa is not here. Papa may never be here again.'

'Sweetheart, do not say that! We must pray that he comes safe home again. Of course there are dangers but we must believe that he will come through them.'

Patience dropped back on to the bed and took her sister's hands, her face distressed. 'I do hope so, dearest, of course I do. But I cannot live my life waiting for his return.'

'Oh, Pattie, it will not be so long! Promise me you will do nothing foolish before then.'

The lovely head drooped and Patience was silent. Nell waited. After a moment, her sister looked at her. 'I promise you, Nell, that I will do nothing I can be ashamed of.'

Nell felt enormous relief. Their upbringing had instilled in both of them a deep sense of what was due from their behaviour. She herself might go against her parents' wishes in this matter of the portrait but not in anything moral and Patience must be the same. 'Thank you, dearest. You will find, I am sure, that everything will work out for the best.'

Patience rose and began to take off her riding dress. 'When you meet Mr Sylvester, you will understand how I feel,' she said.

Had Nell been able to see her sister's expression as she turned away, she might have recognized guilt.

Chapter Twenty-Eight

By the time Canaletto arrived back at Badminton, every muscle in his body ached. If this was what riding was all about, he wondered that any should undertake it for pleasure.

He left his horse in the stables, walked stiffly back to the house and let himself in the side door. In the corridor he came across the young footman who'd been assigned to attend on him. 'Is possible to have hot bath?'

'Of course, sir. Been riding, have you?' the footman asked with a comradely grin. 'I did it once, never again! I'd rather walk. You go upstairs, sir, and I'll bring everything to you.'

It took a little time but eventually a bath was produced together with large jugs of hot water. Canaletto sank into their comforting depths with a sigh of relief.

'You need the waters at Bath,' said the footman, arranging towels conveniently. 'They're a powerful help for all sorts of infirmities.'

'Waters?' Canaletto leaned back and closed his eyes.

'There's hot springs there and folks bathe in them, some of the cures is miraculous, so they say.'

Canaletto remembered what Matthew Butcher had said. 'Baths large?'

'Aye, sir, very large. Many bathe in them together, I hear. One of these days I shall go and see, sounds a powerful entertaining sight, all them men and women disporting themselves.'

All over Europe there were spa towns with mineral waters where cures were sought for a wide range of ailments. There were waters people immersed themselves in, there were waters people drank, Canaletto hoped they were not one and the same.

Later, somewhat refreshed, he finished dressing and stood looking out of his window at the ordered lines of the garden below and his mind went back to the sketch he had showed the duke. James Horton's words reverberated in his head. The fashion now was for less formality, the young man had said, nature would no longer be imposed upon but allowed to inspire graceful vistas. Canaletto thought about this and the continuous programme of works that the duke appeared to be committed to. How long would those ranked lines of trees remain?

Then he went and joined the ducal party for an interminable dinner. It seemed the later part of each day was entirely given over to eating and drinking.

He arrived just as the party moved from the drawing room into the dining room. Canaletto was hastily introduced to two sets of neighbours who had been invited to join the duke and duchess for the meal. As usual, the duke indicated to the men and the duchess to the women where they were to sit. And as usual, the duke waved Charles Sylvester to the position on his right and Norborne Berkeley, his brother-in-law, to his left.

Today, though, the priest had other ideas. 'Sir John

should sit here,' he gestured to one of the neighbours, who immediately demurred. The duke's face darkened as Charles Sylvester insisted on the placement change. 'I shall talk to Signor Canaletto,' he said, moving down the table to sit between the painter and Isaiah. Canaletto was intrigued by the little incident. The only obvious reason for the move was that it gave the priest a better view of Patience Horton at the duchess's end of the table but that hardly seemed to warrant such extraordinary behaviour in refusing the place of honour.

The meal proceeded. Canaletto found the priest monosyllabic if not downright sulky and wondered some more.

After the duchess had removed the ladies, the duke gestured to Canaletto to come and speak with him.

'I have ordered the coroner here today,' he said as the painter hovered by his chair.

'My lord, should we withdraw a little, perhaps?' suggested Canaletto, alarmed that any number of guests were within earshot.

'No need,' the duke said casually. 'All now seem to know that my dear friend met his death in no accidental manner. The duchess asked me about it just before dinner.'

'The duchess?' How had she come to know such a thing?

'She heard it from Mr Cumberledge,' the duke waved his hand in the direction of the young scientist. 'Since there was no longer any need for secrecy, I sent for the constable and the coroner. We shall have the funeral tomorrow. The coffin is ready, my chaplain alerted.'

How had the news of the murder got out? Only Canaletto, Matthew Butcher, and the duke had known. Obviously it wasn't the duke. Matthew Butcher was now back at Bath, which only left himself. And the only person he had told apart from the duke was . . .

Canaletto excused himself with a few words of thanks for the information and went back to his seat. His wine glass had been refilled and he downed most of it in one go. He was seething. How could his apprentice abuse his confidence like this? Now the killer would undoubtedly have been alerted.

Would it also become known that Canaletto had been investigating the scene of the fire at Hinde Court?

'You are upset, I think?' said Charles Sylvester.

Canaletto was surprised. He hadn't thought the young man noticed anything beyond his own concerns, particularly that afternoon.

'It's nothing,' he mumbled.

'I think it is. I hope my lord duke has not cancelled your commission?'

'Indeed, no!' Canaletto was shocked the young man could even think this.

'These aristocrats allow themselves whims,' Charles continued with a note of bitterness. 'They promise one day and retract the next.'

Canaletto forgot about Fanny and the captain's death. 'Indeed,' he said sympathetically. 'I am well acquainted with the, what is you called them, whims? Yes, the whims of the noble and rich. Often commissions promised and not come and when they do, payment usually very slow. Perhaps as priest you find the same?' he suggested encouragingly.

'As a humble petitioner, I have to rely on the good-

will of many. I offer them the fulfilment of a dream.'
Charles waved his glass at a footman for more wine. 'I
offer them the chance to assist heaven to right a deep
wrong.' He sounded a little confused. Or was it because
Canaletto found the language difficult to follow?

'And did my lord duke give you hope he would
assist you?'

Charles raised his recharged glass and finished off
more than half. It was immediately refilled. 'He did
indeed. He, I thought, promised. And then, today, not
two hours ago, he expresses extreme reservation. Suggests my conduct leaves much to be desired. Says that
to me! To me!'

'A man of God as you are,' Canaletto said softly.

Charles looked at him searchingly. 'Indeed, you
say rightly. I am a man of God, his divine right flows
through my veins. And I thought my lord duke recognized this. He has so in the past.' He finished off his
glass yet again and looked around the table. 'This is
a deucedly boring assembly. No jokes, no music, no
ribaldry. Talking of music, the duke has arranged for
a cello to be at my disposal. I shall join the ladies.' So
saying he arose and abruptly left the room.

The duke broke off his conversation with his neighbour and looked at the disappearing back of the priest.
Then he gave a little shake of his head and turned
again to his guest.

Was that how the land lay? Had the duke really
refused his help to Charles Sylvester? If so, would the
man leave Badminton? Or did he still hope to persuade
him?

Canaletto still needed to decide on whether he
should send a message to Paymaster Pitt's agent. But

first Fanny had to be dealt with. Consumed with impatience, Canaletto waited for the duke to break up the party. Charles Sylvester might feel able to leave the room before them, Canaletto did not. He turned to Isaiah. 'I gather, signor, you were able to inform duchess that Captain Farnham died not in accident but was killed?'

Isaiah was morosely cracking nuts and drinking port. 'Why not?' he said belligerently. 'The duchess was lamenting the delay in burying the captain and wondering why the coroner had not pronounced on the matter, such a straightforward accident, however tragic, she said. So I merely told her the matter wasn't as straightforward as she thought.'

'And how you know that?'

Isaiah looked at him in surprise. 'Why, it's no secret, is it? Miss Horton told me this morning.'

Was there anyone who didn't know?

Just as Canaletto was wondering how much longer the drinking and talking were to be spun out, Mr Capper entered and spoke in his master's ear. Immediately the duke rose, apologized to the company, and left the dining room. The constable and the coroner had arrived, Canaletto deduced.

With the duke's departure, the company as one decided the meal was over and left the table.

In the drawing room, Charles Sylvester was playing the cello. Patience Horton accompanied him on the harpsichord in what sounded like a piece by Vivaldi. Both played well.

On a sofa sat Nell Horton with her mother. The sun was low in the sky and the room was suffused with a pearly light that softened the livid colour of the girl's scarring.

The duchess and the two wives of the neighbours sat graciously listening to the music. As did Fanny, who worked on her embroidery

The men clustered in the doorway while the Vivaldi sonata continued. Canaletto thought how much its graceful flourishes suited this most attractive of couples as they bent all their attention to interpreting the composer's intentions. As applause broke out at the end and the cellist warmly congratulated the keyboard player, Canaletto tried to attract Fanny's attention. She saw him and her face broke into an involuntary smile that immediately vanished. He realized that she had not forgotten their dispute. But he was now even angrier with her than he had been that morning.

He beckoned her.

For an incredulous moment, he thought she was going to ignore him, then she rose, sketched a curtsey to the duchess and came and joined him.

'Signor?'

'Fanny, I wish to talk with you,' he said sternly.

Immediately a sparkle appeared in her eyes and he knew she was prepared for a fight.

He didn't care. 'Come with me,' he said and led her to the small room where breakfast was served. There was still sufficient light for them to see each other quite clearly without the benefit of candles.

Canaletto turned and faced her. 'Now, Fanny,' he said.

'Signor?'

'You have told others what I told you this morning.'

For a moment she looked at him without understanding. Then, 'Oh, you mean about Captain Farnham?'

'Yes, about Captain Farnham.'

'But you did not tell me I should not,' she said, bristling.

'I did not think I had to,' he retorted immediately. 'I thought intelligent girl realize I make her, as French say, *confidante* of dangerous information.'

'Dangerous, signor? How could it be dangerous?'

He was incensed by her failure to understand what she had done. 'You alert killer,' he said, spacing out each word.

Fanny stared at him.

'Do you not understand? Before, killer think no one suspect what he did. Death of captain seen as accident. But now he know true facts revealed and that he be hunted.'

'Oh, signor! I am so sorry, I wish you had said something. I didn't think.' Fanny's expression was stricken.

'No, you not think. But why you do this, eh?' Canaletto found that, faced with her distress, the main edge of his ire was blunted. Maybe not much harm had been done. Maybe the killer was so confident no one could discover who he was, he would take no action. Then he remembered how the fire had been started outside Damaris Friend's bedroom and his anger returned. 'Why?' he repeated.

Fanny bridled. 'Why did I speak? Because, signor, you seemed to consider nothing but that the priest we encountered on our way here was the Prince Charles Edward and that he killed, or caused to be killed, the captain. I was sure you were wrong, signor, and so I decided to find out who was responsible.'

She stood and glared at him, her hands resting on her hips, the green silk of her gown and the copper of her hair both aglow in the soft light.

Her words hit Canaletto powerfully. Ever since his visit to Hinde Court that morning, he knew he had made a mistake in suspecting Charles Sylvester. The man, whoever he was, could have had no motive for setting fire to that house.

'And have you discovered anything?' he asked no less sternly than before.

She nodded. 'The captain was having an affair with Damaris Friend, the Horton's cook, Mr Cumberledge said as much. Miss Horton has spoken with her and she admitted all. Miss Horton says Damaris has agreed to speak to you or to me and to tell all about her relationship.'

'She did not tell Miss Horton?'

Fanny shook her head.

'When was this?'

'Why, some little time before dinner, signor.'

'And this cook, she has spoken with you?'

'No, signor.'

'Where is cook?'

'Maybe we should ask Miss Horton,' Fanny suggested. 'But, signor, you do not suggest that she could be harmed, do you?' She sounded alarmed.

'If killer think she has information that could identify him, yes! The fire at Hinde Court, it start outside her bedroom.'

Chapter Twenty-Nine

'Signor!' Fanny sounded thoroughly alarmed. 'This is shocking. We must find her immediately.' She almost ran from the room back to the drawing room.

Canaletto followed. No music now played but Patience hadn't left the harpsichord, she was looking through music with Charles Sylvester, they were laughing together.

Isaiah Cumberledge sat glowering at them. Then he rose and walked out of the room, passing Canaletto without a word.

Fanny went up to Nell and spoke quietly to her. Nell murmured something to her mother then followed Fanny out.

'Signorina,' Canaletto gave her a gracious bow. 'Please, have you seen your servant, Damaris Friend?' It was not an easy name for him to say and he took care over the pronunciation.

'Damaris? Not since this morning. Is something wrong, sir?'

'I hope not. Only, I would speak with her.' He felt Fanny at his elbow, sensed her concern. He was still angry with her but she was his apprentice and partner in this investigation and their foe was dangerous. 'We would speak with her,' he added with a gracious wave of his hand towards Fanny.

'Well, sir,' Nell looked anxious. 'I will find someone to fetch her to you.'

'Please,' said Canaletto. 'Not to speak to other servants about this matter.'

'I shall have to speak to our steward, Thomas Wright, he is in charge of our servants. We are guests in this household, you see.'

As were he and Fanny. It was all a very difficult situation. 'Please, tell your steward you would speak with your cook, nothing else, yes?'

'If that is what you wish, sir.'

'We shall be in breakfast room,' Canaletto told her.

It seemed they had to wait a long time. Hannah came and lit the candles and looked strangely at them. Canaletto offered no explanation as to why they were there.

Fanny walked restlessly up and down the room, pushing the muslin ruffles of her sleeves up above her elbows.

At last Canaletto had to break the silence. 'Have you spent all time at Badminton investigating? Done nothing else?' he asked.

She stopped her pacing. 'I have been drawing, signor.'

'Fetch me drawings. I would see.'

She needed no urging. In less time than he would have thought possible, she returned with her sketchbook.

In silence he studied her sketches. He was impressed both with her draughtsmanship and the

314

power she had managed to get into what were really no more than quick jottings.

'Is very good,' he said. 'Very useful for future paintings, also as exercises. You have good eye.' But it was more than that. 'You see beneath skin. I recognize character in these girls.' He selected one of the several she had made of Hannah. 'This girl, she very involved in her task. She approach all life like that, I think. You make viewer want to meet her.'

She coloured with pleasure.

He fell to studying one of the others. 'This is excellent of cook with apple and knife. She looks intelligent, you found her so?'

Fanny nodded. 'Very, signor.' She glanced at the door uneasily. 'Miss Horton takes a long time finding her.'

Canaletto realized that it was quite dark outside now. He began to get anxious. All the indications were that the fire at Hinde Court had been intended to reduce Damaris along with her bedroom to ashes. It had failed. He didn't know why the cook was the target of such evil intent but Humphrey Farnham had been killed soon afterwards with fire used again to try to conceal the killing. Perhaps most pertinent of all, this woman and Humphrey Farnham had been lovers.

'I think cook have key to killer,' Canaletto told Fanny. 'And killer must despatch her soon, before she realize what she know.'

Fanny collapsed into a chair and hid her face in her hands. 'And I've put her in this danger,' she groaned.

Canaletto sat down beside her and took her hand. 'I, too, to blame,' he said in a constricted voice. 'Better if Fanny and I talk more, not get angry with each other.'

The door to the breakfast room opened and Nell stood there, her face deeply worried. 'No one has seen Damaris since I spoke to her before dinner.'

Both Canaletto and Fanny rose. Fanny's expression was stark.

'Maybe this does not mean anything sinister,' Nell said, coming into the room. 'Damaris,' she swallowed hard then continued, her face a little flushed, the scars no longer standing out quite so strongly against her pale skin. 'Damaris is one of those women who enjoys men. I know she didn't like working with the chief cook here, and perhaps she has gone to some man.'

Canaletto wanted to believe this.

'Signor Canale, while I have been looking for Damaris, I have also been thinking about what you told me about the fire at my home, Hinde Court. It could be that you are right and it was no accident. But maybe it was not aimed at Damaris but at the Horton family.'

'You mean by Walter Cary?' suggested Canaletto.

'You have heard about the trouble he is causing?'

'I hear your brother think he start fire because he want to move village.'

Nell drew out one of the chairs from the breakfast table and sat down. She put her hands on the cloth and studied them as she spoke. 'There is another reason why the Cary family should feel resentful towards the Hortons. When we first came here, I was very interested in scientific research. For some time my sister and I had shared a tutor with my brother, James. Mr Woollard was a member of the Royal Scientific Society and he awoke my interest. My brother, I regret to say, was bored by such matters, as, more naturally, was my sister. My father was amused at my interest. Then, after he heard that the Duchess of Newcastle in the last century had written a number of scientific volumes, he positively encouraged me. He placed a small room in our London house at my disposal and Mr Woollard and I would conduct experiments in the discovery of various properties. When we came down here, I wished to continue these.'

Nell's hand started to brush the heavy, woven cloth that was covered each morning with white damask. 'We met Mr Cumberledge and he told me of a boy he was teaching at the village school who was unexpectedly intelligent. I thought it would be a Christian action to assist his education and gave him additional lessons when his father could spare him from the fields. This was Barnaby. You have perhaps met him?'

Canaletto nodded.

'Barnaby is indeed intelligent and learns very quickly. Soon he was helping me in my scientific investigations. One day,' the flush deepened further. 'One day we had discussed the explosive qualities produced by mixing nitric acid with alcohol. I mentioned that a mixture of sal ammoniac and sulphuric acid could also produce the sort of expansion that would result in an explosion and that I was thinking of designing an experiment involving these media, both of which were available in my laboratory. In the middle of our discussion, I had to leave the room. To the end of my days, I will regret that I had not impressed upon him the dangers inherent in any such experiment, how violent the reaction could be.' Nell's face contorted into a painful grimace. 'When I returned, he was holding a glass vessel with a stopper in its neck and told me he was proving my theory. To my horror, I saw the containers of sal ammoniac and sulphuric acid on the work table and realized that he must have added one to the other. Even worse, I saw the quantities he had used. In any moment the chemicals would start reacting together and produce an explosion of damaging proportions. I tried to tell him to put the vessel carefully on the table and leave the room but even as I spoke, he turned it upside down and shook it! The vessel exploded with such force the liquid hit the ceiling. Both of us suffered flying glass and splashes of acid. Luckily I had instinctively turned my face away and only one side suffered. But Barnaby was flung into the fire and also lost the use of his left arm.'

As she said this, very calmly, the candlelight fell full on the left side of her face, leaving the other side in shadow. Without the compensating softness and charm of her right profile, she looked monstrous.

'Barnaby is no longer of much use to his father. My father gave some small compensation to the family but held that the boy was responsible for the loss of my beauty, such as it was. He said if Barnaby had only waited for proper instruction, both of us would still be whole. My father, though, makes things too simple. He can't see that it was because I left Barnaby excited about the possibilities of the experiment without explaining the dangers, that the accident occurred. We had conducted other experiments that entailed mixing liquids in a glass vessel, some of them with volatile reactions, but nothing so explosive. He was a boy full of curiosity who hadn't been educated as I have. He trusted me and I betrayed that trust.' Again that calmness of delivery.

Canaletto was intrigued by the girl. Great intelligence and great control. What might she not have done had she been born a man!

'Now my father wants to move all the villagers' houses to another, less salubrious part of the estate, so that the approach to our house can be grand. Walter Cary resents this. Indeed, I would resent it. I did not know of this plan until Captain Farnham came and told me the day before you found his body. Then I was deeply shocked. I have spoken with my brother but he is concerned only to fulfil what he says are my father's wishes. So, you see there are two very compelling reasons for Walter Cary to want to burn down our house.'

The hand that had been sweeping the tablecloth was still.

'It is a terrible story,' breathed Fanny. 'Miss Horton, I feel for you. But, one thing I do not understand,' she hesitated for a moment and looked at Nell. The girl looked back at her, waiting. Fanny plunged on. 'I do not understand how it is that Lady Tanquoray can fall out with her nephew over the practice of science and yet remain on good terms with you when you follow the same calling.'

'It is quite simple,' said Nell with a wry look. 'She considers that God has punished me for my blasphemy and that I have learned my lesson. I am afraid she will have a shock when I manage to resume my scientific studies.'

'You will conduct further experiments?' Fanny sounded amazed.

'Oh, yes. If the pain and suffering I and Barnaby have endured is to have any justification, it will be through learning more about the laws of science that underlie all we see around us.'

Canaletto listened with great interest but he also had a question. 'You give good reason why father of Barnaby have resentment against your family. But why he want to kill captain? You say captain tell you of plan to move houses of villagers, the captain surely ally of Cary.'

She smiled painfully. This was something she had obviously thought about. Canaletto doubted there was anything this girl didn't think about. 'I think the captain came in the middle of the night to see Damaris. That was why she was awake when the fire started, she was waiting for him. Perhaps she intended to go downstairs and meet him when we were all asleep. Captain Farnham discovered Walter Cary setting the fire and challenged him. Walter would have had a weapon with him, perhaps a knife. He killed the captain, hid his body and later took it on a cart or some such transport to the pavilion, which he set on fire.'

She made it sound very plausible.

'I think you have given me much matter to think on, Signorina Horton,' Canaletto said.

Nell remained seated. 'Signor Canale,' she said. 'Can you tell me anything of this Charles Sylvester, this priest who does not wear priestly garments and who my sister says has told her he will not be a priest much longer.'

Canaletto let out a long sigh. Fanny looked at him but said nothing.

'We only meet him few days ago. I know nothing of him but duke seem to value his acquaintance.' Even as he said this, Canaletto remembered the duke's expression of disgust as he saw Charles Sylvester laughing so intimately with Patience Horton as they rode towards Badminton.

'Indeed, that is the one aspect of the situation that gives me any comfort. I think that, as a fine observer of life, you will have noticed that my sister seems to enjoy his company.' Canaletto nodded gravely.

'He is a very attractive person,' Fanny interposed. 'I am sure your sister enjoys talking with him.'

'That is my worry,' Nell said in a frank manner to Fanny. 'My mother is much concerned with my young brother and has left looking after my sister to me but I, too, have spent most of my time with Jack. It is only today that I have been aware,' she brought her hands together in her lap and looked down at them before glancing up again at Canaletto, her eyes wide and frank. 'That her liking for this man might go beyond partiality.'

That jolted Canaletto. He had thought the girl was playing with the man. Now this dauntingly intelligent girl was suggesting that the situation could be more serious.

Canaletto made up his mind. Action had to be taken to prevent further disaster at Badminton.

Chapter Thirty

The next day brought the funeral of Captain Humphrey Farnham. Fanny found it a curious experience. Part of her felt detached from everything that happened and unable to concentrate on anything but her fatal quarrel with Canaletto and the fact that Damaris Friend was still missing. But another part of her mind noted every aspect of the congregation.

The duke looked very sad and lost in thought. The duchess, the soul of dignity, sat between her brother and her husband, glancing neither to right nor left.

Lady Tanqueray was there with more feathers in her sweeping black hat than any bird could have comfortably worn and with paint even thicker than usual. Her expression was impossible to judge.

Isaiah Cumberledge, even for him, was untidily dressed and sat as though unaware of the service.

The Horton family sat together, Lady Horton constantly dabbing her eyes with a handkerchief, Nell staring stonily ahead. Patience sneaked little glances at Charles Sylvester, who sat on the other side of the church, soberly dressed though not in his soutane. Occasionally he would send her an intimate smile.

When everyone gathered round the newly dug grave, James Horton stood absent-mindedly clicking his fingers as though waiting for the event to be over as soon as possible.

It was another lovely day. Fanny thought funerals should always take place under grey skies. Rain should suggest that heaven added its tears to those of the mourners. But heaven refused to tone its splendour to the sorrow of the occasion.

After the burial, the company drifted towards the house. It had been announced that a small nuncheon awaited inside but no one seemed anxious to leave the sun. It was as though not their bodies but their souls wanted warming through after the solemnity and sadness of the interment.

Despite the sun and the warmth, Fanny suffered a black depression.

Earlier that morning, the first thing Hannah had commented upon when she brought Fanny her hot water was that the Horton servant Damaris Friend was missing.

'They all say she's no better than she should be and wonder why such a loose woman should be cook in such a respectable household.' Hannah hesitated a moment. 'At least, my sister says it's respectable. Even my mother, and you know what happened to Barnaby, well, even my mother says that, considering it's a commercial family, not landed gentry, like, they behave themselves extremely well. And, having worked at Badminton, she should know.'

Hannah drew breath while she poured the hot water into the porcelain bowl that sat in its stand. Fanny sat in bed and felt all the misery of the previous evening run through her.

'Hannah, is your father a violent man?' The words came out before she could stop them.

The water splashed on to the polished floor. 'What a question to ask, miss!' Hannah made a great business of mopping up the water before it could ruin the polish, using one of the towels from the stand. 'Why should you ask such a thing, that's what I want to know?' the girl looked at Fanny, her gaze belligerent.

Fanny wondered herself. It was hardly the way to get the information she wanted. 'Just a rumour I heard, Hannah. I'm sorry, I shouldn't have come out with it like that. It's just that I have seen so much violence over the years and know what misery it can bring.' It wasn't exactly a lie, anyone who lived in London saw violence at every turn, but she had deliberately made it sound more personal than she really had a right to.

Hannah adjusted the hang of the remaining towels, smoothing the fine linen. 'Dad's no more violent than any other man. Unless someone crosses him, then he's more likely to go in with his fists than try and right it with words. That's men for you, isn't it?' she added. 'At least, that's what my mother says. She's always at Dad to watch himself. Right, that be all, miss? Only I've got to get about, ever such a lot to do with so many in the house and all.'

And she was gone, leaving Fanny thinking about a father who lashed out with fists. But, as Hannah had said, so did many men. Fanny remembered Richard Wiggan, their London landlord. Now there was a chap who valued the merit of a cuff round the ear rather than a verbal warning.

The fact that Damaris had still not appeared made the day seem dark and threatening. Many a time after

Hannah left, Fanny's mind started to replay what had passed between Canaletto and herself after Nell Horton had left the breakfast room, only for her to force it to veer away again.

As soon as Nell Horton had left the room, Canaletto had said, 'I do not trust her account.'

Fanny was astonished. 'What do you mean, signor, she was honest, I would swear.'

Canaletto stood drumming his fingers on the table. 'She stroke this cloth again and again. She not look at me. To me this sign she not telling truth.'

Fanny had tried to control her rising anger. She could not afford another fight with Canaletto. 'Signor,' she said calmly, holding her hands tightly together in front of her. 'Why should she lie?'

'Perhaps two reasons. One, she feel guilt because her cook disappear, perhaps permanently.'

Fanny drew in a quick breath. 'Do you mean Damaris could have been killed, murdered, signor? Oh, please do not say so.'

'If she produce reason why someone set fire to house that has no connection with this cook, then she feel better. After all, did not you say that Miss Horton tell Isaiah about fire and that captain murdered? He then tell others. If you feel guilty,' he looked searchingly at Fanny, 'so may she.'

Yes, Fanny felt guilty and she could imagine that Nell Horton might also feel so. She heard again the girl tell Isaiah that the captain's death had not been an accident.

'Second reason,' Canaletto continued. 'Maybe this lady involved in captain's death.'

Fanny was so startled that for a moment she

couldn't speak. Then she said forcefully. 'Signor, this is not possible.'

'Maybe she in love with captain. Maybe she see cook with captain. She feel betrayed by both.'

'So she sticks a knife into the captain and starts a fire at her home?' Fanny said scornfully. 'Signor I am sure Nell Horton is resourceful but what you are suggesting is ridiculous.'

'Is it?' Canaletto looked thoughtful. 'Signorina Horton is young, strong, active. Did you see her hand and lower arm? It is, do you say muscled? Used to action. If she write as cook, arrange to meet captain in pavilion, not difficult to stab him or to start fire later.'

'And the fire at Hinde Court?' Fanny asked warily. There was, she realized, a terrible logic behind what he was suggesting. She could imagine a certain woman fired up with vengeance because the man she was in love with preferred someone else. So vengeful that she could want both of them dead.

Canaletto shrugged. 'More difficult but not impossible. She has admitted she experiments in the sciences, including explosions. She is intelligent, understands what fire can do. She set it beside cook's bedroom. She not want to burn entire house, not before family gets out.'

'Signor, I can see that a particular sort of woman might well do what you are suggesting but not, I am sure, Nell Horton.'

'How can you be so sure?'

Yes, how could she be? 'Signor, I study people to paint them,' she started. 'I have been commissioned to paint this girl . . .'

326

'A commission you refuse,' Canaletto said grimly.

'Yes, signor. But I am still very interested in her. She tends her brother most caringly. She cares for her sister. She is respectful to her mother, who seems not at all noticing about any of her family. She talks very comfortably with Mr Cumberledge. Her father talked of her true beauty. Signor, this is not a woman who would kill to be revenged on someone who did not love her.' If she had left it there, all might have been well but some wicked devil prompted her to add. 'I try to look below the surface of people for my painting, it's not like capturing the likeness of a building.'

Canaletto thumped a fist down on the table. 'You dare to demean my art! You say you have good understanding of people but did you have good understanding last year?'

If she had gone too far, so had he! The tragedy of last year was with her still. How dare he refer to it in such terms?

'I talk no further with you this evening, go!' Canaletto ended.

And Fanny had gone. She had been so angry, both with herself and with him. How could she have handled the matter so badly? Yet how could he put forward such a ridiculous theory and then speak to her in such a way!

Isaiah Cumberledge came up to her and she wrenched her mind back to the present and the captain's funeral. 'I have just had a long conversation with your signor.'

'Is that why you look exhausted?' His face was

drawn, very unlike the lively visage Fanny was used to seeing.

'If the Spanish Inquisition had been questioning me, they couldn't have done a better job.'

Fanny was both alarmed and encouraged. Did this mean that Canaletto had discarded his theory that Nell Horton could have killed the captain? Had he picked up her initial suggestion that Isaiah had a motive for Humphrey Farnham's death? Or, even worse, did he imagine that Nell had enlisted him as her accomplice? 'Mr Cumberledge, what can he have questioned you on?'

'It was nothing,' Isaiah said hastily. 'I make too much of it, I know. It was just he wished to know what I could tell him of Humphrey Farnham.'

'You were friends, were you not?'

'We lived together in this house for a couple of months or more. But friends? Who could ever know Humphrey?' His shoulders moved restlessly in the way they had. His coat was extremely loose fitting, could it be a hand-me-down from someone larger than himself? Fanny realized that nothing about Isaiah suggested wealth. If she'd met him on the streets of London and not in the splendour of Badminton House, she would have assumed he was an educated young man struggling to make a living. Maybe he was in desperate need of funds.

'When I first met you together at breakfast, I had the impression you were friends,' Fanny said.

'Oh, we dealt together well enough. But it was impossible to tell what Humphrey really thought or meant.'

'That, my dear nephew, is what made him

interesting,' Lady Tanqueray's dry voice broke in. 'As you know, I abhor this modern tendency to analyse and describe every facet of nature and life but Humphrey and I would spend hours arguing over such matters. Did he believe what he propounded? I never knew and I didn't care.' The sun lit up with remorseless cruelty the cracks in her paint but the bright eyes looked at her nephew with lively scorn. 'You wouldn't know anything about that, of course, Isaiah. All you were worried about was whether I was to marry the man or no. And that was only because my fortune would have passed from your grasp.'

'Aunt!' Isaiah gasped. 'Never say that. Your money does not interest me.'

'Say you so?' She gave him a long, assessing look. 'How much I could wish that was the fact.'

'Believe it, Aunt,' he said, fixing her with an impassioned gaze. 'Sign away your estate to the parish if you will, it will not trouble me.'

'I have to doubt that,' she said dryly. 'Maybe, though, we should talk. Call upon me.' She rapped him on the shoulder with a closed fan and moved away to talk to the duchess.

Isaiah's face was a complex mixture of emotions as he made a bow to her retreating back. Then it lit up as he saw Patience Horton. With no more than a muttered, 'Will you excuse me,' he was off to her side.

Canaletto came up. 'This morning I talk with Bob, footman, who attends me and also Charles Sylvester,' he said as though the argument last night had never happened. 'He close friend with Hannah who has sister works at Hinde Court.'

Fanny nodded.

'Bob say Cumberledge,' he nodded towards Isaiah. 'He wish pay addresses to young sister of Miss 'Orton.'

Fanny looked over at Isaiah, now gazing at Patience in a particularly moonstruck way as she talked in a lively manner.

'Young man not have money,' went on Canaletto. 'Sir Robert Horton very, very rich man.'

'I don't think it's her money he's in love with,' said Fanny.

'Good, because Sir Robert not give dowry to younger daughters till Miss 'Orton herself is married.'

'Oh, signor! It will take a very special man to attract Nell Horton.'

'She not take man who is interested in her money, then, you think?'

'No, signor, I am sure she would not.'

'So it may be long time before other daughter can have dowry. And the captain paid court to young man's aunt who also has much money,' Canaletto went on.

'Signor, Isaiah Cumberledge has just told his aunt he isn't interested in her money, he's going to make his own way in the world. Perhaps he isn't interested in a dowry for Patience Horton either.'

'Hmmm,' murmured Canaletto, studying the young couple who now, to Patience's obvious delight, had been joined by Charles Sylvester. 'Very easy say not care about money. But Sir Robert, I think, not give daughter to someone with none.'

'If he was satisfied his daughter cared for the man and the man was in a position to look after her as he would wish, then he might,' Thomas Wright said. The steward had come up unnoticed. 'I trust I do not intrude by saying this, sir.'

Fanny was surprised at the interruption. She had seen the steward around Badminton but hadn't had conversation with him before. He seemed to have met Canaletto, though. She thought he had an open face that, whilst not particularly handsome, was attractive.

'And will Sir Robert accept Mr Cumberledge as suitor for daughter?' asked Canaletto.

'That, sir, you must ask Sir Robert.'

'Most interesting visit to Hinde Court yesterday, signor. The fire there very tragic for building, I think.'

The steward inclined his head in agreement.

'Much drama that night. Very difficult get all people out of burning house?'

'Once all were woken, no, sir.'

'Very fortunate cook not asleep,' Canaletto continued. 'Have you seen her today?'

Thomas Wright shook his head. 'No, sir. The girl is unreliable and so I have told Lady Horton. I fear that when she reappears it will be to find she has lost her job.'

Fanny's heart sank. It looked more and more as though Damaris Friend would not reappear in this life. It would be her fault when her body was discovered. She looked around her. All those trees, all that country. How could anyone find a body if it were hidden in some ditch or out of the way place?

A servant came out of the house with a letter on a silver tray. Fanny expected him to take it to the duke, instead it was delivered to Charles Sylvester.

The young man looked surprised but took the piece of paper, excused himself to his companions, broke the seal and read the message. For a moment he stood motionless, the sun shining down on his well-powdered wig, his face extremely thoughtful. Then he thrust the letter into a pocket of his well-cut coat and returned to his companions, smiling his bright, attractive smile.

Mr Briggs, the butler, started to move everyone inside for the light nuncheon that had been prepared. 'The funeral bakemeats,' said Thomas Wright. 'Not for me, though. I will take my leave of you, Mistress Rooker and Signor Canale.' He sketched a bow and withdrew.

'Very interesting,' said Canaletto, looking after him thoughtfully.

Fanny would like to have followed this up but Nell Horton approached her. 'Good morning, Miss Rooker. What a sad day this is.'

Fanny nodded, wondering whether she was referring solely to the captain's funeral or whether she was including the fact that the cook was still missing.

'My little brother is very keen to have you sketch for him again,' Nell added.

'How is he?' Fanny asked.

'Thank you, he gets better and better. We expect Doctor Butcher again tomorrow but I am sure he will soon be completely recovered.'

The informal repast consisted of savoury pastries and fruit. Soon Fanny took herself upstairs and spent some time entertaining young Jack with sketching and playing various games. His little brother and sister were also there, climbing on the bed, jumping off and generally making a great deal of noise. None of which seemed to trouble Jack.

For a little while Fanny almost forgot her troubles.

She changed for dinner, for once without the help of Hannah. No message arrived to say why the maid hadn't appeared and Fanny wondered if her crude questioning of her that morning had stopped her coming. She had enjoyed the girl's company more than her ministrations and it was almost a relief not to have to submit to her help. She dragged a comb through her curls and added a little lace cap. She hoped that today the meal would not drag out too long. The amount of time that could be spent eating and drinking and talking had been a revelation to her.

Nor did she find the conversation that day particularly interesting. Stories of people she had never heard of, discussions on subjects she knew nothing about. At the male end of the table, talk centred on the duke's intention of hunting the next day. 'Charles,' Fanny heard him say jovially at one point. 'You will enjoy a chase after the buck, we shall have excellent sport.'

Charles Sylvester laughed and said there was nothing he would like more.

'I wonder that the duke promotes such sport the day after his old friend's funeral,' said Lady Tanqueray, who had remained at Badminton for the main meal of the day.

'He does it to please Mr Sylvester,' the duchess said.

Lady Tanqueray did not look much impressed.

'You do not eat much,' said Nell Horton to Fanny. It was the first time the girl had joined the company for dinner. In a dress of plain, bronze-coloured silk, her dark hair simply dressed, she looked elegant and poised. Fanny had been delighted to find herself sitting next to her.

'Do all the gentry consume so much food, Miss Horton?'

Nell's face broke into a smile. 'It passes time as well as providing nourishment. My mother delights in serving as many different dishes as possible. As I told you, we had such difficulties with cooks until Damaris appeared. Then eating became a pleasure. Is it not so for you?'

Fanny looked down at her plate. 'I chose fish as I thought it would be light but the cucumber cream sauce is very rich.'

'I sympathize. Many is the time I would prefer some bread and cheese, eaten whilst reading or conducting one of my scientific experiments.'

'But the dish is delicious.' Fanny didn't want to seem unappreciative of what had been offered her.

'As soon as we are returned to Hinde House, you must come and eat a meal that Damaris has prepared. She has a way with food that you will enjoy.'

'I would love to eat of her cooking.'

Nell looked at her closely. 'I am sure she will return to us soon. Or send word.'

'Send word? Do you think she has left your service?' Fanny was surprised at this suggestion. 'Have any of her things gone with her?'

'All her things were burned in the fire, here she has been dressed in other people's cast-offs. Not that she ever had much, she says possessions weigh one down.'

Later, as Fanny prepared for bed after another evening of music, she wondered about that. She had very few personal possessions herself and most of those were the tools of her profession.

It was an extraordinary experience to be staying in a house filled with so many desirable items. When she was back in the studio with her narrow little bed and the small chest that held everything she owned, would she feel deprived?

No, Fanny decided, she would not. She was ambitious but not for riches, she wanted to attract commissions and receive the recognition of her peers. But she could see that for some the sight of Badminton and its treasures would be bitter. Would such a person kill to gain riches?

Chapter Thirty-One

The next morning Hannah was late bringing Fanny her water.

'Such a bustle there is, miss. What with the duke wanting the hunt to start early, we've been taking water everywhere.' She spoke shortly and seemed disinclined to linger. Nor had she apologized for not helping Fanny dress the previous evening.

The easy camaraderie that had existed between them had gone.

'Hannah, I'm exceedingly sorry if anything I said yesterday has upset you,' Fanny said earnestly, sitting up in bed and hugging her knees.

'Lawks, miss, nothing you say could upset me. I'm not the sort of person who gets upset.' And Hannah was gone with a whisk of her skirts.

Sighing, Fanny rose and started to wash herself. Her window was open and from the stables she could hear hooves clattering on the cobbles and voices shouting as grooms worked with the horses, saddling them and putting on harnesses. There was an air of urgency in the sounds and Fanny found herself putting on her clothes with more than usual speed.

She passed the duke in shirtsleeves and waistcoat coming out of the breakfast room, rubbing his hands in a high good humour. 'Fine day for the hunt,' he told her. 'Not as warm as it has been.'

A small boy rushed up. 'I shall hunt too, Father, shan't I?'

His father laughed indulgently. 'Your pony is being saddled right now, young man. You shall start with us.'

With a whoop of delight, the boy was off again.

'I look forward to Signor Canale solving the mystery of my dear friend's death,' said the duke as he went on his way.

Fanny entered the breakfast room wondering where Canaletto now was in his hunt for the captain's killer.

Isaiah was the only other person at the breakfast table. He rose to acknowledge her presence.

She bid him a cheerful good morning and asked if Signor Canale had already broken his fast.

'I have not seen the signor so far today.' Nothing about Isaiah that morning suggested he was ready for conversation. When Fanny asked him if he would be hunting with the duke, he said, 'Go chase an animal that merely wishes to live its life undisturbed by the baser side of human nature? I think not.'

Not a promising start. But Fanny was determined to take this opportunity of extracting information from him. 'Did the captain hunt?'

'Humphrey? It was not a matter we discussed.'

'I gather from Lady Tanqueray that he was a great conversationalist, did you enjoy talking with him?'

Isaiah stopped eating and looked full at her. 'Humphrey Farnham may well have entertained my aunt with his wit and intelligence. I found him cantankerous, interfering and someone who thought of no one but himself.'

Well, that was frank.

But Isaiah had not finished. 'I'm sorry if you are one of those who think the dead should be wreathed in sentimental recollections. I prefer to say things as I see them.'

'I only know the captain through what others say of him.'

'Then I expect you have a patchwork doll, a figure cobbled together from different parts.'

'Was he, do you think, bitter because of his wound?'

Isaiah gave a short laugh. 'He said he had seen too much of the unpleasant side of human nature to let others profit while he tried to scrape a living. If there was advantage to be taken, he would take it.'

'Such as your aunt and her fortune?'

'Exactly.'

'But I understand you do not want her money for yourself?'

Isaiah gave a laugh that sounded genuinely amused. 'Do you learn interrogation techniques from your master as well as how to paint?' He finished his meat and placed knife and fork neatly together. 'I am sorry to deprive your curiosity but I must be about my business. Good day to you, Mistress Rooker.'

After he'd left, Fanny ate her sweet roll and drank the coffee she was beginning to find delicious, then went to try to find Canaletto.

Nobody had seen him. Finally she went up towards the Chinese room in case he had returned there to work on his view.

Suddenly the door to the Chinese room opened and

out came a slight man of middle height looking very flustered. 'Do you have business with my master?' he asked.

'With Father Sylvester? No, indeed, I am looking for Signor Canale. I am Fanny Rooker, his apprentice.'

'And I am Morrison, manservant to Father Sylvester.'

Fanny stared at him. 'To Father Sylvester? But he has been here days without an attendant. Have you just been taken on or did you lose him?'

Morrison's expressionless face stared back at her. 'I have attended Father Sylvester for a number of years, miss. We got parted, as you might say, but I caught up with him last night. You have not, I suppose, seen Father Sylvester this morning?'

Fanny shook her head.

'And I regret I have not met with your master. The hunt is gathering, perhaps he is in the park.' Mr Morrison walked away in the direction of the stairs.

The hunt! Fanny ran to the landing window. On the grass were a considerable number of sleek horses ridden by men in dark blue coats with buff collars. The duke, similarly dressed and mounted, was moving amongst them and a couple of footmen were passing round charged glasses. The previous day's funeral appeared to have been forgotten. Death had been dealt with, life continued and what a colourful subject was here for a painter's pen.

Turning to go and collect her sketching things, Fanny looked again at the door to the Chinese room. There had been something very shifty about that servant. A little nervously she tapped on the door.

Receiving no answer, she gently opened it and glanced inside. It looked exactly the same as when she had first seen it, the coverlet smooth on the bed, no sign of any occupant.

She closed the door behind her, thinking hard, then went to her room. Armed with sketchbook and chalks, she headed for the stairs. There she met Matthew Butcher. 'Why, doctor, how nice to see you again,' she said.

'And delightful it is to see you,' he smiled at her. 'Almost makes it worth the ride here. A duke's patronage is all very well but the price in inconvenience is high.'

'You would rather tend only those on your doorstep and leave the rich and highly born to fend for themselves?' Fanny laughed at him.

'Enough of that, young lady! If your limbs were as old as mine, you, too, would resent hours in the saddle.'

'Indeed, sir, you must have started early to be here at this time.'

'Early enough,' he agreed. 'Now I must see my patient. I hope he will be well enough that I can discharge him and save myself any more journeys up those infernal hills.'

'Can you spend a little time with us before you have to return?'

He lightly caressed her cheek with the knuckle of his forefinger. 'The prospect of your sunny smiles and engaging conversation have been all that's been keeping me company on the long ride here.'

'You can keep such talk to yourself,' Fanny told him, laughing. Matthew always made her feel more cheerful. 'Go on up to your patient, Miss Horton is having a hard time keeping him abed.'

He moved past her, then stopped and turned back. 'Bless me, if I didn't nearly forget and she so insistent that I deliver her message the moment I arrived.' He put down his medical case and felt about the pockets of his coat. 'Ah, here we are.' He handed over a slip of paper to Fanny. In a large, curving hand, it bore the inscription: 'Fanny Rooker, Badminton House'. It had been neatly folded together and didn't bear a seal.

'I was strictly instructed to give it into no hands but your own. She said her life could depend upon it.'

'Her life?' Fanny looked up at him. 'Who gave it to you?'

'Very strange, it was the young woman your master and I found in the church beside that military body he had asked me to examine and who was then met at the young lad's bedside.'

Hope flared in Fanny. 'You mean Damaris Friend?'

'Is that her name? Whatever it was, she came across me in the hospital in Bath yesterday, apparently looking for a job. I was able to put in a word for her, then she asked if I was going to Badminton again. I told her, yes, and she begged writing implements then gave me that note for you. Also I was not to mention meeting her to anybody else.' He paused. 'She is a most unusual looking woman,' he added.

Fanny hardly heard him. She was reading the message. *If you would hear what I can tell, come to the King's Bath and ask for Dolly Fry.* TELL NO ONE. *It was signed: Your Friend.*

Damaris Friend was not lying dead under some undergrowth or in a ditch. She was alive and in Bath. Almost as important was the fact that she wanted to see Fanny to tell her everything she knew about the death of Captain Farnham.

How much was that?

'What are the baths she talks about?' she asked Matthew, showing him the note.

'They are medicinal waters in which sufferers bathe each day.'

'Do you know where they are?'

He was amused. 'Yes, indeed, everyone in Bath knows them.'

'I must go there, can you take me?' Fanny demanded urgently.

'Take you to Bath?'

'Yes, it is vital.' She took back the note. 'And also vital that no one else knows.'

Matthew looked grave. 'How am I to get you there?'

Fanny was nonplussed. It had never occurred to her that this could be a problem.

'Do you ride?'

She shook her head.

Matthew pushed a finger beneath his wig and scratched his head. 'You know I'll always help you when I can, Fanny, but what are we to do? I can hardly ask the duke for the loan of a carriage!'

'Can't you take me up behind you on your horse?'

'How will you get back here afterwards?'

Fanny shrugged. 'There will be some way. If there isn't a stage, maybe a carter will be coming in this direction, or I can hire some sort of conveyance.'

He sighed. 'If that's your only option, I suppose it will do. But we won't be able to ride fast.' He looked her over. 'Still, you are not much of a weight and he's a sturdy enough animal. You'd better tell Signor Canale what you're doing.'

'No, I can't!'

Matthew put a hand on her shoulder in a fatherly fashion. 'Fanny, as I said, I'm willing to help you all I can but I cannot whisk you away from here without your master knowing what is happening. What would he think? After all, you are his apprentice.'

As if she could forget!

She looked up at Matthew's serious face. He meant what he'd said.

'I will leave him a note,' she said finally. 'I will tell him I have gone to Bath with you to meet this woman.' That would tell him everything – and nothing.

'Well then, I'll meet you in the stables after I have seen my patient.'

She nodded. 'Please don't be long, we must go as soon as possible.'

'I have to be satisfied with my patient's progress, and his mother's.'

Fanny sighed but could do nothing else.

She returned to her room, wrote a brief note for Canaletto and decided she would give it to one of the servants to hand to him at a convenient moment. She would say there was no urgency about it. Then she looked out her little store of money and sorted out a change of linen in case she was detained overnight and tied it up in a large kerchief.

As she went downstairs again, she was filled with excitement. This was her chance to make up for her

343

stupidity in revealing the fact that Captain Farnham had been murdered. She could hardly wait to hear what Damaris Friend had to tell her. Surely it would reveal who had killed the captain.

Chapter Thirty-Two

Canaletto had risen early. Much of the night had been spent tossing and turning.

There had been something quite odd about the tale Miss Horton had told. Canaletto could well understand that Walter Cary might want to hit back at a family that had done so much injury to his but why kill the captain as well? Unless, as the girl had suggested, Farnham had come across him setting fire to the house. But why transport the body such a distance? From the little Canaletto had seen of Cary, he was much more likely to cast an inconvenient body into a ditch.

Fanny's comment that his eye was that of a vedute artist rather than a portraitist's had been a cruel thrust. Was there some truth in it, though? Was he concentrating too hard on the evidence that he could see and ignoring the character of the personalities involved?

And what about Isaiah Cumberledge? Could the young man, after all, be involved?

Some time after dawn, he became convinced there was only one way forward and that was to go and talk to Walter and Betsy Cary.

So he abandoned his tossing, arose and went downstairs.

The breakfast room was empty with no food in

sight. Canaletto found his way to the kitchen. There the air was full of the fragrant smell of bread. A youngster was taking rolls out of the oven and already lined up on the huge table in the centre of the room were freshly baked loaves. Canaletto's mouth filled with saliva, he wanted one of those rolls spread with butter and loaded with a slice of ham. Then he would be ready for the day.

It took no more than a couple of minutes persuasion before the young baker went to a large larder and fetched a cooked ham. Canaletto followed him and through the open door spied wide marble shelves laden with comestibles. Outside, he knew, was a game larder, a stew-pond with fresh fish and a dovecote to provide a source of pigeons.

He left the kitchen clutching a cloth holding his breakfast and wondering about the largesse available. There must be some sort of check kept on all this provender. Would it be by Mr Capper, the steward?

At the back of Canaletto's mind something nagged. Fanny had told him something, something he hadn't paid much attention to at the time because he'd been too involved with the question of whether Charles Sylvester had caused the death of Captain Farnham.

He failed to bring the detail to mind and finally dismissed it. Memory would produce it later in the curious way it sometimes did. In the meantime, he set out for the stables, where the grooms were already getting the mounts ready for the hunt.

Much as Canaletto would have preferred not to submit his aching joints to another assault by horseback, he knew it would be so much quicker if he rode to Hinde village instead of walking and time could be important.

Getting a groom to prepare the quiet mount he'd previously ridden was not as easy as obtaining his breakfast but a word to the effect that the duke wished him to perform a service provided the magic key and soon he was nervously on his way.

With his excellent eye for topography, he found his way unerringly. He jogged gently along, munching on his bread and ham, and realized that his muscles didn't ache as much as he expected. Just before he got there, Canaletto suddenly recalled that James Horton had ordered the Carys off his property a couple of days earlier. Would he be able to find where they'd gone? Then he remembered the look that had passed between Betsy Cary and Thomas Wright, the steward. Maybe he hadn't turned them off yet.

Arriving at Hinde, he slipped down from his horse and found a convenient railing to hitch the reins to.

He was relieved to see signs of occupation at the Cary cottage. Barnaby opened the door to his knock, the scarred face splitting into a grin as the boy saw who it was. Behind him crowded several younger children. 'Mother's milking,' he said after Canaletto asked to speak to her.

Canaletto needed to talk to Barnaby but not surrounded by inquisitive children. He asked for directions to the byre and found Betsy Cary on a small stool, her head close against the side of a golden brown animal, her hands pulling rhythmically at its udders, creamy milk splashing into a wooden pail. Other animals stood waiting for their turn, their breath making the atmosphere warm and fecund.

'Yes?' she said, never pausing her milking.

Canaletto slid a hand over the sleek hair on the animal's shoulder and the cow looked round at him with big, liquid eyes. 'May I introduce myself, signora, I am Antonio Canale, landscape artist, I am interested in views round Hinde Court. Is it true that this village is to be moved?'

Betsy Cary looked up at him. 'What be that to you, sir?' she asked suspiciously.

'Why, to decide a view of Hinde Court, I must know how house will look, not how it looks now,' Canaletto said with open honesty.

'Hmm!' Betsy gave a last few pulls to the udders, shook the drops of milk off into the pail and removed it from beneath the animal. She gave a slap to its rump and the cow trotted off. Betsy got up from the stool and stood looking at Canaletto in what could only be described as a truculent manner.

Now Canaletto could see that she was a stout woman, her rough brown wool dress well worn, a coif over her hair tied in a knot at the nape of her surprisingly well-shaped neck. This woman, he remembered Fanny telling him (what a blessing her chatter had proved to be after all), had been a maid at Badminton and felt she could have been a housekeeper. Now she looked a veritable farmer's wife, not too different from those Canaletto was acquainted with in the countryside around Venice, with full cheeks, ruddy complexion, ample figure.

'Yes, there are plans to move the village,' she said reluctantly. 'All so Sir Robert can landscape the approach to his grand new house,' her voice was caustic. 'We have been promised new houses to the west of here,' she pointed vaguely.

'But what about the land for farming?' Canaletto asked in a sympathetic manner.

'Yes, Betsy, tell him about the farm land,' said an irate voice behind him.

Walter Cary stood in the doorway, a huge, malevolent figure, blocking out the light.

Betsy looked levelly at him. 'Why, we are to be given new and increased amounts of land, adjacent to the new homes.'

'Increased amounts? Tell the truth, woman,' he said belligerently. 'It's land that's useless. If we had ten times the acreage we wouldn't get near what we get here.'

'You say that,' Betsy said impatiently. 'You don't know!'

'If you're a farmer, you know.'

'You are, you say, tenant farmer?' asked Canaletto.

'Aye, as my father was and his father afore him. This land is ours,' he waved his hand angrily towards his holding. 'That woman don't understand that,' he stabbed a finger at Betsy. 'She's not farming stock, don't understand our ways.'

She glared at him. 'Seventeen years I've been your wife. Seventeen years I've worked alongside you, seventeen years I've borne your children. If that don't, doesn't,' she quickly corrected herself, 'make me farming stock, I don't know what should.'

They stood squared up to each other, the small, determined woman, the big, aggressive man.

'You tell me you don't want my children on the land!'

'If they want to farm, I'll not stop them.'

'But you'll try to get them doing something else first,' he insisted.

The woman shrugged. 'That's their choice.'

They seemed to have forgotten that Canaletto was there. He gave a small cough. Both swung round to him.

'Barnaby, your son, he is bright boy.'

That brought another explosion. 'See what I mean, woman?' Walter Cary roared. 'You gave him ideas above his station and now look at him, disfigured and crippled for life, on the rubbish heap.'

'Not if you'd let him continue his education with Miss Horton,' snapped back his wife. 'He's clever enough to get on even with his useless arm and ruined face.'

'There you go again! I told you before, I'll not have that name mentioned in my hearing! Devil's brood they are. Hanging's too good for them.' Walter Cary's face was purple with his rage.

'You try to stick fork in James Horton other day,' Canaletto slipped in.

'Such an idiot as he is,' Betsy Cary snapped, turning on her husband. For a moment it looked as though she might hit him and he backed a step away.

'I visit Hinde Court and look at where fire started,' continued Canaletto. That brought the woman's attention back to him.

'Fire? What's that to do with you?'

'Duke ask me to see if I can find what caused it to start.' Canaletto was stretching a point here but the duke's name seemed to make almost any action acceptable, even beyond the confines of Badminton. 'Sir Robert Horton close friend of duke's.'

Betsy bristled again. 'That's as maybe but you can't suggest we had aught to do with it.'

'Barnaby was found there shortly after fire start,' Canaletto said calmly.

For once both of them were silenced.

Then, 'He raised the alarm,' said Betsy slowly. 'I reckoned he'd gone to watch Walter help our neighbour's horse give foal that night.'

'You always do think too much, woman. First time I saw Barnaby that night was when he came to say Hinde Court was on fire.'

'You with neighbour, you say?' Canaletto wanted to get this completely clear.

'You got cloth for ears?' Walter jeered. 'Gabriel's horse were in trouble with foal, he came over for me around midnight. We wrestled with that foal till just before young Barnaby came over with news house was on fire.'

'You didn't want to do anything, did you? Said it could burn right down for all you cared. It took Gabriel to tell you what an idiot you were being. Can't afford to stand by and watch landlord's property be destroyed, he said, no matter what he does to us.'

So Walter Cary could prove it had not been him that had started the fire. In that case, why had Barnaby gone to Hinde Court in the middle of the night?

There was no point in prolonging his conversation with the Carys. Canaletto took a courteous farewell.

Back at the house he found that there was only the tribe of younger children, none of whom could tell him where Barnaby had disappeared to.

Frustrated, he found his horse then climbed on to the railing so he could get his leg over the animal's back. He needed to talk to Fanny. Despite their disagreements, he could think of no one more able to help him sort out all the various details he had learned. As he rode back to Badminton, he concentrated on trying to recall the morning he had viewed the park and Fanny had chattered away telling him all she'd learned from Hannah and the extraordinary things Mr Cumberledge and Captain Farnham had said to each other. He mightn't have thought he was listening at the time but now he found that some remote corner of his capacious memory had tucked it all away.

Gradually a sinister landscape formed that chilled Canaletto despite the warmth of the summer sun. The killer was more dangerous than he'd yet realized.

Chapter Thirty-Three

Nell still slept on the truckle bed in Jack's room. There was a lantern always lit in the corner of the room and he had only to stir for her to wake.

Meg, the maid that attended upon Nell and her sister Patience, brought up their breakfast and helped Nell to dress. 'Such a sight it is to see the folk gathering for the hunt,' she said, brushing Nell's hair.

'A hunt!' shouted Jack. He was out of bed in an instant and at the window. 'I can't see any riders,' he complained, throwing up the window and leaning dangerously far out.

'Get back into bed,' Nell said, grabbing his nightshirt in case he fell.

'They be all round at the front,' said Meg.

'I want to see the hunters,' Jack protested as Nell carried him back to bed.

'Doctor Butcher is coming this morning and he will say whether you are well enough to go downstairs.'

'He won't come for ages and ages. They'll all be gone by then.'

'Then you'll be able to see them coming back.' Nell helped him climb back into the bed and adjusted the covers over him. 'Poor boy, it's boring for you, I know, but it's not going to be for much longer.'

Nell sat down again. 'Meg, just make it neat and tidy. I'm not going to be moving in company today.'

'You know how Lady Horton always wants you to look your best,' the maid said, rapidly inserting pins into the arrangement she'd made.

'Dear Mama,' sighed Nell. 'Always trying to make a swan out of a goose.'

'You look nice,' said Jack, sitting up in bed and playing with his wooden horse.

Meg finished attending to Nell's hair and went on to tidying the truckle bed and pushing it beneath Jack's.

By the time a knock on the door announced that Dr Butcher had arrived, all was neat.

'So how is my patient this morning?'

'I'm better!' shouted Jack, bouncing in the bed. 'I can get up, can't I?'

'There had better be a very good reason why he can't,' Nell warned the doctor with a smile.

She watched while the burly figure examined his patient.

Nell appreciated the care he was taking. She was sure Jack couldn't be in better hands but she did worry that no leeches had been applied as yet.

'Will you not bleed him?' she asked as the doctor finished his examination and Meg picked up the toy horse that had fallen to the ground.

Dr Butcher shook his head. 'It is not necessary. The boy is recovering very well. I see no reason why he should not get up. No running about, though,' he said to Jack. 'We don't want you falling over again. Quiet games, yes?'

'Can't I play battledore with Kate? She never runs very fast.'

He laughed. 'A gentle game, perhaps. But not today nor yet tomorrow. For two days you go downstairs and walk gently about. Will you promise?'

Jack looked mutinous.

'If you cannot promise, then you must stay in bed.'

'I'll be good, really I will.'

The doctor laughed again. 'Mind you keep your promise, young man. I don't want to have to come all this way to see you another time.'

'You will not attend us again if we need you?' Nell asked in some dismay.

'I shall not be in Bath for much longer, I only accompanied my sister for her cure and to do some research at the baths. Soon we return to the city.'

'Then when we are back in London, perhaps you will attend us there if we are in need?'

'I shall be flattered to do so.' He gave her a small but courtly bow. 'I will give you my card. First, though, I should see Lady Horton.'

Nell told Meg to dress Jack and take him downstairs to see the huntsmen assemble. Then she took the physician along to her mother's room. 'She is much better, doctor, since you gave her that tonic,' she told him.

Lady Horton, dressed in a voluminous morning sack, sat reading. 'How is the dear boy?' she asked as they entered. Reassured as to her son's condition, she submitted to the doctor placing his ear over her back and then her chest to listen to her lungs and heart.

'My lady, you are much restored,' he said, straightening up. 'You have no further need of medication.' Then he eyed her. 'A glass of wine with dinner and one of brandy each evening should settle your nerves excellently.'

She fluttered her eyelashes at him. 'We so appreciate your care, Dr Butcher.'

'The good doctor will attend on us in London, Mama,' said Nell.

'How lovely,' Lady Horton held out a limp hand and he bent over it. 'Have you seen Patience, my darling? She is neglecting her poor mama.'

'Not this morning, I have been busy with Jack and the doctor. Perhaps she is watching the hunt assemble. Have you, though, seen James? As Doctor Butcher soon returns to London, I am sure he would like to have his account settled now.'

Lady Horton sighed heavily. 'James has gone to Bath, apparently it's most important some stone is approved, or not approved, or something. He is never around when he is needed. But Doctor Butcher is not a tradesman,' she said reprovingly. 'I am sure he will submit an account to us.'

'Indeed, my lady, there is no problem about that,' the doctor assured her.

'Will you not have some refreshment before you return to Bath?' Nell asked as she accompanied him to the landing at the top of the stairs.

He shook his head. 'Someone waits on me, I have promised to make haste.'

'I am not surprised, you must have many waiting on your attentions,' Nell said, sorry to see him go.

He looked carefully at her. 'You have not mentioned your own injuries to me, Miss Horton.'

She flushed and one of her hands went automatically to the scarred cheek. 'There is nothing more to be done for them, Doctor Butcher, I regard them not.'

He removed a small pot from his case. 'I have had a salve put up that I think could help your scarring, will you use it if I give it to you?'

Taken aback, Nell found she was holding the jar. Without thinking, she removed the top and inspected the contents.

'Just apply night and morning. It contains healing herbs and oils.'

The pot contained a green ointment that looked soothing. Nell smiled at the doctor. 'Thank you, I appreciate your thoughtfulness, I will use it and maybe it will help,' she said cheerfully without the least hope that it would.

'At least it can do no harm,' the doctor said with a good deal of understanding. 'When you return to London, send me word,' he handed over his card. 'We will see how you go. Please to give my regards to my old friend, Antonio Canale, who is apparently elsewhere this morning. Say I hope to see him soon, either in Bath or London.'

After he'd left, Nell took the pot to Jack's room and put it on the dressing table. She wondered that Patience had not yet been to see their mother that morning. However attractive the prospect of watching the hunt gather, surely she would not have ignored common courtesies?

With a distinct feeling of unease, Nell went along the corridor to Patience's room.

Immediately she entered, she knew there was something very wrong. The bed was disarranged but too artfully. More than half the toiletries rescued from

357

Hinde Court and usually arrayed on the dressing table had disappeared. Instead, propped against one of the remaining bottles, was a piece of paper, folded and sealed, addressed to Miss Horton.

Nell snatched it up and ripped open the seal. *Darling Nell*, it started.

> *Don't be cross but I am obeying the dictates of my heart. Charlie has to leave and wants me to share his life. We are to be married in Bath. I am the happiest of women. Please explain to Mama but not until this evening.*

It ended, *Your ever-loving sister, Pattie.*

At first Nell couldn't believe what she had read. She turned the piece of paper over, to see if there wasn't something that might change the import of this extraordinary message. There was nothing. She looked in the cupboard. Patience's two best dresses had disappeared, together with an overmantle. Also gone was the valise in which Thomas Wright had brought the clothes over from Hinde Court.

Any moment, Nell thought, Meg would be along to air the bedclothes. She must notice nothing amiss. She went back to Jack's room, scooped her toiletries into her apron and returned to the other room. With the extra bottles, the dressing table looked almost as it had. Another trip moved her dresses into the cupboard. It was time she moved back with Patience anyway, Jack could manage without her now.

As she closed the cupboard door, Meg entered. 'Sorry, Miss Nell, did you want to be private?'

'No, that's fine, Meg, you carry on.' As the girl

approached the bed, Nell said in an idle voice, 'Did you not attend my sister this morning, Meg?'

'No, miss, as I helped her undress last night she said that you needed extra attention, what with Master Jack being such a demanding little fellow, and she could manage without me.' Meg assaulted the dishevelled covers with quick, efficient movements. 'That was all right, wasn't it miss?' the girl asked.

'Indeed, Meg. I must find my sister and thank her for her thoughtfulness.'

With a swift swoosh, the feather bed was removed and hung out of the window, the rest of the bedclothes stripped back and hung over the footboard.

'Have you had time to watch the hunt?' Nell asked, reluctant to leave the girl in the room by herself.

'Oh, yes, Miss Nell. They were just moving off as Jack and I got downstairs. Such a sight! Hannah was there too. It's so nice to be here with her, we sisters don't see much of each other these days. There, I'll come back later and make everything straight,' the girl said with a quick look around the room. She seemed to notice nothing amiss.

'Thank you, Meg.'

The moment the girl had gone, Nell subsided on to a chair. What was she to do? If she told her mother, Lady Horton would suffer a nervous decline without doubt. Never had Nell missed her father more. Strict he might be but Sir Robert was always a calming and reassuring presence. He would immediately have arranged to rescue Patience from the disastrous consequences of this terrible action. How could she be such an idiot? To be a romantic was one thing, to abandon family and society for love was something else again.

Nell had no confidence in the statement that they were to be married. If the fellow was still a priest, how could that be? And if he wasn't, then if he could mislead once, he could do it again.

But how to rescue Patience? Nell was sure if she went to the duke, he would help. But where would his loyalties lie? To the daughter of his old friend or to this somewhat mysterious fellow he'd received with singular honour and respect. Would the demands of aristocratic lineage (and whatever Charles Sylvester actually was, everything said he had to be an aristocrat) win out over a friendship with someone of much lesser status?

At the moment she was the only person who knew Pattie had gone. Appealing to the duke would mean several others would be acquainted with the facts and, however much secrecy was insisted upon, these were bound to leak out.

Anyway, the duke had gone hunting.

The person who should help, of course, was her brother, James, in whom her father had reposed his trust whilst he was abroad. But James had gone to see about some stone. Typical of him not to be here when he was needed. He had been useless on the night of the fire also, it had been Thomas Wright who had taken charge.

Then Nell remembered that her mother had said the stone works were in Bath. Thomas would surely know where he'd gone. The steward normally went over to Hinde Court each morning, would she be in time to catch him before he went?

Nell hurriedly descended the stairs. The first

person she found was the cheerful footman who always seemed so willing to help.

'I'll find him, miss,' he said after she asked if he knew if the steward was still at Badminton. 'Shall I send him to you in the morning room?'

'No, I'll be walking about the north front,' Nell said, unable to contemplate sitting still whilst her beloved sister threw away her reputation.

Nell paced the gravel, her thoughts bounding around and around her mind in frustrating circles. Charles Sylvester's intentions towards Patience could not be honourable; if they were, he would surely have applied to James, or even to the duke. If it was essential for him to leave the country (and why should that be necessary anyway, was he fleeing justice of some sort?), why couldn't he return later and court Patience in a proper manner? And just what was the truth about his priesthood? Was he abandoning his calling or had he merely been pretending he was a priest? Either way, Nell considered it said very little for his standing as a man. Faster and faster went round the unanswerable questions and it was a welcome relief to see Thomas Wright striding towards her, dressed in riding clothes, his open countenance concerned.

'You wanted me, Miss Horton?'

'Oh, Thomas, I'm so glad you were here and not over at Hinde Court.'

'Bob caught me just in time. What can I do for you?'

His calm, sensible manner quieted some of her fears. Thomas was so reliable, he would help her find her brother and bring Patience back from the brink of ruin. 'Do you know which stone works James has gone to see?'

He nodded. 'Allen's, just outside Bath.'

'I need you to take me there. I have to speak to James most urgently.'

His expression politely enquired as to why. But, much as she trusted Thomas Wright, Nell felt she owed it to her sister not to betray the full facts. 'Arrange for my horse to be saddled while I change into my habit, and send word to Hinde Court that you will not be there today. How long will it take us to get to this stone yard?'

'As to that, a couple of hours? Less if we ride hard. Is it urgent?'

Nell didn't answer and after a minute he said, 'You know I will always do anything you ask without question. I'll have both our horses ready by the time you're changed. Do you wish me to bring them here?'

'No, I'll meet you at the stables.'

Nell had never changed more quickly in her life. As she discarded her morning gown and tied the laces of her scarlet riding skirt and the matching, black-braided jacket, Nell tried to work out what she should say to her mother. She had to tell her something, Lady Horton could not have both her elder daughters disappearing without word. She decided to keep as close as possible to the truth. She fastened the last, metal cut button then placed the scarlet peaked hat on her head. Patience had persuaded her that it was the perfect accompaniment to the riding habit. As far as Nell was concerned, its chief merit was the fact that she didn't need a mirror to set it upon her head. She was therefore quite unaware of how dashing it was.

She found Lady Horton in one of the side gardens with Jack, the boy trying to persuade her to throw a ball for him to catch, and her two youngest children with their nurse. 'Mama,' she said. 'After spending so much time in Jack's room, I need fresh air and exercise. So I am going riding with Thomas Wright.' She gave her mother a brilliant smile.

'Of course, my darling, your health is all important.' Then Lady Horton frowned. 'But with Thomas Wright? I am not sure your brother would be at all happy with that. You know how he says the fellow has encroaching ways and believes himself as good as us.'

Nell forced herself to keep her temper. 'Mama, Thomas's birth *is* as good as ours. It is his misfortune and our fortune that his income is so small he has to take employment. He is always respectful and I am sure James would find his task of taking forward Papa's plans a good deal more difficult without his help.'

But Lady Horton was no longer paying attention. 'Jack, come back here,' she called as the boy started to run down a grassy walk.

Nell dashed after him and brought him back, told him he ran the risk of being put back to bed and left.

At the stables, Thomas was waiting for her, a groom holding his piebald gelding and her bay mare with its three white socks.

As she started across the cobblestoned yard towards him, she had a sudden thought and approached the head groom, busy organizing the soaping down of harnesses. 'Ned, I understand Father Sylvester left us this morning, did he go by horse or carriage?'

The groom's small, impish face looked at her with his head on one side. 'Right early it was. The duke loaned Mr Sylvester the small chaise. Was you wanting a carriage, miss?' Nell had grown to know the man well enough during her various visits to Badminton to be aware that he was dying to know why she asked such a question.

'Thank you, Ned, but I ride with Mr Wright.'

'Right you are, miss, I see he has your mare all ready.'

'And she is looking in excellent condition, Ned. Thank you for looking after her so well.'

He touched his forelock as she turned away, his face alive with speculation.

An unasked question had been answered. No one at Badminton appeared to be aware yet what had happened, for if they did, word would have spread and Ned would have been knowing, not curious.

Nell allowed Thomas to help her mount and then settled herself, arranging her legs as comfortably as she could on the side saddle, feeling the twist in her back as she faced forward. Thomas swung himself on to his own mount and looked round at her, then something in his eyes held her transfixed.

'What a picture,' he breathed.

She realized she had presented him with the undamaged side of her face. For a moment she was pierced with a deep sorrow for the loss of her looks. 'Come on, Thomas, Bath!' she cried and urged her horse on.

As they rode from Badminton, Thomas seemed to understand that Nell would rather not talk and as soon as they were clear of the drive and in open countryside, they let the horses out into a gallop.

Before coming to Gloucester, Nell's riding had been confined to sedate outings in the parks around London. Gallops were short and required close attention to other riders. Once in the countryside, however, she had gloried in the long rides it was possible to take and she and Patience had enjoyed exploring the neighbourhood.

'Oh, that was wonderful,' said Nell impulsively as they slowed to approach a road. She had almost forgotten the purpose of the ride.

Thomas grinned at her. 'Makes you feel godlike, doesn't it?'

'Is that how you feel, Thomas? Like a god?'

'No, only a lowly mortal, accompanying a goddess.'

'Idiot!' she said happily. It was nice to receive compliments. 'Right, now, which way?'

'Down there,' he pointed with his whip and they plunged down a steep hill.

The Allen stone works were conveniently situated to the north of Bath but by the time they reached the yard, Nell was tired.

Thomas led the way through ranks of stone blocks up to a grand house.

'My,' Nell marvelled, forgetting for a moment the ache in her limbs. 'Who lives here?'

'Quite a sight, isn't it,' Thomas said. 'Ralph Allen has built it to show the potential of his stone. If you will wait for a moment, I will see where your brother is.'

A servant was already approaching and offering assistance to the visitors. Thomas dismounted, spoke with him and disappeared inside the house. After a little he returned. 'James has been here but he left about an hour ago. Said something about enjoying himself in Bath.'

'Oh, no!' Nell cried in despair. 'What do I do now?'

Chapter Thirty-Four

Canaletto returned to Badminton to find a strangely deserted house. He came across Mr Capper and asked where everyone was, only to learn that the duke and all the male guests were hunting and the duchess had gone visiting, Neither Miss Horton nor Miss Patience Horton was available, Mr Cumberledge was at the village school and Miss Rooker was nowhere. 'But Lady Horton is in the garden with the young children, sir,' Mr Capper concluded his recital.

Then he produced a note. 'Miss Rooker asked me to give you this if I saw you, sir,' he said casually.

Canaletto snatched it from him and just remembered his manners enough to say thank you before turning away, opening and reading it.

His first emotion was profound thankfulness that Damaris Friend was alive. Then he realized what else the note said. Fanny had gone to Bath with Matthew to see her!

'What time it take to ride to Bath?' he asked Mr Capper.

'Bath, sir? Two hours, maybe less.'

Canaletto groaned as he thought of such a trip.

He went through the front hall to think about his

options. Would the duke have a chaise he could borrow?

There came a loud knock on the front door and Bob, the footman, appeared to answer it.

A smartly dressed groom said, 'Lady Tanqueray enquires whether the duchess is receiving.'

Canaletto went eagerly out to the carriage. 'Good morning, your ladyship,' he said with a low obeisance. 'How pleasant to meet with you.'

She inclined her head politely. 'Signor Canaletto, I am happy to see you again.'

'Duchess visiting,' he added, just before the groom came back with the same news.

'Ascertain if Lady Horton is receiving callers,' she instructed her servant. 'I very much hope the duke will show me your preliminary sketches,' she said to Canaletto. 'I am an admirer of your art. My late husband visited Venice nearly twenty years ago and would have bought one of your paintings but such was the demand for your work, he would have had to wait what he considered an unconscionable time for its delivery. It was a matter of deep regret to me.'

'It is a regret to me, also, my lady, I like to think one of my paintings is on your walls. Maybe in the future, perhaps?' he hinted delicately.

'Maybe,' she said without conviction. 'Ah, here comes Lady Horton.'

From the direction of the formal garden erupted several noisy children. 'Take them away, Martha,' Lady Horton said. 'I am quite overcome with their noise and Jack must have a rest now.' She came over to the carriage. 'Letitia, how pleasant to see you, my dear. No one told me you were here.'

'A footman is even now enquiring if you are receiving,' Lady Tanqueray said, bending forward out of the carriage to kiss Lady Horton's cheek. 'Since yesterday's funeral I have been too restless to sit at home. So out I came. Signor Canale has been entertaining me.'

'Signor Canale?' Lady Horton looked around absent-mindedly. 'Ah, there you are, my dear sir. Tell me, have you seen either of my elder daughters? Oh, I remember now, Nell said she was to take a ride with our steward, she has been starved of fresh air and exercise these last few days. She does seem to have been gone for rather a long time, though, she must realize I need companionship,' she said plaintively. 'Beautiful as Badminton is, it is not one's home.'

'You depend too much on that girl, Abigail,' Lady Tanqueray said. 'What about Patience? Where is she?'

'Now, there's a thing. I have not seen Patience all morning.' Lady Horton sounded resentful.

Canaletto excused himself and went off to the stables to enquire about the possibility of borrowing a carriage.

'Sorry, sir,' said the head groom. 'The duchess is visiting with the landau and Mr Sylvester took the chaise early this morning.'

'Mr Sylvester?' Canaletto's interest was caught. Had the priest acted upon the letter he'd had delivered to him yesterday? 'Is he to return to Badminton or did he take leave of the duke?'

'As to that, it's not my place to say. I only knows that Mr Sylvester said he would leave the chaise and horses at the George in Bath and to send someone for them.'

The man's voice was expressionless but his eyes were lively with interest. Canaletto wondered why a seemingly ordinary business had whetted his curiosity.

'It's funny, sir, you're the second person to ask after Mr Sylvester,' the head groom said, scratching at his head with a thickly gnarled finger.

'Really, who else?' Canaletto wondered whether to offer a coin. Had he been in London, it would have been essential but this was Badminton and maybe long-serving retainers did not hold out for largesse before answering a perfectly civil question.

'Miss Horton, sir. Then she and Mr Wright set off for Bath.'

Indeed! An incredible thought flashed into Canaletto's mind as he pieced together the fact that Lady Horton had not seen her second daughter that morning with the information that her eldest daughter had set off for Bath without, apparently, informing her parent of her destination. Here could be another reason to visit Bath.

'Thank you,' said Canaletto. 'I shall consider the means of my own trip.'

'And there was Miss Rooker, sir,' the groom volunteered. 'She went to Bath riding pillion to the doctor what come from there.'

'So many folk going to Bath,' said Canaletto in as uninterested a manner as he could manage.

The groom paused for a moment. 'You could enquire of Mr Morrison, Mr Sylvester's manservant, as to his plans, sir.'

'His manservant?' As far as Canaletto knew, the footman, Bob, was attending the priest as he had arrived quite alone.

370

'Joined Mr Sylvester yesterday, sir, and he's to take charge of Mr Sylvester's horse.'

Once again Canaletto thanked the fellow and then walked swiftly back to the house. There he enquired after Father Sylvester's manservant. Soon a quiet, self-contained man stood before him. 'Mr Sylvester, sir?' he said. 'He has left Badminton, sir.'

'And you, you meet him where?'

Morrison looked at him carefully then said, 'At Portsmouth in two days' time.'

'You spend much time chasing him round country-side,' suggested Canaletto and a flash in the man's eyes said that he had hit home but no more information was forthcoming.

Canaletto decided he would have to make for Bath and that a horse was probably the best he could hope for. As he made towards the stables again, he met with Isaiah.

'Good morning, signor,' the young man said courteously.

'A most distressing affair,' Canaletto said, fanning his face with his hat. 'I find myself in a perfect quandary.' It was amazing how he could sometimes find English words so easily and at other times flounder into near incomprehensibility.

'Indeed? What sort of quandary? Can I perhaps help you solve it?' Isaiah didn't sound too interested.

'Well, dear signor, I am not sure.' After a brief pause he added slyly, 'Yet you are such friend to the young lady, perhaps so.'

'Do you refer to Miss Patience, sir?'

'I think so. Certain facts suggest she may have gone to Bath with Father Sylvester.'

'I knew the fellow was a bounder!' Isaiah ejaculated. 'But Patience cannot have been so reckless. You cannot be right. What facts do you refer to?'

'I have just now seen Lady Horton, who says she has not seen Miss Patience all morning.'

'Tush, that is nothing.'

'Shall we perhaps mention matter to Lady Horton?' Canaletto suggested tentatively.

'She will dismiss the idea out of hand,' Isaiah said emphatically.

They found both their ladyships in the small drawing room. Lady Horton was upset.

'Letitia, that's not true, Patience is a sweet, biddable girl,' she was saying as Canaletto and Isaiah entered.

'So biddable she has made herself invisible a whole morning,' said Lady Tanqueray.

'Signor Canale says she has gone to Bath with Father Sylvester,' burst out Isaiah.

Lady Tanqueray looked at him distastefully. 'Such tact, Isaiah!'

Lady Horton gasped and put a hand to her cheek, her expression appalled. 'Patience gone to Bath – with Mr Sylvester?' she jerked out. 'Oh, it cannot be so.'

'Is it indeed so, signor?' asked Lady Tanqueray, who did not look at all surprised at the suggestion.

'Father Sylvester leave early this morning. He take the duke's chaise without a groom or his manservant. He not coming back to Badminton. His manservant say he to meet with master at Portsmouth in two days' time.'

'But no one saw him with Miss Patience Horton?' Lady Tanqueray asked, gimlet eyed.

Canaletto shook his head. 'Groom then say Miss Horton and Mr Wright ride to Bath.'

'Nell to Bath? And with Thomas Wright? Oh, my nerves, my nerves!' shrieked Lady Horton, fluttering her hands.

'Your steward is a sensible chap, Abigail, Nell is in safe hands there, I think,' Lady Tanqueray said firmly. 'Ring the bell, Isaiah, let's get some brandy for Abigail.'

'Brandy, Aunt, when Patience is with that, that . . .' Isaiah failed to find an epithet sufficiently dastardly to describe the priest.

'What would you do?' his aunt enquired in her most acid tone.

'Why, go after them of course.'

'And challenge the fellow to a duel, I suppose?'

'Of course, no gentleman could do less.'

'If you managed to kill the fellow, the consequences could be more than you bargain for,' Lady Tanqueray's voice was unusually thoughtful. 'I take it you, at least, understand what I mean, Signor Canale?'

He gave her a small bow. 'I believe I do, Lady Tanqueray.'

'It won't do, you know?' She turned her piercing stare on to him, the painted face more serious than he had ever seen it.

'I understand, your ladyship.'

'Do you have the first idea where they have gone in Bath?'

'He leaves the carriage at inn called George.'

'The man's an idiot but thank heavens he is. His manservant appears more circumspect, I would suggest Southampton would be a more obvious choice of port for France. Take my nephew and my carriage and see what you can do. If what you say is in fact true, I hold no truck for Charles's conduct. Nor for Patience's but Charles has always had a way with women. They abandon all sense when he looks into their eyes.'

'Aunt!' said Isaiah.

'And your sense is less than that of a rabbit, Isaiah. Go on with you, rescue your lady love but be guided by the signor, understand?'

Isaiah looked belligerent.

'And for heaven's sake ring that bell, Lady Horton is expiring!' she added with extreme exasperation. Abigail Horton groaned and fluttered her eyes and Lady Tanqueray took her hand. 'Hush, my dear, everything will be all right.'

Outside the drawing room, Isaiah looked challengingly at Canaletto. 'If we catch up with that bounder, I'll not answer for my conduct.'

'Come, you tell groom of Lady Tanqueray we go to Bath, then I explain,' said Canaletto.

The foremost question in his mind, however, was how on earth he was going to find Fanny and Damaris as well as track down Patience and Charles Sylvester.

Chapter Thirty-Five

Fanny's journey to Bath was one of the most uncomfortable of her life. The jolting from bumping along behind Matthew Butcher was worse than she'd received in the post-chaise. She spent the time torn between wanting to suggest she walked for a bit and desperate to get to her destination as quickly as possible.

As they travelled, she tried to tell him why she was so anxious to see Damaris Friend. As her story progressed, it seemed that Matthew spurred his horse on faster and faster.

'Well, well,' he said when she'd finished. He brought his horse to a stop at the top of a hill so that they sat looking down on a city built from golden stone warm in the sunshine. Matthew pulled out his pocket watch and flipped open the cover. 'We should just do it. I'm taking you straight to the King's Baths, where your friend is working. They close at noon.' He gave his horse's neck a pat. 'Good girl, you'll have extra oats today.' The mare blew through her nostrils, lowered her head and started down the steep slope. Fanny hung on tightly and prayed that they would reach the baths in time.

Soon they were on the outskirts of a thriving town.

Fanny stared at the handsome houses and the number of folk thronging the streets. Horses gave way to sedan chairs. Shops appeared that would have looked attractive even in London's best areas. Fashionably dressed ladies and gentlemen strolled on the wide pavements, exchanging greetings. In surroundings of urban sophistication, there was the atmosphere of a village.

'I stable my horse here, at the Saddlers Arms, it's convenient for my sister's lodgings,' said Matthew, turning into an inn's stable yard. 'The King's Bath is not far away.' He helped her to dismount.

As he handed the reins over to an ostler, Fanny eased her aching back and wondered if her hips would ever recover. Then, grasping his bag, Matthew set off on foot. Fanny took secure hold of her small bundle and went with him.

Soon they were in a pedestrian area where the only conveyances were sedan chairs. In the shadow of an impressive church was what looked like an orangery. 'That is the Abbey and here is the Pump Room,' said Matthew. 'This is where the fashionable drink the waters and here we have the entrance to the King's Bath.' He plunged down a narrow set of stairs beside the Pump Room and Fanny followed.

Steamy warmth met them and Fanny's nostrils twitched at the sulphurous smell. Matthew asked for Dolly Fry, then guided Fanny up more stairs to a walkway above a huge, open-air bath. 'See if you can see her,' he said. Fanny gazed, astonished, at the scene below. All around the walls were arched niches with people sitting submerged in water so warm it steamed in the summer air. Men and women dressed in linen disported themselves, the men on one side, the women on the other, an elaborate, pillared and turreted edifice rising from the middle. Close inspection revealed that it was hung about with discarded crutches. As Fanny studied the scene in fascination, a woman reclining in one of the niches reached for a little, japanned bowl that floated near her, anchored by a ribbon. She extracted a bonbon from the bowl and popped it into a greedy mouth.

'Already many people have deserted the waters,' said Matthew. 'And soon the bath will be quite clear.' Sure enough, as Fanny watched, more of the bathers were moving towards steps and hauling themselves out of the water.

A woman with a tasselled cap walked heavily through the waters towards the woman with the japanned bowl. 'Time to go,' she said.

'That's a guide, that's what those who work here are known as.'

Fanny looked but it wasn't Damaris Friend, more than half submerged she might be, but she could never mistake this woman's chubby cheeks for the cook's sculptured face.

Gradually the remaining bathers made their way up the steps and out of the baths.

Then a hand tapped Fanny on the shoulder and there was a tall figure dressed in wet linen, a tasselled cap on her head. 'Miss Rooker, you've come!' said Damaris Friend. 'Thank you, Doctor Butcher, for bringing her.'

'Oh, Damaris, I'm so pleased to see you,' Fanny said. 'We thought you were dead!'

'I feared I might be if I remained at Badminton,' said Damaris. She looked very tired and drawn.

377

'What are you doing here?'

'I'm what they call a scrubber,' said Damaris with the ghost of a smile. 'I rub down the patients' limbs with the spa water, it is supposed to do good.' She smiled at Matthew. 'The doctor helped me get the job after I met him when I applied at the hospital. I reckoned looking for a job as a cook was too dangerous.'

'But what makes you fear for your life?' asked Fanny.

Damaris sighed. 'It's a long story but Miss Nell said she thought you could help me tell it.' She looked around at the walkway where they were standing. 'We are too conspicuous here, come downstairs to my domain.'

She took them to a world of narrow corridors and dark rooms, the stonework oozing damp, the atmosphere steamy with moist heat. There were few bathers left. 'Most people come much earlier in the morning,' said Damaris, 'when the baths are cleaner. Soon, now, they'll be empty and then we'll start scrubbing them out ready for tomorrow.' She sighed. 'Making bread dough has to be better for the skin than this job.' She held out her reddened hands.

'But what happened?' pressed Fanny.

Damaris waved towards stone benches. 'Sit down and I will tell you. It's a tale of chicanery and treachery and I'm afraid no one will come out of it looking very good, including myself.'

All around them were sodden cloths, buckets of water and scrubbing brushes, which to Fanny's eye looked little different from those used for washing the floor. Damaris found a stool and sat opposite them. 'I suppose what began everything was the servants' party the Horton household attended at Badminton at Christmas. It was soon after that that I was foolish enough to allow Mr Capper, the steward, to seduce me.'

Chapter Thirty-Six

At Simpson's Assembly Rooms, just off the fashionable North Parade, James Horton found few gamblers. Town was empty, complained one player, and would be until the season started again in the autumn. James began to wish he'd gone elsewhere for entertainment, but what other entertainment was there? He had no interest in mingling with society at the always over-crowded Pump Room, or in promenading the Orange Grove. He didn't know enough Bath folk to make that a pleasurable occupation, nor was he interested in the shops, be they ever so fashionable, or exhibitions of paintings.

The company at the Pharaoh and E.O. tables seemed damned dull, dowagers and mountebanks to a man – or a woman, for there were several females. Just as he was thinking that maybe he would return to Badminton, he saw a couple of bucks he was acquainted with playing dice. They waved him over. Flinging himself into a chair and ordering a cognac, he nodded to the young men he'd met at a cock fight shortly after arriving in Gloucestershire. 'Glad to see you, Stukeley, and you, Clarke,' he added, nodding at the lean and hungry looking man a few years older than himself. 'I hope you'll bring me luck.'

Stukeley, a well set up young man the same age as James, dressed in a jacket of a violent purple embroidered in blue, grinned. 'I need my luck myself, Horton.'

And the luck stayed with Stukeley.

James became more and more morose.

'Snap out of it, Horton,' said Stukeley, gathering in a pile of coin and several notes of hand. 'It's not your day today, tomorrow may well be different.'

'Damn your eyes, Stu, I can't come here every day the way you and Clarke do. And soon I'll not be able to come at all. I had a note the other day that the old man's ship is due in at Bristol any time now.'

'Day of reckoning at hand, eh?' said Clarke in a sardonic voice, preparing to throw the dice.

James looked at him with an arrested expression. 'What the devil do you know about it, Clarke?' he said suspiciously. 'Who the hell have you been talking to?'

'Easy, man! I know nothing about you. But whenever a father leaves a son in charge of his affairs, there is always a reckoning to be made,' Clarke said, throwing with an easy hand. A smile of satisfaction crossed his face as he passed the dice.

'The only affairs I was left to handle are those concerning the rebuilding of Hinde Court. That was all I was trusted with!' James said bitterly. He threw back the last of his cognac and waved at a passing waiter for another. 'Now I have to justify the bills and explain the fire.'

'Fire?' queried Clarke.

Stukely said, 'Catch a sight of that phiz! I wonder she shows herself around the Rooms.'

With a dreadful premonition, James looked towards the door. Sure enough, there was his sister, Nell, accompanied by that upstart steward his father had insisted on hiring. 'Watch your language,' he growled at Stukeley. 'That's my sister.'

Stukeley coloured and muttered some graceless apology.

'James, at last!' said Nell, hastening over. 'We have been looking for you everywhere. But Thomas suggested you would be here.'

'You did, did you?' said James curtly to the steward. He staggered to his feet, anxious to remove his sister as soon as possible from this fashionable arena, and made no attempt to perform introductions. 'Can't a chap enjoy himself after his business is done? What do you want with me?'

'Come outside,' she urged him and took his arm.

'I think it would be as well,' said the steward in a quiet voice.

People were looking at them now and a whisper was running round the room. James was sure it was because of Nell's face. Why the hell did she have to seek him here? Just what was it she wanted?

Outside the door she explained matters to him in a concise manner and quiet voice.

James's head swam as he tried to take in the details.

'Hell's bells! Patience and that Sylvester fellow in Bath?' he said finally. 'Where?'

'That's where we need you,' Nell said urgently. 'I have no idea where they could be but surely you know where he would take her.'

'If you know so little about Bath, how did you find me here?' James said, trying to gain time to think what it was best to do.

'Thomas had heard you mention Simpson's gaming

rooms,' Nell explained. 'Oh, James, what would father say if he knew you spent your time gambling?'

James suddenly felt so angry. 'What do you mean, big sister? I am to spend my entire life incarcerated at Hinde Court, with no one to talk to but silly women or workmen? I can tell you, it is no fun looking after building operations that do nothing but eat money. And you have the gall to follow me here and expect me to jump to your bidding?'

'But, James,' interposed Nell in a shocked voice. 'What about Pattie? You can't see her lose her reputation and honour?'

For the first time James realized Nell's distress. It made him feel thoroughly uncomfortable. Was this really his fault, though? Pattie being mad enough to run off with some well-bred rascal, surely was nothing to do with him. 'What do you want me to do about it?' he asked sulkily. 'If she's gone, she's gone.'

'James! She only went this morning, we have to find her and make her see reason. It is what Father would do.'

James felt even more uncomfortable. Was this to be added to the reckoning he was going to have to make when Sir Robert returned home? 'How can we find her? They've several hours start, they could be anywhere.'

'She said in her note that they were coming here. You know how she has been longing to see Bath. We have only to search the leading hostelries and I am sure we will find them.'

'And you want me to help.' James felt the first faint hope that something might be rescued from this mess.

'You must know the best inns in town,' Nell pleaded

with him. There was nothing pointed in her remark and for once James realized his sister was looking to him for advice.

'I believe, sir,' said Thomas Wright, 'that the George is considered one of the best.'

James looked at him with dislike. Standing there in the background, listening to his family's disgrace, would they ever be able to get rid of the man now? 'Wait here a minute,' he ordered and marched back into the gaming rooms.

'Stu,' he said to his friend. 'I have to go, my sister has some small feminine crisis, some matter of a hat she needs my opinion on,' he added in a moment of inspiration. 'Listen, you're a man of sophistication, I shall need to take her for some refreshment when we have settled the matter. Which is the best inn to bespoke a private room at?' He was very proud of himself for having thought of such a good tale.

Stukeley didn't seem to see anything strange in this request, though Clarke leaned back in his chair with a supercilious smile that might mean anything. 'Why, I consider the White Lion by far the best. Mention my name and you'll be well pleased.'

'Take his word and your sister will be worse off. The George is superior,' said Clarke in a bored manner. 'There's also the Angel and the Queen's Head with reputations.'

'Don't forget the York House,' added Stukeley. 'My mama won't put up anywhere else, at least until she has found rooms.'

James rapidly repeated the names, his head spinning.

'I'll hold these for another time when you can

384

settle,' Clarke said, rustling the notes of hand James had given during their play.

'Of course,' James said with an air of grandeur. Then he hesitated a moment. 'Can't be more than a couple of hundred guineas, I suppose?'

Clarke smiled, 'Nearer six hundred.'

James hoped he didn't look as shocked as he felt. Six hundred guineas lost in a couple of hours!

'You know my direction but I shall not fail,' he said and left with his head held high.

'The White Lion,' he said as he rejoined a worried looking Nell and the silent figure of Thomas Wright. 'That is the best inn in town.' At least that was one in the eye for the steward! 'And if they have not gone there, I have the names of several others, the George amongst them,' he added in a pointed manner.

On their way out of the Assembly Rooms, Thomas Wright stopped a servant and asked for directions, getting the full list of names from James. All the inns were centrally located, none very far away.

Outside, James blinked a couple of times as the sun hit his tired eyeballs. Noon was long past but the light was bright as bright.

'You have your horse?' enquired the steward.

James shook his head. 'I put him up at John's livery stables, they're just off Cheap Street, the other side of the Abbey,' he waved a hand towards the towering edifice. 'You should do the same,' he said in a superior way, glad for once to have the better of Thomas Wright. 'Walking is best in Bath.'

'Oh, Thomas, will you do that?' asked Nell. 'You can catch us up at the White Lion.'

James interrupted her, 'It's near the Market House,

but a step from the stables. But if we don't find them there, we'll try the White Hart next, then the Queen's Head and the Saddlers Arms, lastly the George.'

'Of course, Miss Horton, sir. I'll find you.' The steward mounted his horse and moved off, leading Nell's.

'That's got rid of him,' James said in satisfaction. 'We can walk more directly than he can ride.' He fully intended that if the runaways didn't prove to be at the White Lion, he and Nell would try the George next. By the time Wright caught up with them, if he ever did, with any luck the matter should be resolved. He guided Nell towards the Abbey then led her in the direction of the Pump Room.

'Look,' said Nell in astonishment. 'Isn't that Damaris?'

Damaris? James heard the name with dismay. He'd found her disappearance fortuitous. He looked where his sister pointed but could only see a crowd of people moving along the wide pavement. 'You must be mistaken,' he said authoritatively. 'Why on earth would she be in Bath or at the Pump Room? Come on, do you or do you not want to find Pattie?'

For a moment he thought Nell was going to run off, then she gave a rueful smile. 'You're right, James. It can't have been her.'

Chapter Thirty-Seven

Back at Badminton, after a splendid run, the Duke of Beaufort's horse had gone lame. One of his fellow huntsmen offered him his mount but spoiling someone else's day was not the duke's style.

In any event, he had already taken part in the killing of one buck. If they managed another, that would be a bonus. He walked his mare carefully home a couple of miles through woodland and across fields, humming tunefully to himself and enjoying the day and the countryside. It was looking at its best, the greens set and varied and wild flowers still plentifully jewelling the hedgerows and meadows. There was nothing like Badminton!

But all too soon his mind turned to the unexpectedly catastrophic state of his finances. Influence at court would have brought rich sinecures. Without them the struggle to find enough funds to pay for all his heavy outgoings seemed even more difficult than usual. His steward and his agent had much to explain and he hoped they could do so satisfactorily, the alternative was too burdensome to contemplate. It meant acknowledging that he had been mistaken in where he had placed his trust, a prospect that was too depressing to contemplate, especially on such a lovely day.

He reached the end of the trees before Badminton House and stopped for a moment, the horse pointing its injured foot, and looked at the north façade. It was indeed handsome and he was delighted with the rough sketch Canaletto had produced. The finished painting would be a treasure indeed, proof to future generations of how he had carried on his brother's work. He had never expected nor wanted to take on the dukedom but he carried out the duties and responsibilities as well as he could.

What, he wondered suddenly, if, instead of unexpectedly inheriting, he had been deprived of rightful possession? How would he have felt then? How many generations would the need to reclaim such a title persist? He thought of Norborne, his brother-in-law, and what would undoubtedly prove highly expensive proceedings if he decided to put forward an attempt to reclaim the barony of Botetourt through a tangle of female relationships.

His horse nuzzled his neck, reminding him he needed to get her home. Home, how must it feel not to have one?

He sighed deeply. Charles hadn't appeared at the hunt that had been arranged especially for his entertainment. Did that mean he was leaving Badminton? He'd told Charles the previous evening that it was time he moved on to sound others out. It had been a difficult meeting but the duke had been badly upset by his guest's behaviour with the Horton girl. With her father abroad, the duke felt responsible for Patience and she had neither the background nor the temperament to deal with the dashing Charles.

For a moment the duke wondered if he'd taken the

right line the previous night. But time and again the lad showed lack of judgement.

The duke had been badly disappointed in Charles and he had told him so. He sighed again as he resumed walking. He had sacrificed much to his principles and he expected the same behaviour from others. Charles must learn that loyalty was not blind. The duke did not really think he had come to a watershed in his relations with the House of Stuart but holding back the carefully husbanded sum he had intended to hand over would, he hoped, give the prince a lesson in propriety.

In the stables, the lame foreleg was inspected. 'Poultice, my lord, that's what she needs,' said the groom, running a hand down the swollen limb. 'If I gets it on straight away, she should be wearing well again before you know it. Will you be wanting another mount, my lord?'

The duke shook his head. No catching up with the hunt now, his day was finished.

'I'll get the poultice on then, my lord. Never been a day like today for comings and goings, there hasn't,' the groom muttered as he led the duke's mare away.

The duke entered the house by the side door. Walking along to the main part of the house, he encountered Briggs. His butler was in a state of great excitement.

'My lord, I am glad you are back so early, there have been unexpected developments.'

The duke's heart plummeted. It must be something to do with Prince Charles Edward.

'I think your lordship will be greatly distressed with what has happened and I know not what to tell you but you are awaited in the drawing room, my lord.'

'The drawing room? Make sense, man. What developments?'

'As to that, my lord, I think you will want to hear them from others.' Briggs had this unfortunate habit of hiding behind formality as a way of not breaking bad news. 'May I suggest, my lord, that you repair to the drawing room?'

'Not in my riding boots.' The duke sat down on a chair and held out a foot for Briggs to pull one off. 'You had better get my shoes brought to me and,' he said, lifting up the other leg, 'send me Capper. If you can't make sense, I'll hear what has happened from him.'

Briggs staggered a little as the second boot shot off, then he stood it with its pair, handling the footware with reluctance. 'I regret, my lord, that Mr Capper is not to be found.' He passed his tongue over his lips as though the words had left a pleasant taste.

'Not to be found? For heaven's sake, man, what do you mean?'

'Mr Capper was seen riding off some little time ago. He left no word as to where he was going.' Briggs's tone got rounder and more mellifluous.

'With the hunt taking place today, no doubt he is attending to business elsewhere,' the duke said, unperturbed. He had long ago decided to ignore the feud between his steward and his butler. 'I have to say, Briggs, you seem to be piling Ossa not on Pelion but a wart.' The duke got up and wiggled his toes comfortably in his stockings. 'Have my shoes brought to the drawing room, I'd better see what domestic dramas have been inflated beyond their worth there.'

Briggs cleared his throat, seemed about to speak,

390

thought better of it and went off to find Carter, his lordship's attendant.

The marble floor was pleasurably cool beneath the duke's stockinged feet and as he made his way to the drawing room, his mind was calm, the worst of his fears focused on what scrape the children could have got themselves into.

He was, therefore, completely unprepared for either a tale of disaster or the visitor that awaited him.

A short while later, yet another party set out for Bath.

Chapter Thirty-Eight

Canaletto had felt distinctly nervous when Isaiah first took the reins of Lady Tanqueray's prancing black horses. Nothing about the young man instilled any confidence in his ability to handle such a highly bred and nervous pair. As Isaiah clicked his tongue and urged the horses on, the painter took firm hold of the gaily painted coachwork and prepared to consign himself to the mercy of the Lord.

However, Isaiah quickly showed unexpected skill and the carriage bowled swiftly if not actually smoothly along the rutted roads towards Bath.

Soon Canaletto was able to breathe more easily but it was a long and punishing journey. By the time they arrived, the dust from the dry dirt of the roads thrown up not only by themselves but other vehicles they passed on their way, had given him a throat like sandpaper. He'd tried to talk to Isaiah, but the young man drove on like one who thought his carriage had wings. The horses responded gallantly, their muscled legs galloping up the miles. In the process, the jolting was such that Canaletto had difficulty in keeping his teeth in his head and producing sentences proved beyond him.

Twice they nearly came to grief as an equipage

came towards them in a narrow part of the road. Instead of slowing and seeking a suitable place to pass, Isaiah had whipped up his horses and forced the other road-user into a hedge. Loud were the imprecations that followed them. Canaletto hoped that Lady Tanqueray's carriage was not known in this part of the county but he feared that such a striking vehicle could not escape recognition.

Speed, though, suited his purposes as well as they did Isaiah's. Canaletto could not help fearing that Fanny was in as much danger as Damaris. Even as he tried to tell himself that no one knew of the reason why she had gone to Bath with Matthew Butcher, he saw again the face of the Badminton steward as he handed over Fanny's note. It had been so perfectly blank that Canaletto could not but suspect he had read the letter's contents. True, it had been sealed but care and a hot knife could be employed by those who would read confidential missives.

'The George I think you said?' Isaiah let the exhausted horses slacken their pace down the last of the hills.

Canaletto, hardly able to speak, nodded vigorously.

'Not a difficult place to find.' Isaiah reined in the sweating animals to a gentle trot as they entered a built-up area.

'You know Bath?' asked Canaletto, trying to clear his throat of some of the dust.

'I once accompanied my aunt here while she took the waters. She said a young man gave a woman her age glamour. That was before we fell out over my scientific career.' Isaiah grinned at the memory.

'A remarkable woman, your aunt.'

'Indeed she is.'

'And a remarkable city, Bath.' Canaletto was surprised at the grace and elegance of the houses and streets they were passing through. Built of a golden stone that seemed to absorb and then give out light, he found it one of the most attractive places he had seen since arriving in England. Much more so than London, which was such a mishmash of styles and building materials. Would there possibly be commissions to be obtained here? It was hardly Venice or London, merely a small, provincial town but one with style. It was something to bear in mind.

The George was a busy, bustling place, the stable yard full of comings and goings. Horses were being hitched to, or unhitched from, a vast variety of carriages, people were entering and leaving, riders consigning or reclaiming mounts, ostlers and grooms shouting. But immediately Lady Tanqueray's distinctive carriage appeared, there was a man to run to the lead horse and start stroking its sweaty neck. 'Been travelling fast,' he said cheerily. 'I'll see to them, shall I? Water and oats and a rub down, sir?'

'I don't know how long we'll be,' Isaiah warned, jumping down with enviable ease and then helping Canaletto to descend.

'Not to worry, sir, I'll stable them for now. You just let me know when you want to leave.'

Isaiah patted and spoke a few words to each horse, telling them how well they'd done.

'We like to look and see stables first,' said Canaletto. 'Make sure good enough for horses.'

'You'll find no better in all England,' the ostler said,

but was willing enough to show Canaletto the accommodation for both the horseflesh and the carriages.

All Canaletto needed to see was the ducal crest on a small, closed carriage. Then he followed the ostler back to where Isaiah was holding the horses. 'Is very good,' he said. 'We leave them here, yes?'

'Certainly,' Isaiah said.

'If they are here, it is in private salon,' Canaletto said softly as they entered a crowded tap-room. 'But they may be out seeing sights.' He didn't think so, though. Even taken at a relaxed pace, the drive to Bath would have been very tiring. The couple would surely take the opportunity of a few restful hours and some refreshment. The trick would be to find out where they were and surprise them.

'Wait here,' he said to Isaiah. 'I be back in few minutes.'

On their way into the George's stable yard, he'd glimpsed the window of a modiste offering a display of hats.

A furious bargaining session obtained him a pretty bonnet in a large round carton printed with the modiste's name. A remnant of the season that had recently ended, it was his for a knock-down price after the owner had refused to let him have it on approval. He had no credit with her, she insisted. No doubt his Italian accent hadn't helped, or the lack of any address other than the George.

He had to hand over practically all the money he had on him but he reassured himself the hat would soon be going back for a full refund.

Returning, he found Isaiah downing a glass of ale. Giving him a wink, and longing for the time when he could rid the dust from his own throat, he looked around until he saw a waiter carrying a large tray furnished with covered dishes, obviously destined for upstairs.

Brandishing his hatbox he said, 'I have urgent order for young miss, arranged by master. Must deliver immediately. Which room?'

The waiter looked at the hatbox and, without even glancing at Canaletto, said, 'Follow me.' He headed for the stairs.

Canaletto jerked his head at Isaiah and set off after him.

A first floor corridor offered several doors. The waiter knocked on the first. 'Third along on the left,' he said to Canaletto.

Clasping the unwieldy hatbox as best he might, Canaletto hurried past. As soon as the waiter had vacated the corridor, Isaiah joined Canaletto.

Canaletto rapped on the door the waiter had indicated. 'Service,' he sang out.

'Enter,' said a voice.

Chapter Thirty-Nine

In the labyrinthine surroundings of the baths with their echoing depths and sulphurous smell, Damaris began a tale that to Fanny sounded as though it could have come from *Le Morte D'Arthur*.

Her wet linen garment clinging to her, Damaris had shown no shame in admitting how attractive she found the opposite sex. 'I am a girl who requires male attention, I daresay I should be a courtesan. But I do not choose that path. I prefer to dally where I like, not be at the beck and call of any man.'

In gathering wonderment, Fanny heard Damaris explain that not only had she allowed the Badminton steward, John Capper, to make love to her, 'A masterful man, but one I quickly tired of,' but also James Horton: 'He is selfish with none of the sweetness I first thought was there.' And after him, the Hinde Court steward, Thomas Wright. 'Now there, for a while, I thought I had met someone who could interest me beyond a few lightsome nights. Until he decided his future lay elsewhere.'

'With Miss Horton?' asked Fanny.

'Surely not,' said Matthew in surprise.

'Oh yes, with Nell. That was after her accident when he saw there could be an opportunity for a faithful servant to become something more,' said Damaris with just a trace of bitterness. 'But then I met Captain Farnham, who chanced upon me while I was gathering sorrel for a supper dish.'

Damaris made the captain's involvement with her seem like some story of a knight errant rescuing a maiden who was not quite in distress but definitely suffering. 'He healed the wound Tom had given me,' Damaris said in her soft, low voice.

Another guide, a woman whose skin looked as though it had been pickled in lime and whose eyes were as sharp as pins, erupted from the narrow, dank corridor and curtly told Damaris to return to work.

'She is assisting me with a patient's history,' Matthew said.

The guide looked at him. 'Doctor Butcher, isn't it? I'm sorry, sir, but the baths need scrubbing out, we can't have the servants slacking.'

Damaris got up. 'I quit,' she said contemptuously. 'I need no longer work in this devil's pond.' The woman stared at her for a moment, then shrugged and left. Damaris sat down again. She was shivering, whether from the dampness or from tension it was difficult to decide.

'You should get into dry clothes,' Matthew said. 'Do you have a change here?'

Damaris nodded. 'If you will wait, I will return in a few minutes.'

After she'd left, Matthew looked at Fanny. 'It is quite a story,' he said. 'Not perhaps one for your ears, though.'

'Tush,' she said. 'I've been in prison and heard and seen far worse.'

'You have?'

'Of course, that was before you met the signor. It was he who got me released.'

Matthew looked fascinated. 'Tell me all.'

'It would take too long. It was all a mistake that was righted but never think that I have to be protected from tales such as the one Damaris is telling us. Even without my prison experiences, I have not led a protected life such as the Miss Hortons. I know what men are like and what women can feel.' As Damaris had spoken of her desires, Fanny had relived the heat of her unfulfilled passion for another painter.

Matthew laughed. 'You look such an innocent, young Fanny Rooker. Now I must remember a woman of the world is underneath those copper curls of yours.'

Fanny grinned back at him.

Damaris returned, wearing the buff wool gown Fanny had seen her in at Badminton.

'Where shall we go?' she asked. 'I cannot take you to the friend I am staying with, her room is tiny. There is the Orange Grove nearby that is spoken of as a pleasant place to walk, though it is so popular we could well be overheard.'

'We shall go to my sister's,' said Matthew. 'She has most commodious rooms near Westgate Buildings. It is past the Cross Bath, not far from here.'

As they emerged into the sun, Damaris laughed, 'Oh, am I glad to leave those dank and dark surroundings behind!' she said. 'Now that I am no longer in fear for my life, now that you know what I know, I shall return to being a cook.'

'But we don't yet know what you know,' Fanny said

hurriedly. 'You haven't told us who killed the captain, or who set fire to Hinde Court and nearly killed you.'

Damaris lost her brief exuberance and rubbed her arms as though she was cold. They had to wait to cross Stall Street. Here, unlike outside the baths, there were carriages and riders as well as a multitude of sedan chairs.

'Doctor Butcher,' a voice hailed. An aged gentleman in a chair required his attention. After briefly talking with him, Matthew turned back to Fanny and Damaris. 'Can you find your way to my sister's? It is only a few streets away.' He felt in his waistcoat and took out a bit of pasteboard. 'Here is the address. Cross this street, go down the one you see opposite and past the George Inn. Then it will be on the other side of the road. Knock and ask for Mrs Silence and say that I sent you. I will join you presently. Do you think you can manage?'

'We shall be fine,' Damaris told him.

The surgeon raised a hand and started walking beside the sedan chair. Fanny was sorry to see him go. With him, she had felt safe. For a moment she almost called after him, then told herself not to be silly. If Damaris didn't feel afraid, there was no reason for her to. She slipped her arm through the cook's and crossed the road.

Afterwards, Fanny couldn't be sure exactly what had happened. They had walked along a little way in the direction Matthew had indicated, then she saw a printing shop window filled with etchings and rhyme sheets. She stopped to look at the display, letting go of Damaris's arm for a moment. Then she staggered back as a rushing horse mounted the pavement and brushed past her. It crashed into Damaris then sped on, people falling back before it, sedan chairmen trying to sidestep out of its way in the narrow street.

Damaris had given one scream as the horse hit her then she fell to the ground and lay very still. 'He must have lost control of the horse,' said someone in a shocked voice. 'Who would have thought it, in Bath!' said another, equally shocked.

'Did you see what he looked like?' asked Fanny as she dropped to her knees beside Damaris.

'Big fellow,' said a young man dressed in the latest fashion. 'But his hat was pulled down tight.'

'It all happened so quickly,' said someone else.

Damaris was breathing but unconscious. Blood trickled down her cheek. Fanny was very much afraid she was badly hurt. Oh, why wasn't Matthew still with them?

Then he was there, breathing fast as though he had run all the way.

'My patient in the sedan chair stopped to talk to a friend, I heard the commotion and came to see if you were involved,' he said. 'What happened?' he asked as he knelt on the pavement beside Damaris.

'Someone on a horse ran her down,' Fanny said jerkily.

There was a crowd around them now, pushing forward to see, all curiosity.

'Stand back, please,' said Matthew. 'I'm a doctor and I must have room.'

There was a little movement but not much.

'She dead?' someone asked.

'Not yet,' he said grimly. 'I need somewhere to examine her properly.'

401

'The George is close by,' someone else said.

'Ideal,' said Matthew, standing up. 'Who can help me carry her there?'

Several men stepped forward.

Fanny scrambled to her feet and watched them carefully raise Damaris. How dreadful it was that she should have had this accident just before she was going to tell her who was responsible for the crimes at Hinde Court and Badminton. Then Fanny felt trickles of ice run down her spine. It hadn't been an accident, she realized. The rider with the hat pulled down had to have been the man who'd tried to silence Damaris once before by setting fire to Hinde Court. The man who'd murdered Captain Farnham.

Chapter Forty

Canaletto took firm hold on his hatbox and entered the private room.

It was large, offering plenty of space for the capacious four-poster bed that occupied much of one half, with a round table and several chairs in the other half. On a chest were several items of luggage, including the holdall Canaletto had seen in the Chinese room at Badminton.

Patience sat on one of the chairs. As Canaletto entered, she said plaintively, 'But you told me we were to marry!'

By the window stood an exasperated looking Charles Sylvester.

Canaletto congratulated himself on his timing.

Then Charles saw him. 'Good heavens, Signor Canale! What do you here?'

Canaletto offered the hatbox. 'I think Signorina Horton forgot this.'

Patience looked amazed. 'I brought my bonnet with me, it is my most becoming, fit to be married in.' She shot a look at Charles through downcast eyelashes that was both artless and pleading.

Isaiah erupted through the door. 'Patience, he is a

mountebank. He will never marry you,' he said passionately. 'He is . . .'

Patience rose, an angry flush on her cheeks. 'Mr Cumberledge, what do *you* here? This is a private room.'

Canaletto cursed silently. Without the young man's impetuosity, he might have been able to manage matters smoothly.

'Miss Horton, Patience, you do not know what you are doing.' Isaiah went and grabbed her hands, almost pulling her out the chair. 'Let me take you home.'

'Mr Cumberledge, you can know nothing of the matter and it is nothing to do with you. Please leave us immediately.'

'But, Patience, you don't understand . . .' said Isaiah, still holding her hands.

'I understand that you are intruding, sir.'

'Can you not accept that the lady does not wish to go with you?' asked Charles Sylvester, speaking with regal authority.

Canaletto stood back. There was nothing he could usefully interpose at this juncture and maybe Isaiah's ardour would, in the end, carry the day.

Isaiah's normally loose jointed and unco-ordinated look left him and he appeared every inch as possessed and aristocratic as the other man. 'Do you intend marrying this lady?' he asked quietly.

'The lady knows that I love her and want her to share my life. That is all I have offered.'

'Oh,' said Patience. She pulled her hands away from Isaiah and held them out to Charles. 'But you want to marry me, do you not? That is what I understood you to say.'

He looked sadly at her. 'My darling, I never mentioned marriage. You read things into my proposal that were never there.'

Canaletto put an urgent hand on Isaiah's arm and pressed it warningly.

Patience gazed wide-eyed at Charles, her hands still outstretched. Then tears welled up in her splendid eyes. 'But why?' she whispered. 'If you love me, why can't you marry me? You have said you are no longer a priest.' She drew in a sharp breath and clasped her hands against her breast. 'Is it that I am Protestant, not Roman Catholic? I can convert. I will convert.'

'It's not that, my angel.'

'You can't, surely, be married already?' her voice was piteous.

At that Charles drew her to him. 'No, my darling, no! I am not that disloyal.'

Isaiah could bear it no longer. 'Disloyal? I will say you are disloyal! Disloyal to the love of this dear creature.' He was shaking with anger. Too late Canaletto saw where this impassioned speech was leading. 'On her behalf, I demand satisfaction. You will meet me, sir!'

'No!' Patience cried, breaking away from Charles. 'Isaiah, you cannot! If you love me, you will not fight over me.'

'I do not fight over you, Patience, but for you. For your honour and for your standing in society. All these this, this *bastard* has traduced.'

'Sir, you shall answer for those words,' Charles said, his face contorted with anger. 'No man insults me thus.'

'Sir,' interposed Canaletto. 'If you value your life, you will leave Bath now. Did you not understand the note that was sent you? An agent of the government is here who will arrest you as soon as look at you.'

'You sent that note?' Charles said.

'You'll not leave this place without fighting me,' declared Isaiah.

'No, no fighting,' pleaded Patience, wringing her hands together.

Charles looked round the room as though a government agent could erupt from a wardrobe without ceremony.

Canaletto grasped Isaiah's arm, stood on tiptoe and whispered in the young man's ear.

Isaiah looked at him with incredulity. 'Can this be true?'

Canaletto nodded.

'Then we must call out the guard, at once.'

'The guard? Isaiah, what on earth are you saying?' shrieked Patience.

'Think, man,' urged Canaletto. 'If you care nothing for this lady's reputation, think what you will do to the duke's!'

Charles rummaged in his holdall. A pistol appeared.

'There is no need for that here,' Canaletto told him. 'Only imagine the chaos a shot will bring!'

Patience and Isaiah watched in disbelief.

'I have no intention of firing it now, signor,' said Charles, stripping off his jacket and waistcoat. 'But if what you say is true, it would behove me to have it at the ready.' He placed it on the window sill beside him, drew his soutane out of the valise and slipped it over his head. The pistol went in a pocket. Two saddlebags now emerged from the holdall and Charles packed his toiletries and change of clothes into them.

'What are you doing?' cried out Patience.

'My darling, won't you come with me to the continent? My trip here has been a disaster and I have to return to Paris. I can offer you little but love but much of that.' He looked at her with all his charm, his brown eyes serious, his mouth firm.

Her mouth trembled as more tears welled up. She had never looked lovelier. Her mouth opened but no sound emerged as she gazed beseechingly at him.

A voice came from the corridor. 'Is this the room you mean?' Then in came Nell and James Horton.

The moment Patience saw her sister, she gave a piteous wail. 'Oh, Nell! I've been betrayed!'

Nell gathered her into her arms.

James strutted up to Charles. 'Now, see here,' he started.

Isaiah and Canaletto exchanged glances. Canaletto said, 'Mr Horton, Mr Sylvester is saying goodbye to your sister, he is leaving. There is no need for any action on your part.'

Charles took one look at Patience sobbing in her sister's arms, donned his biretta and hefted the saddle-bags over his shoulder. A moment later he'd gone.

James looked relieved.

Canaletto thought what a useless young man he seemed to be. Full of high-flown ideas about architecture and landscape but incapable of protecting his sisters.

Patience lifted her head from Nell's shoulder and looked with brimming eyes at Isaiah. 'What you must think of me!' she said.

He took her hand. 'You are my life,' he said.

'I do not deserve this,' she murmured and rested her head again on Nell's shoulder, turning her face so that she could look at him.

With the departure of the man known as Charles Sylvester, Canaletto felt enormous relief. There was no reason to doubt that he was leaving England and so no need to inform Paymaster Pitt.

Now he could turn his mind to the matter of Fanny and Damaris Friend. All he needed was to find where Matthew's sister lodged and he would no doubt discover them. Then it was a question of whether she could confirm his theory as to the identity of Captain Farnham's killer and the perpetrator of the Hinde Court fire.

There came a commotion from the street outside the window. Canaletto went across and saw that an unconscious woman was being carried into the inn accompanied by a crowd of interested people.

Then he recognized the woman.

Chapter Forty-One

A shopkeeper produced an old door. Damaris was carefully laid on this then the fellows who had volunteered earlier lifted it up and headed for the George Inn. Matthew was unable to dissuade most of the onlookers from accompanying them.

It was a fashionable crowd. Wigs, hats, silks, damasks, dimities, lace and furbelows were all the height of chic. Perfumes floated on the air, shrill voices in affected accents cut through the background bustle and expressed concern, excitement and outrage in equal proportion. And curiosity! It was curiosity that kept them thronging around the makeshift stretcher, buzzing like a swarm of bees around their queen. And as they travelled the short distance to the inn, so more folk gathered, drawn as if to an entertainment.

As they entered the inn, Matthew stopped a servant carrying several jugs of ale. 'I am a surgeon and we have a badly injured woman,' he said with great authority. 'Where can we take her that is quiet so she can be properly examined?'

'Now, there's a thing!' exclaimed the servant. 'Against all expectation, today we are that busy! All our private rooms are taken.'

'There must be somewhere,' urged Matthew, bringing out a silver coin.

The servant looked at the press of folk and his eyes seemed to reckon on the profit to be gained from the presence of so many. 'There is a small room at the rear,' he volunteered. 'Follow me.'

The corridor was narrow and forced most of the onlookers to fall back. With difficulty the stretcher party manoeuvred their burden through the door he indicated.

Matthew flapped his hands at those who would follow. 'Leave us, the girl needs air and I need room to examine her.'

Reluctantly, they drifted into the tap-room and started to order refreshment.

The room they'd been invited to use was indeed small but it had a table, some chairs and a narrow sideboard.

The door was placed upon the table and the men who had borne it stood back with expressions of relief, easing out their shoulders, cramped from carrying such an awkward load. Damaris lay, pale and unconscious, her right arm stuck out awkwardly.

'How is she, sir?' asked Fanny anxiously. 'Will she recover?'

'I need to examine her first,' Matthew said impatiently.

But even as he bent over Damaris, she stirred. There came a sigh from the watchers.

Matthew looked up. 'Thank you for your help,' he said abruptly. 'Now please, leave me with my patient.'

As he started to feel her head, the men reluctantly filed out of the room.

In their place, to Fanny's amazement, entered Canaletto.

'Signor! How on earth did you get here?'

'Too long to say but we have rescued Miss Patience Horton from consequences of her too romantic nature.'

That made no sense to Fanny but she was content to wait for the full story. It was enough that he was there. No longer did she wish to investigate the murder of the captain on her own, too much had gone wrong since she started.

'What happened?' he asked her.

Fanny turned back to Damaris and gasped as she saw Matthew's exploring fingers covered with blood. 'Is she badly wounded?' she asked.

Matthew wiped his hands on a kerchief. 'She wasn't just run down. Someone tried to knife her or run her through with a sword. I think all he managed was a scalp wound.' He started to unlace Damaris's bodice.

'Knife? Sword?' said Canaletto. 'You have been in fight, Fanny?'

'No, signor, nothing like that. We were walking along the street, Damaris was to tell me everything the moment we arrived at Matthew's sister's house but she was ridden down.'

'Ridden down? Who by?'

Fanny sighed with frustration. 'It was impossible to see, signor, he had his hat pulled down.'

'Think, Fanny! You must have seen something.'

Fanny tried to cast her mind back. Then Damaris groaned and moved her head slightly.

'Doctor Butcher, she's coming to,' Fanny cried.

'Think, Fanny, think!' urged Canaletto.

Matthew said nothing, his hands now feeling Damaris's right shoulder.

'Oh, signor, how can I think!' wailed Fanny. Then she closed her eyes and tried to build up a picture in her mind of, first the print shop, then of the horse brushing by her and finally the cry from Damaris as she fell. What had she seen of the rider?

'He was dressed in a very plain suit,' she said slowly. 'But neat.'

'A suit not worn by gentleman but man who consort with gentlemen?' suggested Canaletto.

'Yes,' agreed Fanny slowly, fitting this into her memory of the rider. She looked at him, appalled. 'The sort of suit Mr Capper wears! And Damaris was bitter about Mr Capper. Signor, you don't think . . .'

But Matthew had finished his examination. 'Her shoulder is dislocated,' he said. 'We need to see how serious the head wound is.'

Fanny held Damaris's hand while Matthew extracted a pair of scissors from his bag he always carried and cut away the girl's hair, revealing a nasty gash.

'I need a bowl of water and a cloth,' Matthew said to Fanny. 'Also another bowl would be a wise precaution. I must set the shoulder. If she recovers consciousness, the pain will be intense and she will undoubtedly vomit.'

Fanny whisked out and found a servant. She asked for two bowls and a jug of warm water to be brought to the back room, then brushed off anxious questions from those of the onlookers who had stayed at the inn to drink.

Matthew bathed the wound and bound it with linen

412

from his bag. He asked Fanny and Canaletto to hold her head and the other shoulder securely while he took the right arm in a strong grip and placed a leg against the table.

A quick jerk on the arm resulted in a sickening click from the shoulder followed by a terrible cry. Sweat broke out on Damaris's forehead as her eyes fluttered open. 'What happened?' Her voice was very faint but she struggled to sit up.

Fanny tried to help but Matthew reached for a bowl and got it in place just in time.

'The first signs are hopeful,' Matthew said as the spasm passed and Damaris opened her eyes again

'You were run down by a horse,' Fanny said gently. 'I very much fear by the same person who set fire to your bedroom.'

'Do not believe a word that woman says.'

Fanny turned and saw James Horton standing in the doorway.

'She is a whore and a liar.'

'I am not,' Damaris rasped out in a much stronger voice. 'I know what I know and it's the truth.'

'I believe you,' Fanny said and pressed her hand.

Matthew put the bowl on the sideboard and covered it with a cloth.

With Fanny's help, Damaris managed to swing her legs off the old door and sat pulling her bodice together with her left hand

'Oh, Damaris!' Nell rushed into the room and flung her arms around her.

Damaris shrieked.

'I'm so sorry, I didn't mean to hurt you,' Nell said. 'I was so worried when Signor Canaletto said you were being brought in but we had to attend to Patience first. She is in such a state.'

Patience herself, clinging to Isaiah's arm, entered the room. 'Oh, Damaris,' she said with a dying fall that suggested the drama was almost too much for her. 'Damaris, what have you done?'

'It's nothing *she* has done,' Nell said tersely.

'She needs laudanum,' said Matthew, retrieving a square brown bottle and a spoon from his bag. 'Get me a glass and some water, Fanny.'

'No,' said Damaris. 'Not laudanum, I must be lucid.'

'You will be lucid enough,' said Matthew.

The last thing Fanny wanted was to have to leave the room just when it looked as though Damaris might be ready to tell the end of her story but she knew better than to hesitate. Never were glass and drinking water so quickly obtained and then she was rewarded for, as she turned back with her trophies, above the sound of the crowded tap-room clamour there came an excited rustle and she caught the words, 'Duke' and 'Beaufort'.

She pushed her way through the crowds towards the entrance. Sure enough, there was the duke plus a man she had never seen before. He was dressed in travel-stained riding clothes of an excellent cut. His face looked faintly familiar but Fanny was sure she had never met him before.

The duke saw her immediately. 'Miss Rooker, thank heavens! We are in the right place. Where is Signor Canale?'

'Come with me, my lord,' Fanny said. She wanted very much to know how he had come to be there and

414

also who the other man was but knew it wasn't her place to question.

Back in the small and now overcrowded room, Damaris sat supported by Nell, her eyes closed. Matthew had arranged her right arm in a sling. What with that and the head bandage and her white, pain-stricken face, she made a dramatic picture.

'Good heavens,' said the duke.

'Patience, what has happened?' enquired his companion sternly.

'Father!' cried Nell.

Patience flung herself on the newcomer's chest and burst into tears. 'Father, everything is horrible, just horrible,' she said.

'Hush, my dear,' he soothed her. 'I'm here now and it will all be all right.' Then he looked round the company gathered on either side of Damaris. 'I understood Thomas Wright came with you to Bath, Nell, where is he?'

'Stabling the horses, Father,' said James sulkily. 'He should be with us shortly. We, well, I didn't quite follow the order of the hostelries I gave him.'

'What about Father Sylvester?' asked the duke anxiously.

Patience buried her head in her father's shoulder and said nothing.

'He has quit Bath and heads for France,' said Canaletto.

The duke looked profoundly relieved. Then he glanced around the assembled company. 'Has anyone by any chance seen my steward, John Capper? He is not at Badminton and since everyone else appears to have come to Bath, I rather expected to find him here too.'

There was a general shaking of heads. Canaletto took a little step forward. 'My lord duke, cook about to tell us truth of Captain Farnham's death. Continue,' he instructed Damaris.

'Yes, speak,' said the duke.

'My lord,' said Damaris weakly. Then she took a deep breath and spoke more strongly. 'It was the steward.'

'Good heavens, John Capper?' ejaculated the duke.

'Telling tales again, Damaris?' Thomas Wright said. Fanny didn't know how long he'd been standing in the doorway behind the duke.

Damaris's eyes narrowed. 'Now that Sir Robert is back, Tom, all your wrong-doings will be exposed. I told Humphrey how you and Harris were falsifying the building accounts and your plan for making great sums of money out of moving the village.'

'Moving the village?' exclaimed Robert Horton. 'My God, James, was that your plan?'

'Hinde Court needs a suitable approach,' blustered his son. 'It is only sensible.'

'Sensible to move folk from their traditional homes! That was not why I put you in charge of Hinde Court.'

James bit the fingernails of his right hand.

'Humphrey needed money,' Damaris continued as though there had been no interruption. 'He had no scruples about how he obtained it, any more than you have, Tom.'

The Horton steward stood rigidly, his gaze darting

from person to person, as though evaluating exactly what they thought of the story being told.

Damaris sighed and leaned more heavily on Nell. 'When the fire at Hinde Court happened, I didn't think it sinister. Nor Humphrey's dying, burned in that pavilion. The shock was . . .' she wavered.

Matthew held out the glass of laudanum and water he'd prepared. Damaris shook her head. 'First I must finish. I was so shocked,' she went on. 'Then I heard that Humphrey had been stabbed to death before the fire had started. That was when I realized what must have happened.' She looked straight at Thomas Wright. 'He blackmailed you, didn't he, Tom? So you killed him. And because you knew that he must have got his information from me and that I would realize you must have murdered him, you set fire to my bedroom. But I survived,' she added with a faint note of triumph.

'You have no proof,' sneered Thomas Wright. 'Who will believe a whore?'

'Oh, Thomas, you cannot call her that,' said Nell. 'But, Damaris, he couldn't have done all those dreadful things, you must be mistaken.'

'More than that!' said Thomas.

Damaris closed her eyes, her face a picture of exhaustion.

'I know nothing of this woman,' said Sir Robert doubtfully. 'And I trusted Thomas. I relied on him to advise and guide James. That was the basis of the very generous salary I pay you,' he said to the steward.

Damaris opened her eyes. 'He cheated you,' she said in a weary voice. 'Thomas courted me then, when he saw there was a chance to gain your eldest daughter, Sir Robert, he dropped me.'

'Which is why you accuse me like this and tell such lies,' Thomas jeered at her.

Anger flashed in her eyes. 'In part, yes! And do you blame me? But I reckoned Nell was worth more than you and so I watched you, determined to gain evidence to prove you were not worthy to act as a carpet for her feet.' Her audience was mesmerized. 'I overheard you talking with Mr Harris, the builder, one day. That set me sorting through your accounts – you didn't know I did that, did you, Tom?'

Vicious hatred infused his face.

'I watched for times you were otherwise engaged and I carefully sifted through them on a number of occasions, sometimes making copies. Then I found that an account from Allen's for stone had been doubled before being entered in the official accounts. Poor booby that James is, he never thought to question the sums. Far too enthralled with visions of frescoes and plasterwork that would adorn the edifice built to the greater glory of the Hortons.'

Sir Robert winced.

'You know nothing of me,' James blurted out.

'I know you, Jim lad, oh yes, I do,' Damaris said softly. 'Just as I know Tom and his desperate desire to live as the gentleman he was born and not have to serve others, especially those he considers inferior to him in both intelligence and standing.'

'Woman speaks truth,' said Canaletto. 'Steward wear boots night of fire when everyone else no time to dress properly. At time I not wonder,' he smote his forehead with his hand. 'Other matters too pressing. But later I put pieces together and hope cook will confirm my suspicions.'

'Stop him,' said Matthew suddenly.

It was Isaiah who grabbed Thomas Wright as he tried to bolt. The steward struggled but Robert Horton was there as well and so was James. The duke looked on as though ready to lend a hand but the man was safely in custody.

'Find somewhere to lock him up,' said Sir Robert Horton in disgust.

'Send for the watch,' said the duke. Then, as the steward was led away, he turned back. 'Sir Robert and I bear one piece of good news for you young Hortons, Puff has been found.'

'Puff?' exclaimed Canaletto. 'What is Puff?'

'Why, it's our cat,' said Patience with delight. 'Jack trod on its tail as he tried to catch it the night of the fire. He wanted to save Puff,' Patience added sadly, 'but all he did was to frighten him so badly he ran back into the house. Jack will be so happy now.'

'Who found him?' Nell asked.

'That young lad with the damaged face, Barnaby, isn't that his name?' the duke said. 'Brought him over today, arrived just about the same time as your father. Said he'd seen the cat around Hinde Court for a couple of days, and this morning he managed to catch him.'

'That's wonderful,' said Nell. 'Surely that's everything explained.'

'Except where the devil my steward is,' said the duke.

'Try the housekeeper's room of your neighbour, Lord Marston,' said Damaris. 'As far as John Capper is concerned, hunting days are holidays.' She reached for the glass of laudanum, drank it down then closed her eyes and sank back into Nell's shoulder.

'We shall return to Badminton,' said the duke. 'There are many questions to be answered but I think we have seen enough of Bath today.'

Chapter Forty-Two

Canaletto wiped his fingers on a rag and set his partially cleaned brushes upright in a jar on the work table. Fanny could finish them off.

He stepped outside his makeshift studio on to the grass and surveyed the scene. The landscape was golden in a late August splendour. Harvesting was in progress and he could hear cries of children as they helped stack the stooks. Hedgerows gleamed with red haws and blackberry bushes glistened with ripe fruit.

Canaletto stretched out his arms, easing tired muscles after a day at the easel.

Fanny came and joined him. 'You have finished, signor?' she asked excitedly.

He nodded. 'Soon we go back to London, yes?'

She gave a small sigh, 'Will you be sorry, signor?'

'I look forward to our studio, to hustle and bustle of the city, the river, the buildings, our friends, no?'

'I shall miss the countryside, signor, and as for friends, I think the Hortons can now be counted as such.'

Repairing Hinde Court's roof sufficiently for the family to return had taken several weeks. In the meantime the duke had insisted that the Hortons remained at Badminton.

Canaletto and Fanny had also remained. It was a luxury for Canaletto not to have to rely on his sketches and memory as he started painting in a room the duke made available.

The Chinese pavilion no longer existed, the ruins had been removed and the duke had announced that its place would be taken by a different design. He had soon had this commission, together with a sketch for a Grecian-style temple he was considering building. Canaletto included both in his painting. On the distant horizon, in life as well as on his canvas, was the decorative banqueting hall, Worcester Lodge.

After he had finished painting each day, it was time to hear the latest details that had emerged of Thomas Wright's perfidy. Sir Robert had organized lawyers to inspect all the building and household accounts and to question Damaris Friend. Everything she had said was proving true.

Then, soon after Sir Robert had returned from London, a lawyer had arrived from Bath with the news that Thomas Wright had confessed all.

It was Nell who gave Canaletto and Fanny all the details. 'You remember Damaris said she'd found those accounts that showed how Thomas and Mr Harris were falsifying the figures?' she said as they took a walk before dinner. 'Apparently she gave them to Captain Farnham, who said that he would handle things. She expected him to approach either James or myself, perhaps both together. The captain, though, had other ideas,' Nell said sadly. 'He needed money and he had few compunctions about how he was going to get it. That last day he visited us, he told Thomas he knew exactly what was going on and demanded to be cut into the deal with the builder. He said there must be more than enough to be shared between three rather than two.' She paused for a moment, 'I didn't realize Captain Farnham could be like that.'

'Money a great temptation to many men,' said Canaletto sententiously. It was another beautiful day, especially now the midday heat of the sun had eased. Always he was to remember his time at Badminton as bathed in sunshine.

'I think you say true,' Nell sighed. 'Anyway, Thomas says that he told him no doubt something could be arranged but he would have to talk to Harris. He had no intention, apparently, of doing any such thing. The following morning, Thomas sent a note over to Badminton to the captain in Damaris's hand. Thomas is a great forger, it has been discovered that he has obtained monies from my father's bank under his signature.

Nell bent and found a stick to throw for the dog who accompanied them. 'Damaris says she taunted Thomas at one stage with the meetings she was enjoying with the captain in the pavilion, saying she had found a better lover. So the note suggested a rendezvous there that evening. The rest you know. When Captain Farnham arrived at the pavilion, Thomas was behind the door and hit him with a rolling pin he had taken from the kitchen. He then removed the accounts from the captain's pocket. Thomas says he reckoned that he wouldn't take the chance of leaving them in his room. He knows exactly how dishonest servants can be!'

'And then he knife him?' Canaletto said.

'Yes. Thomas knew that the captain and Damaris were lovers and he was certain that she must have found the accounts and given them to Captain Farnham. He reckoned that if she heard the captain had been killed, she would work out what had happened and denounce Thomas. He decided a fire outside her room would despatch her. He could alert the rest of the house before anyone else suffered.'

'But surely,' said Fanny, frowning. 'If Damaris was to be burned to death, how were the other servants who slept upstairs to escape?'

'I don't think he concerned,' said Canaletto.

'I'm afraid you are probably correct,' Nell agreed with another sigh. 'As it was, Damaris woke and got us all out. Thomas says that the more damage there was to the house, the more scope there would be for him to cream sums from the building accounts to repair it all. I have never been more at fault in my estimation of anyone!'

'I didn't know him well,' said Fanny, 'but from what I saw of him, he seemed open and honest.'

'Exactly,' said Canaletto. 'So, Damaris not die and steward must make captain's death look like accident, *si*? So she not think he responsible?'

'Yes. Thomas had not only taken the rolling pin from the kitchen but also one of Damaris's knives and that was what he had used to kill Captain Farnham. He'd left the forged note on the body so it would look as though it was Damaris, in a fit of jealous fury, who had killed the captain. So the following morning he set fire to the pavilion to destroy all evidence of murder. Which it might very well have done if it hadn't been for you, signor,' she said, turning to Canaletto.

He thought of the figure he had seen walking away from the pavilion as he'd been working on the landing.

Yes, it could have been Thomas Wright. What a tragedy that he had not been able to identify him at the time! 'Was Betsy Cary involved in plan? Mr Harris her brother, no?'

Nell nodded. 'Thomas says not. He says she would have betrayed something to Walter. The man rushes around like a demented bull, roaring at every opportunity and he would have exposed the plot without doubt. Thomas doesn't know, though, what Barnaby was doing in the garden the night of the fire.'

'I know,' said Canaletto, delighted to be able to add to the sum of information.

'You, signor, how do you know?'

'You know I investigate death of captain for duke. I suspect fire at Hinde Court may be involved and wish to talk to Barnaby about his presence in garden,' said Canaletto. He explained that a couple of mornings after all the excitement of the Bath visit, he'd walked over to Hinde Court, no more riding for him, and was able to talk to the boy alone. 'He says he often wander round the new building at night, even when impossible to see. He not need much sleep, he says, and hates sharing bedroom with brothers. He like to imagine house as it will be, pretend he is living there. He determined to make way in the world.'

There was silence for a moment.

'I will speak with father,' said Nell at last. 'He has to agree that Barnaby can return to being my assistant again and this time I will arrange that he moves into Hinde Court. He can be helpful with errands and in many small matters.'

'What about his father?' asked Fanny.

'I'll speak to his mother and between us we'll per-

suade Walter he must let Barnaby come to us,' said
Nell resolutely. 'Betsy wants a better future for all her
children than they can get from the land.'

'I suppose Mr Harris has been arrested as well as
Mr Wright,' said Fanny. 'Who will look after the
building works now?'

'He has been arrested,' said Nell. 'But father has
already sorted out another master builder and all the
workers are now under his command. We should soon
be able to return to Hinde Court. And Father thinks
he has found someone to take Thomas's place as well.
A man of much experience, considerably older.'

The Hortons had returned to Hinde Court at the
beginning of July and Canaletto and Fanny had gone
with them. An outbuilding with a northern aspect had
been cleaned out for use as a studio and a large window
installed. When Canaletto had queried the expense, Sir
Robert Horton had told him not to worry. 'I am
delighted you will both be working here,' he said. 'After
the new house is completed, we may hope, perhaps,
for you to return and capture it for us.'

Damaris, completely recovered, had returned to
her duties in the kitchen. Sir Robert did not like this
but Nell argued that she must stay. So far Damaris was
still there. 'If he can insist I obey him in certain
respects, it's only fair he should accept my decision in
other matters,' she'd said at one stage. Though the
dining room at Hinde Court was not nearly so grand
as the one at Badminton, the food was as lavish. The
dishes might have been less rich but Canaletto found
them delicious. Damaris Friend was indeed a cook to
treasure.

James Horton had gone abroad. Sir Robert had

arranged for him to serve at his office in Delhi. 'Be the making of the boy,' he'd said when his wife had wailed that it was too far away and the climate too dreadful.

James had declared that he was delighted to be going. 'England is too dull by half,' he'd said. 'I need a challenge. Soon I shall be arranging the importation of goods from the Orient.'

There were rumours that Sir Robert had had to settle large gambling debts and no one apart from Lady Horton seemed too despondent at James's departure.

Certainly not Patience, her spirits had improved as soon as her brother had sailed from Bristol. Canaletto felt, though, that this had less to do with James's departure than with her removal from Badminton. There, Isaiah had hung upon her every word and paid court assiduously. As soon as harvest approached, the children were required in the fields and school was no more. Isaiah spent much time in his laboratory in one of the Badminton outbuildings, but he still seemed able to suggest that Patience and he might go riding, or visit Lady Tanqueray. The quarrel with his aunt had not been forgotten but she now seemed to enjoy sparring with him. Patience declared Isaiah's attentions were all too much for her.

As well as the return to Hinde Court, Patience's spirits were improved by the appearance of a widowed peer on the local scene.

The recently ennobled Lord Branksome, Whig politician, was in his late thirties, charming and lively. He had lost a wife in childbirth two years earlier, had two small children and, to give his peerage the authority he felt it required, had acquired a country seat not three miles from Hinde Court. Intending to spend most of the winter in town, he was happy to enjoy his new status in the country during the summer, especially after meeting Miss Patience Horton. Visit had followed visit to Hinde Court. His lordship enjoyed conversations with Sir Robert, whenever he wasn't in London, and he was genial and friendly with Lady Horton and Nell but it was plain that he was only drawn there so often by the opportunity to spend time laughing and chatting with Patience. They rode together and organized picnics and divertissements that included the younger Hortons and the motherless Branksomes. Evenings were often spent with Lord Branksome playing the violin accompanied by Patience on the harpsichord. Nobody expected the result of these meetings to be anything other than an engagement.

Nobody, that is, other than Isaiah Cumberledge.

'What is one to do?' Nell had asked Fanny one morning. He comes visiting and sits glowering at poor Patience and Lord Branksome.' Fanny had told Canaletto that Nell had been torn between amusement at the ridiculousness of the scene she described and sympathy for Isaiah.

'I think he holds her heart, signor. Do you think there is any hope Mr Cumberledge will realize where his affections should lie?' said Fanny.

Canaletto had shaken his head. 'He treats Miss 'Orton as friend, as colleague. He need romantic vision for love. Miss 'Orton not the romantic vision.'

Remembering this now, Canaletto asked, 'And you, little Fanny, you finish work, yes?'

She nodded, looking apprehensive. 'Sir Robert comes to view it shortly.' Sir Robert had returned the previous evening from another of his London visits.

There had been a furious argument between Nell and her father over the wisdom of the portrait. Eventually she had given in to his wishes but only after he'd asked if she was disappointed a leading portraitist such as Mr Hudson had not been commissioned. Canaletto and Fanny had been sitting with Lady Horton and Patience in the little drawing room off the hall where Sir Robert and Nell were arguing and there was no avoiding eavesdropping as the raised voices came through clearly.

'No, indeed, I would be more than happy to have Miss Rooker to catch my likeness.'

'Well, then, that is all in order,' Sir Robert had boomed out and the matter had been considered closed. There was no doubt that Sir Robert and his eldest daughter were very close and only he could have persuaded her to sit for Fanny.

Sir Robert himself now appeared from the direction of the new construction. This grew larger and more imposing by the day. The plans to move the village had been put quietly on one side. It was no secret, however, that new houses were being built some way away, though not on the site picked out by James. No villager would be forced to move but such were the attractions of the new properties, it seemed unlikely that even Walter Cary would refuse the spacious new accommodation that was being offered.

Dressed in a neat, dark-brown jacket and breeches instead of the long, merchant's robe he sometimes wore, and his small bag-wig looking cool in the summer heat, Sir Robert folded up the papers he had been perusing and slipped them into the back pocket of the jacket. 'So, now we view the masterpiece, eh, Miss

429

Rooker?' It was said with a smile, he and Fanny had developed a pleasant relationship, but there was no doubt that this was the time he would pass judgement as to whether his money would be well spent. 'Does my daughter join us?'

'I do, Father,' Nell said, appearing from the other direction.

'And what do you think of your likeness, eh, Nell?' he asked in a kindly fashion but there was a shrewd look in his eye.

'I have not seen the portrait yet, Father,' Nell said calmly. Canaletto saw, though, that a rapid little tic beat in her left temple.

'Now is the time,' said Fanny. She sounded calm also but Canaletto knew that she was as nervous as Nell.

In the makeshift studio the first things that caught the eye were Canaletto's paintings of Badminton.

'Striking,' said Sir Robert, looking at the grandeur of Badminton House set serenely against a vast sky with highly decorative clouds, their cream echoing the pale gold of the house's stonework. In the foreground was a broad expanse of green decorated with deer and figures. The companion painting of the park had as foreground the stark semicircle of gravel that led on to the same expanse of green parkland, again decorated with all manner of action. Encircling the park were the trees, separated by their avenues. Only the merest glimpses of the wings of the house on either side anchored the viewpoint. The gravel seemed a world from which radiated out paths to all parts of the universe, the centre of which was Badminton.

'Wonderful sense of space you have achieved, my dear signor,' said Sir Robert.

'I love all the characters he has peopled the scenes with,' said Nell. 'See, there is little Henry on his horse with his groom.'

'Ah, the Marquess of Worcester,' said Sir Robert.

Canaletto hoped he wouldn't study the little cameo too closely and recognize that he had gained inspiration for it from a much, much larger picture hanging in one of the Badminton salons. So much easier than getting the child to pose for him.

'And surely this is the duke and the duchess, standing on the terrace,' said Nell excitedly.

Canaletto hoped she wouldn't notice the servant dashing out with a letter. Or that the figure on horseback he was approaching was the prince. He wondered how many at Badminton had been aware that Sylvester was one of Bonnie Prince Charlie's names. The prince had done Canaletto one favour, however. The duke had promised to pay him cash when the finished paintings were delivered. 'I had intended it for another purpose. But I have changed my mind,' he'd said. It was an unusual course of action for any of Canaletto's patrons to take, normally he would have to wait some considerable time for bankers to be instructed to pay him.

'Why, there is Aunt Letitia,' said Nell, looking at the open carriage travelling across the park.

For a little while they enjoyed themselves picking out other aspects of the characters they said they recognized. 'But let's see Nell's portrait,' said Sir Robert suddenly.

Silently, Fanny took them over to where the picture, covered with a cloth, stood on her easel.

431

Canaletto had assisted Fanny in the early stages of the portrait with advice on perspective and technique but the concept had been Fanny's and soon he had been happy to leave her to work on her own. 'I here if you need,' he'd said. But she hadn't applied for further help, neither had she shown him how the portrait was progressing and he had respected her privacy. So his curiosity now was as sharp as the Hortons's.

Fanny carefully removed the cloth and stepped back.

For a moment nobody said anything and she looked anxiously at their faces.

Sir Robert gave a great sigh. 'Now, Nell, my dearest daughter, you see why I wanted you captured on canvas.'

Nell studied the work in silence.

She was shown three-quarter length in her laboratory. She held a large glass vessel and appeared to be showing its contents to the viewer. Her face was vividly alive, her lovely eyes made the most of. All around her were scientific vessels and instruments and in the background was a fire with Barnaby tending it. The light was all from one side, concentrating on the unscarred side of Nell's face. That, though, was the only trick used to minimize her disfigurement. The effect on the viewer was to make them appreciate the dangers inherent in scientific research. It was an immensely powerful and unusual portrait. Though he'd seen the beginning of the work, Canaletto was unprepared for how the picture affected him.

'Your true beauty,' said Sir Robert softly.

Nell gently touched her scars. Whether it was time or whether the salve that Matthew Butcher had given her had helped, they were beginning to fade slightly. 'Thank you,' she said to Fanny. 'This picture gives me status, a standing. In years to come, people will view it and say, there is a scientist.'

Fanny gave her a wide smile. 'Then my intention has succeeded. I hope you are pleased, sir,' she said to Sir Robert.

'Indeed, indeed,' he said. 'I shall have a very special frame designed for it, gilded, of course, with scientific symbols carved at the top and the bottom. No viewer will be in any doubt as to Nell's qualities.' Then he tore his gaze away from the painting. 'Miss Rooker, you have a great future in front of you. You may rely on me to obtain you more commissions. You must give me your studio directions.'

Canaletto suddenly realized that the days when Fanny attended to all his needs were over. Now she would have to set up her own studio, somewhere smart enough for sitters to come. At the start of this project he'd feared he would no longer be able to work in England, now he wondered if he could bring himself to remain. Without Fanny, how would he manage?

Historical Note

Of the two pavilions in the middle ground of Canaletto's view of Badminton Park, the Grecian temple was never built. The other was erected towards the end of the 1740s, then disappeared at a later date. The Chinese pavilion that plays such a part in this book is an invention. The Beaufort records contain no mention of any payments to Canaletto for his paintings.